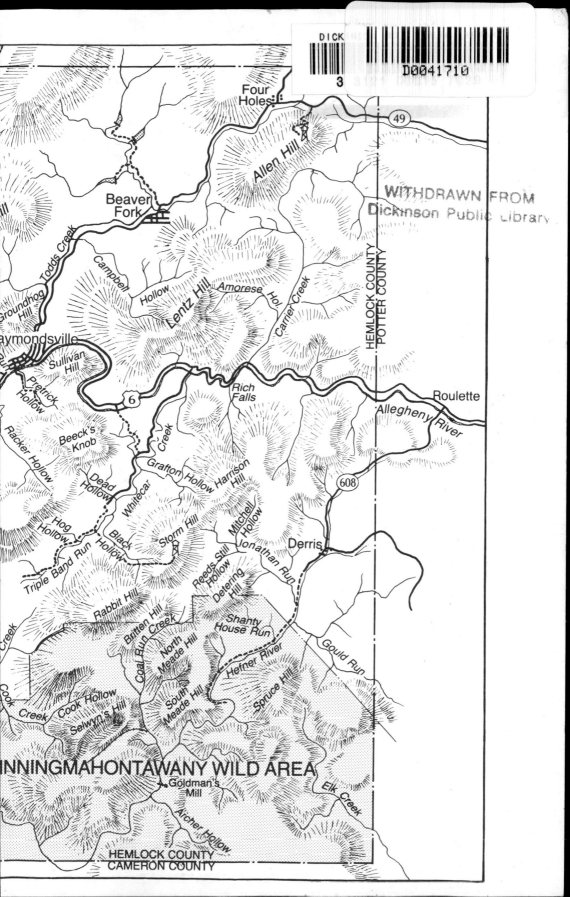

WINTER
IN
THE
HEART

David Poyer

WINTER IN THE HEART

A TOM DOHERTY ASSOCIATES BOOK
NEW YORK

WINTER IN THE HEART

A Tor Book
Published by Tom Doherty Associates, Inc.
175 Fifth Avenue
New York, N.Y. 10010

Tor® is a registered trademark of Tom Doherty Associates, Inc.

Library of Congress Cataloging-in-Publication Data

Poyer, David.
    Winter in the heart / David Poyer.
      p. cm.
    "A Tor book"—T.p. verso.
    ISBN 0-312-85421-8
    1. Corporations—Pennsylvania—Corrupt practices—Fiction.
  2. Environmental protection—Pennsylvania—Fiction.   3. Trials-
-Pennsylvania—Fiction. I. Title.
PS3566.O978W56 1993
813'.54—dc20   93-690
                                         CIP

First Tor edition: June 1993

Printed in the United States of America

0 9 8 7 6 5 4 3 2 1

For John,
Who left too soon
1933–1982

Acknowledgments

Ex nihilo nihil fit. For this book I owe much to James Allen, Laura Benton, Robert Chapman, Phyllis Cook, Tom Doherty, Candy S. Ekdahl, Donald Ekdahl, Kelly Fisher, Doris Peterson Galen, Frank Green, Robert Gleason, Lenore Hart, Frederick Hillyer, Russ Jaffe, Tim Jenkins, Mary Ann Johnston, Anna Magee, John Ordover, Jay Parini, Rick Peroginelli, Martin Pesaresi, Lin Poyer, Gary J. Richards, Howard Troutman, George Witte, J. M. Zias, Robert Legault, and others who preferred anonymity, though generously giving of their time. All errors and deficiencies are my own.

My struggle was always against
an inner darkness: I carry within myself
the only known keys
to my death—to unlock life, or close it shut
forever. A woman who loves wood grains, the color yellow
and the sun, I am happy to fight
all outside murderers
As I see I must.

—ALICE WALKER

WINTER
IN
THE
HEART

Prologue

T he guards woke the old man early, slamming the barred door open with a jangling bang that echoed down the corridor of the cell block. Earlier than he'd expected; he hadn't thought judges and lawyers went to work that soon. They waited as he washed his face and dried it with the thin jailhouse towel and thought about shaving. He'd shaved yesterday, he decided, that should be good enough.

He moved around the cell, slowly pulling on faded green work pants, suspenders, a white shirt his daughter had brought, an old green work cap with ear-flaps. He favored his shoulder, which was still tender where they'd taken the bullet out. Then he sat on the bunk to lace up his boots. The lawyer woman, Quintero, she'd told him to wear a tie, but he drew the line at that.

If I'd of been the kind of fellow owned a tie, I wouldn't of ended up here in the first place, Halvorsen thought.

The breakfast tray came, the same meal as the last three days: oatmeal with raisins, toast, coffee. He wasn't hungry, but he made himself eat the oatmeal.

He was standing at the narrow window looking out at the hills when the U.S. federal marshal came for him. A big friendly-looking fella in a gray suit, but you could tell he was a cop. Another marshal stood behind him. "Morning, Racks," he said. "Ready for the grand jury?"

"Question is, they ready for me?"

The marshal chuckled and jerked a thumb at his deputy. Halvorsen held his hands out without saying anything. The heavy cuffs dragged them down.

"Leg-irons too. And waist-chains."

"Hell, give me a break, fellas. I got a good thirty years on anybody else around here."

"Everybody gets the same jewelry, old-timer. Had a eighty-six-year-old man assault a guard in Montana last year."

When they were done with him he could hardly walk, but he shuffled and jingled out into the corridor after them.

They went out the back of the jail, the marshal holding the door for him. Halvorsen stopped for a minute in the parking lot, sucking in the cold snow-smelling air and looking up at a glazed sky. He hadn't seen much of it for the last couple of weeks. The snowflakes fell toward them between the dark buildings in perfect beautiful silence, glittering fragments chipped from the white glacier of winter cloud. He sighed as one needled his upturned face.

It was winter. The seasons of sun, of green, were gone. Now each thing that lived had to endure. Or die.

"You ready? We got about five blocks."

He cleared his throat and nodded, recalled to the present. Snow crunched and squealed under their boots as the marshals led him to an unmarked car. Another plainclothesman sat in the front seat. The engine was running. "No squad car?" he asked.

"Attracts too much attention. Last year we had that guy was testifying against the Colombians, maybe you read about him in the paper. We took him over in a bakery truck."

The marshal laughed and they got into the back seat. A steel screen separated them from the front. He leaned over Halvorsen to fasten the belt as the driver put the car into gear. As they turned into the street Halvorsen got his hands on the crank after a couple of tries and wound the window down. The fresh air felt good after the closed, overheated, man-thick atmosphere of the Allegheny County Jail.

They drove through the heart of town and turned at the Federal Reserve Bank. The car juddered suddenly over cobblestones. Grant Street, he remembered now. He hadn't ever gotten to Pittsburgh much, not for years now, and hardly ever downtown.

The last time he'd looked up at this granite building the Depression had been on, and brown-uniformed National Guard with doughboy helmets and bayoneted Springfields had surrounded it, holding back a sullen crowd.

"You know," he said, "Last time I was here, Roosevelt was president."

"Roosevelt, huh? Which one?"

He was about to answer, angry—how old did they think he was, anyway?—when the marshal said, "Just kidding. You mean FDR, right? Over there, Bill. Damn, there's a bunch of 'em this time. Okay, here we go."

The car doors opened into a sudden boil of faces, open mouths, a shouting wall of granite-echoed sound. Strobe lights detonated blinding-bright, pinning them with focused lenses. Two or three dozen jostling, elbowing people were shouting at him at once in an unintelligible gabble that let no word through. It sounded to him like a pack of hounds baying after a deer, the way they hunted down South. He kept his face blank, moving with the marshals, who surrounded him now. He caught a glimpse of himself on some kind of electronic screen they'd set up: a slightly stooped, thin old man with a jailhouse pallor, stalking stiffly through the mob in faded old clothes, the too-long chains dragging on the sidewalk.

Then the marshal had his arm, was half leading him, half lifting him up broad granite steps toward brass-edged doors. The snow fell harder now, whirling out of the white sky.

The revolving doors hissed closed on the pandemonium outside. Halvorsen glanced back to see faces and cameras pressed to the glass. Then he stumbled, the chains catching on the step of some kind of walk-through machine. An impassive black woman waved a wand over him, then nodded to the marshal.

At the far end of a low marbled corridor he saw the others. Boulton was sitting on a wooden bench with two men in overcoats. His attorneys, if that's what they were, looked confident, as if they'd just had big breakfasts and a shot of something to set them up. But something had changed in Boulton's eyes. He looked straight ahead, as if blind to anything or anyone around him. There was the Farmer girl, too, an older woman with her, sitting quietly in a corner. Halvorsen tried to catch her eye but failed.

He wondered if somehow the boy could see them too.

Quintero was waiting for him at the door to the grand jury room, her briefcase between her galoshes on the green and white tile floor. She was his court-appointed lawyer, a small woman with a scarred-up face. He'd wondered what had happened to her. It looked like she'd had a run-in with some mean dogs. But he hadn't asked, and she hadn't said. As they neared her the marshals slowed.

The first thing she said was, "You didn't shave."

"You goin' in with me?" he asked her.

"I told you, Mr. Halvorsen, persons called before a federal grand jury testify alone. You're the first witness today. So please, just listen. Are you listening?"

"Yeah, I'm listenin'."

"When you're in there, don't answer any questions about your actions or even your intentions. Just your name—that's enough to establish cooperation. You can answer anything that reflects on Boulton. Gibson will probably start with that to soften you up, make you feel he's on your side. Cooperate with that part if you like, but stay alert. Because after that, when you've set Boulton up, he'll go after you. Understand?"

"I get it."

"When you're asked anything pertaining to your own actions, excuse yourself, leave the stand, and come out here. Tell me what the question is, I'll tell you what to say, you go back in. *Don't say anything without asking me first.* Tell me you understand that."

"It's a pack of foolishness. *You* can't come in—"

"But you can come out and consult with me. That's right."

"Who made up that rule? No, forget it." Halvorsen swallowed. He wished he had a chew, his mouth was dry.

"If you don't want to come out, then take the fifth amendment. Just say, 'I refuse to answer on the grounds that it may tend to incriminate me.' This guy's smart. And whatever he says, he's not on your side. First he'll try to scare you. Then he'll mention immunity, but it won't be a real offer. If he was serious he'd have come to me. Don't try to match wits with him. If you don't watch yourself he'll have a full confession by the time you step down."

"Thought you said this wasn't a trial."

"It's not. But whatever you say before a grand jury can be used against you later, if you *are* put on trial. Understand?"

"I guess."

"Calling William T. Halvorsen," said a bailiff.

The marshal said, "You about done with him, counselor?"

"Remember what I said," said Quintero, taking a fold of his shirt between her fingertips. "Don't say a word about anything you did without coming out and talking to me first. And good luck."

Halvorsen blew out, grimaced, and said to the bailiff, "Let's go."

The courtroom reminded him of a church. Same worn wooden pews. The same let's-get-started murmur from the flock. The tall man waiting up there for him looked like the preacher. Only instead of a congregation, the jury. Ordinary-looking people, middle-aged, mostly women, one colored fella almost as old as he was. More of them than he'd expected. He felt their eyes follow him as they led him down front and took off the cuffs and chains and irons. There was a chair for him at a little table. Halvorsen sighed as he let himself down into it, rubbing his wrists and looking around. A little man in a bow tie sat a few feet behind him, limbering up his fingers, then tapping on a funny-looking kind of telegraph key. Taking down what they said, most likely, because he tapped some when Halvorsen had to get up again and swear on a Bible.

As soon as he sat down again the preacher-looking fella started in. Halvorsen squinted up at him as he began, no smile or word of welcome, just: "Please state your name."

He said slowly, "My name's W. T. Halvorsen."

"The W stands for William."

"That's right."

"Resident of?"

"Hemlock County, state of Pennsylvania. Live outside of Raymondsville."

"Mr. Halvorsen, let me introduce myself. I'm Gregory Gibson, the assistant U.S. attorney for the Western District."

Halvorsen cleared his throat, wondering if he should say he was glad to meet him. Finally he just said, "Uh huh."

"I understand you've been able to consult with a court-appointed attorney. Is that correct?"

"That's right."

"Good. However, just to be sure you're clear in your mind what's going on, let me explain what you're doing here.

"These men and women constitute a federal grand jury. If they think there's evidence you committed a crime, they'll vote an indictment against you. Then the real trial takes place, where the jury decides guilt and innocence, and the judge hands down a sentence. The grand jury has no power to punish. However, false or misleading statements before it are punishable as perjury. Do you understand?"

He nodded, muttered, "I understand." Was it just that he was old, that made everybody want to explain everything to him three times? Hell, he understood what was going on. Understood all too well.

They were going to try to pin it all on him.

Gibson nodded. He strolled a few paces away, as if collecting his thoughts, then came back. Now his voice changed, acquired a threatening edge.

"Mr. Halvorsen, I don't mind telling you we're dealing with a confused situation here, about the events that took place on December nineteenth of last year. And the events that led up to it.

"But first, I want to make sure you understand the gravity of what happened. We're talking about major damages, major impacts on the whole Allegheny watershed. Over seven hundred and fifty thousand people, in seven counties, draw drinking water from the river. For the past weeks they've had to depend on bottled water or emergency supplies for their drinking and cooking needs." Gibson glanced at the jury. "This includes most of Pittsburgh, by the way. A cleanup effort is underway, but it's going to be slow. Estimates vary as to how long it will be before the river is usable again, but even the shortest is in months.

"Mr. Halvorsen, someone is liable for damages. Not just for the expense of cleanup, not even just for fines, but for the dozens of civil suits already filed along the route that poison took.

"I also don't mind telling you that my office is drawing up federal charges against you and your co-conspirators. To make it brief, we're drawing up indictments on federal explosive charges and on dumping of hazardous substances. The knowing-endangerment charge alone carries maximum penalties of a quarter of a million dollars, fifteen years in prison, or both. And then there are the costs of cleanup, which it's quite possible will run into the millions."

Halvorsen took his green cap with the thunderbolt insignia off and put it on his lap. He wished he'd brought a handkerchief, it sure was hot in here. The talk about millions didn't scare him. He just didn't have it, that was all. But to spend the rest of his life walled in, never to see woods again . . .

"Those are the federal charges. I can't speak for the state charges, but they'll be at least as serious. Subject to the decision of a Pennsylvania grand jury, you may be charged with conspiracy, destruction of state property, a separate state explosives charge, reckless endangerment, brandishing of firearms, manslaughter, attempted murder, and murder. You and the others involved will stand trial for those separately from the federal charges. Do you understand that?''

He grunted, ''Yeah.''

Gibson nodded slowly. ''Good. Now let's return to the federal charges, and your testimony.

''Mr. Halvorsen, I personally believe that if you testify fully and fairly about the events of that night, it may be possible to offer you immunity on some or all of the above charges, in exchange for your testimony against others involved in the violation of the Toxic Substances Control Act—those being the primary federal charges in this case. We're counting on you to clarify the reasons for your actions, and to clarify the reasons behind the actions of others. Are you willing to help us do this?''

He thought about Quintero's advice, and his mouth twisted. ''You mean, make some kind of a deal? I say what you want, you let me off?''

''Not exactly like that, Mr. Halvorsen—''

''Because W. T. Halvorsen don't make deals like that. I'm goin' to tell the truth, y'see? Tell you what I done, and why. And I don't need you, or that lady lawyer they give me, or nobody else to tell me what to say.''

He watched the prosecutor's face change; become the face of a man he could trust, a fellow who wanted to help him. ''Let me see if I understand you, Mr. Halvorsen. As a concerned citizen, you're willing to tell us the full and complete story about events leading up to your actions on the night of last December nineteenth, without reservations, guarantees, or any promises on the part of the government as to immunity on any charge that may result?''

He caught a motion from the back pew, and half expected to see Quintero, her scarred face red and white now, waving frantically at him. He turned his head away, just in case she'd got in somehow, and said firmly to the preacherlike man, to the silent jury: ''Yeah. I'll tell you folks ever'thin' I know.''

''All right, Mr. Halvorsen. When you—''

''Long's I can tell it m'self, in my own words, without you interrupting me.''

The prosecutor looked as if he was eating something he hated. But finally he nodded. ''You have the floor, Mr. Halvorsen.''

Halvorsen looked at the ceiling, at the lazily turning fans, trying to get his thoughts organized. Too damn hot to think. Had so much to tell. About Barry Fox, and the Farmer girl, and the doctor woman. About Ainslee Thunner and old Dan and the smooth-faced man who'd taken his place . . . about the little girl . . . the black trucks . . . the men who'd come to Mortlock Hollow with guns and cans of gasoline . . .

But how could he tell it all? Tell it so they'd understand? He felt sweat slide down his back under the stiff white shirt. Goddamnit, he'd told Alma he hated starch in his shirts. Maybe this wasn't smart. Maybe he was just sticking his head in the noose. No business for a man old as he was. Man who couldn't remember right, either forgot things or else remembered too damn much, saw everything, like it was happening in front of his eyes. He didn't want to be here. He hadn't wanted to do what he'd done. All he'd wanted was to be left alone.

But they'd never put it together if he clammed up. Quintero meant well. She wanted to protect him. But if they didn't get everything out in the open now, it'd never get told. Boulton and his pals and politicians would twist and shred and bury it, like cats covering their dirt, till no one knew what was hidden where. And the rottenness would go on, and spread . . . This was what the boy had died for. A chance to tell the truth, the whole truth, and nothing but.

The ceiling was white. At first it looked white as snow, until you stared a while. Then you noticed the brown stains seeping through.

Yeah, Halvorsen thought. A grim faint smile of memory took his white-stubbled jaw. Yeah, that'd been the beginning, far as he knew.

The day it had started to snow.

One

When dawn had come that day he'd been on the road for two hours, hiking downhill through the storm. He had his old-style floppy cap, earflaps tied down. Heavy army-surplus melton pants. Plaid wool coat, the kind not even hunters wore anymore. At each step his boots plunged lace-deep into new snow. And it was still whirling down steadily out of the darkness, lashing his numbed and downbent face.

An invisible pothole made him stumble. This stretch had been bad all winter, and now it was worse. There were springs above it, on the south face of Town Hill, and when they froze the macadam heaved and buckled like a slow earthquake. A few more years and Mortlock Run would be impassable to wheels, relapsed to the foot trail it had been two centuries before, when the names of this land were Seneca.

Well, Halvorsen thought, there's not many use it these days. There wasn't another house from here all the way back up to Mortlock Hollow.

He was resigned to hiking all the way out to Route Six, when he caught an orange flicker deep in the storm. He rubbed ice from his eyelashes.

A snarl of diesels, a creaking rumble of axles, the grating scream of steel on stone.

The lights rose like twin suns, blinding him like a jacklighted deer. The snowplow leaped from the blowing snow as if created from it, huge as a locomotive, yellow and black, the colors of peril and death. Halvorsen stood half facing it, as if waiting to be run down. A horn blatted, the warning echoing from the hills. Then was succeeded by a rush of braking air.

The plow rumbled to a halt. The driver stretched across the bench seat, and the passenger door swung open.

Halvorsen hauled himself stiffly up steel steps into the cab. He untied his hat and flirted snow onto the floor. The interior light showed a pepper of stubble on his cheeks, a rime of snow on his collar. Pale blue eyes closed briefly in the blast from the heater.

"Morning there, Racks," said the driver.

"Hullo, Barry."

Barry Fox eased the truck back into gear. The blade rumbled and boomed, snow hissing off it as they picked up speed.

"Goin' into town?"

Halvorsen nodded.

"Almost didn't see you. Guess winter's here for sure now."

Fox waited, then went on. "Ever ride the plow before?"

The old man shook his head.

"State's got newer now, but these old Loadstars just keep rollin'. Half-ton plow"—he gestured expansively, like a captain at his new vessel—"carbide steel, lasts the whole season. Carry eight ton of three-to-one in the bed. Lever here runs the spinner. Don't need a guy with a shovel like in your day. Say, she's glassy this morning, isn't she?"

Halvorsen sat silent, head nodding as the truck jolted and roared.

Fox said, "Saw a big old buck out here last week. Just caught a glimpse of him before he lined out for the brush, but looked to be a ten, twelve-pointer. Funny, looked like he had a heavier rack on the right side, you know? Ever see a deer like that?"

"Think I know the one you mean."

"Must be pretty crafty, takes 'em a while to grow antlers like that. Got to wonder if he'll make it through the season. Scary thought, you know? Wonder how we'd do, out in them woods, people after us . . . So, you still livin' way the hell up back of nowhere?"

"Uh huh."

"Takes all kinds, I guess. Me, I like people around. We just bought us a house out Finney Parkway. Solid oak floors. Get a paycheck ahead, we'll get some throw rugs from the Big Wheel—"

Halvorsen said, "On Finney? What number?"

"One-twenty-two."

"That was Dick Myers's house."

"Yeah, Myers, that was the name on the title."

"I worked a lease with Dick back in forty-eight. Dottie sold the place, huh? How's she doing?"

"She died six months ago. No, eight."

Fox shifted and the plow began snarling uphill. The headlights transmuted falling snow into spinning cones of gold, the whirly lights flicked it orange. "It was in shitty shape. Had to get the chimney pointed, do all new guttering . . ."

As he talked on, Halvorsen sank his chin into wet wool. He remembered '48. All their rigs, teams, tractors, worn out from the war. But Dan Thunner had driven them like dogs, opening up the gas fields along the Kinningmahontawany. He had a sudden vivid memory of Myers, face white as shitpaper, hauling and cursing at a length of five-inch casing. Dick had a weak heart. Never let on to the foreman, but the team knew and covered for him when they could. Until one day he'd pushed himself too hard in the cold, trying to drag a fallen tree off a pony line out near Hantzen.

The hot air licked at his cheeks, scorched his numbed thighs through long johns. The wipers clapped back and forth, forth and back. Snow blew through the open windows. He blinked, then squinted. "What's that?"

"What?"

"Stuff on the windshield. Looks like oil."

Fox shifted gears. "I don't know what that is. Soon's I got in the hollow I saw it smeared on the glass. Look out there, you can see it in the road."

"Where?"

"There, in front of the blade. See it? Kind of a darkness."

Halvorsen saw it then: a shadow beneath the new snow, two, three inches down. The polished steel whispered into it, peeling up a foot and a half of accumulated drift and sending it roaring away till the wind caught it and blew it back into the cab.

"I sure hope she likes this house."

"Who's that?" said Halvorsen. He'd lost the thread, thinking about the old days.

"The wife. We ain't been getting along too good. See, right after we got married I went out to Beaver Falls on that new particleboard factory. Had the foundations dozed out, then the project folded. I was lucky to get my pay."

"Rough."

"You said it. Things have changed since you retired, Racks. There just ain't nothing around here anymore. My brother, he— Ah, *Christ!*"

The skids juddered and screamed. Fox jerked the blade up. A Scout bolted past them, chains jingling, trailing powder snow like white smoke. "Well, like I was sayin', she and me got married, then I went right out on this job. When I come back it was like she didn't remember me. Kind of depressing, y'know?"

Halvorsen nodded absently, looking out. They were leaving the hollow, coming out into the valley. Empty fields glowed suddenly on the far side of the Allegheny. Bare and flat, they stretched off in shadowed dips and waves to a stand of dead-looking beech and a ruined barn, sunken like a corpse's cheeks. He remembered it; past that was a powerhouse, pumping jacks. You had to be careful up there. The separator pits were easy to see in summer, but they were deadly under snow. On top floated a bubbly rime of grease, dirt, small dead animals; below that was waste oil, and on the bottom, black water. If you made a misstep, if you were alone, you might never get out.

The snow was still coming down when the plow slowed, flashers blasting the wavering curtain orange, white, orange, and pulled over. The driver's door rasped open. Halvorsen climbed stiffly over Fox and let himself down onto the cleared center of the street. The younger man leaned out. "Sure this is okay?"

"You saved me three miles. Thanks."

The door slammed above him, and a moment later exhaust exploded. The truck grunted through a three-point turn, denting the snowbanks. Halvorsen lifted his hand in farewell. But as it came by him again Fox leaned out, mopping at his mouth with a handkerchief. "So whatta ya think I ought to do?" he shouted.

"About what?"

"About the wife. You used to be married, didn't you?"

Halvorsen looked up at the young face, reddened with cold or embarrassment; grinning to deny seriousness; but asking, still, for help. He didn't answer right away, thinking not so much about what the boy had asked but why he'd asked him. As if surviving a lifetime made you an expert at living. He'd gotten some of the oily stuff on his face too, and on his hands when he got out. He took out his bandanna and dabbed at it, considering. Finally he said, "Well, it's hard to know what's in a person's heart, son. Sometimes even for them. Give it time. It'll probably turn out all right."

To his relief Fox didn't take it wrong. In fact he seemed to think Halvorsen was joking. He laughed again, waved, and put the plow in gear. It shuddered and rolled away, leading a motorcade of cars and pickups that had waited patiently for it to move on.

Halvorsen stood alone again, rebuttoning his coat, watching the smooth oblivious faces glide past. God, it was cold. He stood trying to remember where he was going, then turned to stare down the street.

Did he drop me in the wrong town?

It felt wrong, alien, like another country. He stood motionless, his mind gnawing at it. It made no sense. He'd grown up outside Raymondsville. Danced with its girls, gotten rowdy on needled beer in its saloons, lived here for years with Jennie. Why, he'd been in just last month for beans and coffee and bacon.

But though his mind told him where he was, something deeper told him he was wrong.

Suddenly Racks Halvorsen felt afraid.

The details, then. He squinted. Pickard's Drug. Same gold-leafed sign. Only the displays had changed since his boyhood. No longer Save the Baby, Castoria, Black-Draught, but some new hemorrhoid preparation; inside no longer elixirs, paregoric, but antibiotics and stress vitamins . . . Beyond it the railroad embankment, that too the same, the rusty switches, the glass globes of the crossing guard round and red as candied apples.

But then a void, a vacancy in the world as it once was and thus to him somehow still ought to be. He stood blinking in the falling snow, wondering if his next blink would make the old Erie Lackawanna stationhouse reappear. Would retrieve from time's memory its rose-petal brick, the arched portico of sooty gilt and lace-metal, the porcelain drinking-fountain, the solid iron wheels of the baggage-wagons. If another blink would bring back the vanished blocks beyond. In his boyhood they'd been banks, producers' offices, machine shops, beer joints. From his manhood he remembered them as thrift shops, relief offices, and from middle age abandoned storefronts.

Then one day the bulldozers came. The *Century*'s editorials had talked brightly of an assembly plant; then of a shopping center; at last, in a kind of Rotarian despair, of low-income housing.

Halvorsen squinted into the wind till the world wavered in tears. But nothing returned. The town's heart was still. Dead. He wondered what would spring next from that razed ground, sowed with sharded glass as the teeth of dragons.

He shuddered suddenly, and forced his legs into motion. The snow fell like soot from burning icebergs. The Christmas decorations were already up. They hung shabby, decades old, from the lightposts. Abreast of Pickard's he turned for the Raymondsville Hotel. He remembered only when confronted by blank plywood that it too was gone, shot, kaput.

He stood for a moment shivering, brain empty as a jug. Then recognized the door next to it. It jingled gaily as he pulled it open.

"Morning, Racks." As he stamped snow from his boots a short man, fiftyish, came out from behind a stack of secondhand records. His hands trembled as he adjusted his glasses; his eyes, magnified to golf balls, focused somewhere to Halvorsen's left.

"Hullo, Les. How's business?"

"You're first one today. Help you with something?"

"Just come in to get warm, thanks."

Les Rosen, the owner, busied himself behind the counter while Halvorsen presented his backside to a nickeled Amherst. He looked around absently. Worn washboards, a thirdhand dresser with curling veneer. A Kelsey handpress, a bronze lamp without a shade. Engravings of Jesus and locomotives, sepia-toned men in handlebar mustaches with watch chains, grim busty women in black, all either faded or darkened to a contrastlessness that made it hard for him to tell in the gloom what he was looking at.

He strolled over to a wooden ice chest. On it, beneath a photo of the 1937 St. Rocco's women's basketball team, were three Nancy Drew novels, a glass rolling-pin, and a dented metal can a foot long.

"Bet you know what that is," said Rosen, puttering up behind him. His fingers never left the tables, the walls, as if he were hauling himself through the past by handholds.

"Nitro can."

"Yeah, picked up a bunch of those when the blasting company went out of business."

"Sell any?"

The owner shrugged. "They'll move. It's not like I got to worry about overhead. Say, I got one nice thing out of that sale."

"What?"

Rosen opened the ice chest. In it was a wooden box, mitered at the corners, with a walnut handle at the top. Halvorsen took it with both hands—it looked heavy, and was—and turned it over. The letters were burned into the wood. *Hercules Powder Company, 50 Cap Blasting Machine, Connect Wires Only After Charge Is Set.*

"Spark box," said Halvorsen. He lowered it to the floor and drew up the plunger. It came smoothly and he saw that the toothed metal was oiled and rustless. He licked his little finger and then his index. He bridged that hand between the brass screw-posts, then with the other drove suddenly down. Within the box the armature whirred.

He smiled faintly and straightened, massaging shock-tingling fingers.

"Probably seventy, eighty years old. But she works, don't she? What you think it's worth?"

"No idea."

"I'd take fifty for it."

Halvorsen hefted it again, then slid it back into its copper-lined coffin. "Thanks, Les. But I got no use. Now, a bolt for a .30 Krag—that I might scratch up a buck for."

"Sorry."

Rosen puttered his way back behind the counter. Halvorsen lingered for a few more minutes, then drifted toward the door. A loose board gave him away.

"Leavin' already?"

"Got some errands to do. Then I'll probably head over't' the Brown Bear, see if anybody's around."

"Stop back any time."

The door jangled behind him with ominous gaiety, returning him from the safe past to whatever year this was. He'd felt okay with Rosen. But the strangeness had waited outside for him all this time, like a stray dog hoping for a master. Again it stopped him, made him look vacantly down the street.

What in the hell was wrong?

His mind found no answer. Only the snow, the wind, the loneliness of a blighted and dying town.

Halvorsen shivered suddenly. Was it a judgment? Over and over greedy men had torn fortunes from these blasted hills. They'd laughed at the future. Now it was here.

But whatever was coming, whatever he was dreading, he didn't want to meet it. He'd fought hard all his life. He was old now. Tired. He wanted to be left alone.

Closing his eyes, he lifted his face to the sky. To the icy death-kisses of snowflakes on his forehead, on his neck, on his bare still-tingling hands.

Another tremor shook him, of cold but also of something not far from terror. His hands slapped his pockets, then fell back helplessly to his sides. Only now, too late, did he remember that his scarf and gloves still lay on the seat of a snowplow, headed west.

Two

And the snow fell without cease. It whispered down on silent hills; on an old man's upturned face; on the cab of a snowplow rumbling toward the county line. Soft, heavy, endless, it hissed down past the windows of the high school like congealed silence.

Phil Romanelli was sealed off from it by grimy glass into a steamy classroom on the second floor. He sat at one of three dozen identical desks. His face was too thin and his hair too long, and his left leg was twisted like a climbing plant.

At last he lowered his eyes to the note that had reached him a moment before, announced by a pencil-prod from fat Alice Saunters behind him. Miss Marzeau had missed the pass. He held it unopened, trembling a little.

He was savoring the possibility that it might be from Alexandrine Ryun. His explanation, a few minutes before, of why Jim had accepted the challenge of the island might have done the trick. An excited twitch made his leg knock rapidly against the desk.

With infinite care, shielding his hand behind Ed Masters's broad oblivious back, he peeled the palm-dampened paper apart.

KNOCK IT OFF SMART MOUTH read pencilscrawl. OR ILL TEACH YOU TO SUCK MY DICK INSTEAD OF MARZEAUS ASS.

Phil stared at it as the teacher droned on. Lozenge-shaped iron walls were closing on him, glowing-hot. Though half the seats in the room were vacant, depopulated by the first snowfall, the very air seemed suddenly solid with hatred.

He didn't know which of them had sent the note. But he knew the type. They sprawled in the back row with their arms folded, sniggering to each other. They made farting noises with their hands. Technically they were his peers, but Phil had realized long ago they were of separate species. *Jockus americanus*, the common musclebrain, resisted learning as the Dutch resist the sea. While he sat near the front in every class; could not let an idea pass without challenge; could not accept an assertion without subjecting it to the proof of argument.

And could never, ever, be a jock.

His eyes caught snow again, and drifted down with it. Till they found Alex. Two rows over she sat with chin propped on fist, a faint smile touching her lips. Her lips . . . he stared, unaware that his clenched jaw had loosened, his mouth had fallen open slightly. Rounded softnesses shifted beneath her sweater as she tossed back her head, sending that long, long hair back to break in fatal shining surf . . .

The teacher's voice faded to a dull ache. His eyeballs, sandpapered by the dry heat, centered and fixed. A more absorbing drama had taken center stage, with himself—edited here and there, but himself as everyone is most himself in dream—in the title role.

He and Alex had spent the evening at the Dirty Shirt, but neither liquor nor lateness slowed the Stag. He'd parked the Firebird off the road, across a disused spur, and they were screened from midnight travelers by brush and the solid dark mass of the hills.

The first kiss. She moaned. Soon she was panting.

Moonlight gleamed tangled in red-gold hair. His fingers polished soft flesh, slow, maddening. She leaned back, shuddering, and the moon silvered her eyelids. His fingers considered the curve of her breast as he bent his lips to her panting mouth, her long white throat. When his hand dropped she tensed, then gave in with a helpless cry. Her arms came up, round his neck, and drew him downward.

The bucket seats changed magically to a bed. Beyond the window snowflakes fell like cold manna from an opaque sky. She wore a nightgown the texture of fog. His hand explored beneath it, then dipped within. Her flesh was hot and smooth, like incandescent petals.

"Phil, I want you. I need you inside me." Her burning eyes locked with

his in the near-darkness. Her hungry mouth demanded him. His fist gathered gauzy material, and suddenly ripped it apart. Beneath was wanton alabaster, smooth and hairless as Aphrodite in the art books.

He took her almost violently. Not because it was what she wanted. But because it was his desire.

Alex Ryun, the real one, stretched up her hand. Recalled by the motion, Phil wrenched himself back from cool sheets and scented moonlight. Here the air was dull with carbon dioxide, suffused with a high earnest drone of literature, permeated by a glow of hatred like the dry heat from the rusting radiators.

"That's right, Alexandrine. The most interesting thing here is Conrad's use of what's called a 'frame.' The opening and closing scenes are set pieces within which a narrator tells a story. Now, why is it done that way? Who is Marlow, really? Yes—Bethany, go ahead."

The thin eager voice faded, leaving no mark or echo in his hormone-driven consciousness. The crippled boy's eyes glazed over again. Helplessly libidinous as a male mantis, they bored through the shadows that surrounded him to his inmost desire, the fantasy, the lubricious, impossible dream.

Yes, the disease still existed. To the surprise of people he met. It seemed they always had to know exactly what was wrong with his leg, his hip, his arm.

He didn't remember the onset. But the first images he could retrieve of life were of bed, doctors, stainless steel, and pain.

At Strong Memorial in Rochester the specialists hadn't encouraged his parents. There were operations, they said, that might straighten the twisted leg. But there was little chance of the boy's walking. It was Joe Romanelli who'd insisted on surgery. Regardless of cost, regardless of the pain.

The worst operation had been the third, when Phil was seven. Most of his leg muscles were gone, atrophied and resorbed. The surgeon, a quiet balding man, brought hand puppets on his rounds. He pretended they were biting the children's withered limbs and chests. He'd spent six hours teasing out smaller muscles from the undamaged ones in Phil's legs, and connecting them with ligaments cannibalized from the left arm.

After that came endless months of excruciating therapy. Nurses

and therapists, pulling like devils in a Boschian hell, till it seemed
the gleaming machines would tear his joints apart. Endless drill to
retain muscle tissue, to reprogram his brain. A hundred thousand
calf-builders, quad-builders, and stretches. Always stretches. He
still did them every morning. If he neglected them, even for a day,
those painfully rebuilt muscles would tighten back toward uselessness.

In a way, his father had been proved right. Phil was strong. He
could walk for miles. But one thigh would always be too weak for
him to move without a limp. He had to aid it with his lower torso,
hitching it forward from the hip at each step.

Now the boy who'd outlasted the knife was seventeen. He
dreamed, and knew bitterly that what he dreamed could never
happen. In his fantasies he saw himself as the Stag. Awake, as a
virgin, a cripple, and a nerd.

Which of the two did those around him see? Did Alex Ryun see?

It was an important question. He'd thought about it a lot.
Because if he'd never be anything more, he'd decided it might be
better not to live.

Alex had only panties on now, and was daring him to reach across
the aisle by caressing her sweat-slicked belly, when he became
aware of a change around him. He returned unwillingly to the
other universe, the one outside his head. At least, nude or not,
whether she knew he was alive or not, Alexandrine Ryun was in it
with him.

Reality, he thought. Chipmunk shit.

"And that will be due next week," Marzeau's voice, at once
dust-dry and breathless with excitement, concluded. "Any questions?"

Despite the total inattention of what passed for his conscious
mind, Phil found that some obscure part of his brain had retained
the words before that. They were "Four pages, typewritten, double-
spaced." He raised his hand, conscious as he did so of the cessation
of normal classroom sounds—belches, sniggers, undertones—
from the back.

"Philip?"

"Ma'am, I caught everything about that except the subject."

"The subject of your composition is to be an older person,
preferably over seventy. Interview the individual and record his life
story in his or her own words. This is to show you how to bring out

character through dialogue—something Mr. Hemingway was good at."

He nodded, lowered his head. The awareness behind him relaxed. But a flame had ignited inside him. His glance had crossed hers, just for a moment.

Had he imagined it, or had Alex Ryun smiled at him?

The next class was social studies, taught by Mr. Maxwell, a slight man with restless eyes who smoked a pipe in the teacher's lounge. Today's subject was socialism. Phil had been looking forward to it. He'd found the dusty tomes by Wells and Bellamy in the back stacks of the Carnegie. If socialism meant an even start for everybody, justice and equality, he was for it. When Maxwell asked for comments on the reading his hand lofted itself before he was well aware of it. It stalled halfway as he recalled the note, then continued up. He doubted whoever had passed it was in this class too. Anyway it was too late now. I may be a mouse, he thought. But I'm gonna squeak.

"Romanelli, enlighten us."

"Uh, I thought the reading was kind of slanted."

"Interesting. Meaning what?"

"Well, first all that stuff about Utopia. Then the Communist Manifesto; then the thing by Lenin about how terror is great. Isn't that too simple? Like, you can choose capitalism and get freedom, or socialism and get prison camps. According to the book, there's nothing in between."

"You don't think the textbook's right?" said Maxwell. "Well, a hand from the hinterland! Yes—there in back."

"Horse puckey. Socialism, communism, it's the same thing."

"No, it isn't," said Phil, half-turning in his seat. "Communism, the government owns everything, socialism, just the industry and airlines and stuff. But then the country gets run to benefit everybody. Not just people with money, like now."

A different voice. "What's wrong with capitalism?"

"It doesn't do anything for the people on the bottom. Ayn Rand, I read her stuff, she's like the capitalist prophet. But she only writes about rich, super-talented people. How about the ones who aren't geniuses with megabucks? Who'll never have anything, unless somebody helps them?"

"They should get a job."

"Sure, but what if they can't? Like here, the casket factory, it's shut down. And Thunder Oil laid off tons of people. Is it their fault there aren't jobs?" Phil knew he was in too deep now. But he was getting mad. "The Gerroys, the Whites, the Thunners—why do they have so much, and old people who worked all their lives got nothing to eat? Why, if somebody gets sick, why's their family got to be poor from then on? Is that the way it ought to be?"

The kids around him were silent. "Look, I don't want to start an argument," he said, twisting in his chair. A fence of hostile or bored-out faces stared back. "But just because it's in a book doesn't mean it's true."

"You might have a point," said Maxwell. "But we have only a limited amount of time. Phil, can I ask a personal question?"

"Uh, sure."

"You're getting hot under the collar there. Do you just like to argue? Or is that what you really think?"

Some instinctive caution quelled his first attempt to speak; it made him stutter before he said, "I don't know. 'From each according to his ability, to each according to his need'—that don't sound too bad to me. But I guess it didn't work too good in Russia, did it?"

He forced himself to grin at the end of that. Foolishly.

Maxwell waited; then, when there were no more comments, gave a weary smile. "All right—ten minutes before lunch. Just long enough for a little pop quiz. Take out your crayons, kids."

The class groaned.

After lunch the school authorities surrendered to the snow. It had kept coming all morning, in bursts and flurries, and when Phil came out it was drifted to his knees. The wind bit at his face, pushed its icy muzzle down his neck. He zipped it out of his jacket, hugging his books under his left arm. Ahead of him kids hurried toward their parents' pickups or four-wheel-drives, some toward cars of their own. He didn't bother to look. It made him too depressed. His dad's car had a cracked block, hadn't run for years, just sat in the yard rusting.

Christ, he thought, Haven't we taken enough? Why do I got to be poor too?

He was looking at the way the snow had bleached Candler Hill to a faded, ominous gray when he heard the door clack open again behind him. He turned; slower than the rest, he'd thought himself last to leave the locker-lined corridor.

"Well, hell, if it ain't Professor Crip," said "Bubba" Detrick, grinning down at him.

Behind Detrick's red-and-gold bulk was another boy, a senior. Mooney, the bullet-headed shotputter, also in varsity colors.

"Let's go over behind the gym, buds."

"What for, Bubba?"

"What do you think for?" Detrick looked left and right, then gave him a shove that looked effortless but that sent Phil flying. Books hit the snow chuff, chuff, chuff, burrowing from sight like frightened woodchucks. "Come on, jerk, we got deep international issues to discuss."

Behind him, not speaking, the senior stood huge and immobile, screening them from the other students. "Move out. Behind el gym-o, Romanellito."

"Look, I don't want to fight you guys."

"Whoa! That's a relief. I told the Brick here, you sure we want to mix up with that guy? We piss him off, he'll hand us our assholes on a plate."

Behind the school the wind came hard and cold across the buried expanse of the football field, the goal posts like abandoned colossi in a white desert. When they were no longer visible from the lot Detrick moved close. He lifted Phil by the collar and breathed Juicy Fruit into his face.

"We had enough a' your wiseassin', Romo. Romo the Homo. I warned you in comp, but you done it again in Maxwell's class. You got no right to criticize America, buds. Not around us."

"I wasn't criticizing America."

"Shit you weren't! No, don't *explain*. We don't need to suffer through it again." Detrick shook his head wearily. "Okay, like I said, we already warned you."

The punch blasted low into his gut. He gasped and dropped the last book. The ball player hit him again, a careful backhand to the nose, then just below the breastbone. A sheet of light leaped up between him and his body. He dropped to his knees, unable to breathe or see. Mooney pulled him up and held him while Detrick took a few more shots.

Phil was dangling from the shotputter's arm when Detrick said something. "What?" he mumbled, through something slick and salty on his lips.

"I said, got 'nything smart to say now?"

"Yeah, I do. My dad—"

He stopped.

"Yeah, your dad, what? He's gonna come after us for roughin' you up? Hey, I doubt it, jerkoff. We know Pop the Cop. We know he's a lousy drunk too. You send him around any time."

"Fuck both of you guys," Phil said. He hated it when he started to cry.

Pain ripped through his head like a bullet. He tried to scream, but before he could Detrick slammed a ball of snow into his open mouth.

"Listen up, Crip. There ain't no reason you're here. People like you, they oughta put them all away someplace so we don't have to look at them. So do the rest of the world a favor. Keep your fuckin' teeth zipped and stay out of my sight. There's a lot worse shit can happen to you than getting slapped around a little."

"Bubba?" A girl's voice, calling from the lot. For a moment Phil thought he recognized it.

Detrick turned his head. "Gotta go," he said to Mooney. "Think that'll give us a little peace and quiet?"

The shotputter jerked his shoulders. Detrick released Phil's ears and he fell into the snow, face down.

"Wait a minute. He breathin'?"

"You breathin', Crip? Say something."

A boot probed for his kidneys; he tried blindly to roll away.

"He's okay."

Bubba, shouting: "Comin', darlin'!"

"Anytime you want to talk more of that shit in class, have a ball," he heard Detrick toss back over his shoulder. "You want to be a troublemaker, hey, that's fine with us. It's a free country. Just remember, we'll be right behind you."

He lay there for a long time, watching his blood melt slowly into the perfect cleanness of the snow. Perfect cleanness. Perfect cold. Cold as steel. He closed his eyes, but it seemed like his mind went no further than that.

Then the cold blue steel of his father's service .38.

Three

O

h, *there* you are, dear!''

Jaysine flinched, jerked from reverie. At the door of her station
Marybelle Acolino cocked her head, watchful as a crow. She realized she'd been daydreaming in her chair.

"Your two o'clock's here, dear. Don't you think you should be
out front to greet her?''

"Yes, Marybelle," she said, but inside she thought an ugly word.

Her two o'clock looked pale and scared. When she closed the
door on the wind she stood waiting-still, one gloved hand to her
mouth. Her eyes darted like a trapped sparrow's about the busy hot
interior of the Style Shoppe.

Jaysine moved toward her, fitting a smile to her lips. Beyond the
swagged curtains the day was sliding toward dusk. She felt a spurt of
anxiety about the storm, icy roads. Brad had said he'd be over
tonight. Lord, let him get here safe, she thought.

"Karen?''

The girl turned, startled. Her eyes fixed whitely on Jaysine's; her
smile was tremulous. "That's me. Are you the—?''

"Yes. Come on, let's talk in back.''

As they passed the other customers Jaysine saw her glance
fearfully at them. Toweled, awaiting rejuvenation under the whining dryers, they ignored her. Most were three times her age.

They're always so frightened, she thought. What do they think I'm going to do to them?

Still smiling, she closed the door to her station. "Now, why don't you just sit down, Karen? And we'll discuss your little problem and how I can help."

Jaysine Farmer saw herself as too short, not blond enough, and too involved with chocolate and crullers. Her face was full behind Anne Klein glasses; her hips were what the magazines called "generous."

She'd grown up in Four Holes, a mile from the New York state line. Her grandfather had started a dairy store there in the twenties. Till she was sixteen she'd expected to spend her youth behind its counter, mining out Rocky Road and Mint Chocolate Chip with the aluminum scoop, making change, and flirting not too obviously with the customers, until Someone came to take her away.

Then business fell off. When the store failed, her father, a silent man, shot himself one night out in the barn.

After they sold the farm the family split up. Brothers and sisters gone to Richmond and Atlanta, two into the navy. Now only she and her mother were left, her mother still practicing Science in the old house and the store itself bulldozed into oblivion when they widened the road going north.

She'd used her share of the money for a year at Johnstown College of Cosmetology. All the courses were interesting: Personal Hygiene, Hairdressing, Dermatology, History of Beauty. But halfway through she'd read a book on Permanent Hair Removal. About how electrolysis was not just a job but one of the healing arts. And curled up that night in her rented room, looking at the awful before and miraculous after pictures, she'd suddenly known that there, not in fixing hair or doing manicures, was her profession, her calling, and her fate.

As the girl laid her purse and coat aside Jaysine noted the growth on her upper lip; the shoulder-length hairdo, swept forward to hide her face; the dark, slightly oily complexion.

She gave her a moment to look around the station. The only private one in the Shoppe, it was paneled with imitation walnut, dark, professional, rather than the frantic pink of the main salon. She'd decorated it too: a vase with silk nasturtiums, pictures of a covered bridge and of Jesus at Gethsemane, and a cypress plaque, Gothic-lettered with *Today is the first day of the rest of your life.*

And best of all, Eterni-Sealed on woodgrain plaques in front of the operating chair, her diploma from Johnstown and her R.E. certification from the Pennsylvania Society of Electrologists.

"Is this your first experience with permanent hair removal, Karen?"

"That's right."

"Well, let me tell you a bit about our procedure," Jaysine began, leaning forward. *Eye contact.* "Now, there are four things everyone asks. So to save us both time, I'll answer them up front! First of all, it doesn't hurt. Second, hair removed by electrolysis will not come back. It's not like waxing or tweezing or shaving. The root will be dead, you'll never see it again.

"Third, how long will it take? I can't answer that before we talk about your specific needs, but by the time you leave today we should have a timetable for your treatments. The same applies to the cost."

The girl nodded submissively. "Now," said Jaysine, lowering her voice, "How can I help you, Karen?"

"I'm kind of hairy all over, I mean my arms and things. So is my mother."

"I think you look very attractive," said Jaysine, though of course she'd noticed the upper lip right away.

"It's my bikini line."

"The lower abdomen?"

"Yes."

"How high does it extend?"

"Higher than it should." She colored. "I've been taking it off. But when I'm . . . intimate with someone, you can tell. My boyfriend used to say he liked it. But now he doesn't . . . say nice things anymore."

Oh Lord, Jaysine thought. She loved her work, but it dismayed her sometimes, the emotional freight her customers dragged in with them. It was funny. If you had an ugly behind or lousy fingernails you didn't waste time on shame. You fixed them, or diverted attention with accessories. But hair, body hair, seemed to be different.

"It's natural, Karen. Unfortunately, what's natural isn't always what's beautiful. Why don't we take a look at what we're dealing with."

She made her voice businesslike and the girl responded to it, straightening and stopping her sniffle. Jaysine tilted the chair. Karen lifted her skirt, peeled down her panty hose, and gazed without any trace of expression at the ceiling.

"Would you move your legs apart, please? Just an inch, please."

This was no bikini line problem. The pubic hair formed not a triangle but a diamond, with heavy centerline growth all the way up to the navel. Heavy growth on the thighs too. She pulled up a pinch of skin. Fortunately Karen had shaved rather than tweezing or waxing.

When Jaysine looked up her two o'clock was weeping silently. "Can you do anything?" she whispered.

"Look here," said Jaysine. "Sit up. See where my finger is? We're going to take away the hair from here up. Plus all this on the inside of your legs. Make it go away forever. How's that sound?"

Karen nodded. Jaysine turned briskly away and began opening drawers, laying out her equipment.

"This here is the electrolysis machine. I place this tiny needle right into the hair root and press the pedal down with my foot. When we're finished the hair slides right out. I'd like to have you come in twice a week. Karen, I'd say in about three months we'll have your problem down to nothing."

"That would be good," the girl whispered, and for the first time hope showed in her eyes. "I'd like that very much."

Later Jaysine stood outside her station, wiping her hands. The astringencies of alcohol and aloe vera sliced the perfumed air. Marybelle wasn't there. She dabbed at her nose; she'd felt a little feverish for the last week; but it hadn't developed into a cold or anything. Sighing, she perched the tissue on an overflowing wastebasket. Letting her hand fall to her side, she looked down the double row of chairs.

The salon was twice the size of a living room, five stations, with the sixth partitioned off for her. In the infinite multiplication of mirrored walls hundreds of ample women in white smocks bent over shrouded bodies. Hanging plants stretched off into a curving jungle, leaves swaying beneath the overhead fans. At each chair the operator had taped pictures of her children and inspirational knickknacks from Hallmark. The stands overflowed with brushes, curlers, nail polish, pumice stones. Tall glass jars held combs angrily erect in bluegreen Barbicide.

"You want this frosted, just a bit? Here on the side or down the middle? That's very stylish, yes?"

"So then he said, my son, he said a bad word. And I don't care how old he is, I taught him not to talk that way around his mother. And I took and hauled off on him. I tell you it taught him some respect."

"This strand here's the final color. Does that look like what you want, dear?"

Jaysine walked toward the front. Her feet hurt. She felt hot, and wondered for a moment if she was getting sick. She wondered how the older women, Marguerite for instance, could stand it. At least she could sit when she was working. But Marguerite, tan support stockings bulging like sausage casings, stood chattering bright-eyed as a jay from eight A.M. till six and seven at night; and her sixty-eight years old. It was a wonder, that was for sure.

"Hello, Mrs. Teach."

"Hello, Jaysine. I was telling Marguerite here, I told her to go right to the hospital with it."

"What's that, Mrs. Teach?"

"My daughter. She's been getting bad eczema . . . she breaks out all the time. On her face, on her arms. I don't know why, when she was a teenager her skin was flawless, just flawless."

Jaysine murmured something consoling and slid past toward the waiting area. She'd just let herself down, sliding the weight down with a sigh, when the door jingled open. She jumped up, but it was too late; Mrs. Acolino came in, carrying two lidded cups.

"*Jaysine*, dear. Don't you have any more customers? Why aren't you helping the others? How about this lady. Miss, what can we do for you?"

"I'm here for your special pedicure. See, I got the coupon out of the paper." The old woman looked up through cunning eyes, offering the scrap.

"Miss Farmer here will take care of you. Give Alison a break, Jaysine. Trud-*ee*! Here's your coffee!"

Jaysine hated doing pedicures, but Marybelle made her do them every chance she got. She knew why. It was the profits from the electrolysis booth. Marybelle had promised her half after six months, but here it was nearly a year and she was still only getting thirty-three percent.

Jaysine pried the customer's boots off, then peeled free torn knee-highs with black soles of solid dirt. The feet were a mess. The cuticles sheathed the brown-ridged toenails almost to the ends. Worse, it was all too obvious she hadn't washed her feet in ages.

"What are you doing?" the woman snapped.

"This is a bath for your feet."

"I come for the pedicure. I want the pedicure."

"You get a foot bath first. There's no extra charge."

At the corner of her eye she sensed Mrs. Acolino's blue smock. "Is there a problem, Jaysine?"

"No. No problem, Marybelle." The old woman looked unpleasant, but didn't contradict her. Marybelle went in back, carrying her coffee.

Hot soapy water and an antiseptic bath improved the atmosphere somewhat. Jaysine eyed a splendid set of varicose veins while waiting for the cuticle softener to work. At last she tossed her hair back and got down to work, humming, pushing dead skin back with the orange stick.

The old woman muttered.

"What did you say, ma'am?"

"I said, it's a wonder a pretty girl like you isn't married."

She could hardly believe her ears. "What do you mean by that?"

"You know, no ring and all. How old are you, girl?"

"I believe that's my business," she said, thinking, Shave the corn down? Forget it. These feet weren't going to any cocktail parties. She selected a fresh stick and began working under the nail. That hadn't been done for a long time either.

The old woman shifted, then suddenly cried out.

"What's wrong, Miss?" Marybelle was there instantly, glaring sideways at Jaysine while she bent over the customer.

"She *hurt* me. She's diggin' in with that stick—"

"Jaysine, can't you be gentle! You know you can cause infection if you get too far up under the nail. I know you don't like to do pedicure, darling, you think you're above it."

"No, I don't, Marybelle, I—"

"Miss, I'm sorry, I don't know what's on her mind today. Some man, probably. Would you like another operator?"

"She'll do, but she got to take it easy. I'm an old lady," said the customer, humbly; but Jaysine saw the tyrannous spark in her eyes. She glared after Marybelle. What did she mean, that crack about men?

Two hours later she stood outside, inhaling the icy wind with relief as she pulled on her mittens.

The Style Shoppe, her workday universe, shrank to one door out of thirteen between Main and the creek. Her apartment was a block away. She stepped up onto the embanked snow, piled waist-high by the plow, but it was too soft to support her. Her flat Red Cross whites disappeared, numbing her ankles through the hose. She muttered an ugly word. Well, she'd have to change anyway, before *he* got here—

Thinking about Brad made the air suddenly warm. Humming, she swung along as above her the streetlights flickered, buzzed, then detonated copper light into the dusk.

After a hot bath and a half hour in front of her vanity, she perched on the window seat and looked down at the sidewalk. Then lifted her nails, scrutinizing them like a diamond cutter. She wasn't sure she liked Revlon Sunset Russet. But her hair was perfect. Marguerite had bobbed it, highlighting where it lifted off the forehead and sweeping it to one side to lengthen her face. The earrings were two-inch hoops made of old demitasse spoons. Daring, but she liked the effect. She'd made them herself.

She glanced across the room to a small workbench. A vise and anvil, a buffing wheel. A pitch bowl and an annealing pan made from a wok. Above the bench were racked saws and files, various punches, her other silversmithing tools. Her latest project lay on it, half-finished. She got up and put it away, in a drawer. It was a pair of drop-cast cuff links, which she was setting with a banded gray agate.

The things we do for men, she thought.

She went back to the window, waving her hands slowly, reviewing the status of dinner.

She was looking at her watch when the midnight blue two-door emerged from darkness. It slid past half-buried cars toward her block, slowing as it breasted where a pickup had just pulled out. But went on. Turned the corner, its exhaust glowing like evaporating gold in the clear icy air of night on Main Street, Raymondsville, Pennsylvania.

A few minutes later she started at a buzz. Her heels clattered down the stairs. Watch that loose step . . . She swung the door wide, shivering at the blast of cold.

A sudden vacuum pulled their bodies together. Her skin tingled where his car coat, dewed with melted snow, crushed her breasts, her belly. Snow glittered on his hair. Her hands curled into his back. "Brad! I'm so glad . . . I was starting to worry."

"Hi, babe. How've you been? Jeez, let's get warmed up, here."

In the apartment he pulled a bottle from under his coat. "Dom Perignon. Ever tried it?"

"Who are you kidding? If we have a good week at the Shoppe I might drink a Straub's."

"You're not a beer woman, Jay. You're a champagne girl. Get us some glasses, babe."

As they came opposite the kitchen nook she detached herself and unwrapped the bottle. Started to put it into the fridge. He stopped her. "It's chilled enough. I'll open it in a minute. Come on, let's sit on the couch."

"Dinner first."

"I said, the couch." He mock-growled and she squealed as his arms took her off-balance.

The veal was overdone, warmed too long, but the rest of the meal turned out fine. The wine, too, was what she'd come to expect of Brad Boulton: nothing sweet, nothing cheap, just the best.

She watched fondly as he devoured apple crisp with hand-whipped cream.

Brad was the tallest man she'd ever dated. His face was square, with no softness at all in his jawline, no fat, like so many men his age. His eyes were light gray; she'd had to return three lots of agates before she was satisfied she'd matched them. With his dark hair the combination was striking. She hadn't known men's shirts could be tailormade. He wore nice suits all the time, or expensive soft Italian sweaters. He did all his shopping in New York.

She interlaced her fingers, prim now, though she was wearing nothing but her slip, and let flow through her like champagne and honey the knowledge that he was secretly hers.

"Why didn't you call me from Nevada? You said you would. I waited up all week."

"Nevada?" He stared at her, fork poised. "You mean Tucson? That's Arizona. Yeah, I'm sorry, we got bound down in the negotiations, they went late. We're about to close. Going to start interviewing for a manager pretty soon."

"Is Tucson nice?"

"Compared to this, it's heaven. This damn snow . . ." He waved its dismissal. She smiled; it wouldn't have surprised her to look out and see it gone. "It's warm there. Dry."

"I'd love to go out west. Did you go alone?"

"Oh . . . not really."

She was instantly sorry. They had a sort of rule, not to mention his wife when they were together. She appreciated how he'd told her everything straight out, on their first date. He worked in oil, something about marketing. His marriage was loveless, but his wife was emotionally ill. He felt he owed it to her to stay. He had to think of his daughter too. He loved her more than anything else, Jaysine knew that just from the way he talked about her.

She valued that, his openness. It made her the "other woman," but after a struggle with herself she'd accepted that. It was like he'd said once. This was his real life, with her, and what he did with his wife was a masquerade.

He set the wineglass aside. She saw at close range how the heavy dark hairs of his wrist curled as he tilted up her chin. "Hey, almost forgot. You like silver, right?"

"Oh, Brad." She turned it, examining the dull gleam, the tiny hammer-marks. Turquoise, but not a good grade, and the mountings were badly soldered. It looked like something he'd bought at the airport. "It's so . . . heavy," she said. It was all she could think of to praise about it.

"That's Navaho work. Picked it up out west."

Well, it wasn't his fault he didn't know anything about jewelry. "It's lovely. Thank you." She slipped it on, held it out as if admiring it.

"Say, babe. About that bedroom of yours—"

"It's still in the same place."

"Let's just check, to make sure."

His face filled her sight like the sun. Oh, it could be better. His wife could . . . get well, so he wouldn't feel he had to stay with her. He could call her more often.

But she didn't think things like that very often. Jaysine knew how few decent men there were in a small town like this.

She knew when she was lucky.

Later, in the street, Boulton stood beside his car, retying his tie and staring with disbelief at the rocker panel.

Christ, he thought. It's rusting already. There, faint yet undeniable beneath midnight blue, was the bubbled ugliness of corrosion. Not a year old. It's the fucking salt they put on the roads, he thought. Remembering it, he lifted his shoe. They were ruined too, three-hundred-dollar Johnson & Murphys.

God, he hated this hole.

He tucked in his tie, evened the ends of the scarf, and finished buttoning his coat. He looked up and down the street, then stared blankly at the sailor hats the snow had put on the parking meters.

His thoughts went back to what they'd never, even with the woman, left far behind. To strategy, anxiety, and survival. These things never left his mind. That was why he thought sometimes that Thunder Oil ran him more than he did it.

Before he'd taken over it had been run like something out of a history book. Zero debt-load, encumbered with illiquid assets, pensions, and overemployment. After he'd married Ainslee he'd worked like he'd never worked in his life, streamlining, firing, cutting back, divesting.

It hadn't made him Mr. Popular. But it had paid off. He'd turned cash flow around just in time, saving the company when oil prices crashed.

But it was still undiversified. The board called it sticking to their lasts. He called it dangerous idiocy. Thunder was economically marginal, and it was touch and go whether he'd be able to save it.

His mouth tightened. The board. Old farts with a few shares each, fighting him every step of the way. He could smell death on them. For Ainslee, for himself, above all for Willie, he had to destroy them.

The butt of his cigarette hissed as the snow quenched it. The door slammed. The Jag purred into life. As it crunched over the fresh fall he glanced upward. A shadow at the window. Could she see him? Just in case, he mimed blowing a kiss through the windshield.

What a wonderful night, he thought, his hand dropping absently to scratch his crotch. A home-cooked dinner with a small-town hairdresser . . . He remembered New York, the last trip to brief the new ad agency. That PR girl had been wild . . . But Jaysine gave him what he needed. She'd do, at least till things settled with Ainslee, and he could think about what came next. As long as she didn't get possessive.

He pulled out onto Route Six, dropping back from his first burst of speed as the Michelins writhed on black ice, treacherous, invisible till you were on top of it. A moment later his mind was back on business.

Four

The bear towered above the old man like a falling redwood, claws like the poised blades of guillotines. Eight feet of chocolate-furred fury snarled down at him, baring two-inch fangs the color of abused piano keys. He was that close he could smell its rank wild odor, faint now, overlaid with the smells of tobacco and beer and cooking.

Yeah, Halvorsen thought, blinking up at it for the thousandth time, Sonny done a hell of a job on this one.

He stood just within the tavern, squinting past the mounted animal. As his eye penetrated the gloom his hand reached up absently to pat a worn patch of fur.

They'd shot it in the Cassiars just before the war. He and Lew Pearson had put four .375 belted magnum bullets into the huge brown before it had stopped, as Lew used to tell it in his Alabama drawl, "With hits paws on our feet, like it was aiming to untie our bootlaces and start eatin' on us toes first."

So many years ago, yet the bear remained, still upright, still fierce, still awesome as ever. Just as the mountains remained; just as W. T. Halvorsen remained. Though, the old man thought, the less said about his own condition the better.

But Lew Pearson had never come back from Kasserine Pass that disastrous summer of 1942.

Behind the bar a fat man in an apron was stacking pilsner glasses. "Well, look who's here!"

"Hello, Lucky. What you up to?"

"About five feet five."

"Business good?"

"Can't complain. Be a madhouse when them hunters start coming in next week, though. I put in more miles behind this bar than most of them do in the woods."

Halvorsen nodded, looking around. Not much of a crowd for lunchtime. From the street window red-orange neon buzzed STRAUB'S. Uncushioned pine booths divided the room. Two men in Penelec jackets nodded to him over stoneware mugs. He lifted his chin; thought he recognized one of them; raised a hand, just in case. He turned back to Lucky Rezk. "Anybody in back?"

"Couple'a your pals, yeah."

He threaded his way past the cigarette machine into an alcove separate from the eating area and bar. Three old men sat there, hidden from the other customers, beer-glasses and shots of whiskey in front of them. He nodded to Jack McKee, Mason Wilson, Len DeSantis.

"Hey, Racks."

"H'lo, W.T."

"Hullo, boys. Where's Charlie?"

"You know how it is over't that home," said Wilson heavily. "Goddamn nurses won't let 'em take a leak by themselves, much less let 'em out in a snowstorm."

"Coffee," said Halvorsen to Rezk, over the Marlboro ad on the machine. "Fatso, shove over. You're double-parked again."

"Up yours, with a stick," said DeSantis mildly.

Halvorsen wedged himself into the seat, a pine pew Rezk's dad had carried out on his back when the Kluxers burned St. Rocco's. They'd started early, by the smell. But so what? No harm to anyone if a few old has-beens sat tippling away their Social Security checks. No harm.

He sat in silence for a comfortable while, absorbing the warmth from Lucky's big gas-heat blower and looking at his cronies.

McKee had been a tool dresser for the Gerroy outfit. Halvorsen remembered Jack's coarse blond hair, his curt, angry speech, the way he shaped carbon steel like whittling pine. Now he was bald and his hands shook with Parkinson's. Only the harsh way he jerked out his words, as if paying off a bet, remained of the man Halvorsen had gone fifteen rounds with in 1936.

Mase Wilson had worked oil, teamstering, and lumber from the day he turned fourteen. In those days there was no such thing as accident insurance, no workmen's comp, and no guards on the White Timber Company's bandsaws. For twenty years after he lost the arm he'd sold the Buffalo *Evening News*, Prince Edward cigars, and Hershey bars from a tin-sided newsstand on Veterans Square.

DeSantis. Halvorsen had known Fatso for sixty years; had played sandlot with him through the long dusk after his first day of school. A ladies' man once, bulky but a dandy, cheeks talced like a baby's butt as he bent to fit a shoe in the Fren-Le Bootery. Now he was gross, belly bursting his shirt, jowls drooping like a lard-assed hound's beneath whiskey-glazed eyes.

Time, you bastard, Halvorsen thought, you've made fools of us all. We fought the cold, fought this hard land to make our bread. Whipped Krauts on one side of the world, Nips on the other. But who remembers? Those who loved us most are gone. Those who remain—they see us not as we were, but as we are.

His eyes burned; he rubbed at them with a finger, surreptitiously, surprised at himself. Getting sentimental. They said it happened when you got old.

A cup rattled down in front of him. He grabbed for it, then restrained himself, ashamed of his greed for heat. "How much is that these days?" he asked Rezk, turning—no, it was Roberta, his wife. Her merry dark eyes were lost in flesh, like lumps of anthracite tossed into a snowbank.

"Straight coffee, no Irish? For you a quarter, William. You know I like to keep you boys happy back here." She waited as he counted out two nickels, a dime, five pennies onto the wet-ringed wood. "Anything else? Sandwich? Lunch? A little late for it, but—"

"Thanks, I ate out home."

"You still living out in the woods, in that old basement? You ought to get yourself married again. I worry about you, all alone out there. What if you had a fire?"

There was silence around the table. Halvorsen kept his eyes down, stirring in the sugar. "Oh," she said then. "I'm sorry . . . but really, you ought to. Now, I got a friend, she's got a house in town. You like cherry cobbler? She makes the best—"

"Thanks anyway, Roberta."

"Say, I heard a good one the other day," said DeSantis, belching. "Naw, Bert, don't go 'way. There's this guy out drivin' one day, and he goes past the old homestead. There's a farmer out there on his tractor. Guy stops and says, Say, this is where I grew up. Let me plow for a while. So the farmer says okay, and he goes inside for a break.

"When he comes back the guy's plowed the field real nice. All except two places. He's just plowed around them. And the farmer says, Why didn't you plow those two places? And the guy says, Well, right in the middle there used to be a big old willow tree, and I got my first piece of stuff under it.

"And the farmer nods and says, Okay, I understand that. But what about the other place? And the guy says, Well, that's where her mother happened to be standing. Oh, not so good, says the farmer. What'd she say when she saw you? And the guy says, 'Moo.'"

Despite himself Halvorsen had to smile. Not at the aged joke. At DeSantis. From beneath that mountain of fat, from behind the beer-filmed eyes, for just one moment an elbow-poking twelve-year-old had grinned out. And by extension McKee, and Wilson, and he too, were still somehow the same, each man's changeless self lurking and slouching like a night watchman through a vast decaying warehouse, recognizing here or there a shipment lost so long in inventory its destination had passed out of existence. *All else is turmoil'd by our master, Time.* Now where was his old-man's memory pulling that from, so many years before?

Halvorsen shook his head, still smiling, as the boys lifted their glasses in wry salute to the retreating insulted behind of Roberta Rezk.

Phil lay on the field for what seemed to him to be a long time. Long enough for the snow to frost his coat, trousers, gloves with translucent silver.

When he was able to move he got himself first to his knees, his body crimped on the ache in his gut, and then, finally, to his feet. He swayed there, looking down at the twisted, pink-splotched snow-angel his fallen, beaten body had made.

He shivered, and kicked fresh whiteness over the blood. Turning, hunting under the drifts, he gathered up his scattered books.

His hip hurt. He couldn't remember from which punch, or if it had happened when he fell. But it made it hard to walk. That and the snow. He headed down Main Street. He didn't think about what he looked like till an old woman, shoveling her walk, gave him a frightened glance.

Face must be a mess. He paused at the window of Capriccio's News to examine it. Bloody scabs had clotted or frozen to his lip. When he bent his nose with his fingers it hurt. He was a little disappointed it wasn't broken. It seemed a shame to be in a fight and have nothing permanent to show for it—a crooked nose, a scar.

To hell with them, he thought. Detrick and Mooney and all of them. I got a right to say what I think.

He didn't feel like deciding just then whether he was going to use that right again.

Aiming himself like a bent arrow down Main, he observed the street with cold slow hatred, memorizing its every line and flaw. As soon as he could manage, he'd see Raymondsville for the last time.

He limped rapidly past the old City Hall, a brick monstrosity whose cracked foundations bore a yellowing certificate of condemnation. Past an Italian bakery, its yeasty smells calling to him like his grandmother's kitchen; a Texaco station; the *Century* building, the Moose hall, a closed and boarded opera house. Once this town had glittered with the gaslit ostentation of the Gilded Age. Now the faded brick and peeling wood emanated poverty and abandonment. From the carved granite lintel of the Oilmen's Haberdashery, 1889, dangled the tarnished globes of a pawnshop. He passed a plasma center, the Salvation Army store, the Raymondsville Club, where twice a month patient lines of shabby overcoated women waited for surplus cheese and rice and flour.

A sardonic smile twisting his mouth, he limped past it all with a bitter dogged persistence. Behind three-story buildings with false fronts, rows of shabby houses, peeling and gray, plodded up the slopes above the town like defeated and retreating soldiers. He'd climbed their wooden walks, stumbling as rot gave way under his boots. He knew the shrill women with filthy hair, the pale children who lived in those paintless wrecks. He knew the old who sat motionless and hopeless on foundering porches, or stared all day at the blue flicker of mass illusion. Like the dreaming Julian West he saw the faces of the defeated, the forgotten, pass before him.

The land of opportunity, he thought bitterly. Was this remote town part of it, the nation that boasted to the world of its ease, its plenty, and its freedom?

He was looking up at the bank—TIME 3:34 PM, TEMPERATURE 12 DEGREES— SAVE AT FIRST RAYMONDSVILLE— when a door swung out a few feet ahead. He knew the place, a greasy spoon left over from the thirties. The kids called it Wrinkle City. An old man in a red and black coat came out, stood for a moment eyeing the sky, and then turned away, heading down the street.

Phil noted him absently. Then, a moment later, looked up again with renewed interest. The old guy looked familiar. Where had he seen him before?

He hesitated for a moment, then followed him.

"Mr. Anderson?"

Halvorsen plodded steadily on, head down. The wind whistled past his numbed ears, and his bare hands were tucked deep into his coat.

He was thinking again of the grizzly. How it had appeared suddenly around the edge of a rockfall. Like in the old poster, Remington Cartridges, he thought, where the miner on a mountain trail meets the she-bear. He and Pearson had been heading back to camp. Neither of their guns was loaded. The bear had reared from behind the rubble, not fifty feet away—

"Sir? Can I talk to you for a minute?" The voice startled him; it had moved up beside him. He stopped dead, staring blankly at a dark-haired kid with a bruised face and swollen lip.

"It's Mr. Anderson, isn't it?"

"No. Name's Halvorsen. D'I know you?"

"Well, sort of. Don't you remember me?"

The old man's slow blue eyes, blinking against a burning sensation, moved up and down. He saw a thin boy, in clothes too cheaply made for this wind. A stack of books on his hip. Italian, from the nose. "I don't think so," he said at last. "Who's your dad?"

"Joe Romanelli. He's on the force here."

"The force?"

"He's a policeman. My name's Philip."

"I don't seem to—"

"Yes, sir, we met last year."

"Where was that?" said Halvorsen, turning his head to look down the street. Lord, he thought, it's twenty below freezing. He didn't recollect this boy and he didn't know his family. Nor did he know the town police anymore, though he had in his drinking days.

Phil shuffled his feet in the snow, realizing that his pants and socks were wet through. He remembered now that Halvorsen had intimidated him at their previous meeting too. Embarrassed, not sure how to reach this aloof old man who seemed about to turn his back, his mind cast back to summer.

His mom had got a part-time job in "telephone solicitation."

She sat in a rented room with other women and called people to sell them things. Notions, lotions, shoeshine in spray cans, cheap shampoos with French names. After her first day she'd asked him if he wanted to make some money too.

He'd ended up on his three-speed, delivering. He got a nickel for every dollar's worth they bought, and sometimes more, though tipping wasn't a custom in Hemlock County.

Halvorsen; sure, he remembered that run now. Seven miles out, seven back to town, for a nine-dollar order. There hadn't been much traffic and he'd cycled along in drowsy bee-buzzing heat. The road lifted and dropped as it unrolled along the valley. Here the river was smooth-flowing and green, bordered by old farms.

A ways out of town—he had the directions, penciled in his mother's sloppy hand—he took a turnoff to the right. The farms dropped behind. The road narrowed to one lane, crumbling at the edges back into soil, and started rising. It squirmed against the south slope of Town Hill like a climbing snake. The woods closed in as he moved into the welcome shadow, and abruptly his tires ground on gravel.

Even in low gear he was sweating when he got to the top. At the crest was an abandoned lease road, hard-packed and rutted. The trees met over it, and here and there saplings and bushes poked upward actually in the middle of the way.

He ground on, too far now to turn back, swerving occasionally to avoid puddles. Toads spat like watermelon seeds away into the grass. Now and then the trees thinned and he could look out across the hills. They stretched out green-blue, then blue, and beyond that a flat violet gray, ridge after ridge, all the same height as his whirring Ross. Far below a tiny truck had crawled along the valley, going away, away, into the world.

"Well, boy?"

Phil came back to winter, to the steady chill wind starching his wet pants and the old man studying him coldly. They were almost the same height.

"Yes, sir. You live out Mortlock Run. I was out your place last summer, deliverin' some stuff your daughter ordered for you. I think it was soap, shampoo—and boot sealer, yeah."

"Alma buys fool things like that," said the old man. "That boot sealer's no good. Got a can of bear grease does me fine."

"I just deliver it. Anyway I biked all the way out there. Uh—I got an assignment today in English. I have to interview somebody. I thought you might want to talk."

The old man's eyes narrowed. "Talk? What for?"

"Well, like I said, it's for school. Then I was walking home and I saw you and I thought, well, maybe you'd be willing to help me out."

"I don't think I got anything to tell you'd want to hear," said Halvorsen, looking again toward the bank. Was it really two o'clock?

"You're pretty well known in town, sir. Didn't you used to hunt? There's a picture of you with a lion in Fretz's window."

"Puma. Ain't no lions in Mexico."

"You used to hunt in Mexico?"

"Used to."

"I'd really like to hear about it. Sir."

Halvorsen stamped his feet. The itch in his eyes was increasing; he had half a mind to rub them with snow. He said, "I just ain't got the time, son. Got a long way to walk before nightfall."

"Maybe I could come out and talk to you there some time?"

Halvorsen reached into his pants as he considered this, nipping off a thimble-sized chaw of Mail Pouch with his thumb. He almost offered the boy some before he remembered no youngster in this day and age knew what to do with a cheekful. He said reluctantly, "Well, if you got your heart set, guess I couldn't stop you comin' out. Might not be there, though. You'd do better to get somebody else, here in town."

He turned away then, nodding a curt farewell, and bent himself again into the wind. The boy vanished immediately from his mind, replaced by the prospect of seven miles in deep snow.

Phil watched him step stiffly over the piled-up banks, where the sidewalk ended, into the road. Was he really going to walk all the way back to Mortlock Hollow?

He turned too, shifting his books to the other hip, and set out in his own direction. Who else old could he interview? His grandmother was getting too spacy. Halvorsen was his best bet. No one else in class would think of him. And he'd said it was okay to come out.

Phil touched his nose and looked at the glove. The bleeding had stopped.

He decided to go tomorrow, Saturday, and see if he could get W. T. Halvorsen to talk.

Five

illie was alone now. After she broke the bottle with the rainbows in it Miss Stern had given her a pill. Then put her here, in the big room, and told her to play while she and Ainslee had their talk.

And then she'd closed the door. But there was no one to play *with.* Except the animals. And she was afraid of them, afraid even to look at the fierce dead faces.

The little girl stood trembling in the white light from the tall window. After a while she leaned against the curtains. When you looked through them things looked grainy, like a picture on TV. Then she slipped behind them. Suddenly hidden, secret, safe, she smiled dreamily at her reflection in the glass.

She whispered, "Goodbye, Willie." Then leaned her nose against her image. Breathed out. And it was gone.

Outside it was getting to be night. The snow lay white and deep. She wished she could go out and play in it again. Inside here it was warm. There was a fire in the front room. But she wasn't supposed to go in there. There were too many pretty things. Ainslee was afraid she'd break them. Like the rainbow bottle. "I didn't mean to," she whispered. But then she thought: *But I did. And maybe I'll break some more.*

Standing on the polished floor, singing to herself behind the curtain, she suddenly had to go to the bathroom. But there was nowhere to go. Nanna had told her to stay here. And Ainslee wouldn't like it if she disobeyed.

She nudged back the lace and peeped out. But the animals were waiting. Their eyes glittered at her from the walls. She sighed and retreated again to her covert.

Faintly now, through the walls, she could hear Ainslee and Miss Stern shouting. It made her remember how mom and dad shouted at each other. That was before they came to live with Ainslee and Grandaddy Thunner.

She wished she had somebody to play with. In the mornings Miss Stern gave her lessons. They were learning to make letters together. She smiled a hidden smile, tracing her finger across the frost.

"This is an *R*, Williamina. Say it now—'R.'"

"R," she'd said, her mind only half on what she'd just scrawled, imitating the beautiful one Miss Stern had made. She let the crayon doodle, making big curves at the bottom of the sheet.

"Do you like *R*s? Let's do another one. Look at this."

She watched the pen. It made another funny shape, loop, then a downstroke and a backwards loop. A snake. That was a 2, wasn't it? They just did numbers, she'd done lots of them—

"That's not an R," she said.

"No, you're so smart. It's the next letter. Can you guess what it is?"

"No." Sullenly.

"What does it look like?"

"Like a snake."

"Yes! This is what it looks like, isn't it?"

She stared at the pen. In Miss Stern's thin fingers it made an elegant curve, sinuous, then broadened suddenly. Suddenly there was a tongue and two eyes, and looking at her was the snake, real, and suddenly she was kind of scared.

"Doesn't that look like a snake? And how do snakes go, Willie? They go s-s-s-s, don't they. So what letter is this?"

She thought of the one in the book, the apple, and the trees in the yard. "S," she said, putting three fingers in her mouth.

"What a smart girl. Let's make some *S*es, and then I think we'll get dressed and go outside and look at the snow. What letter does snow start with? Can you guess?"

Snake letter, then zigzag N, round mouth O, then funny new letter, down and up and down and up, S N O W sssnow—

She wished there were lessons now. Or something to do. Usually at night she got to see her dad, if he was home. Or else she and Miss Stern played a game or watched *Sesame Street* in the nursery.

But since lunch today things had been different. Bad different. Ever since Ainslee had slapped her. Not *hard*; it hadn't hurt much. She wouldn't have cried, she never cried when she was punished, if she understood why. But just from being so surprised she'd screamed and broken the bottle before she could think.

But all since then things were bad and no matter how good she was Ainslee looked angry. From time to time all that afternoon Miss Stern would do something Willie had never seen her do before: she'd start crying. Not out loud, she'd just keep doing whatever she was doing. But all of a sudden Willie would feel her go rigid, her eyes staring off into a corner of the nursery. Finally, overcome by a dread she had no word for, Willie had asked Miss Stern why she was sad. She'd just looked at her, not speaking, and then a tear slipped down her cheek.

"What's wrong, Nanna?"

"It's all right, Willie," she'd said then. "It's time for your Ritalin now. Then we'll go downstairs. I think it's time I had a talk with your stepmother."

When Miss Stern came back it was long after dark and the animals were gone, their dead eyes and teeth eaten up by the dark. When she turned on the light Willie saw her face was all red and swollen. She stood in the door, looking at her. "Have you been good, Williamina?" she said at last.

"No. I've been bad today," she said remotely.

"What's this puddle on the floor, Willie?"

"It's been snowing," she said.

Her nanny laughed and came to her and hugged her. "Don't worry about that, I'll wipe it up. But why didn't you use the bathroom?"

"You said to stay here."

"Oh, dear, and you were too frightened to— I see. *Don't* say that about being bad, Williamina. It's not true, you're as good as gold and my precious girl. It's time for you to be in bed."

She knew it was past that because she knew what the big hand meant. She asked where her daddy was and Miss Stern said he was still at work, he'd be home late, but he'd be there in the morning when she woke up.

Miss Stern gave her a bath and shampooed and dried her hair. Willie didn't complain or fight as she helped her into her jammies, turned down the covers, and tucked her in. Maybe tomorrow would be better. The sooner she went to sleep, the sooner it'd be here. She stiffened, though, when she saw another face at the nursery door.

"Is she behaving now?" the woman said, looking in.

"Yes, Mrs. Boulton."

"Good. About your termination. I've talked to Jones. He'll drive you to the airport at noon. Your check will be ready then."

"All right, Mrs. Boulton."

"Good night, Williamina." The cool voice was like the bared teeth of the animals downstairs.

"Good night, Ainslee," she whispered.

Willie closed her eyes, wishing her stepmother would go away, but she could feel her watching them as Miss Stern moved about the bedroom. She tucked the blanket in and smoothed her hand over her hair. When Willie looked toward the door again her stepmother was gone.

Miss Stern sat down on the side of the bed. She looked tired, not like Ainslee, who was always beautiful. Her hair fell over her eyes and she looked sad. Willie still didn't know why. But suddenly she felt scared.

Miss Stern smiled. "You look very pretty in your new pageboy. Willie—"

"What?"

"When Ainslee hits you, that's wrong. No matter what you've done. I've tried to stop her. But I can't. I'm sorry but I can't."

Willie was silent. The thought of it made her scared more. She hadn't been Bad. She'd just wanted to move around, wanted to do something instead of just sitting at the table trying to be quiet and still and nice like Ainslee wanted. It was hard to be quiet all the time. She'd wanted to play with Lark or talk to Grandaddy. So she'd whined, she couldn't help it, and Ainslee had suddenly reached right across the table, and the next thing she knew she was on the floor and her ear hurt something awful. Then she was so mad that without thinking she'd reached for the glass thing and Ainslee had screamed—

"Williamina . . . your Nanna's going to have to go away."

She caught her breath. Her mother had *gone away*. To the hospital. And never come back. Was that what Miss Stern meant? She wanted her to stay. She didn't want to be left alone with

Ainslee. But she was afraid to ask now. It was safer just to nod. To make her face blank, like it didn't matter, like she'd just taken a pill.

"You know I want you to grow up to be a good girl. That's why I want you to forgive your . . . to forgive Ainslee. She doesn't mean to do things like that. You'll understand someday."

Willie didn't answer. She turned her face away. Looked around the room, the familiar nursery, and saw that the walls were decorated with bunny rabbits. What did "go away" really mean?

"Where are you going?" she said, digging her fists into her eyes.

"Away, just away. But don't worry, you'll have a new nanny in a little while."

Suddenly, not understanding why, she began to cry. Miss Stern said swiftly, "Now what are you crying about? Don't be a baby. I'll play with you all tomorrow morning. We'll play castles and we'll watch your *Sleeping Beauty* tape. Then Mister Lark and your father and Ainslee will take care of you till you get a new Nanny. Don't you want to sleep now with your old Raggedy Ann?"

"I don't like her anymore. She's for babies, Ainslee says."

"Oh, Willie, not everything she says is right or true." Miss Stern started to cry again. "Oh, *shit* . . . I'm going to miss you, William-ina Boulton. Hey! I want some loving up. Hello! Hug me!"

Willie turned her face and made herself limp and heavy. Finally Miss Stern gave up and tucked her in again. She murmured the same words she always did—"Goodnight, sleep tight, don't let the bedbugs bite"—but Willie didn't say goodnight back or kiss her like she usually did.

When Miss Stern went away Willie lay in the dark for a long time without moving, breathing through her mouth, listening to the whisper of the snow and watching the shadows reach across the wall from the tree outside the window.

At last she got up, padding out of bed so quietly in her jammies.

The air was cold. The floor was cold too. Her closet was full of stuff, old toys, her old clothes, a lot of things. She pushed them aside and burrowed down. At last she found the doll, soft and warm and floppy, and took it back to bed, holding it tight against her chest.

The room was too dark. The pills made monsters come in her dreams. She lay in her bed, staring out at the blackness, panting a little in fear. The animals didn't scare her. She knew they were dead. Grandaddy had explained that. That was why their heads were hanging on the walls.

But the monsters weren't dead. There weren't any monster heads up there at all.

She ducked her head under the covers. It was warm there. She curled into a ball, holding the doll tight. Hurting slithered in her stomach like a sssnake. She curled around it, pressing her face close to the doll's, breathing the hot close air she knew she couldn't stand for long. Soon she'd have to come out, into the cold.

Without knowing why, Willie Boulton, five years old, began to cry.

Six

Saturday, November Twenty-eighth

Dawn filtered down through an overcast sky, through several inches of new snow, to fall at last on the old man's pale blue eyes. Open, as they'd been half the night, laid like a poultice on the two high slits of dirty glass that were the only way the light could find him.

Halvorsen thought: *What the hell is wrong with me today?*

Getting no clear answer from his body, he laced his fingers atop the blanket, looking around in the growing radiance.

The hole he lay in was unfinished, walled with ripsawed planks over fieldstone. Behind that was earth. In the chill air his breath rose slowly, wraithlike, luminous. Opposite him a plank bench was covered with square cans, presses, other things still obscure in the gloom. Beyond it a wooden door was caulked with strips of blanket. To his right was another, heavier door. It gave onto a mud room, and thence up to the open air.

Lying there, he listened. To snow whispering beyond the already covered windows. To the far-off croak of a raven cursing the new day. To a sudden sneeze beneath him, under the bed.

But there was something else too, something unnatural: a huge and malevolent vibration like giant mill-wheels, so low and vast it might be the slowing rumble of a dying universe.

No, Halvorsen thought, that can't be. It's somethin' wrong with me, is all. In my ears, or in my head.

His mind labored slowly through possibilities that ended with the stove. He rolled his head to stare at it. The cold was intense. The pipe, the joint where it met the roof, all looked sound. And Jezebel, he thought, she sounds okay. No, ain't the stove.

Then why in hell did he feel like this?

His mind tired at last of unanswerable speculation. And drifted. What had they been talking about, there in the Brown Bear—yeah. The time he told McElligott he'd be damned if he'd put in another hour without overtime. Now, he remembered that as the beginning of the big strike, there in the winter of '36. But Wilson, he'd said it started later, out at Minard Run . . .

And then without cause or volition there was a picture in front of his eyes, like the instantaneous cycling of a projector: the image of an animal, off-white, suspended in space as if leaping into flight. He mused over it. Then had it, suddenly, the memory more vivid than yesterday or even now.

The Rockies, in '51. They'd spent days climbing, nearly dead from altitude and cold. The goats, the big Dall sheep, toyed with their hunters. Their vision was eight times better than a man's and they went up scree-covered fifty-degree slopes like they were rocket-powered.

Then late one afternoon he'd found himself, after a day spent working his way up a goddamn-near-vertical chimney, looking down at the granddaddy of all goats.

He'd dropped immediately in the snow, focusing his glasses. The face of the mountain gave way, two hundred yards below, to a ledge no bigger than his front yard. The huge old male, with the nose of a Borgia pope and a magnificent curved rack, had been feeding. He could see that from the piled snow in front of its hooves, the dun bristle of forage. But now it was standing motionless, looking out over miles of canyon and beyond that mountains and then the setting sun as if it, the goat, had just created them all and was thinking, It is good.

While the ram ruminated, Halvorsen, on his belly, was inchworming toward a windswept ledge of granite. Only ten yards distant, but it took him fifteen minutes to reach. Twice the animal glanced around, but its motion-sensitive eyes must have detected nothing but snow and rock.

Once behind cover, he'd set the sights on the 7mm Winchester Magnum he was carrying that year, thinking not of the goat, nor of the cold, nor of the hundreds of square miles of desolate rock below them both; but of the shot. For mountain work he favored a Lyman adjustable peep over a scope. It was lighter, and there was no glass to break. But he couldn't make out in the fast-dying light how much drop he'd cranked in. With the 175-grain boattail he'd handloaded—

He lay freezing against gray gneiss, staring down. Not three feet from his face it had opened, blown apart, a hole leading down forever.

His father stood facing him on the far side of the pit. His face was set and white, his mother's negated by a black veil. Above them blue sky burned like a gas flame. Over the hole, between him and his parents, six soldiers slid a wooden box. The letters US were burned into it.

The man they called the Major finished folding the flag. Handed it, like something worth far more than what they had paid, to Thorvald Halvorsen.

The old man took it wordless and stood looking down, eyes empty as the sky, his gnarled farmer's hands clenched on it.

There was a thud as the box came to rest, and then the machine-gun rattle of stones.

Halvorsen closed his eyes, but he could still see it. The little Lutheran cemetery above town, the summer of 1918.

What had Mase Wilson been saying about the strike . . .

When he looked back up from the sights the goat was peering up at him, the wool blowing around its face like the beard of a patient patriarch. The golden eyes unfrightened, even weary . . .

Halvorsen stared up at the rough-hewn beams, breathing rapidly. Getting senile, he thought. That Altschuler's disease. This must be how it started. With this randomness of memory, more real than his empty room. This tremor and nausea, stabbing in the eyes, hammer-slam of pulse. And beneath and most disquieting of all, the deep unending rumble, like mountains being ground to powder.

He dragged back coverlet, quilt, and blanket, and tried to swing his legs out. On the third try he won and sat hunched, coughing and staring at the floor. His hugged arms covered where the union suit gaped.

"Time to rise 'n shine, Jez," he muttered.

The brown-and-black puppy squirmed out and attacked his ankles. He suffered it for a few seconds, then forced himself erect and staggered to the stove. Not even an ember. So it wasn't monoxide poisoning. He rattled the grate, sneezing as fine ash rose. He wadded a newspaper, rested; reached the kindling, rested; then stacked two chunks of beech.

An Ohio match sputtered across cast iron. The flame took paper, then curled under kindling like the fingers of a cautious lover. When the beech started to smoke he clanged the door shut and latched it.

Halvorsen nursed a yellow trickle into a coffee can. The door by the bench groaned open reluctantly. Solid earth-cold met his face. He stood shivering in baggy cotton, looking at the shelves. *Should of bought something when I was in town. Beans or something.* He looked for a time at a pint bottle on the top shelf. Then turned away. Instead he considered over several bundles of dried leaves and roots hanging from a water pipe, selected one, and closed the door.

The tea bubbled presently, sending up a resinous sharpness. He sat on the bed half-dressed, fondling the puppy's ears. At times his chin fell halfway to his chest; then he raised it again, angry at his weakness.

But I really ain't feeling any too good . . .

A mile down the hollow, Phil prodded the body with his boot.

The raccoon lay belly up in the middle of the road. He'd thought at first, seeing from some distance off the crows worrying it, that it had been run over. Then he realized the snow was flawless, unrutted. Only wind-eroded footprints showed beneath it. The ones he'd followed all the way up Mortlock Run.

The coon's eyes were open. One was torn, beaked apart into jelly. The other was glossy-looking and probably, he thought bending slightly closer, frozen that way. It'd gotten down to five above that night. Strange, he thought. Well, even animals must die of disease or old age. Not all of them got eaten.

Phil straightened, circled it—it might have fleas or something—and trudged on up the hill. When he looked back a hundred yards on the birds were back at work.

A while later he came out on top of the ridge. He rested on a stump for a few minutes, then trudged on. His breath drifted ahead of him. It was very cold and he was starting to hurt. He hoped it wasn't much farther.

Half an hour later he paused again, in a clearing. Was this it? Last summer it had been pleasant, grassy, part of the Alleghenies' million-tinted green. Now it was wind-whipped and stark, a flat white nothingness with birches sere and vertical beyond. Only a stand of spruce gave this dead world color.

But smokesmell lurked under the evergreen sharpness, the ozone bite of new snow. He rotated slowly, sniffing. At last he smiled, making out a shimmer in the icy air. Shrugging the pack on again, he followed the all but invisible trail to the steps.

After he knocked he stood for a while looking at the stumpy stovepipe, at the lazily ascending smoke. Somebody was here, or had just been. He knocked again, louder.

The door jarred suddenly against its frame and he started back, staring into gloom. At first he saw nothing. Then something dim, as if it was drifting upward from beneath deep black water. A gaunt face, white hair, stubbled cheeks, bristly and gray as a porcupine. The eyes were red-rimmed.

"Who is it?"

"Hi, Mr. Halvorsen!"

"*Who're you?* I said."

He stepped back before the fiercely repeated question. The frozen earth of the stair-pit stopped him. "I'm Phil Romanelli. Remember, we talked yesterday? In town?"

"What do you want?"

"Well, you—you said it was okay if I come out and talked to you sometime."

The old man blinked, seemed as if about to speak; then disappeared. Phil stood there, uncertain what to do. He wondered if he should leave, then thought: I don't want to walk all the way back right now. I don't know if I *can*. He ought to let me get warm at least.

The old man reappeared. "Might as well come in, get warm."

"That's just what I was thinking."

"What's that?"

"Nothing, sir."

The darkness inside stank of urine. Searching with his hands, Phil found another door. "Close it," came a growl. He turned and shoved it shut. He went through the second and closed that too. Then he stood still and tried to see.

The only light came from two dirty, webbed apertures high on the walls. That, and a yellow flicker from an iron stove. Something was bubbling on it. It smelled vile. As his eyes adapted he saw the old man hunched over, buttoning his fly with uncertain, trembling hands. He was suddenly sorry he'd come, had intruded on this.

"Sit down, boy."

He was looking for a chair when something came at his legs out of the dark. He flinched back, then realized it was a dog. No, just a puppy. It pinned him against the wall, wriggling and whining, nosing his crotch. He put his glove over it.

"Jez, get off him. Chair behind you."

"Thanks."

"Take y' coat off. Want something hot?"

He dusted snow from his sleeves. It was warmer inside than out, but not much. "Uh . . . what you got there?"

"Feverwort tea."

"I think I'll pass, Mr. Halvorsen. But thanks. Thank you anyway."

The puppy came back to his knee and he patted it. It lowered its head and dug its muzzle under his glove.

At last he could see in the subterranean gloom. Opposite him was a bed, actually an old horsehair sofa under layers of grimy-looking blankets. Opened cans lay in and around a wooden box next to the stove. There were stacks of old magazines and newspapers; long cloth-wrapped bundles in racks on the wall; a bench crammed solid with junk. He looked back at the door to make sure he'd closed it and saw a lever-action rifle propped against the jamb.

The old man came back from the stove and let himself down slowly into an easy chair. A stoneware mug steamed in his hand. He had his pants buttoned and his suspenders braced. And old-fashioned half-moon spectacles on his nose. Phil thought he looked less intimidating wearing glasses.

"So, y'say you come out to see me."

"Yes, sir." He remembered the pack and unslung it. "I brought you some stuff. Cookies, some bacon—"

"Cookies, huh?"

"Yes, sir, oatmeal, my mom made 'em."

"Haven't been feeling too good this morning. But I might try one."

Fortunately the old guy seemed to like them. He ate three, sipping the fetid liquid between bites. Phil thought, *Christ, I hope I don't end up like this if I get old.*

"So, y'say you walked all the way up here from town?"

"Not all the way. Mr. Bauer gimme a lift part of the way."

"How's Ernie doing? All right?"

"Yes sir, I think so."

The old man seemed to lose interest after that. He stared into the stove. Phil played with the puppy. It was easier, somehow, to look at it than at Halvorsen. At last he made himself say, "Sir, did you mind if I interviewed you?"

"What?"

"Well, like we talked about back in town. I'd like to ask you some questions. About your life."

The old man shrugged.

Phil was proud of the recorder. He'd bought it for a dollar from the junk box at Ray's Gun and Pawn. The speaker wires had broken: he'd resoldered them, and now he had a working machine, practically free. Electronics, fixing things, he was good at stuff like that. The blue eyes followed him without curiosity as he uncoiled the cord and hunted around for an outlet. At last he found an old two-pronger under the bench. He plugged it in, then stared at the silent machine.

"I don't have no power out here, if that's what you want," said Halvorsen at last.

Feeling his face heat, Phil cursed himself. Of course there was no electricity. Not in this literal hole in the ground. He noticed only now the kerosene lamp hanging from a joist.

"That was pretty dumb, huh," he said. "Real dumb. Well, let's just forget it. I'll just get warm, and then I'll head back."

"This's somethin' for school, you said."

"For composition class." He flushed again, thinking how stupid he sounded. He wished he was lying outside in the snow, beyond it all. Like the raccoon.

Halvorsen sat silent for a moment, then cleared his throat grudgingly. "Well. Long as you come all the way out here, might as well get what you come for."

"Sir?"

But the old man had already pulled himself up by his arms and disappeared back into another room. When he came back he had a pencil, very short, and a damp pad of yellow paper.

Phil swallowed. "Thanks, Mr. Halvorsen."

"So, let's get to 'er," said the old man, settling back into the chair and rubbing his eyes.

"Sure you don't mind? I can come back some other—"

"Let's get it done, boy. I ain't feelin' too good this morning and I'd like to just get it over with."

"All right. All right, sir. Well . . . were you born here?"

"Here?"

"I mean, well, in Raymondsville."

"A little ways outside." Halvorsen collected his thoughts. "Some ways south of here, down Racker Hollow."

Phil began to write.

"Yeah, I grew up on the farm there. There was eight of us, my ma and pa, and I had three brothers and two sisters. My older brother, he died in the Great War. That was what they called World War One then. I was just thinkin' about the day they brung him home.

"My pa was Thorvald Halvorsen. He come over from the old country when he was sixteen. Come over on a boat. They made him shovel coal into the furnace. He didn't mind, 'cause, he said, they gave him cake to eat. It was nothin' but white bread, was all . . . he never did learn to talk English too good.

"My ma's name was Alma. You know where Hantzen Lake is? Used to be a town down in that valley, before they built the dam. Probably still there, hundred, two hundred feet down under the water. That's where he was from.

"We grew potatoes and corn and truck, and on the weekends we'd come into town and sell it. First we had a buggy and then my dad he got himself a used Ford. I saw John D. himself once—"

"John who?"

"Rockefeller. Yeah, ridin' through Petroleum City in a black Packard. And he didn't look a bit prouder than my father looked that day, sittin' up in the cab of that old truck."

"When did you leave home?" Phil asked him.

"Well, first time I left the farm was when I was twelve. Went down to the Kinningmahontawany, trappin' with old Amos McKittrack."

Halvorsen had a sudden image of the old man, little and stocky, his white beard rusty with tobacco juice. He'd meant to look him up once. But he had to be long dead. It was nearly sixty years ago they'd wintered together.

He caught the boy's paused pencil and recollected himself. "Anyway, we went down along Blue Creek, into what's the Wild Area now. We sawed down spruce for the cabin, then split out clapboards and puncheons. Built the chimney out of fieldstones. Then we chunked it up good with mud and moss from the spring.

"We trapped down in the Wilderness all that fall and on into winter. Got us fisher, marten, skunk, fox, once even a wildcat. We had a line of two hundred traps. Oneida Jumps, Victors, Newhouses . . . I still remember how to set a log deadfall."

He sat silent, fingering the worn memories again: remembering how the hemlocks, long gone now except in the deepest, most remote hollows, had stood shadowy and tall as the nave of a cathedral. He remembered McKittrack's hands, so tanned from salt and acid it looked like he was wearing leather gloves. And he remembered how he used to run up the hillsides, leaving the trapper laughing sadly, laboring along behind.

"What did you do all winter?" the boy asked him, and Halvorsen started, coming back again to the basement, to the chill slow realization that now it was he who was old.

"Well, you trap some in the winter too. And hunt. But mostly we'd lay up in the cabin and Amos'd tell stories. He had some good ones. When he was a kid he knew Ben Yeager."

"Uh . . . who's he?"

Halvorsen blinked. "Never heard of Benjamin Yeager? He was king hunter of all northwest Pennsylvania. Yeager was huntin' these woods back in 1820, 1830. Back then this was a howling wilderness. The woods was full of game—buffaloes, elk, wolves, panthers . . ."

"What did you do then?"

"When?"

"After you went trapping."

"Oh. Well, when I come back that spring I was thirteen, so I went to work."

"What jobs did you do?"

Halvorsen nodded approval of a reasonable question. "Like most guys around here then, went out in the oilfields. Slush boy, that's what I did first. Worked six and a half days a week, three dollars a week."

"What's a slush boy?"

"Well, you had your can of rod wax and motor oil, and every morning you'd dip your leather in it and grease the rod lines out to the jacks. You know the jacks, pump the oil out'a the ground? Now they're electrical powered, or natural gas, but when I started out they were steam. They had the boilers in houses, and the steam lines running all up and down the hill. We'd fix barkers—different lengths of pipe so you'd get a different pitch. You could tell that way when the well was pumped off. I packed stuffing boxes, cleaned out the tanks. Stuff like that.

"I made roustabout in nineteen and twenty-eight. I worked at that, then as a driller all over Hemlock and McKean and Potter and Cameron counties. Drilled wells, and put in the casings, and the power and the band wheels. That's what drives the rod lines, looks like a ferris wheel on its side.

"Then later on I was a shooter. You get these torpedoes, they call them, sheetmetal cylinders is all they are, that you pour the nitro into. I shot wells for Wolf's Head and Kendall. Then worked for Minard Run for a while, then for Thunder Oil the last thirty years. Worked my way on up with them, lease foreman, then field foreman—that was highest I ever got. Worked all over northern Pennsylvania, even some down in Texas, showin' them how to drill.''

Phil was writing hard. The pencil was blunt and the light was dim. But he'd resolved, after making a fool of himself with the recorder, to get it all down somehow, and make sense of it later.

"Uh . . . what'd you do during the war?"

"Worked. They didn't draft the skilled men, but they took the rest so we had to pull twelve-, fourteen-hour days. But we knew our boys needed that oil."

Phil decided he had enough about the oil business. "They say in town you used to hunt."

"In them days everybody did. Got your pot meat that way. Rabbits and squirrels when you're little, then you work up to your deer. You hunt, boy?"

"No sir. I don't think it's—"

"And wild turkeys—not like your store-bought ones, they're so dumb they drown in the rain. They look up at the clouds with their beaks hangin' open and they're too stupid to put their heads down again."

"Did you ever hunt raccoons?"

"What? Raccoons? Not since I was a kid. They used to pay good for the fur."

"I seen a dead one on the way up here."

"Dead coon?"

"Yeah. It was laying on the road, down the hill a ways."

"I've seen one or two there myself," said Halvorsen. "Not touched or anything. And possums, and a doe once. Mystery to me."

"You were saying, about hunting."

"Oh, yeah, it took hold of me when I got older. Shot my first deer with m'dad when I was eleven. Later on, when I was workin', I'd save up and go on trips. Mule deer and blacktail out west, Wyoming for the pronghorn, Colorado and Mexico, elk and moose and goat in the Cassiars."

He fell silent, rubbing his eyes, and to help him along Phil asked him where that was.

"Where's what? Oh. Canada. I had trophies—used to be, I had trophies covering the walls of my house."

"You shot that bear in the Tavern?"

"Me and Lew Pearson. Sonny done a nice job of taxidermy on that one, didn't he?"

"Tell me about one of your hunts."

Halvorsen laced his fingers over the nausea. He wished this was over with, so he could lie down.

"Well, I was just rememberin' this morning about one time when I was in the Rockies. Hunting goat. And one day I happened to come up behind one of them. He was just standing there lookin' out over the mountains. And I glanced down to adjust my sight. And when I looked up again he was looking right at me. Once those Dalls see you that's it. So I jerked the rifle up and snapped off a shot. I was aiming at his neck, but the bullet was heavier than I was used to. And so it hit him in the back instead. Made a *thunk*—like that. And a cloud of dust come off his hide, like when you beat a carpet.

"I found out later they do this sometimes, but it surprised the hell out of me that day. See, when he realized he was done for he took about three jumps, slow and graceful, and the last one took him right out off the edge of the cliff."

Phil felt sick. Killing helpless animals—that wasn't his idea of sport. "You said you quit. Why?"

Halvorsen sat silent, holding his belly surreptitiously. *Feel like a gut-shot deer*, he thought.

How could he explain it? Just that at each kill he'd felt more strongly a loss, not a gain. Had found himself looking down at his quarry and thinking not about the spread, how it would mount out, but things he could not admit even to himself. So he'd concentrated more and more on the technique, the tracking, passing up easy kills and taking only the canniest game, the hardest shots.

Not that he'd turned against hunting. He still thought it hardened a man, gave him the tenacity and self-denial without which you were no man at all but something house-kept by women. It was as natural for man to hunt as for the wolf. But man, though he was still mortal, had become something more. He had the power to destroy, and the power to save. And knowing that, he took on some of the responsibility of God.

"Can't tell you, not exactly," he said slowly. "All I know is, one day, after the house, I shot a buck. Plain old whitetail. And lookin' down at it, I knew I wasn't going to do it no more."

Phil kept his eyes on the tablet. There was more to it than that, he felt sure. But he didn't know how to go after it. Instead he said, "What do you mean, after the house?"

Halvorsen didn't answer for a long time. At last he said, "I always wanted a place out here in the woods. We built it together, Jennie and me. Two stories, lookin' out over the valley. Had a big living room, den, all that stuff."

"What happened to it?"

"There was a fire."

Phil waited. At last the old man, turning his face away so Phil could see the furrows in his neck, said, "I was drunk. I was tryin' to pour gas into the chain saw. I spilled some and went to the garage to get some rags. While I was out there, it—well all I can figure is the fumes must of got to the water heater. I tried to get up the stairs but the smoke got to me. I woke up outside, on the grass. She was so proud of that lawn. She was laying beside me."

"She got out?"

"No. Jennie was upstairs. She jumped. Broke her neck."

Phil stared at the pad. The stove muttered to itself, settling. After a moment his hand wrote, *Caused fire that killed his wife.*

"So since then—"

"Since then I been waitin' here to die. An' I think that's about the end of my story."

The old man got up abruptly and staggered toward the stove. Afterward Phil thought he might have been headed for the other room. But he never got to it. Instead he halted suddenly and put out a hand for support. Flesh hissed on red-hot metal.

Halvorsen felt his skin burning even through the sudden faintness, yet could not move. A dark behind his brain was lighting up, dancing in shimmering bands. The Northern Lights. He'd seen them only once in his life, in Alaska. He hunched for a moment, his other hand pressed to his stomach, watching the light and thinking how beautiful it was. Then he went toward it.

Phil stood up when he crumpled to the dirt. *Oh, shit,* he thought. "Mr. Halvorsen?"

The old man lay motionless, like a discarded rag. Scared now, Phil bent over him. Halvorsen was breathing, but so slow and slight it was hard to see. He rubbed his wrists for a few minutes, then slapped his cheek.

Neither seemed to help. Phil straightened and looked around the basement. Nothing offered itself. He fought against guilt and panic.

After a while he bent again. The old man wasn't heavy, but lifting him hurt his hip. He laid him in the chair and stared at the sagging, lined face, the silent eyelids.

At last he decided there was only one thing to do.

He moved rapidly around the basement. The blanket came off the sofa. He found rope and a hatchet, and went up the steps.

When he came back he bundled Halvorsen into his coat and put his cap on him. He looked for gloves, found none, but came up with a gray sweater. He knotted that around the old man's neck and pulled a pair of wool socks over his hands.

When he was dressed Phil staggered with him out the door, up the steps—pushing the door closed on the puppy's muzzle—and laid him on the blanket. After a moment's hesitation he went back down and got the puppy, carried it up whining and wriggling, and buttoned it inside the old man's coat.

Standing in the snow, he picked up the ends of the saplings he'd cut and lashed. A makeshift sling took the weight off his left arm. It was bearable. For the moment. But he wasn't at all sure his leg, his hip, could take it for four miles, even downhill.

He decided he had no choice but to try.

Seven

Brad was hanging his overcoat when his secretary brought in coffee. "Good morning, Mr. Boulton."

"Morning, Twyla. You look great today."

She left smiling. He hung up his suit jacket, straightened his tie, and glanced at his desk. Then crossed to the window, cradling the warm mug.

A new week, already scheduled full. But he was unwilling just yet to look at the appointment book. It was important, every morning, to take a few minutes to remember where he was, and who he was, and to plan what he'd accomplish with this day.

Petroleum City was the largest town in Hemlock County. Five stories below its streets shone like jet in the winter dawn. A yellow PennDOT truck was salting, and traffic was picking up. At the far end of Main the stop light glimmered like blood on the wet asphalt. It was snowing again; would continue on and off all day, the *Times-Democrat* had said, though the trend was warming.

Beyond the two- and three-story office buildings, beyond the new brick branch campus of the University of Pittsburgh, he could make out dimly the real heart of town. It loomed like a tripled steel keep behind the snow: the three twelve-story catalytic cracking towers of Thunder Oil Refinery Number One.

Driving out of town on his way to Raymondsville he often slowed to look down on it. Number One looked as if some deranged deity of machines had torn apart the engine rooms of a hundred ocean liners and reassembled them on two hundred acres of once-fertile valley bottom. One of the engineers had told him it contained forty thousand miles of pipe. By day it was a pillar of steam and smoke, boiling with tank trucks and rail cars. By night it was a twinkling carnival of lights, capped by fire. Three hundred feet above the valley the volatile waste gases were flared off in a roaring yellow-orange flame so bright you could read a newspaper by it anywhere in town.

From a thousand wells scattered through these hills the raw Pennsylvania crude, finest in the world, throbbed down to Number One; from it, by truck and rail, the refined products flowed out to the world. Everyone in America knew Thunder Gasoline, Thunderbolt Premium Racing Oil, Magick Penetrating Oil, Linette Paraffin. Less celebrated steady sellers were "#1" home heating oil and the expanding gamut of TBC Brand industrial chemicals, high-quality feedstocks for the dye, plastic, and drug industries of the U.S., Europe, and Japan.

Number One and the Company had taken a century to build, passed down from the legendary Beacham Berwick Thunner to his son Charles, and thence to his son Daniel.

Now they, and the house above the town, and Cherry Hill, were his. Because of Ainslee.

Boulton turned from the window. He stood for a moment gnawing at the tips of his fingers, then walked quickly across the room.

The cover sheet of the display chart was blank. He hesitated, then flipped to the first page.

On the fifth day of January, the Thunder Oil Company would become The Thunder Group, Incorporated.

The Company as he'd found it was an unlimited-liability, privately held corporation. Seventy percent of it was held in the name of Daniel Thunner. Ainslee voted that. The rest was owned by Thunner's prehistoric cronies on the Board. The financial structure assured family control. But in terms of flexibility, leverage, innovation, Thunder Oil was still nineteenth-century.

Slide two showed Thunder return on net assets over the last decade. It varied from four percent to minus two, and the trend was down. The company was economically marginal and had been for years. There was still oil in the hills, in the deep sands, but to get it out required pressurization or chemical treatments.

It was a classic case of diminishing marginal returns. Only OPEC and the succession of troubles in the Mideast kept crude prices high enough to make secondary extraction economical. He could cut costs only so far. Sooner or later prices would drop again. When they did Thunder was doomed.

He had to diversify. But to do that he needed capital. The company's captive bank had already been sucked dry and their lease lands mortgaged. For a privately held concern, that left only two ways to raise money. He could borrow, issuing notes or bonds, but that meant SEC and bank interference. Or he could get in the venture capital market. But they'd want an equity kicker and a representative on the Board.

He flipped to slide three. His answer was to take Thunder public. A successful stock issue would provide a hundred million dollars in fresh capital. He could modernize Number One and replace the aging motor-oil plant. The biggest change, though, would be conversion of the cat towers to the new Hart-Havelange process for environmentally sensitive gasoline.

Slide four showed the four ways the new fuel, tentatively called "Thunder Green," outperformed conventional gasoline in reducing emissions. First, it was less volatile, reducing evaporation at the pump by lowering butane and isopentane content. That reduced the volume of hydrocarbon fumes released into the atmosphere. Second, it had a better detergent balance than Thunder's previous fuels, making it burn more efficiently in modern fuel-injected cars. Third, the sulfur content was lower, eliminating the rotten-egg smell you got sometimes in exhaust. And fourth, it was oxygenated, which lowered carbon monoxide emissions.

Boulton smiled tightly, sipping the coffee. They'd sent samples to Ford and GM, and their fuels engineering people loved it. With any luck at all, it would make Thunder competitive enough to survive a Mideast peace and a fall in crude prices of 20 percent. If peace didn't happen, then they'd be earning from 11 to 15 percent.

The last slide, five. The second major result of the restructure. The spinoff of Keystone Health Care, Thunder Oil, Thunder Petroleum Specialties, First Raymondsville Financial Services, and TBC Industrial Chemicals into independent divisions would wall off the old board within Thunder Oil. The old-line ownership would be diluted in over a million shares of new common stock.

He stared at it, biting his fingertips, going over for the ten thousandth time how it should happen. One-quarter of the new

offer would go to holders of current Thunder preferred in a
four-way split. They'd be happy; Merrill, Paine and Wheat had
advised an initial tender at $135 a share. Since the last recorded
sale of T.O. stock had been at sixteen and a quarter, that would
instantly double their worth. But he'd also asked the issuing bro-
kers, off the record, to estimate a buyer profile for new petrochem-
ical issues. It went 45% institutional, 21% pensions/mutual funds,
the rest small investor/miscellaneous.

Net effect: the board's proportional equity would be reduced to
the point where he, Boulton, would become the sole decision-
maker.

The new Group board would be his appointees.

He stared unseeing at the neat boxes and flowcharts. Only when
the intercom beeped did he blink. He pressed the button, his eyes
resting for a moment on twin malachite-framed portraits of a
dark-haired woman and a blond child.

"Dr. Patel is in the reception area. Shall I send him in?"

"Who? —Oh, yeah. Ask him to wait, I'm in conference."

"Yes, sir."

He sat down, looking again at his daughter's picture. What
chubby cute cheeks she had!

It had taken him a long time to get used to the idea of a family.
Of people who'd always love you, who depended on you.

There hadn't been much happiness, or love, in his life till then.

To call his father a miner was a guess. He could still recall, if he
cared to, the little apartment above Jackson Street in West Scranton where Marya Boldoronek took her friends. He'd played in the
front room while she went in back with the men who smelled of
sweat and coal dust even though they'd showered after coming out
of the shafts of the Lackawanna Coal Company. They'd treated
him kindly, rumpling his hair and tossing him a coin or a sparkly
piece of mineral. Once his present had been a flat rock with the
outline of a fish on it.

Then two grim women had come, a policeman with them, and
the time when he'd been happy, or at least content, was over.

He remembered the Municipal Home with fear even now. He'd
wake sometimes at Cherry Hill, his cock hard as a boy's in terror,
believing himself in dream still there. Its cream-painted corridors
and iron bunks still labyrinthed his brain. Its soulless parody of
family had been at once blind and all-seeing. At the Home you
were never alone. You fought, hated, and cried in common, one in
a lonely multitude.

At first his mother had come for him at holidays. But then one Christmas—he'd been eight— he'd waited in his room, watching the snow fall, net bag packed with clothes he'd washed in the sink. The building emptied gradually until only he and the orphans were left. He'd never seen her again. When he was in junior high she'd sent him a rambling letter from Wilkes-Barre, in a County Jail envelope. He'd never answered.

Some of the counselors at the Home hadn't minded using the boys, those who had no relatives to complain to, and were too small to fight back.

He'd thought for a long time he'd be a miner when he grew up. He and the other boys dug elaborate tunnel systems in the slag heaps at the edge of town, heedless of frequent cave-ins. Miners were strong and happy. When he'd seen them with his mother they were always laughing. But when he quit school there was a strike on, it had lasted a hundred and twenty days already, and the only way he could hire on was as a scab. Everyone knew what happened to them after the union came back, down there in the dark. So he'd joined the army instead, marched in off the street into the recruiting station with his suitcase and told the sergeant to put him on the bus.

In Germany the Red Cross forwarded a telegram Mercy Hospital had sent to the Home. The chaplain had asked him how much furlough he'd be needing, and he'd said none. He was saving it to sell back when he got out.

He came back to his office to find his hands clamped white on the edge of the desk. He let go and reached for the first cigarette of the day. No use revisiting that. Marya Boldoronek had been a loser, and she was gone.

After Fort Dix he'd served two hitches in Europe. He was a combat equipment MOS in Schweinfurt, vehicle issue, and there wasn't much to do but drink and screw frauleins. His company commander let men off for classes, so he'd begun studying, at first purely to avoid field training.

He took it slow, a year to catch up to where he'd dropped out, and one day a teacher told him he had a good mind; he could be an officer; could be anything he wanted to.

No one had ever said this to him in Scranton. He passed his high school equivalency and kept on with the Armed Forces Institute, studying at night. When he left the Army he went to Carnegie-Mellon under the GI Bill. He'd worked nights and weekends, plant watchman, stacking vegetables, till finally one of his teachers steered him to a loan officer work-study with Manufacturers Hanover.

And ever since it had been sugar. Even his first marriage had worked out, in a way. She'd left him, but he'd won custody.

He smiled. Williamina. He'd been so sure she'd be a boy. Tricked again by inscrutable Fate. But this trick he didn't mind a bit.

And then the incredible luck of being sent out here, and meeting Ainslee—

It was almost eight. He finished the coffee—New Orleans style, between-roast—and glanced around the office. New furniture, new carpeting, on the wall the award from the Hemlock Recreation Association as Booster of the Year. Only the painting of Beacham Thunner with his first well remained of the antiques he'd inherited from Dan. He reached out.

"Yes, Mr. Boulton."

"Send Patel in now. Hold my calls. But say, when Weyandt comes in, tell him we got to talk about ethane before the meeting at nine."

"Yes, sir."

V. Chandreshar Patel turned out to be short and nearly spherical. In a blue suit he looked like a satellite photo of the earth. His smile was full-lipped below thinning hair and his cologne was sweeter than Twyla's. Showing their teeth, the two men came together in the center of the floor, gripping and wringing each other's hands.

"Dr. Patel. Great to meet you. How was the flight?"

"Good, sir, very good."

"And the hotel? You're comfortable?"

"A Holiday Inn is not a Marriott, but I am not hard to please."

"Coffee? —Twyla, get the Doctor a cup. French roast today, you'll love it. Cream? Sugar?"

"Just call me Vinay, please. Sugar, plenty, yes. I have a weakness for it."

They laughed. "Let's sit here," he said, waving at the corner settee. They sat down, crossing their legs toward each other, and chatted for a few minutes until the secretary came back. When she left she closed the door quietly.

"Vinay, I'm glad you came. We badly need more medical talent at Keystone HealthCare, Incorporated. That's our long-term caregiving division. Here, we just got these printed."

Patel fingered a glossy six-color brochure on coated paper. The cover was embossed silver. "Very nice," he said, nodding. He looked, Brad thought, like a sweaty little Buddha.

"Well, let me give you a brief outline of our organization here, and then we'll talk about how you might fit into it.

"KHC's a privately held company at the moment, fully owned by the parent corporation, Thunder Oil. I'm President and CEO. I started the HealthCare Division two years ago with the purchase of an old fifty-bed facility here in Hemlock County.

"To make a long story short, growth has been phenomenal. We have four facilities on line and two more will open next year. We're opening our first Keystone Manor outside the tri-county area, in Tucson, Arizona. We have four hundred beds now and in the next two years we'll double that.

"Our policy is to provide the most efficient long-term residential care possible, bar none, period. We're well positioned for growth. This part of the country is aging rapidly and up to now the only long-term residential care facilities have been the church-owned old folks' homes."

"The local hospitals, they are municipal?"

"Yes. No for-profit hospitals up here."

"That's good."

"It is. Not only are we in an underserved market, but local conditions allow us to staff at minimum wage. Don't get me wrong, without us they'd be on welfare, but let's just say there's no union problem. Along with cost-effective management, that keeps rates low. We're seeing people coming in from New York already. So I feel confident that in four or five years KHC will outperform the parent corporation, maybe not in terms of gross, but in bottom-line return.

"The position we're interviewing for is staff physician. We have one M.D. with us now, but frankly Dr. Kopcik isn't what we need. He's an old-line physician. He doesn't understand the realities of modern caregiving."

"I hope we can come to an understanding," said Patel, nodding agreeably, but with dignity.

Boulton leaned to pull a letter off his desk. "Okay, let's see . . . we contacted you 1 September. At that time you indicated your expected salary would be in the neighborhood of seventy thousand, correct?"

"That's what I was making in my last position."

"Resident at the Veterans Administration hospital in Hampton, Virginia."

"That is right."

"Vinay, I believe in telling it like it is. We're a private company. We can't match government pay scales. In this growth phase, we've got to keep our belts tight. I'm prepared to offer forty, with a review after the first year."

The little man's eyes dropped. Boulton watched his hands. After a moment they lifted, as if to go to his mouth; but they didn't. Instead they took out a cigarette. "Do you mind?"

"Go right ahead."

". . . Just a moment . . . there. Well, Mr. Boulton—"

"Brad, please, Vinay."

"Brad, it would not be fair to my family to accept that. The average income for M.D.s of my experience is currently over a hundred and twenty-five thousand."

Boulton grinned boyishly. "Never sell yourself short! But that's in a major urban area, right? This is a small-town environment. Your expenses will be lower. I might also mention that there'll be ways to augment your salary."

"What ways?"

"Let's talk about that later, after we get to know each other. Vinay, let's not haggle. I just can't start you over forty. It sounds low but I think it'd work out for you. Better than things did in Virginia."

"I'm sorry, I don't understand."

"Hell, V.P.," he said, slapping the other man's knee, "like I said, let's talk straight, okay? I've never heard of a doc being fired by the VA before."

"I was not 'fired.' I resigned."

"What do I know? Just what the clipping service sends me. Mismedication, overmedication, something about mistaking a nerve for a blood vessel during surgery on some old guy's throat. What was all that about, anyway?"

Patel's cigarette trembled. "My assistant did that. We all make mistakes in training. He was a medical officer, however. Air Force. It was more convenient for them to place the blame on a civilian."

"Well, that's good to know," said Boulton. He looked at the sweating fat man for a moment, then got up. "Can I get you something?"

"No. Nothing."

"I'm having one. Keep me company. Johnnie Walker?"

"A small one, then."

"Uh huh . . . Now, let's go back to before your employment at the VA."

"I think we can talk about salary now."

"Not just yet. You're without a position at the moment, isn't that right?"

"I'm in private practice."

"I see . . . you started out in private practice, in Charleston, wasn't it, after you came to this country? Your license was suspended for irregularities in pharmaceutical accounting."

Patel said nothing. He sipped at his drink stolidly.

"After that you worked for a mill in San Juan, the San Marco Clinic, you did what there?"

"Gynecology."

"Gynecology. Why did you leave Puerto Rico?"

"Personal reasons."

"Which personal reason was it? Codeine? Amphetamines? Or the fact you couldn't tell a nerve from a vein?"

Patel didn't answer.

Brad grinned. "Hey! Don't take it personally! We didn't have to go through this bullshit, Vinay, but you came in here gunning for top dollar. I just wanted to make it clear that what I'm offering is a lot more than you could rake off anyplace else. Can we agree on that?"

The fat man sighed. He put his hand over his eyes. After a moment Brad got up. He refilled Patel's glass, then pressed the intercom. "Twyla, call up our executive employment contract. No, make that the consultant's contract. Prepare it for Dr. Patel's signature, with the figures we discussed."

"Yes, sir."

He stared out the window, giving the other time to compose himself. The interview was going as expected. He felt light and aggressive, ready to finish this and charge on to the ethane price decision. Below him, at the corner of Mulholland and Main, a pickup had broken down. He made out the blaze-orange coats, Ohio plates. Hunters, in for the start of the season. He'd never hunted. He considered it a lower-class sport, like bowling.

When he turned the fat man had regained possession of himself. He said, "You hunt, Vinay?"

"No."

"Golf? No? Too bad, we're building a new course out by the club."

The Indian didn't respond. "Okay," Brad said. "Let's go over some other things while Twyla's typing the contract. Policy matters. Say, you feel like this? Want that freshened up?"

"Sure, go ahead."

"I'll leave the bottle . . . we'll discuss this in detail later, Vinay, but I want you to know up front that I run KHC as a profit center. We hold staff to minimum federal standards. You'll be overseeing all four hundred beds in the county. Our nurse-to-bed ratio is one to thirty."

"R.N.s?"

"No, L.P.N.s."

"At night?"

"That's night and day both. Now, some of the things I'm going to talk about are the facility manager's business, but I don't want you to be surprised when you see them."

"I'm listening."

"We provide complete banking services within each facility, coordinated from here. What that means is the residents' Social Security and pension checks go into the till. That also lets us run FICA withholding for the employees through a revolving fund and pick up the interest on it."

"Go on."

"Cleaning supplies, medical supplies, we deal with a wholesaler in Erie. On durable goods, walkers, wheelchairs, restraints, blankets, we buy them, charge 'em off, then resell them from resident to resident as new. We figure on reselling things like that five to seven times.

"Same on food, laundry, so forth, we've got deals worked out with a single supplier. Oh, and a new line of portion-controlled nutrition stuff. We can feed at a dollar eighty a head a day.

"We'll be running you around every so often to churches and town councils to ask for donations. Cash, but food and supplies are okay too. We resell them to another chain down in the south of the state.

"We just had safety and fire inspection last month, so we're clear till next winter. Fortunately they don't check all our locations at the same time, so we can shift gear around to some extent. And once a year the state inspects training, staff qualifications, that kind of thing. Don't worry about them, I know the guy and he's reasonable." Boulton paused. "Any problems with anything I've said?"

Patel shrugged. He reached for the bottle again. "How often is doctor's call?"

"That's up to you."

The intercom interrupted them. "Mr. Boulton, Mrs. Boulton on four-three."

Brad got up. "Excuse me for a minute."

"Of course."

Behind the desk, he swiveled to face the window. He looked out, seeking the confidence he'd felt a moment before. But the towers were out of sight. He took three deep breaths and picked up the phone. "What can I do for you, darlin'?"

The voice was cool and deliberate and angry. "Brad, remember what we talked about last week? About your daughter?"

"Yes. I do. I called, and—"

"You'll have to take her today. I just can't handle her. We've got to get somebody, this is impossible, she's being annoying and destructive."

He closed his eyes. "Destructive?"

"She broke another piece. A beautiful Baccarat *millefiori*."

"Ainslee, she was probably playing."

"Play or not, it cost nine thousand dollars. And then she lied about it." Faintly, behind his wife's voice, he could hear Willie sobbing. "*Stop* your bawling! Brad, I don't know if you realize how sick she is. This child needs special attention. I don't think she belongs in this house."

Oh, Christ, he thought. "Ainslee, listen. You just fired Miss Stern. It takes time to find people like that. Can't you just tolerate it a little longer? I'm sure she's not being deliberately bad. She's only five—"

"I'm not here to *tolerate* things, Brad! She's your responsibility. I made that clear last time this happened. She's your daughter, not mine."

"Daddy?"

Her voice.

"Get off that extension, Williamina, I'm talking to your father."

"No. *Daddy!*" A cry of pain and fear so terrible he flinched.

"Bunny, now listen. Don't bother Ainslee, all right?"

"Daddy, are you going to send me away?"

"Who told you— Never mind." He closed his eyes again. "No one's going to send you away, Willie. Now listen, sweetheart. Be good, stay quiet, and I'll play Chutes and Ladders tonight with you. Yes, and then we can talk. All right? Good. Now let us grownups talk."

The rattle of the receiver. His sense of helpless anxiety grew, and with it anger. But he couldn't give way to it. Not with Ainslee Thunner Boulton. Carefully screening it out of his tone, he said, "Okay. Okay, darling, you're right. But I can't come in now. I'm in a meeting. Can't Lark watch her? Or the cook?"

"I can't leave her with him, Brad. You know why. And the cook has her own work to do. Dad will be up soon and I don't want her bothering him. You'll have to take her."

"Well, I can't come myself. I'll send the car."

"I can't believe you expect me to put up with this."

"I don't, I don't. I'll take her, darling, I'll bring her here. And I'll call the agency again. This afternoon." He remembered Patel, managed a wink. "Okay?"

"Do it now, Brad. I'm warning you."

"Soon as I hang up. We'll get somebody good, out of New York. Okay?" He breathed deep again. "How's Dad doing?"

"He's still in bed. Tell them at the agency we want somebody tomorrow. Fly her out. Charter. I don't care what it costs."

"Okay. Talk to you tonight, Ainslee."

The receiver clicked.

He hung up too. After a moment of silence he uncapped a pen and jotted NEW NANNY. URGENT on a Post-it note and tabbed it to the intercom.

"Family troubles?"

"Oh, my wife and daughter don't get along. Previous marriage. And Ainslee, she's . . . Look, I'm glad to have you aboard." Brad got up, trying to recall himself to business. "Let me tell you something, Vinay. You're coming to the county at an exciting time. The ground floor of a lot of things.

"Don't let the past hold you back. Anybody can make it in this country, if you're willing to sweat a little. Doesn't matter who your parents are. Doesn't matter where you're from. You invent yourself, market yourself. If they buy, it's real. When I was a kid I had nothing. I worked three jobs after school. Newspapers, mowing lawns, an Amway distributorship. Know what I learned?"

Patel shook his head.

"You've got to deliver the goods. Nobody asks you how. All they want is to have the job done. What matters at Thunder right now is a positive cash flow. Everything else is waste motion. I've operated on that philosophy since I took over and I've not only turned the company around, I'm building the Thunder Group."

The Indian nodded. Brad glanced at his watch. "Well, I guess that's about it . . . Twyla, you done with that contract?"

"Coming in, sir."

"Take a desk and look it over. If you have any questions I'll be here till noon." Brad almost asked him to the club, but stopped himself. He'd better prepare the older members first; Patel was pretty dark. Instead he said, "I've got a lunch meeting, but the Oilman's Hotel has a good buffet. Tell 'em to put it on my tab."

They shook hands again and the doctor left. He looked, Brad thought, even more like a loser than when he'd come in. He'd almost laughed in his face when he came up with that average income figure. Hell, he'd been ready to go up to fifty, but it hadn't been necessary.

He stared out. The snow was coming harder, each flake driving down as if competing with its fellows for the swiftest doom. Between him and the house on the hill a curtain was being drawn. Below him Main Street, plowed that night, was turning white again.

Suddenly he felt dread so deep it made him tremble.

Like a general in battle, he'd committed all his reserves. Now he had to hold everything together—the Board's support, Ainslee's, fourth-quarter profits—till the reorganization went through.

But if they held for another two months, through the sale, he'd be set for life.

He gazed out and down. Through Ainslee he owned the towers, lost now in the falling snow; owned the stone and steel around him; owned this town, this county, remote though it was.

Not too bad, he thought, for a whore's kid from Scranton.

He smiled angrily up at the cloud-sealed sky, remembering his wife's imperious voice. Ainslee didn't know it yet. But once he was in charge, he wouldn't need her anymore, either.

The intercom beeped. "Mr. Weyandt, sir."

He brought his palms down. Still smiling, he slid out a briefcase computer and centered it on his desk. He booted up 1–2–3 and looked at the figures one more time.

Scratching himself absently, he said, "Okay, Twyla, send him in."

Eight

The snow blew straight into his face as Phil pushed himself the last five hundred yards up Mill Street. "God *damn,*" he muttered. The wind froze his cheeks, jammed flakes between his eyelashes, turned his nose to wood despite the application of alternate gloves. His left leg dragged like a dead dog. When at last he reached the portico he had to stop, leaning against a pillar, and rest in its shelter.

Weak as he felt now, yesterday he hadn't even been able to get out of bed. The long haul down to the highway, pulling Halvorsen, had done him in. There'd been a scene with his mother about missing Mass. He hadn't felt like coming to school this morning, either, but he couldn't face another day at home.

Leaning there shivering after the two-mile walk from Paradise Lane, he looked up for a long time at the hills.

When he went in the clocks stood at seven-thirty and the halls were filled with kids. The blast of heat as the doors closed behind him was intense, close, instantaneously somniferous. The smells of wet wood, floor wax, perfume, and rubber filled the corridors. He unzipped his jacket and headed for his locker.

The fact that something had changed only gradually penetrated. The kids he passed didn't look at him. Their eyes slid aside. He said

"Hi" to Fred Bisker—they were lab partners—but Bisker said nothing back, just looked away.

Oh, Jesus, Phil thought, something's happened. But he had no idea what it was. And of course no one would tell him. No one would talk to him at all. It made it hard to concentrate on class work. He found himself listening for whispers when he got up to put a problem on the board. He blew it, and Mrs. Brodie warned him she expected more in the way of attention than he'd shown that day.

The next class was Maxwell's. As Phil came in he saw Mooney and Detrick sitting together in the back, saw their eyes find him and their mouths grin suddenly, together. It was the first time anyone had acknowledged his existence all day, and he thought instantly *It's them.* Fear scurried in his stomach, disgusting him with his own cowardice.

He sat motionless for the next fifty minutes. Even Alex Ryun failed to distract him. He sat with his notebook closed, neither raising his hand nor even noticing Maxwell's puzzled look.

He was busy hating them all. He stared out the window, watching snow detach itself from a sky lightless as a gun barrel. From time to time people went by outside. An old woman waded through the drifts, burdened with groceries. Two little kids with a sled. A black dog, more intelligent-looking, he thought, than the brain-dead mutants around him, tail curled jauntily over its ass, its white breath piston-driven. The dog reminded him that the puppy was in the basement. He had to feed it . . . he ought to visit old Halvorsen at the hospital . . .

At last, long-awaited as summer, the bell rang. No one spoke to him in the lunch line. He lockstepped bitterly ahead, eyes stabbing about the seated students. He imagined how many he could get if he had an AK-47.

He was thinking this when an auburn flame ignited. For a moment his glance lingered on it.

Alex Ryun was sitting in a circle of girls. Her coterie, he thought; the beautiful, the socially accepted, in a word the rich, or those who passed for well-off in a small town. One of them, Sheila Hazouri, glanced his way. Their laughter rankled his ears. Only Ryun didn't laugh, looking speculatively at him for a moment.

Phil thought nothing of it. He was a cockroach who craved a goddess. He hated them all, without distinction of sex or race or class.

When he limped out with his tray he faced the problem of where to sit. Now, at last, people had something to say to him: all the seats were saved. He wound up with the commercial ed students. They chattered among themselves while he ate rapidly, eyes on his food.

I hate this fucking town, he thought. This state. This country. This race, human, but so seldom humane.

I hate this fucking life.

English too went badly that afternoon. He frankly didn't give a shit about point of view in fiction. When the last bell rang he shuddered with relief. He slammed his books into his locker, and was limping grimly toward the cold, enjoying his bubble of solitude, when someone called his name.

When he turned he couldn't speak for a moment. Alexandrine Ryun was smiling up at him. He noted through shock that his fantasies had left out her fragrance. She came closer and closer, approaching more and more slowly, and finally stopped a foot away, leaning forward, her eyes raised to his.

"Hi."

"Well, uh, hi. Alex."

"Phil, you're getting an A in English, aren't you?"

He stared at her perfect teeth. "Uh, I'm okay, I guess."

"Can I ask you something? About that book she made us read?"

"Well, sure." The hallway opened to a lobby before the doors. She moved out of the press, and he followed, nudged close by the crowd. Eyes swung; he caught surprise on passing faces. She was saying something. He stared at her lips. Perfume eddied into his brain. The wiring connecting it to his gonads suddenly energized. He got a tremendous erection, and began to sweat.

His face was to her when Bubba Detrick turned the corner. He didn't see the ball player pause, eyes going hard; then shove his way between two kids walking together, ignoring their protests, and go on out of the building.

Alex paused and smiled. After a moment of enjoying this he came far enough out to say, "What?"

"I said, do you think that's the right interpretation?"

"Oh, sure, oh sure."

"Well, I see that now! I figured you'd be able to explain it better than Marzeau does."

"You really think so?"

"Sure. I mean, you're smart. I can tell by the questions you ask in class. Everybody says so."

"They do, huh? Say—" He searched his mind. "Say, do you know why nobody was talking to me today?"

"Oh, that. It was stupid. They say you were in a fight with Greg Detrick, that when you lost you threatened to have him arrested."

"*What?* You got to be kidding. What happened was—"

"I thought so too . . . Well, my folks like me home when it's snowing. Do you need a ride?"

"Uh, thanks, I like to walk." He cursed himself a heartbeat later. He could have ridden in her car, talked some more; but no, he'd blown it. He stared after her, thinking no more than a rock, or a male praying mantis at its final moment of self-immolative transcendence, then trailed her out into the lot. He could distinguish her scent, rare and distinctive, from the schoolgirl dabbings of the others. He watched her unlock her car.

A moment later slush spattered as its wheels spun, pushing her into Mill Street. He ran forward, and a moment later stared down. He'd picked up a handful of the grimy ice her tires had spurned.

Idiot, he thought. But still he smiled. For the snow was suddenly silver, and damaged limbs the only anchor to his soaring heart. Smiling, squeezing dirty water from his glove, he turned for home.

Paradise Lane was a dirt alley halfway up the flank of Sullivan Hill, on the far side of tracks and river from town. You got to it after crossing an iron footbridge, not by a sidewalk—the hill was too steep—but by plank steps that led up from the pavement. In summer the boards were rickety. Now, in winter, they didn't creak—the frozen mud and ice lent structural integrity—but the way was slippery.

He hauled himself upward by handfuls of rusty pipe, the same dreamy smile playing about his lips. He stepped aside once to let an old woman by. Fearing a fall on the glassy hill, she'd simply sat down and let herself slide toward town.

Eleven was one of five identical houses on the lane, a shotgun with broken aluminum siding and three naked posts holding up the porch roof. Beneath it two rusty chairs squatted like freezing beggars. When he opened the outer door the first thing he heard was the television. Then his mother's voice, and then his father's. Only then did the trance lift, suddenly and completely.

Inside, through the storm door, he could hear them shouting at each other. His smile disappeared as he wiped his feet. The tiny front parlor smelled of onions and Lemon Pledge and stale smoke.

In the dining room, through a bead curtain topped with a dried frond of palm, he saw his mother. She was thin, gray early, mouth unhappy. She wore a brown housedress and was eating Planter's peanuts from a can.

His dad was sitting across from her on the couch, smoking a Marlboro and watching a cop show. He was wearing his uniform trousers and a yellowing V-necked undershirt. The tinny blare of electronic dialogue filled the house with false urgency. His parents had suspended the argument as he came in and now glanced up at him, their faces still set for each other, so that it looked like they resented his coming. He took off his coat without looking at them, already reinfected with the anxiety and hopelessness that filled these close rooms like the greasy smell of old cooking. He hoped he could get upstairs without a scene.

"What do you say?" said his mother.

"Hi, Ma. Hey, Pa."

"Cold out?" grunted his father.

"Yes, sir." He got his boots off, padded into the kitchen. Pots were simmering on the stove. He lifted the lids. Red cabbage soup, redolent with meat broth and olive oil and chopped garlic. Beside it was his grandmother's risotto. The steam came up fragrant with basil and tomatoes, rice and shallots and sausage, pepper and Parmesano and butter. At least he could look forward to dinner. "What's for dessert?" he called, but the crash of cars was louder than his father's reply.

"What?"

"Angel food cake," said his mother, her voice tight.

"What'd you say, Pa?"

His father was coughing, hacking away as if to expel some clawed animal lodged in his chest. At last he gasped, "Nothin'. See if there's any more beer in the fridge."

Phil got him a fresh Bud and went back into the kitchen.

"Your mother said you felt bad yesterday," Joe Romanelli shouted to him over the television. "You feel better now?"

"Yeah."

He waited, but that seemed to be all. He looked through the kitchen window. The chinaberry bushes were white humps, as if a battle had been fought there, and the snow draped frozen corpses. He remembered one Christmas he'd been building a snowman, balancing on his crutches, when the Roemer kids, real bastards like their old man, began throwing snowballs from their yard. He'd been unable to avoid the hard-packed projectiles, they came too fast from four arms to dodge; and when he'd lifted his face to curse them, one had hit him in the eye and knocked him down. He'd hated them for years afterward, till the old man died and they moved away. He felt an anachronistic fear even now, when he passed children, that they'd turn on him with jeers, snowballs in their hands.

He trudged up the creaky stair to his garret. It was a converted attic, too low to stand in; he had to crouch or kneel. The room held a bed, a dresser, and cardboard boxes filled with his electronic junk. A single window glowed, arabesqued with frost. He'd be cold with the door shut, the only heat was downstairs, but he shut it anyway.

He half lay on his bed, bracing his kidneys against the wall. Below him the voices began again, his mother's shrill, his father's growling. Two defeated, imprisoned animals, he thought. The same old sins and guilts returned to unendingly, the same old lines a hundred thousand times repeated. He could have chanted them from memory. His mother accusing his father of drunkenness, failure, lack of ambition. His father telling her she was frigid, stupid, to take it to the priest.

Phil mused bitterly on what they'd made of life.

His father had grown up in Raymondsville, his mother in Nanty Glo. His father's family were stonecutters, and his uncle Tony still had a memorial business in town.

Joe, the youngest, had survived Vietnam and drifted into the police. He'd done all right at first, but as Phil's medical bills mounted he'd begun drinking. The old chief, Hodges, had cautioned and counseled without effect. The new one, Nolan, had simply suspended him. They'd nearly starved; suspended, you couldn't even draw unemployment. That, Joe had told his son bitterly, had taught him his place. Now he was on "night patrol," condemned like a ghost to wander the length of each darkness with an iron key round his neck, checking in at each city property. His pay grade after eighteen years was rock bottom.

Well, Phil thought, I better get some work done. He sighed, crossed himself sarcastically, and reached for the yellow pad old Halvorsen had given him.

He hunched over the nearly illegible scratching, then reached under the bed for the Underwood II that Mrs. Skinner, at the library, had given him for cleaning out the back room. He worked for a time, then paused to press a finger against the frost. Melting out a tiny peephole, he stared out, sifting his memory for words.

The old machine threw letters crazily. It ghosted the *T*s, and the bellies of the *P*s and *R*s were solid darkness. But gradually line by line it tapped the life of W. T. Halvorsen faint and hollow against the hiss of snow. Gradually Phil forgot the voices below, forgot his anger and pain. The hole healed with icy intaglio. He was lost in the magic of words.

. . . Can't tell you. All I can say is, one day, after the house, I shot a buck. Plain old whitetail. And looking down at it I knew I wasn't going to do it no more.

He wrestled for a long time over what Halvorsen had said about the fire. He didn't feel right leaving it out. It explained why Racks lived as he did, penitential, self-exiled, alone. But telling it, writing down the deepest secret Halvorsen had, felt wrong too. He'd been sick. Maybe he hadn't known what he was saying.

Phil asked himself why it mattered, and decided he didn't want to offend the old man.

That was interesting. Why? Because he'd saved his life? Or maybe that he identified with Halvorsen somehow. He gnawed his thumbnail. Then thought: Can't happen. I'll kill myself before I live like that.

At last he just put down that Jennie Halvorsen had died in a fire. He pulled the sheets out and clipped them together, feeling relieved.

Now that he was done he felt the cold. His breath hovered near the ceiling as if trying to escape. He covered himself with the blanket and stared up at a piece of plywood. He'd hammered it up that fall; he'd found nuts in his bed; squirrels had been coming in.

Finally he got up and unbuttoned his jeans. Kneeling on the bed he hesitated, listening, then reached up to slip out a magazine.

She was a dark-haired ballerina, posed with one leg extended on the bar. This was his favorite picture in the entire magazine, though he'd loved, in his way, each woman in it.

This time she was showering with him. He held her close in the carpeted bathroom and her perfume made him tremble. She smiled up at him as the Stag unbuttoned his shirt. Her blouse fell open and he kissed her neck as he slid it off.

Her freckles were the color of fawns. They were both naked as he stepped back in the steamy room. She raised her arms and pirouetted, her narrowed green eyes mirroring his lust. Her breasts were tiny but perfect, nipples pointed like Hershey's Kisses.

Beneath the blanket his hand moved and relaxed, moved and moved and moved.

Under the million hot needles she moaned as he soaped her breasts. His fingers slipped over her belly and then between her thighs, moistened with more than water. "Darling," he muttered, into the curve of her neck, into her flame-bright hair, holding her open while the strongest part of him slid upward, into delight. "I want you. Oh, my God, Alex—"

Behind his closed eyelids he saw again the golden explosion that had created the universe.

He was lying spent, the towel clutched to him, when steps creaked on the stairs. He half-rose, realized it was too late, and covered up in panicky haste.

"Philip, are you all right?"

"Yeah, Ma."

"What are you doing?"

"Studying."

"I lit the hot water, you want to take a bath."

"Okay."

"Are you feeling all right today?"

"You asked me that already. I said I was."

The door came open an inch or two. "Don't leave this door closed, it'll get cold up here."

"I'm all right, I said! Leave me alone!"

His angry shout stopped her. After a moment he heard her sigh. The door clicked closed. He heard her shoes thud slowly back down, and then, a few minutes later, a clatter as she set out plates.

He looked for the magazine, and saw with horror that it had fallen face up. If she'd come in . . . but simultaneously came another thought. In his arms through the endless golden moment he'd held, not the dark dancer, but Alexandrine Ryun.

It occurred to him suddenly that he ought to ask her for a date.

She'd been friendly in the hall today. Even he'd known that was no routine question. But could he ask her out? He'd daydreamed rape and bondage, but he'd never considered a date. He knew she'd been going with Mike Barnes, then stopped seeing him for Detrick. He'd figured she liked winners, athletes, and guys with cars. They both had their own, Barnes a used but hot Datsun Z, Detrick a shiny new pickup. While the only car his family had ever owned, the old Fury, had lain for years now rusting in the back yard. His father had never made enough to replace it.

So even if he had the guts to ask her, and she said yes, where could he take her? He had a few bucks left from his summer job at Dopel's Donuts. A movie, then a Coke downtown? Not real exciting for a girl like her.

Anyway, she was terrific. Not just pretty—she was kind and good too. When he thought about how nice she'd been today, when the others were such bastards, he was ashamed of his fantasies. He was a nobody, Failure Son of Failure; she was only the most beautiful and popular girl in the whole class.

Well, all she could do was say no.

He pushed back the spread and buckled his jeans, suddenly sick of this room, this house, himself. He picked up the typescript again. He found two typos and corrected them with a ballpoint. It looked neat, a nice piece of work. In fact it looked so—so *professional*—that all at once he thought of showing it to somebody down at the *Century*.

"Phil-lip—"

"What?" he snarled.

"Dinner."

She sounded hurt and he was sorry again. He had to get control, Christ, he was going to pieces. His parents had done their best. He felt like howling aloud in rage and despair.

He tucked his shirt under his belt and slid down the stairs. His father called his name and without thinking he jerked another Bud from the fridge. His mother wouldn't touch alcohol, literally. He sat between them, blinking in the smoke; his father kept one going in a saucer, snatching puffs between bites. Crockery rattled and he set to work, only now realizing how little he'd eaten at lunchtime. It was good, but he was eager to leave. As soon as he was done he got up.

His mother called after him as he went into the parlor, "Philip— where—"

"Library," he lied, throwing on his coat, wet with snow-melt, his cap, lacing up his boots.

"Here. Take these scraps down to that dog. How long are we going to keep it? I don't want a dog. It whines all the time under there. It'll drive me crazy. I don't want a—"

"For Christ *sakes*, Ma, I told you, just till the guy gets better."

"Don't talk like that, the name of the Lord—"

"Want a ride?" said his father. "Wait half an hour, I'm about to go on duty."

Normally he would have but he was sick of his parents. Besides, he wanted to get there before the paper closed. "No thanks," he said, carefully demodulating his voice.

"Well, be back soon."

"G'night."

Outside it was already night. He folded the pages carefully and thrust them inside his jacket. Then he went around back. The puppy was glad to see him and he rubbed his ears as it ate, thinking again of the old man. As long as he was downtown he might as well drop by the hospital a minute, see how he was doing. The thought made him feel virtuous.

He locked the dog up again and went down the lane to the steps. Pointing his toes, he let gravity slide him down the edges of the ice-covered treads, bump-bumpbumpbump, down the hill toward the lightless snake-writhe of the river, and beyond it the glittering loom of town.

Nine

Seven blue plastic chairs. A wooden bench. Green tile floors, and a bite of wintergreen lingering in the overheated air. The chairs were the same, the tile the same, even the smell was familiar. But the Maple Street Hospital Emergency Room felt different from the plant-hung, magazine-strewn waiting area of the Style Shoppe.

Jaysine stood uncertainly, holding her warmthfogged glasses. Beyond the translucent, swinging doors she could make out nothing but light.

She'd stopped at the front desk, holding her face rigid, and asked casually where was the Monday clinic. She knew it hadn't been her imagination, the look she got with the directions.

At last she chose the bench. She took off her coat and unwound her scarf. Then sat hunched, looking at her boots. She rubbed her glasses with a mitten, put them back on.

Through prescription lenses the room lost its neat astringency. The overhead lamp was one of the giant ice-cube trays she remembered from grade school. Rust bled down the walls, a grout of dirt edged the tile squares. The ashstand was a cemetery of burnt-out filters, some smeared with cerise or strawberry. The wall clock buzzed, hesitated, and jerked a minute farther into the present.

She'd sat waiting like this before. Through nights at the Cow Palace, for someone to need milk or chips or beer. At school, for her turn to do an aniline tint under the gimlet gaze of Mr. De Bree. And last, for him; at her apartment, or places where she felt as if the price tags on her clothes were showing, like at the parking lot at the We-Wan-Chu Motel.

She shivered. Remembering that night, the first time he said he loved her, she felt pressure behind her locked eyelids, straining at the cold around her heart. Like shouts in the distance, she recognized emotion, though she couldn't feel or name it yet.

This can't be happening, she thought for the hundredth time. It felt like the dream she had sometimes, where Marybelle demanded this awful finger wave and she couldn't find the waving lotion, and got it in a tangle, and finally wads of Mrs. Acolino's hair, brittle as uncooked vermicelli, came out in her hands . . . this couldn't be happening to her. *I'm a good person,* Jaysine thought. *I don't sleep around, I've never hurt anyone.*

She glanced around without turning her head. Like her, the others had spaced themselves as far apart as the room allowed. Beside each was a jumble of clothing, coats, hats, gloves, and sweaters, already beginning that process that would end with the ultimate nakedness.

A little boy crept toward her, eyes on her boots. She smiled and held out her hand. But his mother jumped to her feet, snatching the child up roughly, ignoring his screams. Jaysine watched him borne away, their eyes still locked over the rigid back.

The man across from her recrossed his legs, letting his grocery-store tabloid fall open. He wore a loose casual suit like the models in *GQ* and sunglasses and a kind of beret she'd never seen before in Raymondsville.

He glanced up and caught her examining him. "Big crowd tonight, ain't it? This your first time here?"

Jaysine put on her hard, not-interested face and looked away. Instead of answering she took out her compact. She powdered her pores, then searched her bag for lipstick. When she felt safe again she closed her purse with a sigh and pushed it under the chair.

She sighed again, feeling something thick in her throat. Marybelle would be angry. Sick time cost her money in lost appointments. Jaysine was losing money too. She began adding it up. Elizabeth had been scheduled at three, Lucille at three-thirty, then Frances—a third of that, divide by three—

"Jaysine Farmer."

"Here," she said quickly, standing up.

A woman stood in the open doors, the light so bright behind her no face was visible. "Come on back. Booth on the right."

The examining room was even brighter, even hotter than the waiting room. White partitions sectioned it. Her boots made vinyl sucking noises. She drew the curtain quickly. Chilly light glowed over stainless instruments, an examining chair, a steel dresser of medicines, ointments, bandages. A cartoon was taped on the wall, a monkey examining a human skull: *Constant change is here to stay.*

Jaysine didn't smile. She laid her purse on the chair, trying not to look at the stirrups. She'd hated Dr. Kopcik looking up her that afternoon, probing her with cold metal. Again she wondered: had *he* been here? She imagined being a man, holding it out, the act of exposure no vulnerability but an assertion: "Here it is."

Voices approached, and the curtain that walled her off whiffed out. Beneath it appeared two sets of shoes. Black work boots, wet, cracked, salt petrified, confronted by new white cushion-soled running shoes.

"Do you have any discharge?"

"Say what?"

"Discharge. Do you have any bleeding? Does mucus come out of your penis?"

"Oh yeah . . . oh yeah, discharge. Yeah, I got me some of that."

"What color is it?"

"What?"

"What color is the discharge? Is it whitish?"

"Oh yeah. No, it kind of, kind of yellow. I thought I check this out, I might of got me a strain. Can you give me some pills?"

"Injections are more effective. Is it difficult for you to urinate?"

"Oh, when I go to the can . . . yeah. Just a little there, yeah."

"Let's see what we've got."

The boots were covered by brown trousers. They went to tiptoe as the Nikes approached, then sank down again.

"Hooeee . . . you shouldn't to put them gloves on, that plastic sure was cold."

The Nikes left the booth. Two minutes later they returned.

"Mr. Smith, you have gonorrhea. I'm going to give you a shot to take care of it."

"Oh, no. I don't need no shots. You could give me some pills, you want, but I don't take no shots."

"Turn around, Mr. Smith. Bend over, please."

Staring at the floor, Jaysine began to tremble.

· · ·

She saw the Nikes first. Then blond hair. Lightened, but not properly. It looked like a cream, done at home. Last of all Jaysine made out the eyes: tired, brown, set too close. Her mind chattered professionally: *You could be pretty if your posture was better, if we let your hair grow and style it away from your face.* Instead she was all business, no makeup but a passé shade of lipstick, carrying a clipboard, stethoscope, pen.

"Ms. Farmer. How are we doing today."

"Hello. Is the doctor going to be in pretty soon?"

"I'm Dr. Friedman."

"Oh, I'm sorry—"

"I'm used to it. What's the trouble?"

She explained in a near-whisper. Friedman glanced over the clipboard. "Are you married, Jaysine?"

"No."

"Pregnant?"

"No."

"Are you on the street?"

"What?"

"Of course you aren't . . . Do you use needles?"

"Yes."

"I see. What are you on?"

She felt confused. "What am I on? I don't understand—"

"What do you put in the needles?" said Friedman patiently. "What are you on, what do you use in them?"

"I don't put anything in my needles. I'm an R.E., a registered electrologist, I remove hair with them. I work at the Style Shoppe, on Pine Street, by the Odd Fellows Building."

The doctor gave her a glance over the clipboard, as if seeing her for the first time, and then smiled and put it aside. "Let's skip the rest of these. Sit down, Jaysine. Is this your first occurrence?"

"Yes."

"How long have you had it?"

"I noticed something . . . Saturday. I think I, I've had kind of a low fever for quite a while. I thought it was a cold coming on."

"Does it itch?"

"It sure does."

"Sore throat?"

"Yes."

Rubber snapped as the doctor stretched on gloves. She made

Jaysine say "Aah," then examined her palm. Finally she said, "Well, let's see what we've got. You've been in a chair before."

My turn now, she thought through the coldness, removing boots and peeling down hose and panties. As she fitted her arches to cold metal she remembered the women in her homey station, exposing guiltily to her what they concealed from the world. She stared up as a little sun came on above her and tilted up and down and centered itself hotly between her legs.

The doctor's head appeared between her knees. "Spread a little more, please . . . Yep. Something going on here."

"That's what Dr. Kopcik said."

"You saw him? When?"

"This afternoon. He said I'd better come over here, tonight, to the Monday clinic."

The gleam of the other woman's hair, her lowered head, made her think of the way she lowered hers to Brad. He liked to do it other places than in bed. In his car, up at the abandoned lookout tower east of Four Holes; when it was warm, in the woods, on the picnics she packed for them. Once even in the stairwell of her apartment. She'd been scared, listening for someone coming up from the street. He wanted her on every date, sometimes the first thing. She didn't always feel like it then, so sudden, but because he loved her she let him.

She smiled, remembering, and then her lips stiffened as she came back to when and where she was now.

"Let's try for a scrape," the doctor was saying. "There's a place here that looks amenable. Be right back."

Jaysine let the cold light fill her while she waited. Guilt and shame ebbed, replaced by a numbed disgust and fear.

The doctor returned with a silvery shard of metal, eyed her privates critically, and began mining. She fixed her eyes on the light, feeling the tears rise again, a flood pressure behind a frozen dam.

"Okay up there?"

"It hurts."

"Sorry. Got to get some live stuff."

Steel clinked into glass. A silken thread of blood uncurled. Friedman was done with the scrape and was taking blood when the door opened and the attendant waddled in. She got something from a locker and left. "Privacy," said Dr. Friedman, inspecting the full tube, "is not our number-one concern here . . . okay. You can get dressed now. I'll be right back."

The doctor seemed to be gone a long time. Jaysine sat on the table, waiting, once she had dressed.

Friedman came back in. "Well, we'll do a blood test, just to be sure, but the dark-field's pretty trustworthy."

"What do you think it is?"

"This?" Friedman looked toward the curtain; her mind was somewhere away, Jaysine thought, perhaps on another patient, and she felt sudden jealous rage; not even here could she get attention just for herself. "I don't think there's much doubt it's syphilis. Secondary stage. The chancre's inside the cervix, that's why you missed it till the later symptoms appeared. We're probably looking at six to ten weeks after initial infection. I imagine Dr. Kopcik told you that."

"He said—that disease. Yes."

"You've read about it, I suppose."

"Oh, sure. In the magazines, at work."

"Once we have positive tests, we'll start your treatment. Are you allergic to penicillin?"

"I don't think so."

"All right, then. Do I have your number here? I'll call when we want you for the first course of shots. In the meanwhile, I'd advise discontinuing intercourse. If you can't, have the male wear a condom."

Jaysine nodded. "Tell me—"

"Yes, go ahead," said the doctor briskly, glancing toward the curtain.

"How did I get this? I mean, is there any other—"

"Sexual contact. That's it."

She stared at the floor, then took a deep breath. "Would he know he had it?"

"Not always. But usually. Nine times out of ten, at a guess."

Friedman snapped off the gloves and threw them into a bin. One finger caught, hung over the edge like, Jaysine thought, his penis, limp and small after he took it out and reached for his cigarettes. "If you're sure who it was, I'd tell him if I were you. Make sure he receives treatment. Otherwise you leave yourself open to reinfection. And you'll need to take some precautions in your work—I'll want to talk to your employer. Gloves should be enough, just for a few weeks." The doctor smiled, brief, weary, unexpected; then suddenly reached down and patted her with her bare hand. "Cheer up! It'll take a little while, but we can cure this. That's more than you can say about a lot of things."

"No problem," said Jaysine, sliding down and reaching for her clothes.

In the waiting room the seats had grown new people. Instead of leaving she sat down again. Reflected in the face of the clock, her own wore the hard look again. Her mouth was set wry and a little bored. She told herself she'd expected this, or something like it.

When her knees stopped shaking she got up. Pulled the scarf over her hair. Climbed the stairs to the lobby. Then stopped, wondering what to do, where to go next.

The outer door opened and a boy in a knit cap came in. Snow blew in with him from the darkness, lived for a whirling moment in the lobby heat, then vanished. She turned suddenly toward the invitation of night. He held the door for her and she went through it, not looking at him, feeling nothing yet, into the dark and the wind.

She didn't see the streetlights, haloed glows spaced away in the falling snow. She didn't see the icy road beneath her boots, or the headlights at the top of the hill. Only when a horn screamed out and the station wagon dipped, plowing toward her on locked wheels, did she flinch, then hurry forward. She didn't look back at the stalled car, the woman who stared after her from behind the wheel. All that was real was internal, the unanswerable dilemma that drummed in her brain:

He said he loved me.

Then how could he do this to me?

The lights faded behind her as she stumbled on, seeking solitude like a wounded animal. Past darkened, shabby houses, their only light the ghostly flicker of screens. Past an abandoned garage, into a vacant lot, junk and garbage drifted deep with snow. Here, in the darkness, she stopped, leaning against a shattered, roofless wall of icy brick. Sagged to her knees, then on down into the snow where she could smell dogs had been. She didn't care.

He said he loved me.

The whiteness built on her back, her shoulders, her calves. She laid her burning cheek against the icy ground.

I know I loved him.

Her eyes closed and the hard look slipped off her mouth. She lay without moving in the darkness, in the silence, beneath the slowly falling snow.

Ten

Phil wondered what *her* problem was. She hadn't said a word, or even looked at him. A little heavy, but not bad looking. He glanced after her, wondering who she was, but she was already gone.

He forgot her. Waiting for the elevator, he went back over his visit to the *Century* office.

It'd been brief. He'd had maybe sixty seconds with Jerry Newton, and the editor had been preoccupied by a rattling teletype and a screen of text. He'd nodded continually, hurrying Phil through his explanation; glanced at the typescript, then when a phone rang dropped it into the maelstrom that covered his desk.

Well, Phil thought, at least he said he'd look at it.

The elevator stopped. He nosed uncertainly down a hushed corridor. The hospital smell made him uneasy. Visiting hours were almost over. He'd already passed the double room when he realized the silhouette within had been W. T. Halvorsen, sitting up in the dark.

He had a weird sense of déjà vu as he felt his way in. He almost expected a puppy at his knees. When he got to the bed he hesitated. At last he decided, and whispered the old man's name.

Halvorsen had been sitting there, awake, for perhaps half an hour.

He'd napped through all that day, waking only when someone came to do something to him. And not wholly then. Though he remembered injections. But at last, not long before, he'd opened his eyes on a tangible world.

Lying there he touched, very lightly, a needle taped above his wrist. He turned his head, and made out an obese man who lay with his eyes closed, wheezing with every breath.

Funny, he couldn't for the life of him say how he got here. Last he remembered he'd been at home. The boy had come by, the Italian kid, and they'd been talking about the old days. After that he didn't remember anything. Yet here he was, obviously in a hospital, and a window told him it was night.

When he opened his eyes again he caught the shadow. He watched it hesitate, then approach. When it whispered his name he started.

"What are you doin' here, boy?"

"Hi, Mr. Halvorsen. Come by to see you. Uh, how you doing?"

"I don't rightly know. Where the heck are we?"

"This is Raymondsville Memorial."

"Uh huh. Figured so . . . but how'd I get here?"

"Oh. Nobody told you? Well, you remember, we were talkin'? You kind of passed out. I was pretty scared. You wouldn't wake up, so I dressed you and dragged you down to the road. A trucker gave us a ride. Actually, he drove us right up to the emergency room. He was from Texas, talked funny, but a real nice guy."

Halvorsen nodded. Now he remembered. He'd felt suddenly sick, sick to his guts, and had headed for the doorway to puke it up. And after that, nothing.

"What day's today?"

"It's Monday night."

He'd been out for two days. He thought about that. Then muttered, "Guess I owe you a thanks for packin' me out. Must not of been easy, that's a four-mile haul."

"It's okay," said Phil, and after a moment added, "Don't worry about your puppy. I brought her along too. She's up my house, on Paradise, I'm feeding her and everything."

"I thank ye. That's good to know."

They waited in the darkness for a while. At last Halvorsen said, grudgingly, "What was your name, again? Sammonelli, something?"

"Phil Romanelli."

"Uh huh. Well, ought to be a chair here someplace. Can you reach this light, here, up above me?"

The single bulb clicked on, showing them each to the other. The old man's face was drawn and his gray hair looked wet. There was some kind of rash on his cheek. His arms came out of the hospital gown thin and knobby-elbowed. A tube was taped to one of them. His eyes were cavernous in the glare, and shadows hid his mouth beneath a bony skull.

"You're looking better," Phil told him. "What do they say's wrong with you?"

"Well, I ain't talked to anybody yet. Ain't been in shape to. Feel like I just woke up after a bad drunk." Halvorsen reflected on this, didn't like the sound of it. "Though I ain't had a drop. Hey . . ."

"Phil."

"Yeah, would you mind findin' the doctor? I'd like to know how long they're planning on keepin' me here."

Phil found a nurse at the hall station. The doctor would be in on night rounds in an hour, and unless Mr. Halvorsen needed attention, he'd have to wait till then. He took that back and the old man nodded. "No hurry," he said.

"It doesn't hurt, does it?"

"Well, this needle stings some, but I don't dare pull it out. Another thing—" He lifted the coverlet, stared at himself under it. "By jiminy, here's another one."

Phil sat back. He thought, I'll stay another couple minutes, then head home.

"What's it doing outside?"

"Oh, still coming down."

"First snowfall don't usually last."

"Well, it's been cold for a long time. And it hasn't really stopped since Friday night."

The man in the corner muttered, wheezed, and tried to turn over once or twice before giving up.

Phil whispered, "By the way, I got that interview typed up."

"What interview?"

"You know, what you were telling me out at your place."

"Oh."

Halvorsen had been feeling for a while like he had to pee, but he didn't feel right just letting go in the bed. What if something leaked? But with the tube in him down there it didn't seem like he had much of a choice. He glanced at the boy's waiting face. "Oh, those. Just some old stories . . . Did I tell you 'bout Ben Yeager?"

"You mentioned him."

"Old Amos only told me about a hundred stories about him." Halvorsen remembered the sudden pop and sizzle as McKittrack would lean to aim into the fire, his beard swinging dangerously close, and then rear back and make a miser's-purse of his mouth before he went on with whatever tale was in train. He licked his lips. "You got anything on you to chew?"

"What?"

"Never mind." He should have known. He remembered how the trapper had started him in on Navy Cut out there in the Kinningmahontawany, and how his mother had a fit when he come home, thirteen years old, with a bulge in the side of his face like a chipmunk.

"Well, I better be goin'," he heard the boy say.

"Nah, sit down, let me tell you one of 'em." Halvorsen suddenly wanted to talk, maybe because he was alone and sick and maybe even a little scared. He felt weak, but talking didn't seem to tire him. "Did you ever hear about—"

"Just a minute," said Phil, getting up. When he came back he had a pen and a note pad. "Okay," he said, grinning shyly at the old man; and he saw Halvorsen's face move, just a bit, in what might have been meant for a smile.

"Now, I told you Yeager was king hunter all around here back in the old days. Amos—you remember Amos?"

"The trapper."

"Yeah. He knew Yeager just after the war, the Civil War, and Ben was seventy-one then, so that would born him around 1794, '95. His dad moved out here from the Amish country on the Purchase of 1784. He had the first still west of the mountains. This was wilderness, wasn't a dozen white men in northwest Pennsylvania back then."

"Uh huh."

"So he started huntin' around 1810. When Amos knew Ben he was kind of fat, but still tough as ironwood and fast as a thunderbolt. Used to wear a old-style huntin' shirt and buckskin breeches. Then he had a big leather belt, and stuck his mittens in that, his bullet-bag, and his big bowie. And squirrel-lined moccasins.

"Yeager was what they used to call a professional hunter. He told Amos he'd killed three hundred and fifty bears, probably three thousand deer, exactly sixty-four panthers and two thousand one hundred and five wolves, and then of course elks, and wildcats, fox, and so on. He knew the numbers 'cause in them days the state paid eight dollars for every wolf or panther scalp you turned in. That was real money then.''

Phil's pen scratched. In the corner the other man shifted again, but his eyes stayed closed.

"Now, what are you? Sixteen?''

"Seventeen.''

"When he was a year younger than you he was out huntin' with the Senecas. They adopted him into the Turtle clan, and he burned a white dog with 'em. I don't know what that means. But they taught him to call wolves. One time he called 'em so good a pack surrounded him. He got two with his old muzzle-loader and killed another one with his knife before the rest ran off over a hill.

"That same winter he was hunting down along Falkiner Creek, out where Ironfurnace is now, and he shot a deer with his last pinch of powder. Now in them days all they took was the pelts, they left the meat unless they wanted some right then. Well, he had it dressed out and was ready to head home when it commenced to snow.

"And it snowed so heavy he couldn't see. So he tore down some boughs and bedded down under a hemlock, there's always a dry place there, covered himself up with the hide and went to sleep.

"Well, he woke up around midnight, and felt around, and found that he had sticks and leaves all over him, and the hide he was under smelled of cat sign.''

"Cat sign?''

"Cat piss. He knew in a minute what it was. Some mama panther had claimed him, and was gone to get her cubs for dinner.''

Phil, listening to the old man's flat mutter, felt a sudden chill. He imagined himself huddled in darkness, half-buried in boughs and above that snow; around him the stink of the cat's staling. Beyond that only utter night, icy dark, black as blindness. Yet in it something moved, huge, powerful, night-eyed, and hungry.

"And he didn't have any more bullets?''

"No more powder. Anyway, he pulled that hide back over himself and gathered some of the dry needles and struck him his steel and got a fagot lit. And he hid that and waited.

"Pretty soon, sure enough, Ben hears her comin' over the snow, pad-pad-paddin' toward him. He waits till she's sniffin' the hide and then he suddenly throws it aside and pushes the fire into the cat's eyes. It gave a scream, its whiskers caught, an' it was gone. He nursed that fire all night, but she never came back.''

Halvorsen smiled. Something in him felt completion, passing

these tales along. He knew it was sentiment, telling this boy as he had been told, as McKittrack had heard them from Yeager himself a century or more before. But at his age, he figured he could afford a little sentiment.

And the boy deserved it. He'd come asking for stories, now hadn't he?

"Now, bears. There's still bears, but not like they used to. I remember once when I was livin' in town one came down the street one night, killed two dogs that come out to chase it. I was on the porch loading my thirty-ought-six when Pete Riddick got it with two barrels of buckshot." He paused, frowning up at the light. "No, wasn't Pete—he dropped a can of nitro in '36. Anyway, yeah, these woods used to be full of them. Full-grown, yearling, cubs. Yeager took 'em all."

"He killed cubs too?"

"And skinned them. And sold 'em. Sure. It was his business."

Phil's initial admiration for this Yeager character was ebbing. "He sounds pretty rough."

"Oh, I imagine he was. There was a whiskey shanty out in Medicine Spring then, that's what they used to call Petroleum City. One night some fella from Philadelphia disagreed with him, said you couldn't call a wolf, they were too smart. So Ben grabs a jug of dew in one hand and the fella that mouthed off in the other and heads up Dale Hollow.

"So they're going through the woods in the middle of the night, up above Cherry Hill, and they hear a dog-wolf howl some distance off. Ben says, 'Stop, and be quiet.' And they hear a slut-wolf answer, closer to them.

"So they go in that direction, an' Ben he gives a bark every once in a while, and the bitch keeps answering. Finally after an hour they come to a blown-down oak. The she-wolf's under it. See, Ben knew that when the pups were small the dog-wolf would bring food back to the den. So he crawls under there and gets eight pups out from it and kills six and scalps them. The old wolf comes out showing her teeth, and the guy was going to shoot it with his pistol, but Ben stopped him. He said, 'I've got three litters out of this bitch, don't stop her now.' And he took the live pups back with him and sold 'em, and the city fella paid his whiskey the rest of that night."

"She let him take the pups?"

"They say a wolf won't fight for its young the way a bear will. I don't know, they've been gone here since Amos was a kid. They killed one over in Potter County in 1890, but they ain't been seen in Hemlock since the Civil War.''

"Those panthers—painters—sounded like the meanest.''

"Yeah, guess they was. Eleven, twelve feet long. A panther could kill a bear. Yeager shot the last one down in Reeds Still Hollow. They still call that Painter Rocks, where he got it.''

"Yeah, I heard of that. Only they call it Painted Rocks now.''

"No, it's 'Painter,' not 'Painted.'''

Romanelli made a note.

Halvorsen lay motionless for a time, staring down at his hands. "Yeah, they killed 'em,'' he said. "All the buffalo, all the wolves, all the painters and catamounts and wildcats. Just deer and a few bear now, what they can hunt with no trouble. And then they cut down the woods.''

"What do you mean, cut them down? Who cut them down?''

He lifted his head. "My God, boy, don't you know that? The Campbells and the Gerroys and the Goodyears. Why, Christ, there was white pines here a hundred feet high and two hundred years old. Hemlock higher than that and thick as a man's tall. There was hardwood, chestnut and oak where the ground was good, and ash and hickory and maple and birch everywhere. On the hillsides you had poplar, and linnwood, and down low the butternut and sycamore and elm. That's what these old short-line railroads was for, that's how they hauled it out.''

He closed his eyes as he spoke, and the picture came still terrible though it was sixty years gone. They'd been bumping southward along the rutted track in McKittrack's old Model T, and come round through Grafton Hollow and then the road dropped, the scrub pine dropped away, and he'd gone to stone in his seat.

Before them was desolation to the blue horizon, fold on fold of hills stripped like battlefield dead under the autumn sun. Their sides were littered with stumps and briars and slashed with the Shay engines' right-of-way. The old man, cursing in a whisper, told him how the timber companies had bought politicians, lied and cheated and forced Indians and small owners off their land; then in ten years whipsawed, toppled, and stripped for tanbark twenty-eight million acres of virgin forest. They'd never replanted, just moved on west, and now nothing was left, nothing.

McKittrack had told him then greed would be the ruin of the land. That where the ancient forests had fallen no tree might ever grow again, and for certain none as darkly and broodingly majestic.

Now, two generations later, Billy Halvorsen nodded slowly. "I seen them cut down those woods. And I seen what come back. Aspen and gray birch, maple and spruce and beech . . . it's woods, but it ain't the same. It'll never be the same."

They were sitting there together in silence when Dr. Leah Friedman came in. Behind her was a woman Phil recognized after a moment as Alma Pankow, Halvorsen's daughter.

"Hello, Racks." The doctor flicked on the room light and perched on the bed. "Is this your young friend? The one who brought you in?"

"That's right. Alma, want you to meet Phil."

The woman's round face was reddened by cold. She looked tired, older than she ought to be. At Halvorsen's introduction she looked at Phil, but said nothing.

"We met before," Phil told her. "You work there at the unemployment with my sister. And then last summer, you ordered some stuff for your dad over the phone, and I came by your house for the money—"

"Oh yes." She sat down, placing herself in the chair like a heavy bag of groceries.

Friedman took Halvorsen's wrist. "So you're back with us at last."

"'Fraid so."

"How are you feeling?"

"Tired."

"Um hum. What have you been eating out there in the woods, Mr. Halvorsen?"

"I eat all right. Do a little garden. Alma brings me things in the winter, potatoes and canned stuff."

"Do you take vitamins?"

"Not out of no pill," said Halvorsen. "Start feeling slow, I'll brew me some hemlock tea, or feverwort, somethin' like that. I doctor myself."

"You'd get C and B complex from those." She switched her gaze to Phil. "You were with Mr. Halvorsen when he had his episode."

"Yes, ma'am. I'm Phil Romanelli."

"Leah Friedman, Phil. Have you felt faint or weak? Then or now? Skin troubles, rash anywhere on your body?"

"No."

"Have you two been spending a lot of time together?"

"I wouldn't say so," said Phil, and looked at Halvorsen. The old man shook his head. He looked back at the doctor. "Maybe two or three hours, all together."

"He ought to move into town," said Mrs. Pankow suddenly. They all looked at her. She was staring at the floor, at the muddy footprints from her boots. "I've tried to get him to move in for years. Fred's got a extra room over the garage we could fix up. It's warm, he could help out around the pumps. But he won't listen."

"That's not your fault." The doctor patted her twice, with a sort of professional compassion, then folded her hands on her clipboard. "So let's go on . . . You didn't eat anything that might have disagreed with you?"

"Can't think of nothing."

"Have you been around any pesticides, any recently sprayed areas, any chemical spills?"

"I been out at my place, that's all, mindin' my own business," said Halvorsen shortly. "What're you getting at? What's wrong with me? I figured it was my heart, or maybe I was goin' crazy."

"Your heart? They tell me how you go tramping through those woods, up and down those hills. I don't think it's that. And you're certainly not crazy. But I don't believe it's diet-related either."

"Then what?" said Alma.

"I don't know." The doctor pressed her lips together and looked toward the window. "Snowing like this, I hope people wear their seat belts . . . Okay, here's what I think. I only get traces from the urine, but they're pretty odd. It's a little like cases you read about in the shipbuilding industry, where workers are exposed to organotin paint. And yet it's like pesticide poisoning. That rash you've got is a chemical eczema. And last, I see signs of heavy metal toxicity."

"You're saying, some kind of poison?"

"That's right, Mr. Halvorsen. That's the diagnosis."

"Am I goin' to live?"

She smiled. "This time. What I want to know is, where did you pick this stuff up?"

Halvorsen lay quietly, reviewing the last few days. He'd puttered around in the basement, oiled his old .22 Hornet . . . Thursday he hadn't done much, gone for a walk down the hollow . . . Friday he'd walked into town, had a coffee at the Brown Bear, and got a ride back with Fatso. And Saturday he'd woke up sick. "Can't think of any place I might of got sprayed with any chemicals," he said slowly.

"Try."

"I *did*."

"All right, all right!" She smiled wearily. "Phil, can you contribute anything?"

"Well, not really. He didn't look too good when I got out there, and he just got worse and worse. But I don't know why."

"So, when can I get out of here?" Halvorsen asked her.

"I'd like to hold on to you a few more days. Let you get your strength back. That reminds me, are you hungry?"

"Still a little queasy, but funny, I ain't hungry." He lifted his arm; the tube followed it. "I figured that was what this was for."

"That's right, that's sugar solution, but you should get some solid food in you too. You don't look like you've got a lot in reserve. Maybe a milkshake, would you like that?"

"I'll give 'er a try."

Friedman got up. She crossed the room and felt the sleeping man's pulse; touched his forehead gently; made a note on her clipboard. Halvorsen, growing tired of the light, covered his face with his free arm. All that talking had taken more out of him than he'd realized. When the doctor came back she murmured, "Mrs. Pankow, Mr. Romanelli, I'll tell the nurse you can stay past visiting time if you like. I've got to finish my rounds."

Alma nodded; Halvorsen whispered, "Thanks." Phil hesitated, then jumped up and followed her out into the corridor. She was leaning over the counter, talking to the nurse, and his eyes slid up her leg. Old as she was, she had a nice ass. She finished and turned to him, brows lifted, and he said, "Say, Doctor, I had a question—"

"Go ahead."

"What kind of chemicals are these? That you think he's been exposed to?"

"They're pretty dangerous. Toxic, mutagenic, carcinogenic. That means poisonous and cancer-causing. He's past having children, fortunately."

"What are they used for?"

"Pesticides, insecticides, nerve gas, and various industrial uses."

"*Nerve gas?*"

"Among other things."

"Well, how would he get any of that? He lives way out in Mortlock Run."

"That's what's puzzling me, Philip. I'd hoped one of you could help me find out, but no luck, I guess."

"The thing is"—she paused, tapping her foot and frowning—"this isn't the first case like this I've seen this year. There've been several eczemas and gastrointestinals with no clear-cut etiology. I mean, no obvious cause. There's only one case I've been able to trace. A family out in Chapman bought a load of cut-rate heating oil from somebody in a truck. The stuff was full of cadmium and lead."

"Mr. Halvorsen burns wood."

"Right, I know." Her wrist shot out and he jumped before he realized she was only checking her watch. "Well, look, gotta go."

"Wait—is he—I mean, what's going to happen to him?"

"He's pretty weak now, but he's in good shape for his age. I know he doesn't have much of a pension, and I don't want to eat up his savings, if he has any, but I don't want him to go back to that basement. I know he's the hermit type, but he should have some-body around to keep an eye on him." Friedman hesitated. "Alma would take him, but I don't know how Fred really feels about it. Anyway, he needs professional care. I'm going to recommend he be transferred to a long-term care facility."

"A what?"

"A nursing home. But that's up to his daughter, and to him." She patted him, the same quick double pat she'd given Mrs. Pankow. "Okay, really got to go now. Good night."

"Good night."

Head down, Phil retrieved his coat, said goodbye to the old man and his daughter, and walked thoughtfully out into the night.

Eleven

In the winter night the grimy snow glowed scarlet, as if dyed by the neon light with humming radiance. Beneath her boots cinders crunched like the dried husks of locusts. Slower, and slower. Then stopped, and she stood still, looking up.

By day Sherlock's looked abandoned. Its windows were dirty dark, ragged with the portraits of long-defeated politicians, and the brick-look siding had cracked away from rotting wood beneath. But by night it changed, spread its wings and lived and fed. It was open now, ready for whoever might need.

Jaysine shuddered involuntarily as the door sealed behind her. In the moment before vision fogged overhead fans peeled spirals off a slab of tobacco haze. Balls clicked, backed by a steady throb of Charley Pride. The men wore wool shirts and jeans, boots and hunting vests. She heard their voices as if through cotton. They were talking about their first day in the woods, about deer.

But none of them looked her way, and she moved forward, reassured. The moment she slid onto a sparkly plastic stool a huge round man in a red shirt was in front of her, hands like two rashers of bacon to either side of hers on the bar. "Evenin'. What can I get you, miss?"

"Straub's."

"What's that? Couldn't quite hear you."

"I said, Straub's."

"Are you all right?"

"What do you mean? I'm fine. Just bring me what I asked for, please."

The next thing she knew he had her hand. It took her a moment to snatch it back. A spark of anger flared through the numbness, like a match struck in a frozen forest. "What do you think you're doing?"

"Sorry. But you look froze through." He winked slowly. "Tell ya what. I'm bringin' you a ginger brandy first. After you drink that you can have your beer. And I want you to sit over here, okay?"

Close as he was, she could see him without her glasses. Big and old and bald, with a big wedding band with a cross cut into it on his thick fingers. He didn't seem threatening. So she moved obediently to where he pointed.

And gasped, blinking up into a blue hell. The heater above the bar was angled down, aimed right into her face. Its breath dried her eyeballs and scorched her neck as she unbuttoned her coat. When she looked down again, a long-stemmed glass gleamed in front of her. She tipped it and the fiery spirit stripped down her throat.

After another sip she took off her kerchief, shaking out her hair to let it bake. She realized suddenly she'd nearly frozen to death. She rubbed her glasses with a damp paper napkin and put them back on.

To her left were foosball games and pool tables, surrounded by the hunters. She looked away, but not soon enough. One of them glanced up as he positioned his shot.

"How much is that?"

"Ladies, ninety-five cents. I were you, though, Miss, I'd stay here a little longer. Don't have to drink. But you ought to warm up some 'fore you go out again. You know they closed Route Six?"

"Closed it?"

"Uh huh. Pileup at the overpass. Four cars. It was on WRVL."

"Who was it? Was anybody hurt?"

"They didn't say."

She couldn't think of anything else to ask. She stared past the bottles of Carstairs and Bankers Special into the mirror. I'm too heavy, she thought. I need to lose some weight, maybe cut my hair different . . . Then her mind stopped.

None of that mattered now. She was different. Diseased. And cured or not, she'd never feel clean again.

Jaysine gripped the glass. She wanted to throw it. She wanted to shatter things, destroy, destroy. Instead, when the man came back, she said, turning the gleam of silver and turquoise around and around on her wrist, "That was so good. Give me another one of those, please."

Some time later she put down a five-dollar bill, straightened her skirt, and went out again.

Her face felt warm. I'm drunk, she thought, a little amazed. The street was dark and unfamiliar. The snow came down, snow she remembered from when it had tried to cover her up. Alone under it she had thought and thought and finally come to a decision. Only now she couldn't remember what it was.

She giggled. As if in sympathy, water chuckled to her left. She found herself on a little bridge and paused there, leaning over the iron rail.

The stream was frozen. The ice was opaque and white as frosted glass. But below it somewhere the creek still flowed. She could hear it.

Some time later she paused again, calf-deep in heaped snow. The plows had thrust it aside and left it, burying the parking meters. Main Street was deserted, silent, under a burnished hennaed light.

She lifted her eyes to the streetlamps, remembering all the times she'd stared down at them from her window.

They lit the descending snow in blurry halos. Blue nearest the bulbs, then green, and last and outermost a rose gold like the old bartender's ring. The endless snow came down out of the darkness, was lit for a moment, falling, and then passed as silently out of her sight. If you didn't look close it was just snow. But now, her vision slowed, she saw that each individual flake had its own path. Some were falling, some rising, some zigzagging as if undecided, or as if each had to guess or calculate its own way to the ground. From far off came the howl of a dog. That and the harsh pant of her breath were the only interruptions in the white silence.

Above the five and dime her window glowed welcome. She could see her dried flowers and beyond them on the wall a corner of the forest print. She stared up at it for a while, shivering, before she understood why the light was on. She walked a few paces on and looked down Pine Street.

The midnight car was parked in front of the Keynote.

She climbed the stair slowly, clinging to the handsmoothed rail. Then, with her key out she hesitated, listening through the door.

She heard an argument, a shot . . . No, it was television. She unlocked the door awkwardly and pushed it open.

All her lights were on. He was sitting on the couch in his shirtsleeves, watching TV with his feet on the coffee table. His coat and scarf hung on her workbench. A bottle stood at his feet, foil scraps littering the floor. As she came in he turned his head and gave her an angry grin.

"Where've you been? I've been waiting for you for hours."

She didn't respond; couldn't think, through the ice, of anything to say. From the mist before her eyes his face emerged suddenly: gray irises flecked with blue, dark nostril-hairs, stubble on his jaw-line. He smelled of cologne and cigarettes and wine.

"So where were you, babe? I called the shop but they said you were out today. I been here since six. Left once, but the road's blocked, so I come back. Good thing I had a key. Where the hell you been?"

"Out."

"What do you mean, out? Monday night—that's what I said last week, right? When you say you'll be here I expect you to be here. I have to fix these things up in advance."

She didn't answer. After a moment he let go her shoulders. "You eat yet?"

"No."

"I could stand some spaghetti, or something. That veal last week was great." He reached for the bottle, then swung back. His eyes moved over her face. "Are you all right? You look like you're getting a cold."

"Should I be all right?"

"What?"

She stripped off her mittens and threw them on the couch.

"What did you say? Never mind. Mm, mm. I know what you need. Let's have a taste of those lips."

She closed her eyes and bent back her head obediently as his mouth fastened on hers. Her arms lifted, then stopped, hovering an inch from his back. After a moment his lips moved on. The room began spinning around her. His hands found the zipper of her dress.

"Brad—"

Before she could think or react he'd unhooked her bra. His fingers were cold. "Don't," she whispered. The couch came up beneath her. She tried to close her thighs but he was too strong.

His fingers left her suddenly and she lay limp. She felt dizzy and sick. The air was cold and she tried to cover herself with a hand. The other went to her mouth.

Through the numbness, slowly, like the outlines of the hills emerging from night, she was beginning to feel.

"Hey, babe, what's that I smell? Brandy? Well, you're already primed, let's have a party."

She opened her eyes. A foot away his member strained toward her, the head vein-shot, questing to and fro like a blind snake. Then his hand was pulling her head forward. She felt warmth at her mouth, pushing back her lips.

"Ouch! God damn it!"

He'd jumped back, staring down at her. He looked huge and angry. Then, suddenly, started to laugh. His penis wilted, nodding disconsolately toward the carpet. His laughter filled the room, rattled the windows and the glasses on the shelf. She put her hands over her ears.

"You little bitch! Christ, you startled the hell out of me. Any harder and you'd have bit it off!"

She said thickly, "Brad . . . listen. We got to talk."

"Talk? Sure. Let's play first, though." His hands found his penis again; he pulled it upward, stroked it.

"Get away from me!"

She screamed it so loud her throat hurt. He paused, and something changed in his face.

"What the hell's wrong with you tonight?"

"Wrong with me. With *me*. It's always somebody else, isn't it? What's wrong with *you*?"

He stared around the room, his face little-boyishly puzzled. "What's going on here? I was looking forward to dinner, a little kissy-face, but suddenly it's very unfriendly."

"I wonder why."

"I wonder too. What's the story? There's nothing to eat; you've been drinking and you look like hell. You're all wet and there's some kind of dirt in your hair. Leaves, and dog shit, or something." Her hand moved to it automatically. "I'm not used to being treated like this. Let's get to the bottom of it, right now." He zipped himself and sat down.

"You poor man. I don't appreciate you."

"Wow. I've heard this before. You sound like my fucking wife."

"Do you? Fuck your wife?"

He said softly, "Jay, seriously, what the hell is going on?"

The hurt tone reached her even through her anger. She remembered suddenly how hard he worked, how many jobs depended on him, how much he gave up and suffered to have one night a week with her. No one else understood him; no one else, except of course his little daughter, loved him. A warmth ran through her chest, as if her heart were melting. She put out her hand to his hair. He put his over hers, and they sat like that for a moment, not speaking, just looking unhappily at each other.

"I'm sorry," she whispered. "I'm not acting very nice."

"I can see something's wrong. Tell you what, tell me about it, and then I'll fix it up."

Her eyes stung suddenly, her breath caught in a half-sob. "I was down to the doctor's this morning."

"Oh." He shook his head, looking, she thought, relieved. "What's the problem?"

"Dr. Kopcik sent me to the hospital. The Monday clinic."

She saw, then, something she'd never seen before. It was as if a little piece of steel slid across behind his eyes, like a man closing a peephole.

"What is it, Jay?" he said quietly.

She told him. He sat with his eyes on the carpet, swinging his shoe. It took all the courage she had to ask, at the end, "Did you know you had it?"

"Well, I felt kind of itchy now and then. And there were these little blisters. I didn't think it was anything."

"Where?"

"Well, you know."

"Brad . . ." She shook her head slowly. "Did you ask anybody about it? Did you go to the doctor?"

He shrugged. "What the hell, it went away. I wouldn't worry about it."

"Brad, this doesn't just 'go away.' I read, it's still there, you can give it to people, you can die from it, you've got to get it taken care of. I read—"

"Well, that's if it's not treated, right? But if they can take care of it, what's the problem? We'll just get it taken care of."

She stared at him. He didn't understand at all. "Brad—listen. People looked at me in the waiting room. There was a mother there, she wouldn't let her baby near me!" She felt herself losing control, and said in a rush, to get it all out at once before she did, "And you're saying . . . you knew you had something, you had, had these *blisters*, and you just went ahead and put it in me anyway. Without using anything. Without telling me."

Boulton shrugged. He glanced toward the kitchen.

"Anybody who thought he had something, maybe he might not tell people, but he, he'd go to the doctor. Or use something. Oh, God, Brad! Not keep right on exposing his girlfriend. Or whatever I am to you. What if it was something worse? Something they couldn't cure?"

"Calm *down*. Christ." He made a dismissing motion, a flip of the hand. "Look. This is not what you seem to think. Seriously. What do you say we have some dinner?"

"There's no place open this late," she said, and then realized what he meant. Her voice climbed again. It was bewildering; she hated him, then the next second it felt like love again, and then hate. "You want me to *cook* for you? *Now*? I don't believe this."

"Well, look, I'm sorry. Believe me, honey, the last thing I had in mind was hurting you. Do you need anything?"

"What?"

His suit jacket was beside him on the couch; he reached for it. "Two hundred, will that help? For the doctor." He put four fifty-dollar bills on the coffee table, then smiled across it at her, still holding the wallet. Something about that smile made her remember the blade Dr. Friedman had held up, glittering in the light. A thread of blood, uncurling in glass . . . After an endless moment during which she could not reply his hand moved again. "Two fifty. Okay?"

She whispered, "Brad, why are you giving me money?"

"Well, you had to take off work, right? This is to make up. I want you to be happy, Jay."

"Why do you want me to be happy?"

"I want everybody to be happy."

"But why do you want *me* to be happy?"

"Well, I told you before."

"Tell me again.

"I'm crazy about you. If it wasn't for my wife being the way she is I'd be here full time. You know that."

He smiled up at her, the gray eyes crinkling gently at the corners, the sincerity clear and pure and she saw, all in one killing moment, how very very false.

"If you loved me, you wouldn't have given me this."

"Let's not get into that again."

"Why not? That's what this whole, this whole *discussion* is about. If you cared about *me* at all, about my *happiness*, you'd have gotten it checked. You'd have used precautions, you'd have told me—"

She felt, to her horror, the tears start. They'd make a mess of her mascara. She looked around for a Kleenex. There weren't any. She was about to ask him for a handkerchief when he sighed and got up, tightening his tie.

"What are you doing?"

He didn't answer, only took the billfold out again. Another picture of Benjamin Franklin joined the others and he picked up his jacket.

"What are you doing," she said again, sniffling.

"I don't have to take this."

"What do you mean?"

"There's motels here. The Antler'll be full, but the Gerroy—"

"No, wait." She heaved herself up and stumbled toward the kitchen. "I got some lasagna frozen, I can—"

"Eat it yourself. You're not such a great cook, either."

She forced her lips into a frightened smile. "Don't get so mad. I'm sorry, Brad. I was upset, it was such bad news. I'm—I'm okay now."

"Forget it." He finished the glass and turned it in his hand. "This one I bought you?"

"Yes."

He balanced it for a moment more, as if deciding something, and then threw it against the stove. It burst heavily, fragments skittering along the floor, and she cried out before she could stop herself.

"You want to know something? You've got a little mind, Jaysine. You've never been anywhere or done anything and now you never will. Fat thighs and a little brain, like a chicken. Me, me, me, that's all that's in it."

Filled with sudden terror, she started toward him, forgetting she was half-naked. Her hose were tangled and she fell over the table. He was heading for the door. At it he turned, his hand moving in his slacks. She thought for a moment that he was about to undress, come back, make up. Then something glittered in the air between them. It hit the rug, bounced, vanished under the couch.

"There's your key. Give it to some shoe clerk. You had your shot, Jaysine. I was going to take you to Tucson. But I was wrong. I think you belong here."

Anger and terror fought in her. Why would he say that about her thighs—he said they rubbed him where it felt good, he— "Brad, no, don't leave me, not now! Take the money. I don't want it. I need *you*—"

She looked up to an open door. The room rolled suddenly, like a boat in a gale, and she hit the jamb hard and clung. Down the stair his shadow paused against the light from the street. She flattened herself at his shout like a rabbit at the hunter's approach. "Keep it. *Keep it!* That's what you wanted, isn't it? You're a cheap little cunt, you even smell cheap. A cheap little disease kind of fits."

The words hit her like a thrown glass, bursting into edges that cut inside her head. "Brad," she gasped, "I'm sorry, don't—"

The street door slammed, and glass shattered and tinkled on concrete. I'll have to pay for that too, some detached part of her mind said. The rest was numb again, numb and empty.

She sagged into the jamb. Cold rose toward her step by step. She sagged farther, mouth coming open, staring into the dark. Her stomach lurched then, at last, like a frozen river beginning to break.

Twelve

The kitchen window was still dark as Phil, sitting at the table in stocking feet, gulped the sugar-slush his mother called orange juice. He shivered; the linoleum floor was ice-cold, the air only slightly warmer. His leg jiggled nervously. He shook open the paper and frowned at the front page.

"Philip, you want some eggs?" His mother, from the bathroom.

"No thanks, Ma. I got cereal. We need new milk, this's goin' bad."

"Put a drop of vanilla in it and it'll taste all right. Scrambled, or sunny side up?"

He hated his mother's eggs. She drowned them in margarine and they tasted greasy and stale. He'd asked her not to a hundred times, but it was like there was only one way eggs could be done. And then her ultimate argument would follow: Joseph liked them that way.

The toilet flushed. She came in in her robe and went to the refrigerator. He glanced up. Sure enough, she was examining gray celled paperboard . . . "Mom, I said I don't want any eggs!"

"Don't shout at me, Philip. I'm making some for myself."

"Oh." He was suddenly filled with self-loathing. "I'm sorry."

She didn't answer and he felt even worse. He was trying to think of something nice to talk about with her when a headline caught his eye.

COUNTY EMPLOYEE FOUND ILL

Barry Fox, 29, of 122 Finney Street, Petroleum City, is reported in critical condition in Bradford Public Hospital with frostbite and exposure. Mr. Fox is employed as a road clearance operator with the Pennsylvania Department of Transportation, Hemlock County Division.

Fox was discovered Friday night in his stopped snowplow west of Bagley Corners. He has not yet regained consciousness. Century reporter Sarah Baransky has ascertained that hospital authorities suspect exposure to chemicals may be a contributing cause of his collapse.

In a possibly related case, Mrs. Molly Selwin was treated and released at Raymondsville Hospital for pesticide exposure. Mrs. Selwin had been treating her home with insect foggers from Fishers Big Wheel. Dr. Leah Friedman asked us to remind our readers to read the fine print on chemical products, and not to remain in the home while insecticides are being released.

Dr. Friedman also said that several other cases of toxic effects had recently come to her attention. Anyone knowing about possible sources of contamination or hazardous waste in the area should contact her or responsible city authorities immediately.

Phil stared at the print. There was a Jack Fox worked nights as a dispatcher, his father sometimes mentioned him.

"Say, do you know a Barry Fox?" he said to his mother, in the next room now.

"Not so loud, your father's asleep. Isn't that Jack Fox's brother?"

"Yeah, I thought that's who he was. It says here he's sick."

"Everybody's sick. It's this weather. What's he got?"

"They don't know."

"It's the weather. Do you want some more orange juice?"

"No, thanks."

When he turned to the second page he immediately saw something odd. There seemed to be space at the bottoms of the stories; in fact here and there were blanks, as if snow had fallen on the page. He was flipping toward the comics when he thought for a moment he'd seen his name. His eye went back. FORMER OILMAN AND HUNTER RECALLS OLD DAYS, it said.

Underneath it was his interview. He read it without breathing. They were the same words he'd typed upstairs, but in justified columns beside the pork prices they looked different. He noticed that some words were misspelled that he didn't think he had, but it still looked nice. His eyes went back to the cutline: *As Told to Philip J. Romanelli.*

He lifted the paper, not looking at the dish his mother slid in front of him. "Hey, they published my article."

"That's nice."

When he was finishing his third reading his mother said from the living room, "How are your eggs?"

He stared down at them. Yellow grease congealed like candle wax at the lowest point on the dish. He messed them up with his fork and dumped them into the garbage.

He picked his coat off the wall and carried it into the parlor. "What'd you say, about an article?" she said as he bent to buckle his galoshes.

"Nothing."

"I thought you said something. Were the eggs good?"

Phil took a deep breath, then let it out. "No, I didn't say anything. They were awful, Mom, can't you cook them without so much butter?"

"They stick to the pan."

"Don't we have a Teflon pan?"

"Your father likes them that way."

As it was in the beginning. So it is now and ever shall be. World without end amen, he thought. His elation drained away; the gray depression flooded back. At that moment there was a muffled whine directly beneath him, beneath the floor itself. "Oh—oh, the dog, I forgot, can you feed it for me?"

She sighed. "I knew I'd end up taking care of that thing."

"Never mind, then! I'll get it!"

"No, no, you go on to school, you'll be late."

Hearing her sigh again, he gave up. He had to get out, get out before he went nuts. He pulled the storm door shut behind him and stood for a moment on the porch, pulling on his gloves and taking a first cautious lungful of the icy air.

It was still dark. Across the valley Town Hill lay long and low, like a capsized ship. Above its barely visible prickle of leafless forest the sky was the color of spoiled salmon. The streetlights bounced light up from the snow, the sagging clouds reflected it down again. None of it can leave, he thought, none can leave nor can any new light come . . .

The snow crunched and squeaked as he pushed his body gradually into motion, like some long-unused machine. His lips drew back from his teeth. The first hundred yards were straight agony. At night he'd wake sometimes, recalled from sleep by the tightening of his calves and thighs. Every morning he had to stretch them again, like woolen sweaters washed too hot. He was glad his day started with a downhill. Though he'd pay the price coming back.

By the time he got to the footbridge his legs were moving better. Boards rattled under his boots. In the spring Todds Creek rose to an ocher torrent, covering the planks, tumbling along saplings, stumps, floating trash. Now the ice was like cast iron. Leaves and sticks lay a few inches down, preserved like mobsters in concrete. He pulled his scarf over his mouth and nose, warming the icy dark air he drew in thirty times a minute and then pushed out, through the wet wool, back into the wind.

The side streets were empty. He pushed his way through ankle-deep powder on walks shoveled the day before. The plows had come through in the night, tossing up long ramparts, like the frozen bow waves of speedboats. He vaulted one clumsily, sinking to his hips, then fought free and struck along through an inch of loose crystals above ash and salt, and under that hard asphalt, jarring him with every pace.

He paused at the corner of Main, and looked at Raymondsville on a dark winter morning. Down the street came the wind. A gelid, invisible glacier, pushing before it an occasional tardy flake. Through it the streetlights shone untwinkling. Through it, too, came a steady parade of shadows, like an army on the move.

He hiked along the side of the road, facing them as they rumbled past. Pickups, Scouts, Broncos, each packed with hunters. Headlights silhouetted the racks of bolt-actions and lever-actions, pumps and over-under combinations.

Seven A.M. and Main Street was wide open, windows tossing out light like they had no use for it. He limped past Ray's Gun and Pawn, crowded with hunters buying maps and Jon-E warmers. Past the Brown Bear; past the Odd Fellows Building, with a sign, HUNTERS BREAKFAST 4–7; past Mama DeLucci's, the door as he came abreast of it pushing out on a hot rich breath of fried ham and buckwheat biscuits and then two men in blaze orange, carrying their weapons muzzle down. Past him without cease whined and jingled the heavy vehicles, taillights ruby and amber, streaming out of town east and west, north and south, aimed at the blank grayness of the predawn woods. None of the drivers noticed him, hunched over his books, dragging himself down the street under the first ominous foreglow of day.

Bastards, he thought. A couple of years before he'd picketed one of the gun stores with some of the other kids. When the black-and-white had dropped him off at home his dad had pulled off his cartridge belt, taken him into the back yard, and whipped him savagely, without a word of explanation. He hadn't understood then. Now he did.

They were all interlocked. The store owners, the ones who sold the guns, the ones who ran the town, they were who his father really worked for. He read their ads in the *Century*, in the Season Supplement that came in the Sunday sports section all November. Come to Hemlock County, home of good hunting. Buy in Hemlock County, home of friendly merchants. Kill your deer by aiming at the lungs and heart. Butcher your animal like this, but tie off its genitals first. Bank at First Raymondsville, use Thunder Gasoline, buy a Winchester at Ray's, a new snowmobile at Stan Rezk's. After you've bagged your stag dine at the Hudson Grill, at Nero's Villa. The Hemlock County Recreational Association spared no effort to lure out-of-towners into the county. They were a resource. Like the trees, the animals, like all this dark land. The exploiters' universe consisted of what they could convert to money. Nothing else mattered.

He had a sudden image of the valley as the old man had described it; the great trees, the great cats, the swarming of deer, elk, and bear. Down it now streamed the glaring, jingling monsters, trampling the hills underfoot, powered by the dark fluid sucked from beneath them; cabs crammed with the race that had displaced the Indian, destroyed the forest and all the beasts without speech, but whose greatest conquest had been the subjugation and denial of its own soul.

He turned the corner for the final stretch, and staggered as he met the full force of a wind like an icicle crammed into his teeth. He recovered, bent, and stalked forward, gasping. It was too cold to breathe. He pulled the cap lower over his deadened ears, and yanked his leaden legs upward again and again.

The school loomed through the snow-pale dawning like a hostile fortress. The kids streamed past him. They chattered, but no word came to him. He smiled bitterly; sure, he'd been silenced. How he hated these fools, these shallow pricks, these happy blinded cretins, these willing stupid bourgeois victims.

But *she'd* spoken to him.

Suddenly he remembered that this was the day he was going to talk to Alex Ryun. Then he thought: Why bother? He was crippled, ugly, poor. Be real, Romanelli, he sneered at this dreams. Why ask for more humiliation?

Replenished with rage, he levered himself forward like a cartridge, and was lost a moment later in the hurrying hundreds of Raymondsville Central High. He noticed as he struggled that the corridors were lined with tile exactly like the bathroom walls.

He realized something else before the day was an hour older; that the memory of man is imperfect, or maybe that in some hearts lies forgiveness. More likely, he thought, they just got bored with it. Still he was grateful when Fred Bisker looked up in chem and said, "Hey, Phil," before going back to his lab notes. Another boy complimented him on his newspaper article.

In Marzeau's class he glanced at Alex from the corners of his eyes, yearning like a Zen monk toward a less tangible Good. She was wearing a pale blue sweater; her legs were crossed back under her chair. His eyes fastened themselves to her ankles. She looked wonderful, impossible. Yet she'd seemed to like him . . . he felt like Cortez at the Pacific. Or was it Balboa? Anyway, he realized then he was gonna try. Crazy as it sounded. She'd probably say no. He expected that, actually he'd be relieved.

He just hoped she didn't laugh.

That left the question of timing. He considered this carefully. He'd never asked anyone out before and he wanted to minimize the chances of blowing it. He could ask her between classes, in the hall. No, too public, and they'd both be in a hurry. At last he decided lunchtime would be best. Then too it was comfortably distant, two hours away.

But two hours later, when he picked up the wet tray in the lunch line, he felt as he had in the final minutes before an operation. Scared shitless, the way little kids get scared when they put the mask over your face, smile, and tell you to breathe deep. And you know that when you come up, you'll be screaming.

He loaded his tray with some crap or other and wandered out into the seating area.

The noise was deafening, as usual. He saw them right away, Alex and Sheila and the rest. Their table grew slowly before him, like a rogue meteor just before it smashes into the starship *Enterprise*. His tray wavered, trying to deflect him. He gritted his teeth and swung it back on course. *Warp speed*. Ahead of him one of the girls, Cindy something, saw him. She squeaked and put her fist over her mouth. The way the tables were arranged he couldn't face Alex directly, so he stopped behind her, presenting his right side. His tray was in his right hand, and he had it supported unobtrusively with his left, the one he couldn't lift.

"Hi, Alex."

The girls were deadly silent. After a moment Ryun twisted. She looked surprised. He felt his face flush and had to look away.

"Why, Phil. What a surprise. Are you going to eat with us?"

A sibilance passed around the table, a sigh or whisper without words.

"Well, no, thanks. One of the . . . guys is waitin' for me. I was just wondering, uh, if you'd like to see a movie sometime. Like maybe Friday night."

He'd hoped to keep this private, but they were all listening. He glared at Cindy and she dropped her eyes; two of them turned their heads as if to say something to the others; but none of them spoke. He turned his attention back to Alex. Those lovely green eyes, close up . . .

"Why, Phil, I'd love to." She was drawling out the words, a little louder, he thought, than necessary. She glanced around; the other girls stiffened, their eyes flickered. Then the tension broke, and they all stared openmouthed up at him. He realized he'd missed something. He jerked and said guiltily, "I'm sorry, what'd you say?"

"I said I'd love to. Friday'll be fine."

"Alex!"

"*What*, Sheila?"

"Oh . . . well. Nothing."

The other girls looked dismayed and uncomprehending, though they tried to dissemble it by a sudden interest in their food. "I'll pick you up at seven," he said, preparing to move off.

"Oh, we'll still be at dinner then. Could you make it seven-thirty?"

"Sure. Seven, uh, seven-thirty. Right."

"Thanks, Phil. See you then."

"See you, Alex." He got a new grip on his tray, smiled nastily at

the other girls, and headed for the Commercial Ed table. He
glanced back once, and saw them all staring at him; all except Alex
and the one called Sheila. Ryun was smiling down at her tray,
beatific and mysterious as a plaster Virgin. Hazouri was getting up,
dark eyes slashed narrow.

He was sitting with the geeks, listening to one explaining the fine
points of his after-school job at the Pik 'n' Pak, when he saw a
familiar bulk rise from the training tables.

Bubba Detrick moved through the press like a bear through low
brush, his jaws still chomping. His eyes roved over the bent heads,
the busy forks and mouths. Phil dropped his attention to his
carrots but Detrick bulled over to him, pushing kids into the edges
of their tables. Bubba leaned over and put his elbows beside him.

Phil noticed then that the sound level had dropped. He could
actually hear Detrick when he said to the others, not very loud,
"Ain't you jerks got the word?"

"Hi, Bubba. What word?"

"Shithead here, nobody sits with him. Pound sand."

The other boys got up at once and took their trays toward the
scullery, eating with their fingers on the way. The fattest one
tripped over a chair and there was a clatter of metalware and
plastic.

The ballplayer pulled out one of the vacated seats. He studied
Phil's tray. At last he selected a slice of carrot. He placed it and then
several more in a row on Phil's shoulders, like stars on a general,
then took a fingerful of mashed potato and smeared it into his ears.
"Turn your head," he said, and filled the other too.

Christ, Phil thought, can she see us? No, thank God.

"Can you still hear me?"

"Yeah."

"Good. Look, Crip, you and me we got a kind of a personality
conflict going. That means I find your personality a royal pain in
the ass. Right?"

Phil nodded.

"Now, we already discussed your steady stream of useless bullshit
in class. Brick and me we got our views across last week, I think,
'cause you ain't wisin' off the way you used to. So that's good."

"Thanks."

"Shut your fuckin' lip! But somebody just told me you asked
Alex for a date. Is this real, or am I dreaming?" He picked up the
mystery meat and put it on Phil's head. Phil took it off.

"Put it back on.

He put it back and sat there, feeling numb. Grease ran down his neck and into his shirt.

"Yeah, I asked her."

"Well, I guess you ain't no homo. But you're stupid as shit, Romo, stupid as a box a' rocks." He shook his head slowly. "You got this attitude that somebody else got something, and you don't got any, they oughta share it with you. Life don't work that way. The way it is, guys like me got it, and guys like you don't. Period. And it ain't ever gonna be any different, so you might as well get used to it.

"Now, you know we're goin' together, me and her. So why you annoyin' her? And how do you expect to breathe after I tear your stupid fucking lungs out, Romanelli?"

He didn't know where he got the guts to say it. Maybe just because she liked him. But he said now, "You're not going steady with her."

"I'm not?"

"No. She's going out with me Friday."

Detrick had had something ready to say, it looked like, but now he didn't. He sat there a moment, then took out a pack of Wrigley's and offered Phil one. Phil shook his head. Detrick was thoughtfully unwrapping his stick when one of the monitors, a senior named Berenger, came over. Detrick scowled up at him. Berenger said, avoiding the ball player's eyes, "Romanelli, take that shit off or you're getting detention."

Phil took it off. "Put it on," grunted Detrick.

Phil put it on. "Last chance," said Berenger.

He didn't move. "Okay," said the senior. "Playing with food in cafeteria, one period of detention." He moved off, looking relieved.

Bubba regarded him moodily, chewing gum and picking his nose. "Romo, you got balls. But it ain't gonna help you. You probably figure I'm gonna trash your face for sniffing around Ryun, right?"

"Yeah."

"Well, I'm not." Detrick belched. "Hell, let the best man win! This is entirely, you know, separate.

"See, Phil, it ain't that you're crippled I got a problem with, or being a certified nerd. It ain't the way you jerk when you're happy, or the weird way you hug yourself. Lots of guys, they overcome handicaps like that. It's that you're stupid. And I told you why.

"Now, that can hurt you in life. So I'm gonna do you a favor, I'm

gonna teach you how stupid you really are. You're a meathead. So
you'll be wearin' that meat from now on. For the rest of the day,
and after that tomorrow, no, tomorrow you can put on fresh. But I
see you without a piece of meat on your head, you're fucked. Your
little lesson last week'll be nothing compared to what I'll do for
you. Got that?''

Phil nodded. His tongue was too thick to answer.

Detrick flicked his ear painfully with a finger. Potato flew, spat-
tering a boy and girl at the next table; they wiped it off silently. He
heaved himself up and left. Back at the training tables he and
Mooney bent their heads together. Copper glinted as the shotputter's shaven skull turned and they both grinned at Phil across the
cafeteria.

He sat alone, unable to decide whether to be happy or terrified.
At last the bell rang and he drank his milk quick and turned in his
tray.

He wore the meat to the next class, but Maxwell made him throw
it in the wastebasket. As he walked back to his desk Mooney shook
his head sadly, and Bubba kissed his fingers, patted his rump with
them, and waved Phil a regretful goodbye.

Thirteen

Jaysine jerked awake, instantly angry at the hateful buzz. She rolled over, lids glued shut, and thrust out an arm. The crash as the clock's cord took the bedside lamp down with it made her moan.

She opened her eyes, wincing at daylight. For a moment her mind wobbled forward to routine: tea, weigh herself, breakfast, off to work . . . instead she lay back, blotting out morning with her wrist. She had to pee, but she couldn't get up. She had a sick headache, and awful sour dryness in her mouth.

Then she remembered, and struggled up onto an elbow.

Her bedroom was tiny and dark. Through the door she could see the front room, the couch, where beer bottles lay in a litter of magazines and wadded-up potato-chip bags. The shiny paper flickered, an electronic glow. She stared at it for a long time before she realized it was reflecting the television. Her clothes lay piled in the doorway; underclothes too; under the sheet she was naked.

She saw, then, the little pile of money on the coffee table, and everything came back at once, the night before and the day before and the night before that. Her head hammered and she sank back. Her arms crept out to the empty side of the bed. When they found the other pillow they pulled it to her, holding it tight.

· · ·

When she woke again an hour later she thought immediately of work. She rolled over with a grunt and pulled the phone toward her across the floor by its cord. A nearly empty wine bottle and the crumpled foil of a half-pound Nestlé's Crunch came with it. As she listened to the brrrr she hoped Mrs. Acolino wasn't in yet.

"Style Shoppe, Marguerite speaking."

She spoke slowly, trying not to sound hung over. "Margie, this is Jaysine. Would you please tell Marybelle I can't come in? I'm still sick today."

"Jaysine, honey, I'm sorry to hear that. But you know, Marybelle's awful upset you been out two days already. She wanted Trudi to try doing one of your appointments but she wouldn't, she's afraid of electricity."

"Well, I'm not feeling good," she said, thinking, *It's true, too.*

"Why, what have you got, Jaysine?"

"A cold. A real bad one."

"You don't sound bad."

"Well, I feel awful. Maybe I'll be in tomorrow. Will you tell her?"

"Yes, I'll tell her."

"Thanks a lot. You be good now. Goodbye, Margie."

Next she dialed again the same number she'd tried a dozen times the day before. She didn't have to look anymore. Her finger went 2–3650 without search or hesitation. The line clicked, making the connection between Raymondsville and Petroleum City. When it began to ring, a modern electronic-sounding note, she reached for the wine bottle. The dregs tasted warm and flat, like someone else's saliva.

"Good *morning*, The Thunder Group."

"Hello. This is Jaysine Farmer, calling for Mr. Boulton."

"Oh, Miss *Farmer*. I *don't* think Mr. Boulton will be available today either . . . let me check. Can you hold?"

"Yes."

She held for fifteen minutes, then hung up and called back. The same woman answered. "Good *morning*, The Thunder Group."

"This is Miss Farmer. You put me on hold but nothing happened. Is Brad there?"

"Oh, I am *so* sorry, Miss Farmer. Mr. Boulton won't be in today, I'm sorry."

"Do you know when he'll be back?"

"No, I really don't. But if you'll leave your name and number I'm sure he'll get back to you."

Jaysine slammed down the receiver. She got up slowly, holding her face like a fragile, unset opal, and staggered into the bath-room. When she turned on the light she saw she was crying again. Her face was puffy, her eyes hopeless and swollen, hair straggled down in limp rat's-tails. She glanced at the scale by the bathtub, looked quickly away.

She took a deep breath. Her eyes caught a little plaque over the commode: *Today is the tomorrow you worried about yesterday.*

"Shit," she said. It felt so good she said it again.

She forced herself into motion. After emptying her bladder she brushed her hair and washed her face. She bathed her eyes in the icy stream from the faucet, then dripped Visine in them. She took aspirin and vitamins. She felt both hungry and ready to throw up.

She wandered out to the couch and lay down, pulling his over-coat off the rack to pillow her head. He'd forgotten the coat when he left, just stormed out in his suit jacket. She stared out at the overcast sky, at the television antennas on the buildings opposite. At last she decided she might be able to keep down something sweet.

Fortunately there was a quart of pistachio Sealtest in the freezer. The color was nauseating but she covered it with semi-sweet bits and sliced almonds and that helped. Till she was done. As soon as she put the bowl in the sink she felt bloated.

I ought to clean up, she thought, wandering into the front room again, looking emptily at her workbench. I ought to wash all those dishes . . . pick up, vacuum . . . ought to put my finger down my throat and barf up all that beer and wine, chocolate and ice cream.

He wasn't taking her calls. She wasn't surprised. She'd handled this whole thing wrong, she realized that now. God, she felt so small when she remembered the scene she'd made. No, no more crying, Jaysine.

She stopped, looking at the cuff links. They were almost fin-ished. She'd looked forward to surprising him with them . . .

Suddenly she had a plan. She put water on for tea and went back into the bathroom. When she came out, showered and her hair washed and blowdried, it was whistling. She made dark strong Earl Grey and drank a cup and then put her apron on and pulled her stool up to the bench.

She finished setting the agates, then turned the links over. She'd already built the swivel frames out of 18-gauge sheet silver. Now she soldered them on carefully and then attached the swivel. She drank another cup of tea while she waited for the metal to cool.

You didn't want to do too much finishing on drop-cast jewelry—formlessness was its charm—but she buffed it down with Tripoli compound, then switched to low speed and highlighted the front and findings with rouge on a muslin wheel. Then tucked a loupe into her eye.

She smiled to herself. The frosty surface of the silver set off the deep gray sheen of the agate. No one could resist anything this beautiful. It was the best thing she'd ever done. She packed cotton wool into a little box and dropped them in.

All right, now for herself. She went through her wardrobe. Nothing clean, nothing new.

She looked at the money on the table.

She got back from LaMode at ten and showered again and did her hair in a braid. Then she took that apart and did a quick roller set, brushing up from her forehead and then down, into a whirlpool of ringlets. She gave it a spritz of sculpting spray, then froze it with ultrahold. She did her face carefully, torn between holding down the powder and the need to cover; finally she shrugged and covered. On the eyes, dark shadow. She found her alligator heels and rubbed them with a rag.

She slipped into the new dress in front of the mirror, glad she'd allowed an extra size. Her eye clicked critically from crown to toes. She tilted her chin, raised an eyebrow; shook her head violently, and watched her hair settle back on her shoulders.

At last she nodded. She pulled on boots and picked up her coat. Carrying the jewelry box and her heels, she hurried down the stairs. Her car was almost buried; she hadn't driven in days. While she was scraping the windshield she remembered his overcoat.

She smiled. He'd be back.

She rammed the little Toyota back and forth till she had space to turn. It was a used two-door her brother had bought in Florida for her. There was rust now on the hood, and lining hung from the ceiling like flypaper. But it ran, as long as she asked the man to put in oil every other time she got gas. She left the snow tires on all year and now when she put it in Drive it jumped forward just like, she thought, a little snowplow.

She left Main behind, slowed for the overpass, then accelerated to pass a car full of hunters. As the town dropped away she turned on WRVL for music and then news. From time to time she saw more hunters, their pickups turning back onto the highway from side roads. Route Six curved and recurved along the Allegheny. From time to time black rock thrust itself up from the level, snow-covered ice, but aside from that there wasn't much to see. The road writhed between the hills, the ridges constant and reassuring on either side, as if her little car was a white marble rolling peacefully and inevitably along a track.

She saw a dead deer by the side of the road, just lying there.

In Petroleum City she stopped at a Thunder station to ask directions. She'd been to P.C., as people called it in Raymondsville, a few times, but she'd never been to his office.

She was unprepared for its size. The Thunner building dominated the west end of town like the refinery did the east. She found a parking space, refreshed her perfume, and checked her face one last time, feeling nervous but eager. She slipped on the heels and clicked over the steaming pavement toward the door.

The lobby was vast, with mirrors and a huge modern chandelier of hundreds of glass rods. She felt intimidated, till one of the mirrors gave her back herself. She smiled again, and went on.

There was no one at the fifth floor desk when she came out of the elevator. She followed her instincts down a corridor. A dark little fat man was sitting in a side office reading a magazine. She put her head in. "Excuse me. Where's Mr. Boulton?"

"End of the hall, ma'am."

"Thanks." She continued, emboldened by the smell of fresh-brewed coffee.

He was sitting at a table with other men in suits. She looked through the open door, rapped, and when he looked up, smiled sweetly.

The office he showed her to was larger than she'd expected. There was a vase in the corner as big as she was. The rest of the room matched it, all light wood and polished things, spotlessly clean. It impressed her. His face looked different too. "All right," he said, closing the door. "What is it?"

"Aren't you going to ask me to sit down?"

"Sure, sure, make yourself at home. You've already interrupted my reinsurance meeting."

She sat slowly, crossing her legs. She felt cool and self-possessed. The men with him had glanced at her coming out. She'd seen the interest in their eyes.

"It was rude, the way you wouldn't talk to me on the phone."

"I was out yesterday."

"Your secretary said you were out today, too. But I had something for you."

He stood behind the desk, looking stolid and, she thought, rather defensive. "What?" he said.

She brought out the little box, then, when he made no move to take it, opened it and set them out facing him. They gleamed dully in the white light from the window. "I made them," she said. "For you."

But when she lifted her gaze she saw with a shock that she'd erred. His eyes were much darker than the stones she'd picked with such care. Dark as oxidized silver.

He shook his head slowly, glancing out the window; then sat down. Pressed the intercom. "Twyla."

"Yes, Mr. Boulton."

"There's a woman in my office. Without an appointment. How'd she get here?"

"I was away from my station for just a moment, sir. I'm sorry, she must have come in then."

"In the future call the floor guard if you have to leave the elevator area."

"Yes, sir."

He let go the button. "Okay, Jaysine. Make it quick, I've got a lot to do. You didn't come up here to give me the damn cuff links. What do you want?"

She was hurt, he hadn't even touched them, but she put that aside and said, "All right. I came to say I'm sorry."

He picked up a gold pen and started to play with it. He didn't look at her. She had to make him meet her eyes. Then he'd be halfway back. She took a deep breath and made her hands stop fidgeting. "I've been thinking about it, what we argued about. I decided you're right. I know things like this happen. It's not really anybody's fault, is it?

"Anyway, I wasn't very nice. So I'm sorry I shouted at you, and I brought the money back—except for what I spent on this dress." She slid it onto the corner of his desk.

He flicked his eyes to it, then away. But he still hadn't looked at her. She wanted to keep talking. But he had to say something first.

"That it?" he said.

"That's it. Oh, and—I thought I'd make some fettucine Monday night." She managed a smile. "So. Can we make peace?"

"I don't think so."

"Brad, lovers quarrel, that happens. It'll be even better, once we make up."

He got up suddenly, but kept the desk between them. He shoved the cash back toward her, pushing one of the links off the desk. "Let's make this short and sweet. I'm dropping you. Or however you want to put it. Go back to Raymondsville. Do whatever you want, but don't bother me again. Don't call and don't come here. Understand?"

She looked at the carpet. At the silver gleam down there, almost lost. Unwanted.

"Don't cry, for Christ's sake!" He came around the desk, toward her, but stopped a step away. That close she knew he could smell her perfume. He'd always said it made him lose control . . . but he looked so cold now, so angry, she couldn't believe it was the same man. "Another thing. We had our laughs. Some women would try to use that against me. I expect you to keep quiet about it. If you don't you'll be sorry. That's pretty clear, isn't it?"

"It's perfectly clear," she said through frozen lips. The numbness had come back, but this time it was more fragile, thinner; only a thin sheet of ice between her and the world. Not solid, like before.

"Then why are you still here?"

"Because I don't think you mean it."

"What are you talking about?"

"You aren't treating me like you should. As soon as we get close, you look for a way out, a way that hurts me. Why is that, Brad? Is it because I'm a woman"—she thought suddenly about what he'd told her once—"and your mother, she—"

She could see that hit something. He leaned forward. "Get out of here."

"I'm not going anywhere till you apologize."

He reached back to the desk, pressed something, and a moment later a black man filled the doorway. He looked at Boulton, who said, "Lark, escort this lady out of here. And take her dime-store jewelry with her."

A moment later she was out of the room, her arm held so tight she thought it would break. She was so surprised she couldn't speak till they were in the corridor. Then she shouted, "Brad, wait! I'm not through talking to you!"

She fought him, dragged back, but the black man didn't say anything, didn't hurt her, just held her off as if she was a pet dog with a fit. He marched her out a back way, instead of through the lobby, out into the flat scarred concrete of a loading dock. He thrust the box at her, and the door closed. She whirled, and scratched at it till she broke a nail. But there was no handle or knob from the outside; no way in to him, no way in at all.

Five stories up he sat silently, swiveling back and forth, and watched the bedraggled little figure move slowly up the street. She got into her car, pulled out into traffic, went north, disappeared.

It was over. He felt relieved. A nasty little scene, right in his office too. But he'd done the right thing. She'd gained weight already, God knew how she'd packed herself into that cheap dress. It had just gotten too hard to pretend he was interested in her TV programs and her magazines and all the latest news items about the girls at the shop. He'd toyed with the idea of setting her up, introducing her to some other fellows at the club, older guys whose wives no longer satisfied. But that wouldn't be a good idea now.

He looked at the money and thought, I'll wait a couple of days and then send it to her. With a couple hundred more. She'd cool off. It was the best thing for her too.

Still he sat thinking. What she'd said . . . no. It didn't make any sense. Take his first wife. He'd been fair to her, a generous settlement, more than enough for her pills and psychiatrists. More than she deserved, she'd betrayed him and left him. Bitches! They all left sooner or later.

Gradually his anger ebbed and his thoughts moved on. He didn't like the way things were trending in the county. The *Times-Democrat* understood his position on alarmist reporting, but he hadn't gotten the story wrapped yet in the *Century*. And Raymondsville was the county seat. Over time he'd bring them around, though, through the ad department if not more directly, through Pete Gerroy.

He sat staring at the distant towers, thinking one by one of people who might have a reason to interfere with the disposal deal, and how well set up his firebreaks were. Finally he decided there was no point in getting worried. Not yet.

But it might be wise to let things cool for a while.

He closed his eyes, tapping his fingers, then reached for the phone. He patted his pockets as he waited for the connection, then slid open his desk and went through it, frowning. Where was his appointment book? Then Twyla said "Newark, sir," and he waited for her to click off and said briskly, lifting his head, "Hello, John! Brad here, at Thunder Oil."

The distant voice said, "Hold on a second. Who's that? Boulton? Okay, go ahead."

"Hi. John, look, we need to hold your shipments up for a few days."

"What do you mean?"

"The natives are getting restless." He glanced at the closed door. "Not to worry, but I think it'd be best to take it easy for a while. Let it die down."

"How long you talking?"

"A few weeks should be enough. There's a lot of hunters out in the woods now, roads are traveled a lot more."

The voice dropped. "You trying to back out, Brad?"

"No. I'm acting in good faith. You'd let me know if there was a problem at your end. I'm doing the same. Our arrangement's good for both of us. I'm trying to keep it going."

After a pause the voice said, "I don't think so."

"John—"

"Listen. We're paying you the money, we expect the service. Every business works like that, don't it? Don't yours?"

"Sure."

"Let's see, you're scheduled for a payment on account pretty soon. Do you want to hold that up too?"

Boulton felt himself start to sweat. "Well," he said. "Well, no."

"If it's serious, now, I guess maybe we could reroute," the deliberate voice went on. "Or slow down for a while. But I got no place to put this stuff. I can't keep it here. Tell you what, I'll look at it and get back to you."

"Thanks."

"But till then things go as scheduled. I appreciate the call, but it's got to be something major for us to stop shipping. Local shit you take care of. That was how I understood it."

"Yeah, sure, I understand. See what you can do."

The voice changed. "No. *You* see what *you* can do, Mr. B. Control the situation. That's what we're paying for. Transport we can get anywhere. If you can't cope, let me know. Don't use the phone, no fax, send the details overnight mail. I'll send a guy out, he'll figure what to do on the spot. Understand?"

"That's good advice. I'll think about it."

"Yeah, you do that. So long."

He was sitting with the receiver in his hand, muttering, "Shit,

shit, shit," when the intercom said, "Mr. Boulton, your wife and daughter are here."

"I'll be right out." He jumped up, brushing at the shoulders of his suit, and was out of the office in three strides.

"Willie!"

"Daddy!"

At the elevator a dark-haired woman hung back, smiling coolly within gilded steel as the little girl hurled herself forward like a blond comet toward the sun. She hit his arms and he swung her up, up, both of them laughing, and then dropped her and her doll tumbling and shrieking through space before he caught her again and snuggled her up. He felt his heart move, felt it physically contract within his chest with sheer love like he'd never felt for another human being. Her hair, fine as angora, tickled his nose. He burrowed into it. Nothing else smelled as good . . . "You'll never go away, will you?" he whispered into her ear.

"You're silly! Go where, Daddy?"

"Noplace. Just kidding." He cleared a sudden thickness from his throat and, still holding her, turned back to the elevator. "Hi, darling. Everything okay out at the Hill?"

In the middle of the reception area Mrs. Ainslee Thunner Boulton had stepped out of her coat. She glanced in the mirror, touching her hair and straightening her sleeves as the secretary hung the fur. Then crossed her arms as she watched father and daughter, that same cool distant curve bending her lips once again.

"Better," she said.

"Dan doing all right today?"

"Dad's—as usual."

"Anybody call yet about the nanny?"

"I was going to ask *you* that, Brad. I can't believe it's taking them this long. Perhaps you ought to think about calling another agency. The cook's had her since breakfast. So I brought her in. You can take her for the rest of the day."

"Sure, sure, no problem." He hugged the child again; she squeaked. He pulled back, his mouth an O of surprise. "What does *that* mean?"

"It's mouse talk."

"Is that right! And what mouses have you been—"

His wife said, "I hate to interrupt such a charming scene, but are you ready to talk?"

"To talk? About what?"

"About our plans for Thunder Oil, Brad. Or have you forgotten about those too?"

He flushed, but his voice was still hearty as he said, "No, they're going real well. We'll talk about them, sure. Maybe you can give me some ideas on a couple sticky points. Just let me get somebody to look after Pooh Bear—*how* you been? And how's Annie?" He ruffled the fringe on the doll's lolling head, but he couldn't take his eyes from his daughter's. They were bluer than anything in the world.

"Oh, okay."

"You say hi to Twyla? You remember Twyla."

"Uh huh. What's the matter, Daddy? You sound funny!"

"Well, so do you, so do you, punkin!—Twyla, take charge of this bundle of beauty, will you?"

"Any time, Mr. Boulton." His secretary came forward smiling and Brad offloaded the child into her arms.

The turn of the corridor cut off sight of the tall man, the dark-haired woman, from the little girl's suddenly thoughtful eyes. She sat on the big sofa beside Twyla's desk, holding a grownup magazine and looking at ladies in pretty clothes. Twyla was pretty. She looked like one of the ladies in the magazine.

On impulse she said, "Twyla, do you like my daddy?"

"I like him fine, Williamina. Why do you ask?"

"Ainslee doesn't. They fight."

"I'm sure you're wrong, Willie. Grownups fight sometimes, but it doesn't mean anything bad."

Willie Boulton put her fingers on one of the ladies in the magazine. She had dark hair, like Ainslee. She hoped Twyla was right. She pushed her finger, and it went right through the lady's middle. She shrank on the big sofa, suddenly frightened. *Destructive*, she thought. That was the word Ainslee used. *Destructive. Hyperactive. Going to send you away.*

But no one said anything, and she turned the page, hiding the ugly tear. A moment later she was prattling to herself, not even hearing, over the sudden rattle of the typewriter, the raised and angry voices from the inner office.

Fourteen

Halvorsen patted the bear's muzzle, peering past it into the gloom. Five days into the season the Brown Bear was packed. The coatracks were buried under hunting caps and jackets. The air smelled of wet wool, gas heat, frying meat, and whiskey. A throbbing roar of voices warmed his cold-numbed ears.

The door hissed shut and he sidled in, tugging his cap over the bandage on the left side of his face. He was halfway to the back when a jolly voice called, "Well, look who's here!" It was Roberta, puffing under a tray of fries, burgers, and the shots of White Seal that with a bottle of Straub's made a boilermaker.

"Mornin', Berta. Business good?"

"You kidding? Look at this crowd. You're spending a lot of time in town these days, ain't you?"

Halvorsen grunted; she laughed and went on. He recollected the plug in his cheek—first thing he'd done was stop at Capriccio's for a pack of Top—and got rid of it in the men's room. At last he gained the alcove and sank gratefully into the pew. He was the only one there. Probably still too early, he thought. But it was sure nice to be out.

The nurses had cleaned his clothes and hung them in his room, but they'd locked his wallet and watch up somewhere. When he'd

discharged himself of course he couldn't ask for them, so all he
had was what change had been in his pockets.

As it was he'd had to sneak out, watching the corridor till it was
empty, then shuffling quickly round the corner to the fire door.
The steel steps were slick, unshoveled and unsalted, and he'd
nearly fallen, saving himself with his burned hand. But at last he'd
reached the ground, panting into the cold air, and immediately
swung into a stride that said, *Mind your own business; I'm minding
mine.* Only when the hospital was out of sight did he slow, tilt back
his cap, and aim himself downhill toward Main Street.

Nursing home, like hell, he thought. W. T. Halvorsen wasn't
going to no old folks' home to die. He thought of the wolves they'd
had over to Kane, years ago. Wild wolves penned up like pigs,
yellow eyes burning crazy through the wire mesh. No thanks, he'd
draw his last dollar out in the woods, just like he'd lived.

After buying the chew he had fifty-six cents in his pants.

"What'll it be, Racks?"

He didn't open his eyes. "How much is coffee?"

"Short today? Guess we can spare a cup. Got to make new
anyway. Cream an' sugar, right?"

"Well . . . okay. Yeah, thanks."

She brought it in a stoneware mug. He sipped at it cautiously,
then tipped more sugar over it. The little flap lifted and a white
stream poured out. He didn't like the way it wavered. Whatever
he'd met up with, it'd taken something out of him. He felt every
year of his age and then some. He felt bad, weak, chilly even
though he knew it was hot in the tavern. I should of waited till after
breakfast to leave, he thought. Least I'd of had a full belly then.

The question was, how had he gotten sick?

Sitting there, pondering, his mind cast back over sixty years in
the county. He knew every foot of it from trapping, hunting,
oil-drilling, gas work.

He concluded at last that there was one man he ought to talk to.

"Hey, W. T." Fatso DeSantis grunted as he let himself down.

"Hello, Len."

DeSantis stank of whiskey, even—Halvorsen glanced toward the
bar, missing his watch—at eight in the morning. His eyes blinked
deep in an unshaven face. Dirt showed at his collar and his belly
bulged alarmingly between his suspenders. Lucky showed his face
over the machine; DeSantis grunted, "Beer," and licked his lips.
He took an envelope out of his shirt. Unfolded it slowly, examined
what was inside, then put it back and rebuttoned the pocket.

"How you holdin' up, Billy Boy?"

"Okay, Fatso."

"Been doin' any hiking?"

"I try to stay out of the woods this time of year. Too many crazy flatlanders out there shootin' at anything that moves."

DeSantis jiggled his jowls quietly, then frowned. "Say, didn't somebody said you was in the hospital?"

"Few days, yeah."

"Guess you must be all right now."

"Well, I ain't ready for no knockdown dragouts. Starting to feel my age, I guess."

"About time," said DeSantis. "Want a beer? No, I forgot. Well. Anythin' else new?"

"No, how about with you?"

"Not much."

They sat there for a while. DeSantis drank a Black Label and then another. At last Halvorsen said, "Say, you still driving that Willys of yours?"

"Sure. An' I still got the spotlight on it, too. Remember when your grandson told me to get rid of it. He used to get on my nerves. But don't get me wrong, I'm sorry he's gone."

"Uh huh," said Halvorsen. "Well, look, think you could give me a lift?"

"I don't know, s' gettin' pretty deep. Might not be able to get you all the way up Mortlock. Guess I could try, though."

"I ain't going straight home. Goin' out to Cherry Hill first."

The filmy eyes blinked. "What for?"

"Got to see me a man. See old Dan."

"Dan Thunner?"

"Yeah."

"Old Dan," mused DeSantis. "I remember once he come in to the Bootery, wanted me to fit him to a pair of half-Wellingtons . . . That was, Jesus, that was before the war and he was old then. Size ten. He ain't still alive, is he?"

"I don't know what shape he's in, but I ain't heard nothing about him dying."

"He's old as Charley if he is. Well, hell, even if he's still kicking he ain't gonna see you."

"Just drive me out there," said Halvorsen.

"Say please."

"I'll buy you a beer."

"The way to my heart." DeSantis belched. "I guess so, okay. Can't say I got nothing else much pressing to do today."

"Loan me a five," said Halvorsen.

"What?"

"I'm busted. You want me to buy you a beer, loan me a five."

"You always was the generous sort," said DeSantis.

The yellowed side curtains of the old quarter-ton flapped and roared as DeSantis shifted again and again, flogging it toward a desperate thirty-five miles an hour. Halvorsen, sitting stiffly in the passenger seat, looked into the back. Empty bottles, rusty tools, empty Quaker State cans shifted sides at each curve. He couldn't watch when DeSantis drove. Fatso liked the crown of the road, moving maybe a foot for oncoming trucks. Cars came up rapidly behind them, swerved suddenly when they realized how slow he was going, then skidded around them on the left or right, sending snow drumming on the torn fabric top.

"Can't you go no faster, Len?"

"We'll get there. Way these young puppies is ramroddin' it, only place they're goin' to beat us is to hell."

He gave up and looked out through cracked plastic at an aged world. Young puppies . . . he'd have to remember to get Jezebel back from the boy . . . had to get dog food too somehow. Gerroy Hill rose to its triple peak on the right of the moving truck, and to their left he looked down on the frozen river. Back in that direction, way back of Candler Hill, he remembered one winter they'd drilled twenty holes, all dry, twenty wells in two frozen months, all because of some foulup the attorneys had made; mineral rights reverted to the landowners in February if it wasn't developed; Thunder had to pump crude or lose the lease. So he and McKee and Nate Green and the other guys on the rig had busted their tails working round the clock.

Halvorsen remembered that winter in his hands. Fisher Fifty was out on the clearout rump of an unnamed hill and the wind came straight down the valley like, McKee said once, the whole Boche Army with fixed bayonets. There was no road so they'd bulldozed one up Hog Hollow. The grade was too steep to haul rotary equipment, so they'd told Halvorsen to break out one of the old cable-tools.

A cable-tool didn't rotate; it pounded its way down into the ground like a giant chisel. For each well they had to bolt together seventy feet of derrick. The stem assembly was hoisted with cable by a bull-wheel driven off a twenty-horse steam engine. It swung in the wind high above the crew; sometimes when it snowed it was invisible. The bit worked like a whip, the walking-beam nodding up and down, the spring in the line cracking it against the bottom. At first you could hear it under your feet, smashing its way through shale and sand and limestone, but gradually the impact grew fainter, till at last the bit plunged downward into bottomless silence.

It was a hard way to make a hole even in good weather but in winter it was hell. The shaft was full of water, and when the bailer came up it spewed it all over the rig and the men and it froze; they slipped and slid over the muddy ice, and the sludge froze and their faces froze and their fingers froze to the temper screws and gudgeons, the clutch levers and pipe tongs. The off-shift men slept in a trailer heated only by their bodies; the cook quit, taking the cookbook, and they had to live off corned beef sandwiches, cold; the only place you could get warm was if you stood right beside the boiler, but you didn't get much work done that way.

Rothenberg, their geologist, had been number two on the Music Mountain strike. Halvorsen always figured finding three and a half miles of oil had gone to his head. On Fisher Fifty, he predicted a trap along the corner of the hill at about a thousand feet. They'd drilled the first four holes on this assumption, but there hadn't been one showing. Under good conditions a cable-tool could make ninety feet a day, but six hundred feet beneath the frozen blackberry snarls they hit a conglomerate that dulled and jammed the bits and slowed them to three and sometimes only two feet a shift.

Halvorsen had looked at that, and concluded they weren't going to make deadline. So the next time Rothenberg came up he'd suggested they start another rig at the top of the hill. If there was oil down there they'd get to it quicker. They could bust through the conglomerate with a jack-squib and nitro.

Rothenberg had laughed. Said there was crude there all right, sure as there was gold in Fort Knox, and they wouldn't need to blast if Halvorsen, the foreman, would get his lazy bastards to put their backs to it.

He'd asked the geologist quietly if he wanted to take back what he'd said about his crew.

Now, clinging to the dash with one hand, he worked his fingers as a grin etched his lips. He'd been standing over Rothenberg when the black Chrysler had purred up out of the hollow and Dan Thunner had jumped out.

A high, square silhouette loomed ahead, a slush-caked tractor-trailer. He stiffened, waiting for DeSantis to give way. But he didn't, not an inch, and at the last instant the wide-eyed teamster wrenched his wheel right. The cab turned but the trailer didn't, and a steel wall slid sideways toward them.

"Christ, Len!"

The Willys missed the taillights of the trailer by a foot. They skidded off the cleared road along the berm, slamming and slowing as the flat nose threw snow. The windshield went white. Then it cleared suddenly, showing them a miraculously empty road ahead. DeSantis giggled. Halvorsen, looking back, saw the trailer switching like a cat's tail. At last the driver got it straightened out and back on the road.

"You almost killed us!"

"Teach him to crowd a man."

"You go off the right-of-way here, Fatso, we're done for. There's slime pits along here ten foot deep."

DeSantis shrugged. Halvorsen stared at him a moment, then faced front. He was sweating, even in the icy wind.

A few miles past Petroleum City he pointed DeSantis onto a cleared but unmarked road that struck off up a hollow. The quarter-ton downshifted. A mile on it left behind a snow-drifted field, abandoned farm buildings. Then the woods closed in. Halvorsen made out white oak; beech; farther up on the hill, the blue prickle of spruce. Snow lay still on them and on the slopes, and the only mar on the white silence was their own motor growling back from the hillside. The road narrowed, curved left and then right. Above them Cherry Knob was a bulbous mass of rock and earth, a massive nipple on the hill's breast.

"Wow," said DeSantis.

"Watch the *road*, Len."

"Man, look out there. You can see all the way to the lake."

Below, as they whined along the contour line, a stream lay rigid among rocks and fallen boles and the pale polished trunks of birches. Brows of hemlock and spruce suspended white masses above rock-choked ravines. Ideal snake country, and he'd put money on trout in those pools. Beyond that, as Halvorsen lifted his eyes, the valley sloped down till the gray bare treetops turned blue.

No town, no curl of smoke nor sign of man interrupted that rolling sea till far off, maybe twenty miles distant, a white patch marked where Hantzen Lake had backed up behind the dam.

Every hundred feet, on either side of the road, the woods were posted.

"I never been out here."

"Slow down," said Halvorsen. "I think this is it comin' up."

DeSantis put the truck in neutral and coasted the last few yards uphill to the gate. Black-painted iron, twice the height of a man, it extended across the road from two piers of mortared fieldstone. On either side barbed wire stretched away into the woods. Its only marking was a bronze plaque that said PRIVATE DRIVE.

"Man," said DeSantis after a moment. "You know, I was in Germany in forty-five. Quartermasters. That's the only time I ever seen anything like this. One of the Krupp estates down in Bavaria. What do they call this again?"

"Cherry Hill."

"So what now? You gonna climb it?" DeSantis snickered. He groped grunting under his seat and at last came up with a bottle. He unscrewed the cap and sat back as Halvorsen got out.

He found a little grille and a button underneath it. When he pressed it a voice said, "Yes?"

"Dan Thunner, please."

"Mr. Thunner's not receiving."

"Tell him Racks Halvorsen's here to see him."

"Racks—"

"Halvorsen. I'll wait."

The grille went silent. Halvorsen went back to the jeep and leaned against the mudguard. DeSantis had turned on a gas-fired heater. The fat man cut his eyes at him but said nothing. At last a buzz came from the grille, and the gate clicked. He strolled over and leaned against the bars. When they swung wide so did DeSantis's eyes. He almost flooded the motor getting it started.

They drove slowly up a circuitous road toward the top of the hill. The trees got bigger and farther apart as they climbed. At last they saw lit windows, then the house. Four or five buildings set close together. DeSantis pulled over at a carriage entrance. He set the brake, then aimed the bottom of the vodka bottle at the overcast sky.

"Want to go in, get warm?" said Halvorsen.

"No way. Say, Bill, you don't really want to go in there."

"Why not?"

"Ain't our kind of place. Nor our kinda people. Why do I get the feeling you're mixin' in things ain't your business?"

"Maybe you're right," said Halvorsen. "Guess I'll find out, though."

"Well, I'll jus' wait out here."

Halvorsen slowly climbed the steps. When he got to the door someone opened it from inside. He looked up.

And up. The man was about seven feet high and as wide as the hallway behind him. His neck was thick as a well casing. His teeth looked like they could drill rock. He was black as asphalt-base crude.

"Mr. Halvorsen?"

"Hullo there. Where you folks keeping Dan?"

"I'll take you to him. Just follow me."

"Ought to take these boots off, get this nice floor wet—"

"Don't worry about that."

He followed the man down a long hallway. The floor was little pieces of wood fit together in a pattern, so shiny he could see his face. I don't look real good, he thought. Should of shaved. He stared at a mounted cat's head, slipping his cap off.

"Through here."

Beyond was a sun room, all glass, and Halvorsen skirted the tiled edge of a pool. A row of lamps, some bright, some deep red, glowed down from the transparent ceiling; the sky looked dim beyond their incandescent glare. Potted palms in terra-cotta tubs circled the shallow end. He unbuttoned his coat as he walked and at last had to take it off. On the far side of the palms, in a ten-foot-wide spot of light and heat where the lamps focused, an old man sat in a wheelchair by the pool.

"You can sit down here," the black man said, moving a lawn chair a little closer. "I'll take your coat."

Halvorsen eased himself down. Piano music was playing somewhere. He blinked in the glare and looked at the man in the chair.

"Red?"

It took him a moment to recognize Dan Thunner. The bones of his jaw had grown out but his face had fallen in, cheeks and eyes sunken as if everything vital had been pumped out from under them. His shoulders were hunched forward and his legs were just wrinkles under the plaid comforter.

"Hullo, Dan."

"You're the last person I expected to see today."

"Been a while, ain't it?" Halvorsen blotted his face. A finger inched out along the arm of the chair; touched a button; several of the lights died. "Thanks. That's pretty hot when you come in from outside."

"So," said Thunner, and his head came forward an inch or two. "How do I look? Pretty good for ninety-two, eh?"

"You look bad, Dan."

"Ain't that the truth . . . Let's see, when was the last time we were together? That hunt up in Katahdin. Remember the moose I got?"

"Sure was a beauty." Halvorsen smiled slowly. "Them things take gettin' used to just for size. Eight foot at the shoulder. How big were the racks, again?"

"Sixty inches."

"Holy smoke."

"Yeah, that made Boone & Crockett easy. Say, you never saw my heads, did you?"

"That's all right."

"You never would go out to Africa with me."

"Too rich for my blood."

"You could've afforded it. See that leopard in the hallway? Got her in Kenya." Thunner raised his jaw slightly. "I see you met Jones . . . Lark, get Red somethin' to drink."

Halvorsen turned his head; the black man had stayed, standing just behind his chair. "No, nothing for me, thanks," he told him.

"Not drinking? You were antifreezed up good in Katahdin, I remember."

"I quit." Halvorsen remembered the Top in his pocket. "I'll have a chew, though, if you don't mind."

"Be my guest . . . I'll have a short one. The single malt." Jones left them.

"So." Thunner studied him. "You been doin' any hunting?"

Halvorsen put the plug back in his pants. Around the fresh stiff tobacco he said, "I quit that too."

"Quit *hunting?* You'd be the last one I'd guess that of. What happened? Heart?"

"It ain't that. I just got tired of it."

"Haven't turned into one of those anti-hunters, have you, Red?"

"Don't know any so I can't say. I just don't do it no more."

The man came back, and held a brandy glass to Thunner's nose. The old man's nostrils hovered over it for several breaths; then his eyes sank closed, and he nodded. Jones carried the glass to the pool. The ripples chased each other across the blue water, glittering in the hot light.

"It's hell being old," mumbled Thunner, "as you'll find out . . . Can't believe it, Red Halvorsen off the sauce, off hunting. You quit fighting too?"

"I try not to anymore," said Halvorsen. "Unless somebody don't leave me the choice."

"I remember the time you knocked that rock-guesser down . . . What was his . . ."

"Rothenberg."

"Yeah, that stuffed-shirt Jew. I felt like knockin' him down myself when I saw how he was spotting those holes. You were right, we should of started from the top and blasted through that shale."

Halvorsen emptied his cheek into one of the potted plants. "Then why'd you fire me?"

"Hell, I couldn't let my foreman go around knocking down the salaried. Especially you, with your Bolshie reputation. And you got to admit, I hired you back next day." Thunner chuckled. "What was that? Second time?"

"Third."

"I remember once in '36—and then—"

"Washington field."

"You deserved it that time. Goddamnit! Still makes me mad. What made you go down in that well?"

"Only way to get the tool out."

"But hell, Red, to go down on the line—eight hundred feet—"

Halvorsen didn't like to think about it. He'd been a young fool, and realized it halfway down: jammed so tight in the eighteen-inch pipe he could barely expand his lungs to breathe; the dead dark, the clammy smell of mud and oil. He'd had nightmares about it for years. But he'd got the bit free, saved two weeks of work. "You were right."

"Course I was. We had our differences. But we always fought fair. Didn't we?"

They looked at each other. At last Halvorsen shifted a little in the chair and said, "I think *you* always did, Dan. Some of your boys, though, they must of thought different."

"Well, we had a good time." Thunner turned his head slightly; Jones came around behind and pivoted the chair. Halvorsen realized Dan could only move head and fingers. The old man stared out at the quadrangle, the smooth plane of snow, and beyond it the rise of hemlock-dotted hill. "I miss it. I miss the drillin', the gamble there was something down there nobody'd found before. Business was fun then. Now it ain't. No oil left, hardly, got to squeeze it out. It's lawyer crap, sales meetings, tryin' to shave a hundredth of a penny a barrel off your refinin' costs." He sighed. "I'm glad I'm out of it, Red."

Halvorsen said, "I remember all that. And them picnics the company used to have. You used to welcome us, make a speech, then we'd have games for the kids, softball, all the beer you could drink . . . Why'd they stop havin' those, Dan? All the guys, they loved those picnics."

"Ah, my son-in-law said it cost too much. Said it was old-fashioned."

The two old men sat silent for a while. Beyond the glass a few flakes zigzagged down. The fingers crept out and the lamps blazed on again. "Well, anyway . . . say, what's that bandage for, Red?"

Halvorsen straightened from spitting. "That's what brung me up here, Dan."

"Got something to get off your chest? Shoot."

Halvorsen told him about his collapse and hospitalization. He told him what the doctor had said. Midway through the explanation Thunner began shaking his head. When Halvorsen was done he said, "I don't know nothing about that. Why'd you think I would?"

"They make a lot of strange stuff out of oil these days. Not saying the company's responsible, but it's a place to start."

"What'd you say it was called?"

"They ain't sure. PCB was one of them."

"We don't make it, I'm pretty sure. Just gas and oil and feed-stocks, your basic fractions, fluid catalytic products, and some polymerization. But, see, I ain't really in charge of T.O. anymore, Red. I passed it on to the board about ten years back, then my daughter got married, and now she and my son-in-law, they run it."

"Who's he? Maybe he's the fella I ought to ask."

"His name's Boulton, Brad Boulton. Comes from Scranton, his family was in coal there. He's a hardnose. Done a lot for the company. Not all of it I like, but like I say I'm out of the business now. I doubt he's here, he spends most of this time in the office, or at the house in town." Thunner paused. "But he might be back tonight. And like I say, my daughter, she's pretty well up on things. You might want to talk to her. Lark?"

"Yes, Mr. Thunner?"

"Is Ainslee here?"

"Yes, sir, unless she's left in the last hour. She and Miss Williamina are over in the West Wing."

"You won't join me in a little snifter?" Thunner asked him. "My style?"

"No, thanks."

"Another single malt, Lark. Then I think I'm 'bout ready for my nap."

"Yes, sir."

As Jones wheeled Thunner away from the pool Halvorsen went to the window. He pressed his forehead to the glass and looked out at the hills.

Jones came back. "Did you want to see Mrs. Boulton?"

"If she's here."

"This way."

They went back down the corridor, through several rooms, then through a glassed-in walkway to another building. Halvorsen, looking out, saw a white plume drifting from the Willys's tailpipe. He hoped DeSantis wasn't hitting the vodka too hard. Headlights flickered between the tree trunks, coming up the drive.

"Mrs. Boulton? A Mr. Halvorsen to see you," said Jones, and stood aside.

A fire snapped in a fieldstone hearth. In the corner a twelve-foot Norwegian pine glittered with gold tinsel. The paneling was burled walnut, nice enough, Halvorsen thought, for gunstocks. Along the walls were glass things, vases, cups, glowing and glittering under little ceiling lights like jewels. He didn't know a thing about glass but it looked like an expensive setup. The woman on the sofa was expensive-looking too. No more than forty, but as hard-looking a one as he'd seen in his life. He could see Dan in her, sure enough.

He realized too late he should have gotten rid of his chew.

"So who are you, and why were you annoying my father?"

"No, ma'am, he seemed to enjoy seein' me again. I'm W. T. Halvorsen. We hunted together, and I worked for him back on the—"

"Jones tells me you have a question. What is it?"

"Yeah. It's about some chemicals I got sick from. Seems like there's a lot of it going around."

"See our public relations staff." She got up. "Thank you for coming by. Jones will show you out."

Halvorsen stood his ground, trying to work the chaw around so he didn't need to spit so bad. "Well, I thought maybe you could help me figure out where this stuff's coming from, Mrs. Boulton. I come up to see Dan because I put in all these years with Thunder Oil, I figure I got a right to ask—"

"Maybe you don't understand where you are, Mr. Halvorsen. This is our home. Not our office. I don't know why my father let you in here. Since his stroke his behavior is erratic. But whatever impression he gave you, we don't keep open house at Cherry Hill for our pensioners. Do you understand me?"

Halvorsen's pale blue eyes studied her. "I reckon I do now."

"Show him out, Jones."

He turned for the door, and stopped. A dark-haired man stood unzipping a leather car coat. He raised his eyebrows at Halvorsen, glanced at the woman. "Hi, darlin'," he said. "Who's this?"

"I'm Racks Halvorsen. You must be Mr. Boulton. Dan told me about you."

Boulton looked him up and down, not offering to shake hands. Halvorsen was abruptly conscious of his grizzled whiskers, his suspenders over worn green cotton shirt; most of all of that he was shaking like a kitten, not from nervousness or anything like that, but because he was still so weak.

"Don't bother, he was just leaving," he heard the woman say behind him.

"What was he here for?"

"Something about some chemicals, he got sick."

The man looked at him, Halvorsen thought, a little strangely. "Tell me about it."

He said awkwardly around the tobacco, "Well, what your wife said just now, that's about it. I got put down for a week." He held out his wrist, showing the hospital bracelet. "Doc said it was a reaction to a chemical of some kind."

"What kind? How'd you get it?"

"They don't know. Whatever it is it's gettin' around the county, other people than me's gettin' sick from it."

"What'd you say your name was?"

"W. T. Halvorsen. Thirty years with Thunder Oil."

Boulton seemed to relax. "I see. Well, Mr. Halvorsen, if you have any complaints just have your lawyer get in touch with us. Lark, see him out."

"Yes, sir, Mr. Boulton."

Halvorsen felt the colored man's hand heavy on his shoulder. It helped him pivot around and he nearly slipped on the polished floor. Jones walked behind him on the way back. When they got to the entrance he held out his coat. "Sorry if I was rough, old-timer. But let me give you a piece of advice. Whatever your problem is, don't come around here with it. These people don't like to be bothered."

"I noticed," said Halvorsen.

He paused on the steps and unloaded his cheek into the bushes. The Willys shuddered as it idled. DeSantis's alcohol-glazed eyes peered out at him through the curtains like the puppy's when she played hide-and-seek. Then he fumbled them apart, thrusting his reddened face out. "How'd she go?" he mumbled.

"Not so good."

"Talk to Thunner?"

"Little bit. And his daughter. Jesus."

"What you gonna do?"

"I don't know," said Halvorsen slowly, looking up at the house. "I just don't know."

He spat one last time, as much for luck as anything, and climbed in.

Fifteen

For the two days since he'd made the date with Alex, Phil hadn't been able to think of anything else. Or only one thing. He still had a couple of brain cells left over to dread his next meeting with Bubba Detrick.

He wasn't proud of how he'd avoided him so far. After Maxwell had made him take the meat off his head the ball player had come up behind him in the hall. "Out back, Romo, same time, same station." But instead of going to the field after the last bell he'd gone out the front, as fast as he could limp, and cut this way and that through side streets till he felt sure Detrick couldn't find him, even driving his truck. So that had been one evening safe. The next day he'd just cut the last class and left early. Today—Friday—he hadn't gone to school at all, just faked a sore throat till his mother called the office.

No, he wasn't proud, but as far as he could see getting beaten up tomorrow was better than getting beaten up today. There was always the chance Detrick would choke to death on a fishbone, or be born again and stop beating on people. Or something.

He spent the day in bed studying and came down around four. His mother was humming as she ironed. He looked at her face closely; she looked happy.

"What's wrong, Ma?"

"I'll let your dad tell you about it. Are you feeling better?"

"Yeah, lots."

"You'd better gargle again."

He sniffled a little, for effect. "It really feels better. The salt water helped. When's supper?"

"Soon as your father gets home."

"Gets home? Where is he?" Joe usually worked from six P.M. to three in the morning, then slept till dinnertime.

"I'll let him tell you."

He thought about that for a minute. Then dismissed it as another family mystery. "I got a date tonight. Going to the movies. I got any clean shirts?"

"Look in your drawer," said his mother, humming to herself.

When his dad came home they sat down to supper. Phil kept checking his Timex. "Is it still going?" said his father at last, holding his cigarette away from his plate as he helped himself to scalloped potatoes.

"What?"

"Your watch."

"Oh. Yeah. I got a date tonight."

"A date?" said his mother. "What kind of date? Where are you going?"

"I told you about it, Ma."

"Well, I didn't hear you. And you're not going to enjoy your evening very much if you eat so fast. You're going to get a cramp."

"Ah, I could eat anything when I was his age," said Joe.

"I'm not that hungry," said Phil.

"I didn't say to eat more, I said not to eat so fast."

"Okay, okay!"

"Raise your voice to your mother again, you won't be going anywhere."

"Sorry." He finished his pie and jumped up. "'Scuse me. Got to get ready."

Behind him he heard his father say, "Get ready? What's he got to do? Kids don't dress up for dates anymore. Is it mental preparation, or what?"

"I don't like him going out with the girls from that public school. He's only seventeen."

"I had a talk with him. He knows what to do."

"That's not funny, Joseph. He's not that kind of a boy. But I don't trust those girls."

In the bathroom Phil examined his chin. Was that the beginning of a beard? He decided it was. His father's razor was on the sink. He lathered his face and began scraping.

Even getting ready for a date with a girl like Alex Ryun was scary. He still couldn't quite figure why she was going out with him. Then he thought, Who cares *why*? Even a one-timer would help his social stock at school. Which so far was zip.

He nicked himself on the upper lip, then on the neck. Not good. He tore out little squares of toilet paper and stuck them over the blood, like his dad did when his hand shook after a hard night at the bar.

Upstairs, crouching in the too-low space, he pulled off jeans and sweatshirt and threw them on the typewriter. He looked through his closet, shivering as the air goosebumped his arms. What would she like? He tried on several combinations before deciding on brown slacks, a pale yellow shirt, and a red patterned sweater. The bulky sleeves would hide his arm. He evaluated the result in the dresser mirror, then took everything off and changed his under-shirt and put it back on again.

When he was satisfied he checked his watch again. Two after six. Closing his door and moving to the bed, he reached up and felt around guiltily. He doubted he'd need them, but it was best to be prepared. He tucked the foil pack into his wallet.

He checked his watch again, thinking he'd have to call the cab pretty soon, but it was still only three minutes after six.

"Phil!" From below.

"Yeah, Dad."

"Come down here."

"I'm busy."

"Get down here! I want to talk to you."

He went down unwillingly. His mother had cleared the table. His father was sitting in his T-shirt, a just-opened Bud smoking in front of him. "Yeah?" Phil said.

"Sit down. Here's to your first date. You're pretty young for it, though."

"I thought it was kind of late."

"Maybe . . . guess I just didn't think you were interested in that kind of stuff. When you picking her up? What's her name, anyway?"

"Look, I got to get moving—"

"What's her *name*," said his father.

"Alex Ryun."

"Alex?"

"Short for Alexandrine. She's beautiful."

"You're sure she's a girl," said his father, in the voice he used when he was trying to make a joke.

He didn't answer and after a moment Joe went on, "Well, say, how are you going to get her there? Gonna walk?"

"She has a car, but I figured I'd pick her up in a taxi."

"That's not too cool."

Phil shrugged. His father sucked down half the bottle and gazed at the bubbles. "Cancel it," he said. "Take the black and white. Here's the keys."

"C'mon, Dad, that's city property. I don't want to get you in trouble."

"I been in it before." His father narrowed his eyes at the window. "But things are turnin' around a little. Nolan's puttin' me in for day shift, and I might get my stripe back. So don't argue. Just be careful, for Christ's sake. Just to the movie and her house and back."

"Well . . . okay." He weighed the keys in his hand. "That's great news, Dad. And thanks."

"Don't mention it. Say, see if there's another pack in my shirt, by the TV, would you?"

Outside it was crisp and clear. It had stopped snowing and the wind was light. The patrol car was parked down on State. He started it and let it warm up, checking the controls to make sure he knew where everything was. He'd barely passed driver's ed; they wanted two hands on the wheel.

He thought about where he was going then, and though he was nervous about driving he hugged himself with anticipation. Then sobered. Better not do that around her. She'd think he was a geeko for sure.

At seven-twenty he was parked across town, listening to the ticking of the block as it cooled. When his watch said seven-twenty-six he turned off the courtesy light and got out. 263 was a two-story ranch with attached garage. An illuminated Santa waved from the lawn and colored lights blinked along the eaves. When he pressed the bell a chime tolled far off. A middle-aged woman with faded auburn hair came to the storm door.

"Uh, Mrs. Ryun? Hi, I'm Phil."

"What did you want?"

"Well, Alex and I got a date tonight," he said, thinking, She must still be getting ready. "Are you her mom?"

"Yes." The woman examined him through the glass. "A date, you said?"

"That's right."

"She didn't mention anything to me. But come on in." She disappeared, leaving him standing on one foot and then the other in the living room. He noted the depth of the carpet, the heavy oak furniture, all matching, all polished; he strolled around to examine books ranked on shelves built into the wall, a grandfather clock in a recess. Its indolent tick made him realize how quiet the house was. The air had a cedar freshness.

Mrs. Ryun came back with a glass of milk and a plate of imported butter cookies. "She'll be down in a few minutes, Bill. Please sit down. Won't you have something while you wait?"

"It's Phil. Sure, thanks."

"What was your last name, Phil?"

"Romanelli."

"And where did you say you were going?"

"Just to the movie downtown."

"That sounds good."

"Yeah, thanks." He looked at the clock and then at his Timex. "Is she coming down pretty soon?"

"I imagine so."

"Hi, Phil."

She stood on the stairs, pulling on her mittens. He got up. She was wearing green, with a cream cashmere pullover and a kind of matching hat. "Wow. You look great," he said.

"Thanks." She was giving him the same frown her mother had. "What's that on your lip?"

"What?"

"On your neck, too."

He realized then what she was talking about. He jerked the paper off and felt the cuts sting and start to bleed again. Oh, Jesus, he thought. Her mother left the room and came back with a Wet One while Alex stared in silence at the blank television.

At last it clotted. Alex let him help with her coat. She kissed her mother.

"Now don't stay out too late. Bring her home early, Phil. And have fun, both of you."

She laughed when she saw the squad car. "What's this? Are we going in *this?*"

"Sure. My dad let me have it for the evening."

"Weird. I never rode in one before. Not sober, anyway."

He laughed and held the door. As she got in her hair brushed his arm, sending a funny thrill up it. He saw a flash of her knees, slim and hollowed beneath, by the courtesy light. "Watch the nightstick rack," he said.

"Where're we going, Phil? You told me, but I forgot."

"Oh. The movie."

"What's playing?"

He told her. She said, "Oh, I saw that already. We rented it. Wouldn't you rather go to Cresson?"

"Gee, I don't know. My dad—"

"That's where everybody goes Friday night. The Heathen Creeps are playing, and F K U might do a late set. What do you say, let's go to the Shirt."

He glanced over at her. She was so beautiful; the smell of orange blossoms and of her hair easily put to flight the squad-car funk of Camels, sweat, old vomit, and leather. He wondered again why she was with him. Then thought: That's just your problem, Romanelli. You don't think you're good enough. While obviously she did.

So maybe it could be that he was wrong and she was right, and maybe he deserved love, deserved happiness, after all.

He felt the same sudden joy he'd felt on Sullivan Hill, releasing the brake on this magical night. As for taking her to Cresson, he didn't want to, but he couldn't say no. Not to her. He wanted their first time to be perfect. She reached across and hugged his arm, lifting her eyebrows, and somebody else, maybe the Stag, grinned suddenly and gunned the engine. "Okay," he said. "Sure."

"Great! Now, show me how to put the siren on."

"Christ, Alex! Wait till we're out of town, at least."

Cresson wasn't a town. It was just a crossroads a mile across the state line from Four Holes. But the cops looked the other way when kids drank there, as long as it didn't get out of hand. So tonight, despite cold and snow, the lot by the low log building was full, and cars and trucks lined the side road too. He found a place and locked up; that was the last thing he needed, to have somebody rip the car off. They waded through tracked-up snow to the door.

"So, what would you like?"

"Michelob Light."

The place was wall to wall. Phil got her seated at a table at the far end from the band and pushed his way toward the bar. It took him a while but at last he got two bottles and shoved his way back through groups, between couples, bumping, apologizing. He hoped she didn't want more. After the cover and the beer he had six bucks left. The band was rattling the glasses above the bar with a bass beat he could feel in his guts. The air, solid with smoke, was just like home.

When he got back two other girls were talking to Alex and he had to stand around until they saw him and shoved their chairs over. She'd gotten a cigarette somewhere and was lighting it off one of theirs. He saw right away they weren't going to do much talking here. Well, maybe they could get away, park someplace quiet.

He tilted the bottle and let his tongue pickle for a while before he swallowed. Alex's lips moved and he leaned toward her. "What?"

Something inaudible. *"What?"* he shouted, leaning in front of the other girls.

"Dance," she screamed directly into his ear, deafening him. He grinned and bobbed his head. She took a last drag and handed the cigarette to her friend.

There was an excuse to take her hand as they moved through the crowd, and he used it. Her palm was sweaty. When they reached the floor she let go and spun. Her hair came out in a firework wheel and he saw, with mingled pride and pain he'd never felt before, that she, and he with her, were instantly the cynosure of a hundred eyes.

For the first time he tasted what it might be like, to be a man.

When the number started the strobes cut on and suddenly her body reappeared as sculpture, melted by hot darkness and then refrozen from inchoate black a dozen times a second. Each pose was graceful, abandoned, and different. He stared at her as he danced, conscious as always of his withered arm and faulty legs, but not caring anymore. He was with Alex Ryun, and she was with him.

A bolt of joy burst up from his feet into his heart, and he lifted his face and danced.

They stayed on the floor through the whole set and when they walked off he was wringing wet. Someone had cleared or stolen their drinks and he bought two more. Her girlfriends, he noted with relief, were gone. It was just possible to talk over the canned rock and he leaned over and shouted, "You dance great."

"Thanks." She upended the beer and looked past him. She didn't seem to like looking directly into his eyes. He shouted, "You look really terrific tonight."

"Thanks."

"You know," he shouted, "I was really looking forward to this. Maybe after this we could go someplace and talk."

"Oh, I got to get home early."

"What?"

"I got to go home. Maybe one more beer. We're all going out to Hantzen tomorrow, to the lodge. Skiing."

"Oh. Well, anyway, I think you dance really great. And you look beautiful."

"Thanks," she said, looking past him.

He tried to see what or who she was staring at, but couldn't; there were maybe two hundred people in the Shirt, and its far end was impenetrable with smoke. He got up and she looked at him then. "Where are you going?"

"Find the can. Be right back."

She nodded. "Bring me another one, okay?"

"Uh, yeah."

He was filtering through the crowd, heading for where he figured the john ought to be, when he came face to face with Bubba Detrick and Brick Mooney. They were leaning back with their elbows on the bar, holding bottles of Killian's Red and looking bored. Their faces lighted when they saw him and Mooney said, "Whoa. Look who's here."

"It's our pal."

Emboldened by beer and the crowd, Phil said, "Get out of my face, Bubba."

"You little prick, you played your mouth to me once too often," said Detrick, and came off the bar at him. Phil was trying to get his sweaterfront unwadded from his fist when a just slightly less massive body than Mooney's slid itself through the club sandwich of people toward, then between them. "What you want, Stein?" Detrick asked him.

"Take it outside, Bubba. Them's the rules here."

"You heard the man," said Detrick, shoving him toward the door. "Let's go, Romanelli. I'm through fuckin' with you. This time you're dead."

Outside the wind was bitter and the stars were a thousand

pinpricks in a black tent. Engines vroomed and a group of boys staggered by, arms linked. One fell down, screaming, and all the rest did too. The snow squeaked under their boots as Detrick propelled him along the wall, out of the light.

"So, Crip, what the hell're you doing here?"

"Having a few beers."

"That's great, I like to see the retarded have a good time. How come you been avoiding me?"

"I been sick."

Detrick shook his head sadly. "Nah, don't *lie*, Romo. It might come true. Lemme ask you something, you ever have fits?"

"What?"

"Fits. You know, fall down, kick around, shit like that."

"No."

"Good," said Detrick. "'Cause you have seriously pissed me off, and I'd hate to do this to somebody who might throw a fit on me."

He hit him in the mouth. But Phil was ready this time. He got his head out of the way, then, surprising himself more than Detrick, he punched back. But even as his fist thumped on the other's chest he felt how weak the blow was. Detrick grinned and jabbed him twice in the face with his left, then put him on the ground with something so low and fast he never saw it, just folded over like a jackknife. He writhed around in the snow, seeing nothing but slow red flashes.

When he got his legs under him he went for Detrick's waist. He had his good arm around him and was hanging on to the back of his belt when he heard the ballplayer laugh and then his knee came up and smashed into his mouth.

"Thought you said no fits," said Detrick. "Come on, Wop, get up. We ain't even started yet."

"What's going on out here? Is that you, Bubba?"

Headlights swept across them as Detrick turned, a black cutout with clenched fists. They went on, wheeling across the tops of the trees, and into the returned darkness the ballplayer said, "Who's that?"

"Me. Alex."

"What are you doin' here—no, *wait* a minute, now I know. You're with wimpy-dick, ain't you?"

Coldly: "He brought me out here."

"Yeah, well, what about that? I heard it but I didn't quite believe it. What is this shit?"

"There's no shit involved. He asked me to come here with him and here I am."

"But Romanelli . . . Christ, Alex, I thought we were steady."

"I thought so too, till Sheila passed on a little item about you and this sophomore. What a bastard you are! What's her name, Greg? Does she put out good for you?"

Phil found that he was bleeding from the mouth and that two of his incisors were wobbly. He dragged himself backward through the snow. When he hit logs he pushed his upper body into a sitting posture. He could hear dimly through the wood kids screaming and laughing. The beat of the band tickled his loose teeth.

"You know you're it, Alex, you're the one I want. But you don't come through, a man's gotta get it where he can. She's nothin' to me, it was just for fun."

"And you're nothing to me. Not if you're going to humiliate me in front of the school for some little bitch who's probably taking guys on for lunch money."

"Yeah, but . . . I don't get it, Alex. From first string to the ugliest little cripple in school." Detrick made a helpless gesture with his hands. "Don't you *care?*"

"Why not? It was just for fun."

Slowly, Bubba grinned. "Wait a minute. *Wait* a minute. Why do I get the idea you wanted me to see you with him? And he's the only one who's far enough out of it to go out with you when I'm on the scene. Right?"

"Maybe. Something like that."

Suddenly Phil saw the two shadows melt together. "Greg . . . why are we playing these games? Why are we hurting each other?"

"I don't know, babe. People like us, we belong together. C'mere, you little slut. Pull this up. Rub those against me."

"It's cold out here. Warm me up."

"Sweet Alex."

"My Wolf."

"What a touching scene," said Phil thickly.

"Shut up down there, Crip, or I'll kick your fucking teeth in."

"Let go of her, Detrick. She's with me."

"Greg! Don't hit him anymore. He can't fight you. He can hardly dance."

"Make up your frigging mind! Are you with me or him? I got the truck, I got knobbies on it, I got a case of Stroh's. Let's see if we can make it up to the lookout tower."

"Just a minute." He heard the crunch of her boots; caught his breath; but though she leaned over him she said nothing, just put her hand on his hair for a second, then turned away.

Alone again, he stared at the stars for a while, breathing shallow and touching his front teeth gently with the tip of his tongue. At last he wadded snow and packed it under his lip.

When he could move without crying out he got up and staggered across the lot. His shame and rage had passed, gone like mists burned away by summer sun. He had nothing again. In a way it felt better. He wanted nothing. No pain, no longing, no tears.

There was a way he could never be hurt again.

He had the keys. He had a car to get home. He knew where his father kept his service .38.

He started the motor, floored it, and pulled blindly out onto the road.

Sixteen

Hand over hand, Halvorsen hauled himself up the ice-slicked hillside stairs. He moved slowly, but without cease. Only when he reached a temporary leveling did he stop, pulling in the cold air over and over, and look around him.

It had seem warmer to him that day, but as soon as the sun set the air whetted itself again to a tungsten edge. Below him the town was a rhinestone glitter. But up here night was relieved only feebly by the clear bulbs under white tin reflectors that had been the latest thing in outdoor lighting in 1931.

Wonder why they don't answer their phone, he thought, clinging to the handrail to stay erect.

An engine yowled and a moment later a police car shot past. His head jerked round after it. It skidded from side to side on the ice, but kept on climbing, until at last it swerved out of sight.

Fifty steps on was another landing. He paused there too, breathing hard. He was hungry and from time to time the hill tried to spin away beneath him. But he still had a way to go that night. A long way, in the cold.

He spat onto the snow-slick bricks, and forced himself again into the immense lean of the earth.

• • •

A few hundred yards above him, Phil touched the gun.

His father's Smith & Wesson, hanging behind the bedroom door. He listened again to the empty house, then pulled it slowly out of the patent leather holster.

It was heavy and old. The blued barrel was gray at the muzzle and the grips were worn checkerless. His father had carried it for sixteen years. But Phil knew it worked. Joe had taken him out in the woods when he was thirteen, and with great solemnity shown him how to use it.

Standing in his parents' bedroom, he pressed the latch and swung the cylinder out. He slid six nickeled cartridges out of their loops, loaded the gun, and closed it. Then held it for a moment, looking around the house for the last time.

His mom and dad had left a note; they'd gone out too, to the same movie. Shit; they'd give him grief about not seeing him there. The next moment he smiled bitterly. No, they wouldn't.

The woods started two hundred feet above Paradise Lane.

He considered leaving a note himself. But even his hatred had dimmed, melted like everything else he'd ever felt into the gray despair. Even writing a note would keep him here longer than he wanted to stay.

Let's do it, he thought. He dropped the gun into his jacket and went out, closing the door carefully behind him. He dropped the car keys in the mailbox and turned up the hill. For a moment he thought he saw someone at the bottom of the lane. But when he looked again, no one was there.

The climb pulled anew at his legs. His mouth hurt and he could wiggle his front teeth with his tongue. The revolver dragged at his side. Woodsmoke filled the dark air. It smelled good.

Upward, upward . . . the last house. Yellow rectangles of light lay quietly on smooth snow. He waded through them and left them behind. He climbed a cut bank and was in the woods.

The sky was no longer completely overcast; here and there stars burned down from a frigid sky. He recognized Jupiter, brighter than the rest. Around him as he labored upward the planet's light showed him the winter-stripped trunks as black verticals. Snow crunched and moaned beneath his feet. First a thin crust; then, under that, softness; last, the yielding resilience of dead leaves. He sucked the freezing air through his teeth. It's a ways to the top, he thought. Why go any farther? He could have done it at home, but he didn't want to cause his parents problems. Out here the end would be clean.

Thinking this, that he'd come far enough, he stopped and turned, panting a thin warm stream back into the icy river of night.

Below him, between the black trunks, the valley was a pit of darkness among the hills. At its bottom, lapping up the slopes, the parti-colored sparkle of town surged and glittered. He could see the parallels of lights on Main Street; the on-and-off glow of the time/temperature sign in front of the bank; the blue-lit cross atop the Baptist church; here and there the red-orange flicker of a bar. Like planets among the fixed stars crept the twin white flares of automobiles, red as they receded. Above it all low clouds, trembling with a yellow reflection, passed slowly between him and heaven.

For a moment he wondered if it could be true, if there was a life beyond this one. Then his mouth twisted. That was a tale, a fable the governing classes had made up to numb the weak to injustice, insult, and pain.

But he'd had enough. He looked around. The silence of the trees, the slow soundless passing of the clouds mirrored the emptiness of his heart. People moved below him in the glitter, like angels the corridors of the stars, with smiles and money and straight strong bodies. They laughed and danced and said, *This is happiness. Be like us and you'll be happy too.*

But he couldn't. It wasn't just that he believed in different things, in justice and equality and truth. It wasn't even that he was crippled. The thing he couldn't change was the one thing they would never forgive: his conviction that, no matter what they thought, he was better than they were.

The hammer caught on the lining as he drew it out. He freed it carefully, not wanting to tear his coat. Muzzle-down, the revolver's weight drew his arm to the ground, like a dowsing rod pointing to where he would fall. The butt was cold and hard through his glove.

For a moment, looking down, he wondered if the town itself might be the root of it. He'd always planned to leave as soon as he could. Maybe what he needed lay elsewhere.

Then he thought, It's not Raymondsville. It was he who was different, who was unhappy, who was so poisoned with rage and inferiority he could no longer bear to see or speak to another human being. The problem was not below him. It was within.

Oh, Christ, he thought. If only she hadn't patted my head. He

could live with pain, he could live full of hate. But he couldn't live
with pity.

He cocked the gun awkwardly and lifted it to his ear. "Goodbye,
you bastards," he said aloud, staring down at the town that had
seen his birth, his struggle, seventeen years of a life he now judged
not worth the breathing for. He closed his eyes.

"Yo!"

The voice came from below him, not far distant. He opened his
eyes and crouched, instinctively merging with the earth. Amid the
trees a shadow moved, hesitated, moved again. Someone was
climbing toward him between the naked trees, under the glowing
sky.

He didn't answer. The shadow stopped a few feet away. He
couldn't see a face, but it seemed to be looking at him.

Phil brought the gun, still cocked, around in front of him and
extended it, feeling the trigger creep inward.

Halvorsen was so tired he could hardly stand. "Who's that?" he
said doubtfully, thinking about the click he'd just heard. The
shadow ahead was bulkier than the tree boles, but it didn't move.
Then after a moment it did; stood up, and became a human form.

"What're you doing, boy?"

"Nothing! Is . . . Mr. Halvorsen—is that you?"

"Yeah, it's me."

"What are you doing out of the hospital? What are you doing up
here?"

"Lookin' for you."

"How'd you find me?"

"People leave tracks," said Halvorsen. "Say, don't you folks ever
answer your phone? I been callin' from my daughter's since sup-
pertime."

"I wasn't there."

The boy's voice was high, quavering; he was afraid, or angry, or
maybe near panic. The click, Halvorsen thought, had sounded an
awful lot like a hammer going back to cock. Cautiously he moved
up a step and said again, "What you doing up here, anyway?"

"Just thinking. I got a right to go off and think, be by myself—"

"Don't get upset! Sure you do. I just wanted to talk to you."

"What about?"

He took another step up the hill, feeling with fear the weakness
in his legs, the shallow patter of his heart. The kid sounded hostile

now. What the hell was going on? He glanced quickly around, thinking he wasn't sure what. But they were alone, just the two of them high above the town. "I got me a problem. But sounds to me like you got one too."

"What's that mean?"

"Sorry, couldn't hear you." Halvorsen took another step up the hill.

"I said, what does—"

He took one last step, and the stick he'd picked up to help him in the climb whipped down. A sudden flash and report shattered the night; fire leaped past his cheek. He lurched forward and got the boy in a bear hug, locking his hands behind him. "Just take it easy a minute 'fore you hit me," he muttered into his ear. "You can knock me over with a feather, but then you'd have to carry me back down to the hospital all over again. What you doin' up here with a gun, all alone at night? I didn't know better, I'd think you were fixing to do some silly-ass thing like shoot y'self."

Halvorsen felt the thin body go rigid; tightened his grip; then heard a short, choked exhalation. The boy's face burrowed into his shoulder. He held him close, in the darkness, and said after a moment, "Go on and cry, boy. I done it myself lots of times. Just go on an' get rid of it for a while."

The sudden flare of yellow phosphorus pulled pines toward them out of the darkness, then swayed them back. A slip of flame grew hissing from the pyramid of twigs, then winked out; but beneath it blue tongues licked with increasing hunger at the heavier sticks.

"Seems to be goin' now," said the old man. He slid the matchbox closed and put it in his pocket. "You'll find them lowest branches on your pitch pines, they'll stay good tinder all through the winter. Just feather 'em up with your knife like I showed you."

Phil sat on the rock. He felt empty. Crying had embarrassed him, but only for the first moment. Then he'd given way and bawled. The old man had held him stiffly against his doggy-smelling coat the whole time, and the shame had disappeared, then the rage, and last of all the hurt.

Now he felt like a Thermos bottle. A brittle skin of self, wrapped around a vacuum.

His eyes followed the firelight over the old man's face. He squatted stiffly by a scooped-bare patch of forest floor, feeding in a stick now and then. The fire ate them greedily, snapping and popping, and steadily grew. In its leaping light his face looked emaciated and evil, like a skull with gray stiff whiskers and a bandage. The curved butt of the revolver poked out of his pocket.

Halvorsen fed the fire another pine twig, feeling awkward. At last he cleared his throat and said, "You ready to talk?"

"It's nothing. It was stupid."

"Maybe stupid, but couldn't'a been nothing. Only fella I ever knew to shoot himself, on purpose I mean, had just lost title to fifty producing wells in a poker game. Was it somethin' like that?"

"Not exactly."

"Couldn't be women."

"Sort of." He flinched.

"That's about the dumbest thing I ever heard of," Halvorsen told him. "Shoot yourself over a woman. My advice'd be to find another one. A nice fat one, they're best when it's cold."

Phil thought of Alice Saunters and had to smile. "Maybe you're right."

"Anyway, better pull yourself together. I need some help."

"Is that why you came after me?" He flinched again.

"Told you it was. What's the matter with your mouth?"

"I was in a fight. It hurts when I say 'f'."

"What, your teeth loose?"

He nodded.

"Well, quit playing with them, your mouth'll swell up and hold 'em in. You was in a fight, huh? Over the girl?"

"Sort of."

"You lost?"

He nodded.

"You land one?"

"One."

"Ain't no shame losing, long as you can dish out a couple while you're goin' down."

Phil stared into the fire. Thinking of it as a fight over a girl made it better somehow. After a moment Halvorsen went on, "Anyway, you want to hear about this? Why I come up here after you?"

"I guess so."

"Reason I need help is I'm still some feeble." He hesitated. "I don't know, my mind don't seem to be as good some ways as it used to—fact is, I remember you told me a couple of times, but I can't recall your name."

"It's Phil. Phil Romanelli."

"Okay, Romanelli, you remember what that doctor lady was

telling me about what made me sick. What gave me this rash, and knocked me out the other day when you were out at my place.''

''Yeah.''

''Well, it made me mad when I figured out what she was sayin'. What it means is, somebody's using this county as a dump. Bringing things in here they don't want and spreadin' 'em all over where we live. Now, I don't like that, 'specially since I—well, if you hadn't of been there, I'd probably froze to death by now.''

The old man turned his pale eyes to Phil's. ''Now, I don't like to mess with people much. Just as soon leave them alone, have them leave me alone. But this kind of stuff gets under my hide. Fact is, I wouldn't mind getting my hands on the sonsabitches who did it.''

''Yeah, I can see that,'' said Phil. ''Look, talking about that, I read—''

''So I was sittin' down at the Bear this evening, warming up before I started for home, and I started going back over everything I done before I got sick. My mind's clearer now than it was Monday.'' Halvorsen pondered. ''Anyway, I remembered one funny thing. Friday, day before you come out to the Run. You remember, we had that heavy fall that morning?''

''Yeah. But look, Mr. Halvorsen, I saw—''

''Don't interrupt. Like I was saying, I was sitting there thinking, and it just come to me that I got a lift in that morning from a guy in one of the snowplows. He took me from the foot of the run right down to Rosen's.

''Now, I remember him telling me about this oily stuff under the snow. I looked and seen it too. Didn't think anything of it then, but some of it must of come blowing in the window. With the snow. I recollect having to take out my handkerchief and wipe it off. Had to wipe it off''—the old man's hand came up to the bandage—''right here, off the left side.''

Phil couldn't contain himself any longer. ''That was Barry Fox,'' he said.

''Drivin' the plow? Yeah, Fox, that's who it was. Now if we look him up—''

''He's in Bradford Hospital. With the same thing you had, sounds like, only worse. They found him out by the county line, passed out in the plow. He'd of frozen if somebody hadn't stopped.''

''Is that so?''

''I read it in the *Century*.''

Halvorsen nodded reflectively. After a moment he reached into his opposite pocket. Bit off a piece of tobacco. "Makes sense," he said. "Dump it on the road. That'd be easy to get away with. The way the old cars leak around here there's always that oily line down the center of the lane. Warm weather, you'd never notice. Only see it when they made a mistake, tried to dump it on top of fresh snow."

"So who's doing it?"

Halvorsen looked up at the stars. "You got me . . . I figured the place to start was out Cherry Hill. You know what that is?"

"Sure. That's the Thunner estate."

"Right. Anyway I went out there today."

"You went to Cherry Hill?"

"Uh huh."

"Wow. What was it like?" Phil blushed suddenly, glad for the dark. "I meant, who cares what it was like. It's all stolen from the workers. What did they say?"

"It ain't *stole;* old Dan put in a lot of years in the fields. But he's out of the business now. His daughter's got a swelled head. But it didn't sound like either of them had anything to do with it. Thunners got more money than's good for 'em now, can't see them doing something like this. They got to live here too. No, I figure it's somebody from out of the county."

"So what do you want to do?"

"Well, first I thought, what business is it of mine? And then I recalled all the animals dyin' out Mortlock; and how I got sick; and now you tell me that driver did too. Maybe there's more we don't know about. I don't mean to bother anybody, I just wanted to be let alone. But they aren't leaving me alone. So I figure I'm gonna try to find out where this stuff is coming from.

"Now I got some friends, but they're getting kind of long in the tooth. Even when they're sober. So I thought you might maybe want to help."

"Uh huh."

"Well, what do you say?"

"What would you want me to do?"

"Well, I figure we might post a lookout along one of the roads. Find someplace where we could stay warm, keep an eye on things, and sit out a couple nights."

"What would we do if we saw something going on?"

"Depends," said Halvorsen. "Get a license number and report it, I guess. Didn't you say your pop was a policeman?"

"Yeah, but he—"

"What?"

"Nothing. Yeah, he's a policeman."

"Well, there you go. I thought about calling Bill Sealey, over at the State Police barracks, but I'd like to have something better to give him than some old guy's suspicions."

Halvorsen dropped his eyes and Phil nodded slowly; seeing suddenly how the world might look to another human being. He's alone, he thought, lots more alone than I am. Maybe things aren't so good for me right now, but I can look forward. He can't even do that. He felt like saying something to cheer the old man up, but he couldn't think of anything that didn't sound stupid or patronizing. So he just said, "I guess I could help."

"Good, that's good."

"When do you want to start?"

"Oh, anytime. We could take every other night." Halvorsen squinted up at the stars. "Gettin' late . . . be warmer tomorrow. I need to head on home, but I wanted to talk to you, and oh yeah, get Jez. I hope she ain't been too much trouble."

"No, heck, it was fun playing with her."

"Good, well, thanks. I'll just take her off your hands then." Halvorsen stood up, brushed snow off his trousers.

"You're going to walk back to Mortlock?"

"Ain't got much of a choice."

Phil stood up too. "I can give you a ride. Down to the run and part way up it, anyway. That'll only leave you two or three miles to walk."

"That'd help," said the old man. He stood and looked down at the fire. After a moment he pulled the revolver out and handed it to the boy. Phil took it as silently and stuck it into his belt.

Halvorsen cleared his throat. "Say, don't feel right asking you this, you done so much for me already, but . . . well, I left my wallet at the hospital. Think you could let me have something to take out there with me? Something to eat?"

"How's frozen soup sound? And we got canned stuff."

"Yeah, that's the ticket. Till I can get out and get me a rabbit or something."

"I thought you didn't hunt," said Phil.

"Don't unless I got to, to eat."

"I guess that's okay . . . well, come on. I don't think my folks'll be back yet, I'll get you some tuna and beans and stuff. And your dog. Then we'll go."

"Sounds good." The old man dragged snow over the fire with

his boot. The flames hissed and steamed, fighting for a moment, then died beneath crystalline whiteness, knit of ice and cold beneath the glittering stars.

Together they turned, and headed down the hill.

Seventeen

FOUR WAYS TO FORGET THAT
MARRIED MAN YOU'VE BEEN SEEING

One: Do something NICE for yourself. Go away for a week-end somewhere you've always wanted to go. Give yourself a "new look" with a makeover and new outfit! Start a project you've been dreaming about for a long time. Do something absorbing and above all DIFFERENT from what you usually do with your time.

Two: Reinforce your "social web" by calling an old friend. Make a date for lunch or a movie. Talk about good times you had together—BEFORE you met Mr. Wrong.

Three: Begin the "uprooting process" by consciously not thinking about HIM. Throw out or at least put away out of sight all your old photographs, the gifts he gave you, mementos of places you went together.

Four: Most important, DON'T go right out looking for another man! You're too vulnerable at this stage. Give yourself time to heal!

Jaysine let the magazine sag to her lap. She stared past it, past the wineglass beside her on the window seat, down at the street.

The weather had definitely turned. A passing truck threw out a
spray of dirty slush. The snowpiles were smaller and looked rotten
soft. She sipped at the wine and reread the last paragraph.

Deep down, you have to admit you knew this day might
come! It's part of the HIGH PRICE of loving a married man.
However, it doesn't mean you're a failure, a "homewrecker,"
or any of those other names people used to throw at the
"other woman." As clinical psychologist Ella M. Bernstein of
Chicago told us, "Every 'failed' relationship has within it the
seeds of regeneration. Each is, or should be, a learning experience that will lead to a fuller understanding of ourselves and
our drives. Your life isn't over when a man leaves you. In a
sense, it's just BEGINNING again!"

The sun came speckled through the glass and she thought
vaguely, I ought to clean this window. Shadowed patterns fell
through the peperomia and pothos, warming her thighs under the
robe. She remembered how he used to pull it down over her
shoulders and pin her arms . . . she shifted uncomfortably.
She'd had her second shot yesterday . . .

She threw the magazine across the room and stood up and threw
the wineglass after it. She threw the pothos next. Its pottery weight
balanced in the air and then exploded in a scatter of leaves and dirt
against the wall, next to her workbench. Next to the shattered
agate, the chunks of silver that had been fashioned so lovingly for
him, now mere flattened masses, hammer-marred, battered out of
shape back to shapelessness.

She stood rigid, fingernails digging into her eyes. I don't want to
forget him, she thought desperately.

You can't have him. He doesn't want you anymore, someone inside
her head answered.

What can I do about it?

You can kill him.

She froze, horrified. Had *she* thought that? She didn't want to
kill anyone. Did she?

Hesitantly, like a woman considering a drastic makeover, she let
herself think it.

She found that she wanted his blood spilled on her carpet like
dirt. She wanted to make him beg her to take him back, and then
kill him. She remembered a movie about a woman who'd had an
affair with a married man. He'd jilted her. She'd kept calling him

up, then started threatening him, and at last murdered him with a butcher knife. She saw herself in violent fantasy, steel shining in her hand, plunging it again and again into his chest.

It was incredible, what she read in the magazines. Apparently men did this all the time. The advice columns were full of letters, no, screams of pain from women who'd been strung along for years by men with wives and families.

Oh, she thought, it's evil and it's wrong. How can they do that to other human beings? He'd said he loved her. Said when his wife got better he'd think about a divorce. But it was a lie. She wouldn't be surprised if the rest was lies too. What if his wife was fine, not mentally ill, if he was just . . . having her on the side, because he was bored?

She felt sick. She went to the bathroom and waited there on her knees. But nothing came up.

At last she got the dustpan and whisk broom. The pothos's pale-gleaming roots curled helplessly on the carpet. She remembered when she'd bought it, before she met him. She'd wanted something to brighten the apartment, something to take care of. And now she'd killed it. Well, maybe not. She repotted it as best she could, muttering apologies as she watered it and put in some Jobe's Spikes.

She wondered if she should go in to work. Saturday was a full day at the Shoppe. No, she couldn't go in now, with wine on her breath. Maybe that afternoon. If she felt better.

Jaysine, you have to do something, she told herself. You can't just sit around here reading magazines and swilling wine and thinking about killing him. That's useless. But that part of her that had answered her back wasn't listening. She sat in the window and looked down at the people plodding up and down the street, and found herself plotting ways she could get back at him.

She could find his car and slash the tires. Break the windshield. But where did he park? Downtown P.C., in front of his office, probably. But there were always people there. She could go to the house, the one he talked about, Cherry Hill. They'd probably have guards there, though. She remembered the black man at the office. All of the things she thought of were too dangerous. They were physical things, what a man would do. She wished she had some poison, in a ring, like that Italian princess.

She wished she could think of some way to really hurt him, as much as he'd hurt her. It didn't seem right that he should just walk away.

Maybe, she thought then, If he lied about his wife . . .

He'd never given her his home number. But it occurred to her now that she might have it. She'd gone through his overcoat the night before, after she came home. The one thing she could think to do was burn it, and she had. Taken it down to the alley and poured strawberry-scented lamp oil over it and watched till it was a smoking tissue in the snow.

But she hadn't burned the little book.

She slid open the drawer by the sink. It was under the potholders. She hadn't looked at it close, but it had his card in a pocket in the front, and yes, his home number too. Without pausing to think—if she did her voice would start shaking—she dialed. Waiting, she thought: What if he answers? Then she'd just hang up. She remembered the woman in the movie again and smiled. Doing that a few times might be fun.

"Cherry Hill. Who's calling?"

It sounded like the black man. She said as coolly as she could, "Mrs. Boulton, please."

"Who's this?"

"It's about her, her styling appointment."

She was congratulating herself on her quick-wittedness when the line clicked and a soft voice said, "Ainslee Thunner Boulton."

"Mrs. Boulton?"

"Yes, who's this?"

"You don't know me, but I know your husband."

Mrs. Boulton didn't answer immediately. Then she said, "Wasn't this about my tinting appointment? Are you calling from Anthony's?"

"No."

"Can you hold a moment?" There was a click on the line. Then she was back. "All right. Who is this?"

The soft voice was businesslike now. Jaysine thought then: This is no helpless madwoman. She almost hung up. Then she remembered how *he* had thrown her out of his office, how he'd infected her, and never even said he was sorry; and she said quick and short, "Mrs. Boulton, I'm your husband's mistress."

"I see. Have we met?"

"No. No, we haven't."

"Why are you calling me?"

"Why? . . . Well, to tell you that Brad's been, he's been having an affair with me. For a long time, almost a year."

"I see. Was that all?"

For a moment she couldn't respond. Had she really said that? Was she crazy after all? "Maybe you didn't understand me, Mrs. Boulton. I said your husband has another woman."

"Oh, I understood you perfectly. What I should have said at first was—when you said you were his mistress—I should have asked, 'Which one?'" Laughter tinkled on the line. "*Esprit de l'escalier,* the French call it—the comeback you think of after the party, going down the stairs. Was that all you needed to tell me? I was getting ready to swim, I swim for an hour each morning, then— Well. I don't imagine you care about that. I should tell you, though, that if he hasn't paid you, you're wasting your time calling me about it."

Jaysine closed her eyes. She was being forced farther than she wanted to go. "Yes. Wait. Yes, there was something else." Maybe the woman already knew. Obvious, perhaps, but it hadn't occurred to her before. I'm a little tipsy, she thought. But then again, maybe she didn't know. In that case she'd be doing her a favor.

"It's about—this disease he gave me. I just found out about it."

"A disease."

"Yes."

"Do you mind telling me the name of it? Or do you know yet?"

Jaysine told her.

"How perfectly awful for you, dear! But you must have known something like that might happen. If he'd cheat on me with you, odds are he'd fuck anybody else who offered, too. Don't you think?"

Jaysine hiccoughed suddenly. She couldn't think of anything smart to say back to that. She heard the static again.

"But you say he gave it to you? Recently?"

"Yes."

"You're quite sure?" The voice was interested now.

"Oh, yes, I'm sure. I haven't been with anyone else for, for over a year."

"I see." The line hummed as Jaysine poured herself another glass of Gallo. Let her chew on that, she thought viciously. That should light a fire under his home life.

"Would you care to testify to that?"

"I'm sorry?"

"I'd make it worth your time. Look, Miss, I don't know your name—"

Jaysine didn't say anything. Suddenly, unaccountably, she felt frightened. Maybe it hadn't been such a good idea to call from her own phone.

"Well, you don't want to say right now. I understand. I don't blame you for the other either, he can be a heartbreaker when he wants to.

"Let me put it this way. Brad and I haven't been intimate for some time. I suspected he's been having his little amours, but I didn't have any details. So I'm glad you called, Miss X." The laugh was like icicles falling on concrete. "How would you like to make some money?"

Jaysine wavered, the glass in her hand. She set it carefully on top of the refrigerator. "I don't think I understand."

"You don't? Really?"

"No."

"Well, don't be offended, dear, but Brad does tend to avoid women who challenge him intellectually. I'll spell it out. I'm considering a suit for divorce. I haven't decided yet if I'm going through with it, or when. But if you'd be willing to repeat what you've just said, we could recompense you for it. You wouldn't have to appear in court, nothing public. All you'd have to do is sign an affidavit. My attorney will meet you. This week, if you like. Anywhere you say."

"Oh, no. I don't think so," she said. "I mean, I couldn't do that. My mother lives here. I couldn't let people know that."

"We could keep your identity secret."

"I can't risk it."

"As I said, I can make it pay for you. What do you do for a living? Was it hair styling, you said? You can't make much money there. Surely you could use a little something extra?"

Jaysine felt sweat roll down her nose. Something evil was creeping through the telephone line, closer and closer to her.

"Hello?"

She hung up, rattled the receiver to make sure it was down, and backed away. Her hand, groping among the cereal boxes, almost knocked the wineglass to the floor. She held it in both hands and drank it down and refilled it. *God*, she thought, staring at the phone, and shaking. *My God*.

She wished now, too late, she'd never touched it.

She managed to go back to sleep till noon, then got up and heated a can of potato soup. She had a headache, but she felt stronger. Outside the window workers were putting up more decorations. It looked dangerous, high on a ladder with cars going by, and she watched while she spooned up the soup. When she was done she washed the bowl and then took down her old copy of *Science and Health*. She carried it to the couch and opened the worn soft pages at random.

> If you believe in and practice wrong knowingly, you can at once change your course and do right. Matter can make no opposition to right endeavors against sin and sickness, for matter is inert, mindless. Also, if you believe yourself diseased, you can alter this wrong belief and action without hindrance from the body.

She sat for a long time staring at the repotted plant. Wasn't this just what she'd done? Fallen away and sinned; believed in disease; and sure enough it had come to her. She closed the book and opened it again, and stared at the page.

> I am wholly dishonest, and no man knoweth it. I can cheat, lie, commit adultery, rob, murder, and I elude detection by smooth-tongued villainy. Animal in propensity, deceitful in sentiment, fraudulent in purpose, I mean to make my short span of life one gala day. What a nice thing is sin! How sin succeeds, where the good purpose waits!

She shivered. Did she know someone like that?

Seen in Science it was easy to know what to do. I should forgive him, she thought, then never see him again. I sinned, so I suffered. She saw it all clear when the book gave her the answers. Hatred and revenge were just new sins, and they didn't injure him. They only ate at her own heart.

She'd done wrong again in calling his wife, and in saying the name of a "disease" aloud. She closed her eyes, trying to pray for the first time in years.

But it was like talking into a phone with no one to accept the call.

The air outside was almost warm. She took a deep, thorough breath, losing herself in the antiseptic smell of melting snow. Unbuttoning her coat, she stepped carefully among piles of translucent slush. A little man in a coat longer than he was stood in front of the bank. He was always there, every day. He shuffled his feet as she approached and winked, as he winked at everyone who passed, his eyes secret and afraid. She looked away at first, then looked back and smiled at him. He smiled too.

On Pine Street the loudspeaker outside the Keynote was playing "God Rest Ye Merry, Gentlemen." She smiled again; it was time to start thinking of gifts. This year there was a new little baby to be auntie to, if only by mail.

The door of the Style Shoppe jingled shut behind her.

After her week away it looked dingy and crowded. She hung her coat and went down the aisle, through the close scented air, saying hello to the girls. Marguerite said, "Are you feeling better now, Jaysine?"

"Yes, thanks, a lot."

"We missed you."

"It's nice to be back," she said, and meant it; she was eager to get back to work. Making people beautiful, removing things they were ashamed of—that was good, that was helping in the work of the world. She remembered the dark girl, Karen. She'd made her appointments Saturdays at three, and it was almost three now. Jaysine opened the door to her cubicle and stopped.

Marybelle Acolino was sitting in the operator's chair, reading a book. She placed her finger in it to mark her place, then glanced up over her glasses.

"Why, if it isn't little Jaysine. Hello, dear."

"Hello, Marybelle."

"You're coming in to work?"

"Yes. I have a three o'clock. If you'll excuse me, I need to get cleaned up in here, get ready for her."

"Well, there's a problem with that, dear."

"What's that, Marybelle?" She was instantly on her guard. "There's no problem. I've been sick and now I'm back. You said we got ten sick days a year. I only used six so far."

Mrs. Acolino laid the book deliberately aside on the equipment stand. Jaysine saw the cover. It was her manual on the short-wave machine.

"The fact is, Jaysine, we got a call about you."

"What are you talking about?"

"Why, about what you were sick with. You know you never told any of us, dear, just exactly what it was."

She stood in the doorway, unable to wholly enter; she had a sense of not being wholly there. The shop was silent behind her. She heard herself say weakly, "I told you, it was a cold."

"Well. All I can say in response to that, Jaysine, is that's not what the doctor said it was."

"Doctor? What doctor?"

"I don't remember her name. The doctor from the hospital. But she felt that, since you were employed in a health-related profession, we should know as a matter of public responsibility. So we could take precautions." Mrs. Acolino pursed her lips. "I'm so sorry. But I know you'll understand, you always cared so highly for your clients' welfare."

"*What* are you talking about, Marybelle?"

"Why, just that we have to maintain our standards of sanitation, Jaysine, like anyplace that gives personal care. You can pay me the rest of what you owe on the renovations later. Till then, we'll just"—the older woman motioned at her machine, the magnifier on its movable arm, the chair, the needles and lotions and powders—"just keep these, as security. And of course we'll need them to continue helping our customers who desire hair removal services."

"You can't do that. Look, Marybelle, I'm not going to give anybody . . . anything, doing the electrolysis. You can't just . . . *take* my equipment."

Mrs. Acolino's look went iron. Her voice rose too. "Yes, dear, I understand that, but the fact is that once they know just what you have, they'll stop coming in at all. You know how people are about . . . *those* kinds of diseases. And you owe me money, dear. I put four hundred dollars into this fancy paneling and so forth in here. But your income hasn't covered that yet. So really I can't let these other things go out of the shop." She got up from the chair. "Do you want to see the accounts? I have them right in the back."

"I don't want to see the accounts! I want to keep working. You have no right to fire me!"

"I'm not firing you, dear, don't take it that way." Mrs. Acolino's eyes glittered behind her spectacles. "You've always been one of my favorite girls. But really, wouldn't it be better if you resigned? We can't have you infecting our customers, can we?"

For an endless second Jaysine fought an impulse to slap her. Instead she turned her head, and saw with sudden horror that everyone in the shop was listening. They were all, girls and customers, all staring at her. She switched her attention back to Marybelle, lowering her voice, though she knew it was too late. "You old . . . *witch*. You're not going to get away with this. Give me my paycheck."

"I'm holding that too," said the owner inexorably. "You want to call names, do you? I knew what you were from the minute you walked in here. You can shout all you want to, Miss Farmer, but we're on to you now. No party girl is going to work in my shop. And no cheap little tart is going to jew me out of what's mine."

"Give me my book. Give me my diplomas!"

"Oh, no, we'll have to keep those as long as you're still officially employed here. Trudi, Trudi can—"

"No!" she screamed then, shocking even herself. "No! All right, I quit!"

"What was that, Jaysine?" The shop owner cocked her head, eyes glittering like a raven's.

"I said I *quit!* Give me my things!" She snatched the book from the old woman, making her gasp, then reached for the diplomas. The cord behind one snapped and it came down off the wall, smashing down onto the rack of instruments. She snatched it up and turned for the front door.

It was a hundred miles away. She moved past chair after chair in the hot silent waiting, past eyes that followed her, the whispers beginning already in the rear of the shop when she was halfway to the door. Only Marguerite said in a low voice as she went by, "Give us a call, Jaysine."

She couldn't respond, couldn't speak. It felt like someone had her by the throat. The sunlit window ahead, the pale faces of the waiting customers wavered as if they were underwater. One of them was the dark girl, Karen. She stared at Jaysine in horror.

Jaysine found her coat and fumbled her arm into it. She dropped the book, picked it up. No one spoke at all.

She found herself in the street. The loudspeaker was playing "Good King Wenceslaus." It was December, but the air felt as warm as her tears.

Eighteen

Below Boulton the empty streets glistened like wet coal. Not a car moved; nothing moved the length of town. Above him the hills were just as still, slopes streaked with brown beneath the steady cold drizzle.

Sunday morning, he thought. They're crouched in their little churches, praying for their little souls, or home under the covers, waiting out the rain. The hunters snug in motels, recovering from a week of tramping the woods, no doubt cursing the steady erosion of their precious snow.

"Your turn," said Williamina, giving him an annoyed push. "Pay *attention*, Daddy."

"Sorry, Punkin." He swiveled from the window and leaned over the game. He was sorry now he'd bought the thing. It looked simpler than it was. Sixty-some little wooden blocks. First you piled them up into a tower two feet high. Then you started taking them away. The tower got shakier as its supports weakened. He selected a block near the bottom, poked it out and laid it aside. "Okay, kiddo, you're up."

While she studied it he leaned back in the Execuliner, tapping his pen against his teeth.

Behind them the office was empty; the whole building was shut down. The only lights that burned were here, in the suite of the president and chief executive officer. Brad liked to come in on Sundays. It was his time for reflection, the only opportunity he got to do long-term planning.

"There," the little girl said, triumph in her voice. He glanced at the tower, noted a sway to the left, and removed a block from the right, near the top.

Not that he felt much like planning at the moment. His mind kept going back to yesterday.

He'd come home after a liquid lunch to find Ainslee waiting for him like a hungry predator. He'd known from the first sentence out of her mouth what had happened. The Farmer cunt had done exactly what he'd told her not to. He couldn't get any details out of his wife, but that didn't surprise him. He'd find out what she knew only when she had the bag over his head and the wire around his throat.

He sighed and glanced at his watch. An hour till Patel arrived. He patted his pockets, wondering again where his notebook was. In the process his eyes met the flip chart. He looked at it for a time, then glanced at his daughter. She was still studying her next move, brow puckered intently. He got up, crossed to it, and flipped to the last graph.

The spinoff slide, showing the pyramidal structure Thunder would assume when it went public. Keystone HealthCare, Thunder Oil, Thunder Petroleum Specialties, First Raymondsville Financial Services, TBC Industrial Chemicals.

It occurred to him that there was room for another block. Perhaps he might restructure one of his current relationships, rather than terminating it.

He recalled an article he'd read in *Forbes* about hazardous waste disposal. Very few of the industries in the East had anywhere to dispose of the toxic byproducts of chemical manufacture, outdated stocks, medical wastes, and products withdrawn from the market. There wasn't any legal place to dump, or only a few very expensive ones, far to the south and west. That was why the people in New Jersey had stepped in.

A waste disposal company would fit beautifully within the Thunder Group. The local environment was ideal: rugged, distant, poor, with an aging, conservative population. The local chamber would give a party for Lucifer if he brought jobs with him. There'd be soreheads, but they could be dealt with.

As he'd dealt with the *Century*. Pulling ads hadn't worked, but he'd had a talk with Pete over martinis. Gerroy owned it, third generation. Owned WRVL too. Hadn't been a peep about myste-rious illnesses since. That suited him. They could scream as loud as they wanted after this stock sale. It would be a fait accompli then.

He realized his daughter was staring up at him, her eyes blue and innocent. "How you doing there, Punkin?" he said.

"Daddy, what are you thinking about?"

"Business, honey, just business."

"What's business?"

"Just . . . business. What I have to do so we can live in Cherry Hill, in a pretty house, and have nice things." He smiled tenderly at her puzzled expression.

"We don't *have* to," she said.

"What's that, Punkin?"

"I don't *want* to live there. We don't need a big house. I don't like Ainslee and she hates me. I'm scared of her. Daddy, let's *go away.*"

He chuckled and picked her up. "Sure, sure."

"Daddy, I mean it. Let's leave and go back to Pip-burg."

"Pip-burg! That's great. Go ahead, Punkin, move."

A sigh. "I already *did.* It's your turn, Daddy."

He set her down by the desk and studied the problem. The column was shaky now. It swayed perceptibly, all its weight bal-anced on one block near the bottom. He selected another near the top, began edging it out, but something went wrong. He tried to steady it, but the touch of his hand was too much. The tower twisted, tottered, broke, and fell apart, clattering across the pol-ished oak and bouncing on the carpet.

"Okay, Willie, that's enough. No, not again. You take them out front and play quiet, build yourself a play house, okay? Daddy's got to do some work this morning."

When she was gone, carrying the box with her, he pulled a file folder toward him. A few minutes later he took the computer out and called up a spreadsheet.

The doctor came in at eleven. Boulton got Willie bundled up and they went across the street for the buffet. He'd promised Patel a look at the new facility in Beaver Fork, and after brunch he packed his daughter and her doll into the back seat and the Indian in front. He pulled the Jag into the street, flicked on lights and wipers, and aimed it north, noting with mild amusement Patel trying to fit the seat belt around his paunch.

"By the way, thanks for taking care of my little . . . medical problem, Vinay."

"My pleasure, sir."

He glanced sideways at the little man. Patel was wearing the same cheap suit he'd had on at the interview. Brad realized he'd worn it the whole week he'd been in P.C.; it must be the extent of his business wardrobe. Hell, he thought, if I'd known that I'd have offered him less. But he only said, "Don't call me sir. Or boss. This is America, right? Just call me Brad."

"You are right, there," said the Indian, looking out the window at the speeding hills. "It does not look like India, that is for sure . . . maybe a little like Patna. But not very much like that either."

"Did you say your family was due up from Hampton Roads?"

"They shall be here tomorrow."

"Flying in?"

"No. No, we rented a truck. My brothers decided it would be less expensive to move our possessions ourselves."

"Your *brothers?* How many people you bringing up here, Vinay?"

"Eleven. My wife, my brothers and their wives, and our children. I have two daughters. One of them is about the same age as yours, as a matter of fact."

"That right?"

"Your daughter, she's beautiful. You must be very proud of her. And it is nice that you spend so much time with her."

"Well, thanks, but that's sort of temporary, we're short a nanny." Boulton cleared his throat, dismissing the subject of the Patel family. Below them as they climbed the refinery came into view, a maze of storage tanks, pipe stills, fractionating towers, condensers, percolators, holding tanks for finished fuels and lubes. Steam and smoke rose in lingering plumes, and above it all the flare-off flickered. Number One worked around the clock; letting those miles of pipe and equipment cool overnight, or over a weekend, would cost hundreds of thousands of dollars in fuels and repairs.

The valley dropped back and hid itself, and his mind moved on ahead. "Think you'll like the layout up at Beaver Fork."

"What kind of building is it?"

"An old mansion, built back in the boom days. Last time I was up the walls were ripped out and plumbing and wiring was going in. Should be pretty near complete by now. We're calling it Beaver Manor. It's already ninety percent booked."

"I look forward to seeing it."

Brad glanced into the back seat. Willie was playing with her doll, twisting its arms and singing to it. He couldn't make out the words. She wasn't listening to them, but just to be sure he found the Erie FM station and turned up the back speakers. He flicked Patel a man-to-man grin. "Only one thing: there's a girl out there I hired for food service, Gloria, don't get any ideas about her."

"Oh? I thought the woman who came up to see you, in your office—she looked very nice—"

"Who? Her? Well, I suppose you'd go for the well-padded ones, come to think of it. She's a loser, Vinny. Don't get mixed up with her."

When he glanced over again the Indian's head was going up and down, like one of those spring-necked toys he'd bought Willie when she just started crawling. He seemed awfully jolly. Well, he was probably looking forward to his family's arrival.

Family . . . he didn't like the way Ainslee was acting. She'd never taken to Williamina, but now she was actively hostile. He didn't like to think of the effect it was having on Willie. When he'd asked Ainslee to marry him he'd figured it would be good for the kid. Replace a crazy female role model with somebody strong. He wanted her strong, she'd have to take over after him and hold what he'd won. Ainslee was that, all right. She was the only woman he'd ever met who scared him.

But he couldn't let this latest flareup worry him too much. Ainslee needed him and they both knew it. Not in any personal way, that hadn't lasted long after the ceremony, but to save Thunder Oil.

But though he told himself this he still couldn't shake the worry. Ainslee kept talking about sending Willie away. He'd never do that, he'd see Ainslee and everything she owned in hell first, and she knew it. And other things too disquieted him, things that had come up at meetings of the board . . .

He came back to Route Six to find his knuckles pale on the wheel. They were climbing the long shoulder of Gerroy Hill; on its far side was Raymondsville. The speedometer needle trembled at 25. Practically parked ahead of them was a truck, the bed full of what looked like crushed glass. Cars kept coming toward him on the two-laner. He couldn't pass. He leaned on the horn, a long blast just for the hell of it.

"Do you mind if I smoke?" said Patel.

"No, but crack the window. Smell gets in the sheepskin."

"By the way, Brad, you were going to tell me what you expected of me for the extra income you mentioned."

He nodded, recalled now firmly to the road, the present, and the destination. He checked in back again, but Willie was still deep in her fantasies. "Uh huh. You remember what I said about running KHC as a profit center?"

"Yes."

"Okay." Ahead of them the truck's brakelights glowed for a railroad crossing; Boulton ticked up a finger from the wheel. "Number One. Our Medicare loading right now is seventy-three percent. That's guaranteed cash flow, there's no place else they can stack 'em.

"So I want you to concentrate on the private bodies. Remember, they always get wheeled out for visitors. Don't let outsiders back of the desk. The ones out of their minds, we've got them double-bunked and the family thinks they're in private rooms.

"Number two, I don't know if you've run into this angle in the VA, but Medicare pays us according to what they call a DRG— diagnosis related group. No one goes into a KHC facility without a diagnosis. I'll get you a copy of the disease/reimbursement schedule so you can act accordingly."

"All right."

"Along with that, we've got deals with some professionals around the area. There's a diet therapist, a chiropractor, an acupuncture guy—you'll like Chao—and this real weird lady shrink who does a biofeedback thing. Anytime you refer a patient to them instead of the local AMA twenty percent of the billing comes back to us."

"How much of this is mine?"

"Half."

"Okay."

Boulton saw an opening. The Jag accelerated smoothly, pressing them back in the seats, and he gave the truck driver the finger as he passed. At eighty he cut back in just in time to avoid a van. "Okay . . . next, we all know that despite our best efforts people die in nursing homes. I'll give you a number to call before you release the news to the family. The bodies go direct to Ron Whitecar's. Ron shoots us back ten percent of gross. His dad Charlie's county coroner, so if we scratch their backs that covers our butts on questionable death certs. Understand?"

"Sure."

"Next, I want you to liaison every week with Mrs. Suder, our accounts receivable person. We don't carry dead meat. If a resident can't pay, their insurance coverage is exhausted or their family's past due, dump 'em to the public hospital. Put makeup on them and ship them out."

Patel nodded.

"Now, we can make money in the facility pharmacies, but we've got a fairly tough state code here. I want you to keep the controlled substances books yourself."

"How do we shave it?"

"Couple ways. First, I've got a guy in New York who ships us expired pharmaceuticals from the city hospitals there. They write it off as destroyed. We use it and bill it as new."

"Who thought of that?" said Dr. Patel, lighting another Benson & Hedges.

"I did."

"Very nice."

"Thanks . . . oh, hell."

The rain came. It lashed suddenly against the windscreen, a storm, a deluge. Drops shattered and danced on the hood, and the wipers flailed like birds pinned against the glass. The car bored steadily through, steel and leather muting the water's roar. Boulton hardly raised his voice. "Well, I guess that's about it . . . Oh, yeah, while we're on the subject. Once money loosens up, I'm thinking of putting in a hospice unit for the county. That'll get us PR points for social responsibility. Plus, the government's loosening up on some of the hard stuff for terminal patients. Figure an angle on how we can work with that. I know people, can sell whatever we can supply."

Patel inclined his head to the window. The slipstream sucked smoke from between his lips. The road began to climb. As they entered the woods the rain slacked off. After two miles he cleared his throat. "I understand that, and I can do it, Brad. But, do you mind if I ask you something?"

"Shoot."

"I need to know, I suppose you would say, where to stop."

"Stop what?"

"I am not saying I would not do something because it is wrong. I suppose that is bad karma . . . whatever." Patel shrugged. "But I work for you now. You tell me what I do. What should I not do?"

"Let's let the legal system define that, Vinny."

"The legal system?"

"That's right. Why are we in business? To make money, for our stockholders and ourselves. I don't recognize any other limitations on that than the legal system. You play by any other book, you're handicapping yourself, and a sharper operator will cut you down.

"Now, we got to pay these staff shysters anyway, why not use them to cover our butts? We comply with legal minimum requirements. Except, of course, when they're not enforced."

"And you are saying, in that case, what?"

Brad turned his head. The doctor was passive in his seat, looking down at the empty hollows, packed with fog like pill wadding, that stretched off into the hills. "Don't get sanctimonious on me, Jack. I don't respond well to that."

"Believe me, I had no thought of that, Brad. I just wanted to know if you would back me in any questionable situations with my patients."

"You want to know what I think of your patients? They're a profit opportunity. If we don't take their money somebody else will. I think of them as no different than I think of myself."

"How is that?"

"People are scum. All of them—us too. Only we're riding in a Jag while they're pissing in their sheets. If they were in my place they'd do exactly the same. Now, I hired you with the idea you share that view. Do you or don't you?"

"Yes, sir, I do."

"Then we're partners. And in that case yes, I'll back you, a thousand percent."

Boulton downshifted. The car wound through patches of forest, curving down the long grade that brought Route 49 out of the hills to the Beaver Valley. Trees leaned over them; caught in their branches like Spanish moss, the fog trembled above the polished black glass of the road. Instead of slowing he flipped his lights to amber and held his speed.

"No, Vinny, I can't afford to get sentimental. Not now, with things coming up to crunch point.

"Maybe it sounds heartless, or cold-blooded, what I'm telling you. Well, I've been called that before. Doesn't bother me a bit. What I'm doing will help, down the line, everybody who lives in this county. It'll bring in money and jobs. That's not why I'm doing it, but that'll be the end result.

"So I'll tell you right now what makes Brad Boulton run. If push comes to shove I'll sell you, I'll sell myself, I'll sacrifice anything to keep Thunder Oil afloat. That's what I'm drawing my pay for and that's what I'm going to do."

Patel did not respond or answer. The world glowed orange as fog clamped suddenly down, dropped from the trees. Two silent men and a child engrossed in play hurtled in their metal shell through a world created moment by moment from nothing, and that was sucked back into nothing, into whirling mist and rain again, behind the speeding car.

Nineteen

The rain fell invisibly from darkness into darkness, less water passing through air than a fog-sewn mist, trapped and floating between black velvet hills.

Phil hunched shuddering at the edge of the road. Above him a cheap poly tarp snapped in the wind. Occasionally, when it gathered enough water, it suddenly purged itself into the ground beside him. Below him a blanket oozed when he shifted his weight. Behind him was the forest, invisible, but alive with the drip and patter of a million raindrops through a million pine needles; and ahead of him, also dark except for a far-off glimmer from the Kendall station at the crest of the hill, was Route Six.

The main road through Hemlock County was two lanes of asphalt, not in good repair. Frost heaves took their toll every year, and the trucks that hauled out coal, stone, oil, lumber took theirs too. The Blue Star Highway meshed with the Allegheny's writhe like an ardent eel for seventy miles traversing the forty miles from east to west. The state legislature had postponed improving it for more years than Phil had lived. So it carried traffic all winter and was plowed, and then all summer and was patched, over and over until the patches were patched, and the county crews had repaired the same potholes so often they'd given them names.

He pulled his jacket tighter and wiggled his fingers. Since his talk with Halvorsen they'd stood watch here all through the night. He, Phil, was on from sundown to midnight. When the hands of his Timex pointed toward the treetops the old man would come swinging out of the darkness. They'd nod to each other and turn over the things—the flashlight and the pad and the shampoo bottle he'd scarfed from his sister's beauty junk—and then he'd climb back on his three-speed and head for home, geared down for the hill, but after that coasting the next three miles clear into town.

Tonight was their third night on guard. At first it'd been kind of exciting, like the late shows, where the hero was radioing in the position of the tank column. But now he was wet as well as freezing. Missing half his sleep was starting to get to him. Nor was he getting any homework done.

But he didn't mind. After what he'd nearly done up above Paradise—well, getting a C in chem didn't seem real earth-shaking anymore.

Headlights showed far at the end of the road. He waited, looking to the side so he wouldn't be dazzled. They came on fast and low and he made it as a car. Halvorsen said they didn't have to worry about cars, but Phil lifted the binoculars, old German things the old man had dragged out of some corner of his basement, just to make sure.

It hummed past and dwindled up the hill. He yawned, looking down at the yellow pad. Fifteen trucks so far tonight. Sunday night there'd only been five. Yeah, things picked up on weeknights. But nothing you'd call suspicious.

He sat in the rain and yawned again, hugely, and snapped his mouth shut like a weary dog.

Lights came up the road. Repair truck, Penelec, license Pennsylvania ALA–216. He took off his glove to log it and shivered again, this time so deeply his teeth clattered.

He didn't feel different, though. Which was funny. In school he said hello to the kids he knew and they said hello to him. Alex smiled at him once; he'd looked away. Detrick and his gang ignored him, as if their encounter on the far side of the border had erased his existence.

And he himself, that complex assemblage of molecules that thought it thought, sat shivering and alone, thinking:

I ought to be dead.

In the midst of night he lifted his hand before his eyes and saw nothing. Was this what they saw, the dead? Or did they wander the earth, like in that book by Aldous Huxley . . . No. Death was nothingness.

He looked at his watch for about the fiftieth time. The flashlight was getting dim. He wished he'd brought something hot, cocoa or something. But he'd had enough trouble getting out of the house. He'd padded the bed, the old dummy-sleeper trick, and snuck out the back door while his mom and dad were watching TV. They seemed to be getting along better, anyway. He figured it was his dad's promotion.

Headlights gnawed anew at the rain. He made it as another car. The lights dipped and swayed, first right, then left, lighting the dripping branches above his head. Suddenly they died, into ruddy sparks, into blackness. The car rolled off onto the berm and stopped.

The dome light came on. The driver sat there for a while, too far away for Phil to see much of him. Finally he got out. The light went out and the hollow slam of the door bounced off wet tree trunks.

Another roadside whizzer. Why did they all pick that spot, fifty yards up the road from him? Probably the same reason he was there: you could see a long ways both up and down the road. So people's headlights wouldn't catch them with their dick in their hand.

He sat and listened to the motor idling, an uneasy murmur beneath the cat's-feet patter of rain. After a while there was another *thunk*. The lights came on and accelerated up the hill toward town.

Romanelli shifted on the blanket as his mind went back to his interrupted death. What did it mean? That he'd been given a kind of reprieve?

Because he'd been ready to do it. His finger had been tightening on the trigger. He'd wanted it to end. But then old Halvorsen had showed up, just when out of all his life he'd needed somebody most.

Of course it was coincidence, but still he had a weird feeling of being somehow redevoted. Born again, though not into anything religious. The old man was right. No wonder, he'd been through some shit too. If they wouldn't leave you alone you had to fight back. His life, renounced, forfeited, was devoted now to a Cause.

A new set of lights. He was reaching for the binoculars again when the grinding clatter of gears changing down and then a hiss told him it was heavy, and it was slowing, just as the car had done.

A sixteen-wheel whizzer. He grinned sardonically in the dark-

ness and raised the binoculars. He noted the number, then sat
waiting for the truck to start up again.

A flashlight vanished and reappeared, swinging over the road
around the back wheels. A black outline knelt, flicked the yellow
circle over the axles. Diesels grumbled. Checking his tires, Phil
thought. The shape stood, the light went off. Then came on again,
just for a moment, showing him a gloved hand turning a valve.

He stopped breathing, steadying the binoculars.

The light moved forward, up to the cab, and went out. A door
slammed. Then the motor bellowed, gears meshed, brakes hissed
off. The headlights came on full bright and the tanker eased out
onto the pavement, clumsily positioning itself for the pull up the
hill.

The binoculars thudded onto the blanket. Two quick steps,
hardly enough time to limp, and he snatched his Ross off where it
was propped against a pine. His tires ground on gravel and then
sizzled, gaining speed, over wet asphalt.

Fifty yards ahead the tank truck, rumbling into the first rise of
the hill, shifted gears. He pushed hard, standing on the pedals.
Going to be close, catching up before it hit its pace. But the hill
would help. He slacked for a moment, then steadied again, aiming
between the taillights. Then thought, No, the valve's there, my tires
will be going right over the stuff coming out; if it's slick . . . he
bore left, just behind the taillight.

A gust of rainsoaked wind hit him as they emerged from the
shelter of the woods, rocking him, peeling scarlet-lit veils of spray
off the curved hull ahead. He bent his head, blinking, and drove
on. The first pain shot through his hip. His open mouth sucked
exhaust. The tires whined in his ears. They were beginning to kick
up spray. The running lights, ringed with blurry haloes, showed
him swaying mudguards decorated with girlie cutouts and there,
right above the yellow Pennsylvania plate, a black thread coming
down. Coming out slow, like a half-cracked kitchen faucet. But
drive for a few hours, through woods, back roads, up hollows . . .
that would empty it. Sure.

The vehicle ahead shifted and so did he. They were hitting the
grade now. The gear-change slowed him but not as much as it did
the truck, and he put everything into a last sprint. The final ten
yards narrowed to one, and he grabbed for the big pressed-steel
fender.

He missed, wobbled, dropped back into the spray. He gnashed
his teeth in the roar of tires, pedaling savagely, and closed again

inch by inch till he could make a second and, he knew, last lunge forward.

His hand closed on gritty steel. Beneath him huge tires whined in the dim light. The stack snorted and roared above him. His milling feet slowed, then relaxed as the truck, and his extended arm, took up the drag.

Now, too late, he realized he'd need two hands for this job. One to hold on, and one to manipulate the bottle. Instead he leaned forward. His chest on the handlebars locked the front wheel, and his chin hooked painfully over the fender. He fumbled at his jacket, then extended his arm.

This close he could see it clearly. Black, heavy, curling and drooling downward as its viscosity varied. His hand entered it. Warm and slick, like a heated bath oil. He could smell it too, under the odors of exhaust and rubber, rain and pine woods.

No time to analyze. He flipped up the bottle top and jammed the plastic rim right up under the valve. Held it there till his head felt like it was coming off, then let go the fender.

The bike wobbled wildly. He almost lost it, but managed to straighten. He dropped back, losing speed against the uphill, snapped the cap down and thrust the bottle into his jacket. The truck was drawing ahead steadily when he realized that all this time his generator-powered headlight had been on. Whoever was driving the tanker, if he happened to glance into the rear-view—

A rushing hiss came from ahead and the truck slowed, too suddenly for him to react. The bike slammed steel, then went down so hard it threw sparks. His knees slammed into asphalt. He went down too, too fast to think, except that his hand snagged the fender, and that was all, probably, that saved him from going right on under the wheels after the Ross.

The truck dragged him about seventy feet. When it stopped he let go and lay there on the cold roadway, face down.

"What the *hell* ya think you're doing?"

He didn't look up, just kept trying to breathe through the pain and shock. Hard hands grabbed his jacket. They stood him, whirled him, and slammed him against metal. His bike lay like a stepped-on insect some yards down the hill.

"I *said*, what ya think ya doing, ya little asshole?"

Phil mumbled, "Just hitchin' a ride."

"What?"

"Goin' home . . . it's late."

"How long you been back there?"

"Take it easy, Mister. I just come around the bend. Saw you goin' up the hill. Thought I'd catch me a free ride."

The big pale face swung back; hard small eyes studied him out of it. Doubt and rage struggled in them for a moment. "Fucking kids . . . well, can't say I ain't done it myself. But god damn it, I hope this teaches you it's dangerous."

He nodded.

"You walk?"

He nodded.

"Get outta here."

He stumbled away as the teamster swaggered back to his cab. The truck fired up, then resumed its caterpillar climb. The tail-lights shrank to mist-smeared pinpoints, hung for a moment at the crest of the hill, then disappeared.

He tried a step, then another, and so crossed the road. His knees were scraped raw, hurt like hell, but he didn't think the damage was serious. Bending to the bike, he dragged it off the paving. He suddenly remembered the bottle and grabbed for his pocket. It was dented, but the plastic popped out again. The cap was secure.

Holy shit, he thought in dawning wonder. I did it. I got some!

He looked at his watch. In fifteen minutes the old man would be there. Limping, exultant, he moved toward the trees.

Halvorsen showed at midnight, striding down stiffly from the Run. He built a fire, examined Phil's legs, then wiped his hand off thoroughly with wet leaves. He gave Phil his down bag. When first light came they struck camp. They dragged the tarp, their wet gear, and the mangled bike back out of sight from the road.

They stood on the berm together in the drizzle, thumbs turned out in the dawn. At last a pair of middle-aged men in a Wagoneer pulled over. They looked curiously at the man and boy, but mentioned only the wretchedness of the weather.

They got out at the foot of Maple Street and hiked up to the hospital together. Neither of them spoke. At the desk Halvorsen asked for Dr. Friedman.

"She's not in yet," said the fat lady.

"Well, look, Doris, we need to see her—"

She frowned and extended her lower lip. "Do I know you?"

"Why, ain't you Doris Wiesel? Judge Bob's daughter?"

"It's Doris Hull now, but that's me. And—wait a minute—I know who you are!"

They began talking. Phil stared at the walls. He examined a colored print of some doctor scraping something off a cow. Next to it was one of a guy in a bow tie cutting somebody's tongue off. When the conversation got around to modern times he drifted back. The fat lady was saying, "Yes, sure, I'll let her know. And where will you be? Sure, Racks, I'll call you there as soon as she comes in."

They went out onto the street again. Phil looked at Halvorsen, shivering. Didn't the old man tire, didn't he feel cold, or hunger, or the rain? He didn't move fast but he never seemed to stop for long.

"Well, guess we got to wait around. Doris'll call me when she comes in. You look like you're ready for some breakfast, get warmed up a little?"

"Sounds good. Where do you want to go?"

"Well, I told her we'd be over to Mama DeLucci's."

"Okay."

The restaurant had five stools in front of a dark wooden counter. The deep fat fryers were caked with carbonized grease and so was the overhead fan. The two women behind the counter were both ancient, dark, and thin, with the same black hair-nets and identical noses. They greeted Halvorsen with shrieks. Phil smiled derisively. He'd seen Mama's from the street a dozen times, the old folks huddled in the steamy heat like tropical flowers, but he'd never come in; no more than one of them, probably, would go into the Pizza Den. But now he realized he didn't feel self-conscious, the way he would have before. He didn't care anymore if his classmates saw him sitting here, eating hash browns and bacon in the window opposite old Racks, in his boots and suspenders and his crazy-looking hat, with no one there under sixty.

"So which one is Mama?" he asked Halvorsen.

"What's that?"

"I said, which one of them is Mama?"

"Oh. No, the old lady, she died when I was a kid. These are her daughters." Halvorsen mopped at a yellow run of egg with a triangle of toasted Sunbeam. "They was some lookers once, believe it or not . . . So, ain't it time for you to be gettin' to school?"

"Not today. You and me, we got things to do, right?"

"What time you supposed to be there?"

"Oh . . . eight."

"Finish your breakfast. Then you can head on over."

Phil thought, Well, guess I go to school today.

"What you grinning at, boy?"

"Nothing."

He reached for his pocket, but the old man said, sounding angry, "I got it. I got three bucks left out of my nickel jar, and I'll stop in the post office today, pick up my check. You just go on."

When the boy left, Halvorsen unbuttoned his shirt and sat back. The smells of onion and garlic opened up his head, and he blew his nose deliberately in a paper napkin, one nostril at a time. Skipping school . . . Kids nowadays had no idea what it was like breaking your back with a shovel. He'd done without an education, but the world wasn't what it was in his day. Maria came over and he counted her out the coins and asked for a refill. As it steamed in front of him he stared out at the street. Rain, rain . . . this was exactly the weather he'd choose if he was dumping waste oil on the roads.

He remembered dumping things. Hadn't been no environmental protection when he worked in the fields.

He sat in the heated air, warming his hands around the heavy mug, and remembered how it was, in the winter, back then.

At fourteen he'd been full time on Don Ekdahl's lease on Portage Creek. In those days you were on the job at seven, sunup or not, whether you had to ride or walk or crawl. In the icy dark the men would set about getting ready for the day's operations. With guttering torches, rags wrapped on sticks and dipped in the crude, they'd begin thawing out the rod lines to the jacks. And he remembered, so many long years before that it seemed like a previous life, building the fire under the storage tank, scraps of wood, oil-soaked batting, whatever offered, to gently heat the inflammable crude to the seventy degrees it needed to flow . . .

He remembered when there was a hole at every well, and if you got paraffin out of the settling tank you dumped it into the hole. And there was a man come around with a horse and wagon and picked it up. Then later they didn't want it, but the gaugers wouldn't pump your oil unless the tank was clean on the bottom, so you had to climb down and shovel it out.

No, there was no such of a thing then as an environment, he thought. The paraffin and scum and dirt went down the hill and like as not right into the creek, just like everything else: used acid, salt water, washout water, and a good lot of crude too, and it didn't make no difference, nobody cared. The oil came out of the ground mixed with natural gas but they just let that evaporate, or it howled out of the well pure and colorless and they flared it or just blew it away in the air. In the woods the seepage from the wells and separator pits made the ground marshy and foul as a pigyard. And they built the refineries on the creeks so they could dump what they didn't want.

So in those days Whitecar Creek, and Falkiner Creek, and Todds and Cook and the Allegheny too were all covered inches thick with chocolate scum. It lay on the flat shale banks when the river fell and stank. Sometimes someone would burn it off, or it would catch fire on its own, and burn for days, sending a black cloud up behind the hills. Downstream of the refineries the rocks shone with bizarre colors, purplish red, silver, brass, weird metallic greens. The air was sweet with the oily tang of crude petroleum. It was a smell W. T. Halvorsen had always liked. It meant home.

He thought, But the woods was so big then. Oil was down in the ground; you brought it up on top, that was all, and if you didn't need something you threw it away and there was room for it, didn't seem to matter much whether you tossed it in the creek or burned it off into the clear sky. So much room. The world itself was bigger, seemed like.

Yeah, he thought then, but crude never hurt nobody. He remembered his mother rubbing it into his cropped scalp when he got lice. Some people drank it, hell, that was all mineral oil was. It didn't do the bushes much good when it got on them but the next year they were back same as before. Never hurt no deer, no animals. Course, the fish in the streams, yeah. Anybody who fished in Hemlock County in those days was crazy.

But this stuff in this little bottle was different. The doctor said it'd kill you. Give you cancer. Make women miscarry or worse. No, this was new, to the earth unnatural, to his mind monstrous.

But we shouldn't of done the other either, he thought. It was just like Mase Wilson losing his arm. In those days nobody made you put guards on bandsaws. So nobody did. It was pure ignorance, that and people crazy mad to make the money.

Probably the same reason those midnight trucks were rumbling through the county, too. Root of it didn't change, anyway.

Maria came by. "Phone for you in back."

"Thanks."

It was the woman doctor. She listened silently to his explanation, and said, "Come on over. I'll be in my office."

• • •

Friedman's office was on the second floor, down a part of the hospital he hadn't seen before. Young people in green cotton eyed him curiously. He rapped at the door of 233. When she looked up from a littered desk she smiled, looking tired already, though it was only nine in the morning.

"Our escapee returns. Come on in."

"Thanks."

"You gave me a scare, Mr. Halvorsen. But if you were in good enough shape to walk out, I guess it wasn't my place to keep you here."

He didn't say anything. She went on, "Anyway, you left this. Here it is. With both dollars still in it. And—oh—your watch."

He accepted his belongings gravely. "You mind if I close this here door?"

She nodded, and they sat. Halvorsen fumbled in his coat, then produced the bottle. He centered it on her desk. After a moment she flipped it open and waved a hand over it, pushing the smell toward her nose.

"Whoo. Some kind of aromatics in there."

"Powerful, ain't it?"

"The boy got this off a truck? Whose?"

"Tank truck," said Halvorsen. He leaned his chair back and glanced at the door again. "He couldn't see who owned it. Too dark, too rainy. But he got a tag number."

Dr. Friedman raised one eyebrow. He let his eyes dwell on her face as she poured some of it out into a little glass. Cool now—it must have been going through a heater before the valve—it was gelatinous. Dark, but when the light hit it right green tints gleamed. Its smell seeped into the room. A petroleum smell at first. He could pick out the heavy fraction, like a heating oil. Then a tang like acetone, but beyond that something else.

He'd smelled indigo once. This was something like it: a honeyed reek that warned you not to come too close; that here was something you might like too much for your own good. A smell like the smile of a whore.

He asked her, "Well, what you think it is?"

"No idea. But give the lab people an hour or so and I should be able to tell you pretty accurately." She crossed to a file cabinet and slid out a paper. "Meanwhile you can start on this."

"What is it?"

"A reporting form."

Halvorsen laced his fingers over his stomach. "I guess you better do that. I've got about as far into this as I want to go, Doc."

"What? Why? Are you afraid?"

"That ain't it. I just don't care to get caught up in all this stuff."

"Whoever's dumping this almost killed you, Mr. Halvorsen. Do you want them to keep on? Maybe kill a child?"

"Well, no."

"Then I recommend you report it. *I* can't; I don't know where it came from. I didn't see your sample taken. And they'll need your assistance to track it down. I'll help, Racks, and the hospital will too. But eventually somebody's got to put his name on the dotted line."

Halvorsen looked at her for a while. At last his hand dipped into his pants. He fitted the glasses slowly to his face, slipping the wire rims over one ear at a time. "All right," he said. "You got you a ink pen?"

He was sitting there still, thinking about a chew, when she came back. "Jackpot," she said.

"How's that?"

Friedman picked up his form, clipped a printout to it, and tossed them into a wire basket. "EDB, PBB, vinyl chloride and chlordane; trace mercury, cadmium, arsenic; all in a heavy base, maybe used motor oil. The boys tell me it'd burn in an oil furnace."

Halvorsen nodded. He unhooked his glasses. "So what do I do now?"

"Not a thing," she said. "I'll fax this in to the proper people. They may want to call—I mean, go out and see you, to follow this up. You might want to stay close to home. I have a feeling things will move fast once they read this analysis. But basically you've done your duty as a citizen, and I for one thank you."

"And the boy. I put him in the write-up too."

"Yes, him too." Friedman smiled and stood up. "By the way, your face looks better."

"Thanks," said the old man. He had risen too, when she did, but when he got to the door he paused and turned. "That reminds me. How much I owe you? For the hospital?"

"Don't worry about it."

"Don't worry about it?"

"Don't worry about it."

"I don't take charity."

"This isn't charity."

"It isn't?"

"No."

Halvorsen stood in the doorway for a moment more. But he couldn't think of anything else to say. So he put on his hat and went out again, back into the rain.

Twenty

T he old Thunner mansion stood alone above the town among massive oaks, granite-solid on what had once been a forest bench and was now terraced lawn. Buttresses of yellow light streamed from its windows, footed on the soaked grass. Through each golden slant darted the rain.

It was built in Gothic Romanesque of an intricately carved local stone. Two-storied, but a turret reached to four, and the clustered columns of a huge porch gave the effect of an arcade. Behind beveled glass and falls of damask, shadows moved, pausing now and then to lift glasses, to talk. Music came faintly across the lawn, but died in the misty air before it reached a spike-topped wall.

Boulton stood at the window of the garden room, looking out. Security lighting picked out the walks and cold frames. Past that was the dim bulk of the arbor, and the pale glow of the fountain Colonel Charles Thunner had imported from Chioggia. But beyond and above them was only the blackness of the hill, bare at first, then forest.

He was remembering how three years before his father-in-law, still walking then, had taken him to the mountain. Not far above them was the long-abandoned site of the first producing well in the Seneca Sands, drilled in 1869 by the legendary Beacham B. Thunner and his hunchbacked partner Napoleon O'Connor at the very outset of the company's history. Back then it was the Sinnemahon-ing Seneca-Oil Company. After O'Connor was killed in 1874 in a boiler explosion, it became Thunner Sinnemahoning; then Thun-der Sinnemahoning; then, and for the last hundred years, just the Thunder Oil Company. Old Dan, leaning on Lark Jones's arm, had stood for a long time silent, looking out over valley and hills and the distant towers of Number One, before he'd said: "So you want to marry Ainslee."

He took an icy swallow of martini and turned back into the house.

In the study the quartet was finishing the last movement of Pachelbel's "Spring." Violin and bass viol penetrated century-old stone and timber like incense. Fires crackled in the bar, the living room, the dining room, the upstairs den. In the foyer hung steel engravings and oil portraits of Beacham Berwick Thunner, Colo-nel and Mrs. Charles Thunner, and Dan and Lutetia Thunner; the latest was of Ainslee, aged ten. In the dining room was a Bronzino portrait, a small Jean Clouet, and a Correggio Amazon.

Above, in the master bedroom, his wife lay under the valances with an arm over her eyes.

In the bar Dr. Patel, Peter Gerroy, and his third wife, Melizabeth, were listening to Vince Barnett, chairman of the Recreation Asso-ciation, tell fishing stories. In the billiard room, where Charles's massive slate table had once stood, three people in their early twenties—sons and daughters of the older guests—were gaping up at the head of an African elephant. In the oak-paneled dining room, imported from a Tudor manor house in Kent, Rudolf Weyandt, Charlie Whitecar, and a Deep Pit businessman who was a member of the State Ethics Commission were discussing capital gains taxes with a real-estate woman and a young Frenchwoman visiting from Paris.

And rising now from their folding chairs in the study were the chamber group, from the University of Pittsburgh at Petroleum City, and the rest of the evening's guests, including Dr. Kopcik, Mayor White, several university department chairmen, the chair-man of First Raymondsville Bank, Rogers McGehee, a former county Republican Party chairman, a visiting Episcopal bishop, the presidents or their representatives from most of the local manu-facturing firms, and most of the other people worth saying one knew in Hemlock County.

As they moved past him into the dining hall Brad shook hands, inviting them to help themselves to after-dinner liqueurs, desserts and coffees, or to refresh themselves at the bar. He waved the mayor aside and told him smilingly that if he didn't want to cause a divorce he'd have to take his cigar into the garden room. White guffawed and headed for the rear of the house, trailing a tangible aroma.

He ran his eye over the fireplaces, the bar, the catered tables, the stolid women who stood behind them. Everything looked fine. Still he wished Ainslee was here. This was his third pre-Christmas party at The Sands, a traditional occasion for opening the house in town to a wider hospitality than the family's, but he still didn't feel entirely used to it, entirely at ease.

He chatted for a while with the banker and then some of the board members' wives, then made a leisurely orbit through the house. The barman, borrowed from the club, was doing a brisk business. The French girl was playing Gershwin on the Steinway. Through the window, out on the lawn, he glimpsed the silver-sewn arc of the security guard's flashlight. He put his head in the kitchen; the cooks and servers were having their own late dinner.

He'd decided to have another martini when a round thirtyish man put his hand on his arm and said, "Jack asked me to tell you, he's sorry he couldn't make it. He hopes he can next year, but with the tax vote coming up, he wanted to stay close to first base."

Brad nodded and smiled; DeSilva was Jack Mulholland's chief of staff. "Well, I'm glad you could come, Andy."

He started to move away, gin still foremost in his mind, but the aide touched his arm again. "Got somebody I want you to meet. Took the liberty of bringing him along."

"Sure, hell, more the merrier. Who is it?"

"Name's Nicholas Leiter. He's from the executive side"— DeSilva winked—"but he keeps in touch. Nick! C'mon over. Here he is, right here."

Leiter was slim, young or young-looking. Brad thought it couldn't all be the round tortoiseshell glasses and bow tie. They shook hands warmly.

"Well, what brings you to P.C., Mr. Leiter?"

"I thought we might talk for a minute."

"Oh?"

"Mr. Leiter's from one of our alphabet-soup federal agencies," said DeSilva, tapping his foot as the piano segued to the "Maple Leaf Rag." "He just got in from Philly. Gave Jack a call before he arrived. Professional courtesy."

"I see." He thought about that. "Looks like you could use a refill, my friend. Join me?"

"I'm okay," said Leiter, examining his glass and then raising his eyes quizzically.

"Well . . . let's go up to the den."

He'd had the turret room redecorated the year before. There was a fireplace there now and a small bar by the curved window that looked down on the terrace and the garden. The walls were covered in aubergine suede. He'd left Dan's pictures, though: wildlife and Western studies by Charles Deas, Stanley, Remington, and Russell. He hitched up his slacks and sat on the corner of the desk, nodded to a wing chair. "Grab a seat. What can I do for you, Mr. Leiter?"

"I thought I'd ask you that." The young man took out a pipe. "You mind?"

"Go ahead," said Brad, watching him.

Leiter began stuffing the pipe; he touched the tobacco only with the tips of his fingers. "Mr. Boulton, I work for the Environmental Protection Agency."

"Is that so," Brad said after a moment.

"Yes. It's like this. We got a report that hazardous wastes are being dumped in this county. Not just once, appears there've been several instances. It might be an ongoing operation. We've seen the profile before. Often there's mob involvement."

"What kind of wastes?"

Leiter shot a glance up at him and said, a trifle louder, "Hazardous chemicals." He lit the pipe, waving the lighter over the bowl.

"Go on."

"I'm not a regular investigator. The agency's shorthanded. As usual. Anyway, on the flight up I happened to think of Andy. So I called him from the airport."

"DeSilva's a good man. Where do you know him from?"

"Friend of a friend. He suggested I stop in and see the Thunners. So I went over to your estate this afternoon to talk to your father."

"Father-in-law, actually."

"Uh huh. But your butler, or whoever he is, told me he wasn't in charge anymore. That you are. So I called Andy back and he laughed and said I was at the wrong house, that you had two places, and you'd be at this one today. He said to come over here and he'd introduce me."

He'd been wanting that drink more and more and now he

crossed to the bar and poured a brandy. He listened to the distant piano. Below, in the garden, a flashlight came on, probed around, and went out. He said, keeping his voice casual, "You said something about having a question."

"Well, I'll make this brief, Mr. Thunner—"

"Boulton."

"Sorry. Mr. Boulton. Somebody's dumping waste on the roads up here. We've got a chemical analysis by a reputable source. Evil stuff, all right. It's apparently affected some of the local residents. Now, as I said, we've seen midnight dumping before. And dealt with it. The director regards it seriously. She's just put two men away in Georgia. They bought a warehouse, piled five thousand drums of banned pesticides, hexane, and paint sludge in it, and set it on fire. Fifteen years each."

"What's that got to do with me?"

"Exactly." Leiter blew smoke toward the track lighting. "What has it got to do with you? Seventy-one percent of toxic waste comes from the chemical and petroleum industries. In this county that's you, Mister."

Brad grinned. He swallowed the rest of the brandy and set the snifter down. "Have you visited our plant, Mr. Leiter? Come by anytime. Thunder Oil's had an outflow monitor in place for five years. We employ a Ph.D. in chemistry to keep an eye on it. Monthly reports. On file.

"As to toxics, we don't make 'em, and use very little in our business. We're a fuel, lube-oil, and feedstock company. I don't want to sound smug, but I'll match our environmental responsibility against any other small refinery in the United States."

Leiter nodded. He smoked his pipe for a while and then said, almost sadly "We've got an eyewitness."

"To what?"

"A Thunder Oil truck doing the dumping."

"What? When?"

"A week ago. Monday night."

Brad reached for the bottle again, then withdrew his hand. He sat down behind the desk and looked at Leiter. "So," the young man said, "That's about it from my end, sir."

Brad put his fingers together. He looked out the dark square of window, conscious at the periphery of sight of the younger man, relaxed in the wing chair, looking blandly at him while he tamped his pipe. Okay, Mr. Philadelphia, he said to himself. Are we playing chess here, or poker? He decided it was chess.

He went over what he knew. The man was not a regular investigator. He knew Jack Mulholland. He also knew, or had taken the
trouble to look up, the name of his home-office aide. When he
added that up he got a lower-level political appointee. Limited
tenure. He'd be out next election, if not sooner.

Next, Leiter hadn't started the investigation yet. He didn't have
the specifics. Nor did he give the impression of caring too much
about them.

He sat for a minute more, going over everything again to make
sure there were no gaps in his reasoning. Then he stretched in his
chair and said, "Do you like saunas, Nick?"

Leiter looked surprised for just a moment. Then he smiled. "I
love saunas, Brad."

Stripped, they sat opposite each other in the cedar-scented atmosphere. The electric grate ticked softly; he'd set the thermostat at
eighty-five, comfortable in bare skin, but not high enough to make
them sweat. He looked at Leiter again; slim, pale, bony legs, a long
thin dick. His biggest handicap in whatever was coming off here
was twofold. He didn't know exactly who Leiter was, and he wasn't
sure Leiter knew who Brad Boulton was. He decided to start the
ball rolling on the latter and see how the other reacted.

"I guess you know, Nick, I'm on the Committee to Re-elect Jack
Mulholland."

"I didn't, but that's great. We need more fiscal conservatives like
Jack on the Hill."

"I contributed to Senator Buterbaugh's campaign, too. And
Thunder Oil's a contributing member to several PACs and to the
state victory committee."

Leiter nodded. Brad stared at his placid face, suddenly annoyed.
"The point being, Mr. Leiter, that if you plan to come into this
district with wild accusations against me or my company, you won't
find yourself in very good standing with the Republican Party."

The other man smiled around the pipestem. "I'm not too
worried about that. I'm not a Republican."

"Christ. Then what are you doing here? Put them on the table,
Leiter, or get out of my house and do your God-damned snooping
on somebody else's time."

"Okay. You know Richard Mill."

"The columnist? Of course."

"I'm his son."

"Mill?"

"He was married to Norma Leiter at one time. Actually it's Nick Leiter-Mill, but I dropped the hyphenation."

"Well, well, well." Brad nodded. "Any political ambitions?"

"Watch."

Brad thought for a while more, then turned the thermostat down. "Ready to get dressed?"

While they were buttoning their shirts he said, "I suppose I should thank you, then, for coming by here. It'd be good press for you to crucify me."

"It certainly would."

"I'm not saying whatever was reported to you has any foundation in fact."

"I understand that."

"But this isn't a good time even for rumors. Please treat this as confidential. The company's going into a major reorganization. As part of it there'll be a four-for-one split and a new floater of a million shares of stock. The initial price will be a hundred thirty-five." He paused. "Let's say a hundred shares of that goes into an account with a number I call you with next week."

Leiter chuckled. Brad felt his nose flare; the little snot was laughing at him. He was about to turn on his heel when the other man said, "This *is* back in the sticks, isn't it? I can't accept stock in your company! For Christ's sake, Brad, this isn't 1880!"

"Why not? If it's for a campaign contribution . . ."

Leiter just smiled and kept shaking his head.

"Well, I can't make it as much if it's cash."

"Now we're going *way* back. I don't want cash either."

"Well—I assumed . . ." He stopped, his sense of danger suddenly reactivated. Yet he'd seen the man naked; and he knew there was no possibility of bugging the house. "Look, maybe I'm off base here. Then what do you want?"

"First let's make sure we're straight on the main issue. Am I going to hear any more about this dumping?"

"No. You won't hear another word," said Brad. "I'll make that a personal guarantee."

"There you are. So why make a big deal of it? Investigations, litigation, that costs the government money too. But what I could use . . ." He paused. "Have you ever heard of something called soil remediation?"

"No."

"It's new. Promises to solve a lot of problems. You know we've got all these Superfund sites, a lot of contaminated soil around the country, they've got to be cleaned up. But how? We thought once we could burn it, but nobody wants a huge incinerator in their back yard. The Agency's really on the spot for this one."

"I don't know. And I don't care."

"Genetically engineered bacteria, that's how, Brad. The contaminated soil's scraped up and trucked to remediation plants. They tailor the bacteria to the waste and turn them loose. Friendly little germs, eating up the bad chemicals and turning them into harmless dirt. Who pays? The government will be happy to pay. The federal government will be *overjoyed* to pay."

"You're starting to interest me, Nick."

"I suspected I might. Well, some people have gotten in touch with me. One of them a friend, we went to school together, Yale. They've got the process. A fantastic new development. Their bugs multiply a hundred times faster than anything anyone else can show. As it happens, I'm in a position to award contracts for a pilot plant. All we need is a place to try it out."

"I see," said Brad, thinking it out. Remembering his own thoughts about how to expand in years to come. It was as if his own foresight had brought Leiter to him. "Well . . . I could talk to them. On one condition."

"Which is?"

"I'd like to reserve some of the stock in that partnership, or corporation, or whatever form it takes, for later distribution. You won't be at EPA forever, now, will you? And after you've started that political career you mentioned, campaign donations will be acceptable, won't they?"

"I think we understand each other, Brad. In broad, general terms. The specifics you can discuss with my friend."

They shook hands. "I'm glad I came out here to meet you. I thought we could help each other," Leiter said. "But now, I imagine you want to go back to your guests. So I'll just head back to the hotel."

"Well, it's been interesting. Oh. By the way."

"Yes?"

"You mind telling me who reported this? The dumping?"

"No problem, it's public record." Leiter pulled a folded paper from his sport coat. "Keep that, it's a copy."

"Thanks. Stop by the bar, take a bottle of Pinch with you."

"Can't do it. But thanks. Good night."

When Leiter left Brad poured himself another brandy. He was

pondering the paper when there was a knock. He slid it into a drawer. "Yeah!"

"Mr. Boulton, somebody want to see you."

"Thanks, Melissa . . . Well, come on! Don't stand around out there, don't be a weluctant wabbit!"

It was Williamina, sleepy-looking and pouty in blue pajamas and her mouse slippers. He filled his arms with her, felt her hands warm on his neck. He lifted her and buried his nose and lips in her golden hair. She clung like a little monkey, and he laughed, forgetting everything but her.

"How's your new nursie, Bunny? You and Melissa getting along?"

"She's nice. She sings to me."

"Well, that's good. And what do you think of her, Melissa? She behaving herself?"

"She about the nicest child I ever did see, Mr. Boulton."

"Uh huh, between the two of us we'll spoil her good. Is it time for bed already?"

"Lord, Mr. Boulton, it's way past ten o'clock!"

"Is it? Well, Punkin, guess we got to say good night."

"No. No, Daddy!"

"Willie, darlin', come on now. Give us a kiss, then let's see the last of you till morning."

The child began to cry. "Oh, now. She excited," said the nurse, coming forward and holding out her arms. "It's the party and all, Mr. Boulton. Come on now, let go your daddy."

He kissed her one last time, feeling tears hot on his lips, then disentangled her from his neck. He was surprised to feel his eyes burning too. He said, "I'll look in after the party, see if she's asleep. Good night, now, Punkin. Daddy loves you."

Pouting, the little girl did not reply as her nurse carried her from the den.

After things wound down, a little before one, he went through the house. He found two of the young people in the guest bedroom, and closed the door on them quietly. Jones was sitting pensively in front of the dying embers in the Tudor fireplace. Brad asked him to check the rest of the rooms and the grounds, then he could turn in. He pulled his tie off, poured a nightcap, and hoisted himself slowly up the stairs again.

Ainslee was lying face down on the bed, almost as he'd left her at eight, but she'd taken off the dress. He stood uncertainly above her. "You awake?" he muttered.

"No."

"How's the headache?"

"Shitty. Go away."

He looked down at her for a while, noting the wide muscular shoulders, so unexpected on her small body; the smooth swell of her calves. She kept herself in shape, you had to say that. At last he sat down beside her and began tentatively rubbing her neck. Her skin was softer than the silk slip. She didn't say anything so he kept on rubbing, his mind moving to the way the French girl's eighteen-year-old breasts had swayed as she hammered out Scott Joplin. When his hands got to hers she said, into the pillow, "Don't bother."

"What's wrong now?"

"Nothing's wrong. I just feel rotten and I don't want a drunk in my room."

"Did you take your—"

"Go *away*. You smell like a distillery."

He took his hands off her and sat there for a while, wishing he knew what to do with her. Or just what to do. At last he went into the shared bathroom and brushed and flossed his teeth. When he came out he pulled the chair up to her bedside and said, "That new nurse seems to be working out."

"We'll see. I didn't expect her to be black. How did the party go?"

"All right. We had a problem surface, though."

After a moment she said, "What?"

"Andy DeSilva got me aside and introduced me to a guy he brought. He was from the EPA. Had a report about midnight dumping. I took him up to the den, we talked, and I resolved the situation, I think."

Ainslee Boulton rolled over and sat up. She put one hand to her left eye and dark hair whispered down over bare shoulders like an eclipse. "Oh my God. You paid him off?"

"Well, not in so many words."

"My God, you *idiot*! What if he was wired?"

"I made sure he wasn't."

"I don't see how. How much did it cost us?"

"Nothing. He wants me to talk to a friend of his. About some kind of government-funded chemical treatment plant. It sounded interesting. So I said, okay."

"That's all?"

"That's all. Oh, and to hold some of the stock for him."

"You know it won't stop there."

"Well, I don't know. Why shouldn't it?"

"Who reported it?"

"Apparently two people off the street, right here in the county."

"Did you get their names?"

"Yes."

"Well, that's a break, anyway."

Her tone was a little warmer. He hesitated, then moved onto the bed. She turned her shoulders, inviting his hands like a pampered cat. He rubbed her back for a while, then said, "I'm thinking of pulling out of that business. It's getting too dangerous. People reporting it . . . I promised Leiter I'd stop it."

"Stop dumping," she said, her voice muffled by the pillow, "Or stop them reporting it?"

"I don't know . . ."

"You don't just 'pull out' with people like that. They'll never let go a sweet deal like this." She was silent a moment. "But you're right, once the reorganization's complete, we won't need them anymore. But then how do we get rid of them? Anyway, till the stock issue's sold, what would we use for cash?"

"I don't know. Borrow it."

"Brad, wake up. We can't borrow without losing control."

When he didn't say anything she pushed his hands off and got up. She rummaged through the drawers of an Art Deco dresser, found pills and swallowed two. "This goddamn migraine . . . Brad, one of these days my father is going to die. And then we'll have to fight for our lives. I don't know if you realize it, but Weyandt and those other jerks you keep around have all got their knives pointed in your direction."

"Rudy's our friend."

"Rudy makes fucking Machiavelli look like Pope Pius the Twelfth. Plus you've got Pennzoil, Quaker State, Kendall crowding us. If we lose any more market share in motor oil, K-Mart and Walgreens will drop Thunder Premium. Our dealer network's crumbling away. We lost ten stations this year to the cut-rates and we only built three. If we falter they'll defect all at once. And we can't fall back to being a producer anymore. Our lease lands are security on what we've already borrowed."

"I know that, Ainslee."

"If a company stops growing it starts to rot. My father never realized that. He thought he could park Thunder Oil in 1949. I thought you'd see that things were different, that they had to change."

"I do." He looked around her room dully. "You got anything to drink in here?"

"You've had enough. Sometimes you scare me, Brad. This reorganization won't just happen, it's got to be rammed through. At the same time we've got to take the old-liners on the board with us. You're the rammer; I'm the legitimacy."

"I understand all that."

"Then I shouldn't have to tell you that we've got to keep dividends and net worth up so the offer sells. That means you've got to keep Newark, and the nursing homes, and the other cash cows on the line." Her tone had passed gradually into scorn. "Is it getting too rough for you? Is that it?"

"No."

"I wonder. Somebody reported you to the government. Get serious! My family didn't build this company by letting nobodies kick us around! If you can't find the guts to run a company you can go back where I found you, turning down high school boys for car loans."

Seeing her now, straight and proud and angry, he suddenly felt sad. He was tired of fighting. For a moment he wished he could tell her everything. To his surprise he heard himself mutter, "Well, sometimes I get scared."

"What?"

"I said, sometimes I'm not sure I can handle this. It's getting too complicated."

"Are you serious? Is that why you got drunk?"

"Yeah."

She came over and stood above him, smoothed his hair, smiling distantly. "Well, it won't be for long. Once the divisions are in place we can get some decent middle management. Then you won't have to do everything yourself. We'll be able to sit back and kibitz from Cherry Hill, or New York if we want."

Somewhere in his drink-slowed brain he wondered if she could mean it. That was the trouble with Ainslee Thunner. You never knew. It sounded nice. Get decent executives. Sit back in Manhattan. But it wasn't him. Once he had his own board in place he wasn't going to let go. And Ainslee sure as hell wasn't either. After three years with her he knew that.

It didn't matter, he was too close now to worry about it. Once

The Thunder Group was a reality he wouldn't need her fucking "legitimacy." He didn't even like the word . . . But even drunk he knew he couldn't say that, couldn't so much as hint it. If she ever suspected that she would truly become dangerous.

It occurred to him then, feeling her hand smooth his hair, that once the reorganization was over she wouldn't need him either. What was she thinking? What did that dark head contain, not two feet above his own, but inaccessible as the far side of the moon?

But the room was spinning, and he was so tired that the thought slipped away. Her hand paused; she was waiting for a response. He mumbled, "I hope we can do that, Ainslee. You and me and Willie."

"We will." Her hand patted him, once, then he heard her move away.

He took a deep shuddering breath. "I wish you and Williamina got along. I wish we still loved each other."

"It's kind of late for that, Brad. Let's just try to keep what we have."

He realized as he pulled the sheets back in his own room that he hadn't looked in on his daughter. But it was late, and he felt dizzy and sad and he thought, tomorrow morning. The huge old house was quiet around him; and outside, in the garden, the flashlight swung over the netted humps of the bushes, over the ancient fountain, and then winked out.

Twenty-one

The librarian looked at her, Jaysine thought, as if she'd proposed sharing the disease with her, instead of asking for a book on the subject. "If you have one," she finished, lowering her voice still more.

"I'll see. Something like that would not be in our open stacks, of course."

When she went away Jaysine straightened, sighing, and looked around, unbuttoning her coat.

The Raymondsville Public Library had been endowed ninety years before by a Scottish millionaire. Since then the busts of Ben Franklin and Chief Cornplanter, the models of clippers and locomotives in glass cases, the chromos of David's "Death of Socrates" and Rembrandt had aged. Even the librarians looked as if they could use a good meal. Or maybe, she thought, drinks all around.

"This way, Miss."

She followed the assistant's upswept hair out through the reading room—there was only one other person there, a boy reading magazines—and back into the stacks. The narrow dim aisles smelled of steam heat, book dust, and oxidizing paper. The woman reached up from time to time to pull strings that dangled from the ceiling. Finally she stopped.

"This is it. Our restricted collection. Anything we might have on, that kind of thing would be filed here."

Jaysine accepted the key and looked at the wire-mesh door. The footsteps tapped away into mortuary hush. At last she turned the key in the old-fashioned padlock and stepped inside.

Phil stared fascinated at the *National Geographic.*

A town near Detroit had discovered 33,000 drums of wastes from steel mills, chemical plants, and refineries, and ponds filled with millions of gallons of polychlorinated biphenyls, cyanide, and hydrochloric acid. It was leaching into the town's reservoirs with every rain.

The sewers had blown up in Louisville, Kentucky, when an animal-food plant used them to dispose of used hexane.

The government had bought a whole town in Missouri because a contractor sprayed dioxin-laced oil on the streets to control dust. It was evacuated and paved over, but former residents were still dying.

A company in Los Angeles had built a secret pipeline to discharge into the city's sewer system.

A pesticide called EDB had been banned because it caused mutations. But American companies still sold it overseas, and it came right back on imported fruits and vegetables.

Apparently anyone who wanted was free to make defoliants, herbicides, pesticides, DDT, PBP's, dioxin, chlordane, without any supervision at all. It was illegal to dispose of them without rigorous safeguards. But there were only thirty inspectors in the whole United States, and they were powerless to arrest dumpers even if they caught them in the act.

Toxic chemicals, he read, caused miscarriages, cancer, birth defects, liver damage, nervous disorders, brain damage, blood diseases, Hodgkin's disease, convulsions, seizures, nosebleeds, hyperthyroidism, and death. PCB persisted so long it would still be measurable in the great-great-grandchildren of those exposed. Dioxin was two hundred times more lethal than strychnine, and its first sign was a skin rash.

He thoughtfully examined the rash on the back of his hand.

Since there was no legal place to put it, organized crime had taken over. They accepted waste, got paid for disposing of it, then sprayed it over regular trash and shipped it to city dumps. They pumped it into abandoned mines. They rented warehouses, filled them, and torched them. They mixed it with heating oil and sold it; forty percent of the oil sold in New York City was laced with PCBs or benzene.

He read with a shock of recognition in the *Reader's Digest* about tank-truck dumping. The drivers opened their spigots along the Jersey Turnpike in rainy weather. Others had been caught doing it further north, in rural Connecticut.

He scratched his hand, wondering if he'd die. Probably not. But one article said sometimes chemical rashes never went away.

He leaned back in the deserted library and watched a lone fly wander among the light-globes. Only the one directly above him was lit.

His musings were interrupted by a woman who came out of the stacks carrying a book. He watched as she looked around, then came over to his table. She was short, blond, and wore glasses.

"Hi."

"Hi."

"This is the only light. Do you mind if I read here?"

"Sure, go ahead."

She sat down and he looked back at the article. She looked familiar. He glanced up from the page, but couldn't place her. She was older than he was, but not bad-looking. He tried to see what she was reading, but couldn't make it out.

There wasn't much in the special collection. Was syphilis really incurable? Why was she taking shots for it, then? She turned to the front of the book and saw that it had been published in 1920.

She put it aside, glanced at the boy, and turned it so he couldn't see the title. She looked around. There was no one else in the library. The wall clock said four-thirty.

She took the notebook out of her purse.

It looked expensive. Limp leather binding and snap-out, replaceable pages. She flipped through them. Each had a printed date at the top.

Apparently he used it to list things to do, meetings to go to, inspections, appointments. There were a lot of chemical names. One page had a rough drawing of some kind of equipment. She flipped past it. There were also figures. Money stuff. *Bond yield, Hanover Trust, 1,500,000, 7.24%* was typical. She couldn't make much out of it. She wondered if the book had any value. Whether he missed it. She hoped he did, hoped he was going crazy missing it.

Jaysine wondered what she was going to do.

She didn't have any money. Fifty-nine dollars in her checking account and her rent was due next week. There were two other shops in town, both smaller than Marybelle's; she didn't think there'd be any openings there. Well, there were other jobs. She'd bussed tables at school. She could sell dresses—no, she couldn't do that either, she suddenly realized. The first thing every woman in the Shoppe would have done when she left was tell the first person she met how Marybelle had thrown her out. And why. It was all over town by now, of that she was sure.

What could she do? Where could she go? Back to Four Holes? She couldn't stay there. Her mother didn't make enough practicing to support them both.

No, she thought with dread, I'm going to have to leave. Go someplace they don't know me. Maybe Norfolk; her brother could put her up for a couple weeks, she could help with the new baby till she found a place in a salon. She'd have to start all over again, get relicensed, buy new equipment.

But even a bus ticket would cost more than she had.

That left drawing unemployment. She didn't want to do that. But it wasn't as if she had a choice. She thought, trying to steel herself: If you've got to, do it. Go over and put your name in. Now, before they close for the day. It wasn't her fault. It was his, when all was said and done.

She wished Brad Boulton would die.

She sat motionless, remembering her other alternative. Signing Ainslee Boulton's piece of paper. It felt wrong. It felt like a temptation. She didn't like the feeling that had come over the phone line. Maybe she should have asked how much she was willing to give, to sign it.

She decided not to make up her mind just then, and looked at the notebook again. All this about chemicals. What did it mean? Then she thought, Who cares. She was looking around for a trash can when she noticed one of the boy's magazines was *Chemical Engineering.*

"Do you read that?"

"What?" He looked up.

"Do you read that magazine? Do you know much about chemistry?"

"I'm taking it in school," Phil said cautiously.

She shoved the notebook across the table. "Can you read this?"

He examined the open page, then the next one. "Well," he said, "I can't tell you what it all means, but it's about oil. Ethane, pentane, octane, those are things you make out of it."

"Like at Petroleum City? The refinery?"

"Sure. Like, it says here, under November 9, *Ad agency: campaign for Thunder steam turbine oil,* and over here it talks about cutting premium unleaded with methanol." He glanced up at her. "Where'd you get this?"

"Found it."

"Uh huh . . . Well, you could probably mail it back to Thunder Oil and they could find out whose it is."

"I know whose it is."

"Oh." He thought about that briefly, then dismissed it. He scratched his rash and riffled the pages. For November 14 there were notes about laundry contracts and about a drop and then something about electric power conservation. He was about to ask her where she'd found it when she looked at the clock, took it back, and stood up, reaching for her coat. "Thanks," she said.

"Sure," he said. When he looked up again she was gone.

Mrs. Skinner came back not long after and told him he had to leave, they were closing. He went reluctantly, limping out into a cold wet wind.

Someone had made new stars, or polished the old ones; they glared clear and brilliant down through a billion miles of space. He pulled his scarf up and headed up the street, pondering what he'd read.

Mr. Maxwell talked about interest aggregation, how political parties picked up what people wanted and if they got voted in they did it. But it didn't always seem to work that way. Sometimes democracy got polluted.

That didn't surprise him, that special interests got their way. What surprised him was how nobody seemed to care. If they cared they'd get action eventually. Like on air pollution, or air bags. But on this they didn't. You couldn't exactly see increased cancer rates, or more miscarriages, the way you could bad air. That was pretty much what the magazines said, too.

Anyway, the question wasn't what other people were doing about it, but what he was going to do. He wondered what Dr. Friedman had found out about the sample. He wished there was something exciting he could do meanwhile. Check out the license number? He thought fleetingly of using the squad car radio, but his voice was too high to fool anyone.

He fantasized his way down the street, daydreaming holding his father's gun on the trucker who'd jerked him up off freezing asphalt and said, "Whaddya think you're doing?"

But after a while cold penetrated his boots, bit his toes, made his fingers and dick numb; and he saw lights on in the building where his sister worked. He decided to go in and say hi, warm up for a minute, then head home.

Jaysine moved slowly through the line. All the others were men. They smelled of old sweat, tobacco, liquor. She clutched her purse and when she came up to the little window said shyly, "Hello."

The woman behind it said, "Where's your card?"

"Card?"

"Are you here for the first time? Did you just lose your job?"

"Yes."

"You're in the wrong line, but you're lucky, the counselor's still in. Wait over there and I'll find her."

She was sitting in full view of the men when the swinging door opened and Karen came out from behind the counter. Jaysine saw her face go still, then flush. Her own cheeks heated, and she looked down at her purse. "Well," said the dark girl after a moment, "Jaysine. What are you doing here?"

"Applying for unemployment. What are you doing here?"

"I work here. Come on back."

The desk wasn't private. They sat down. "Well, you were there," Jaysine said after an awkward pause.

"Yes, and I thought it was terrible. I thought you were doing a wonderful job." Karen turned even redder and fussed in a drawer. She whispered, "I know you were helping me."

"I didn't know you worked here."

"It's only till I start school again."

"Oh. Well, I don't have any money saved. So I guess I thought, well, I'll apply for unemployment."

Karen's eyes went past her shoulder; she waved to someone. Jaysine didn't look because at the same time she asked, "How long had you been working at the Shoppe?"

"Almost a year."

"And why did your employment terminate?"

"You were there. Didn't you hear?"

"This is for the form."

"Oh. Well, I quit."

"Yes, but . . ." Karen's blush grew still deeper. "The thing is, if you . . . See, the rules say you have to be laid off to get unemployment assistance. If you leave voluntarily you're not eligible. And we have to verify that with the employer before we issue you a card, to draw benefits."

Jaysine sat still. Too late, she saw how cleverly the old woman had manipulated her into saying the very words that would hurt her most. How Marybelle must hate her!

Karen looked unhappy.

"I wish I could help some other way. A recommendation, or something. Let me know if I can."

"That's all right," said Jaysine again. Then, to her horror, she began to cry.

Phil stood uncertainly behind the woman, looking past her at his sister. He'd recognized her as the one from the library. From what little he'd heard it sounded like they knew each other, so he thought it was okay to come up to the desk. But now she was crying, and Kay looked flustered. "Hello, Philip," she said.

"Hi. What's going on?"

The woman twisted around. "Oh. It's you . . . I just lost my job."

"Oh. That's too bad. You'll pick something else up, though."

"I don't think so. Not around here."

"Did my sister help you?"

"Who?"

"Kay. She's the counselor here."

"Oh, Karen. Are you his sister? No, she couldn't help." She looked away from them both. "Doesn't seem like anyone can. I don't know what I'm going to do. I don't have any money to go anyplace else, or live on . . ."

On impulse he said, "Here."

"Phil!" said his sister, in a shocked voice.

"It's my money, Kay . . . It's not much. I was saving it, but I don't need it. Go ahead, take it."

"I don't want your money."

"Go on. You can pay me back when you get another job."

She wouldn't take money from a strange man, even if he was only a kid. She said, "No. But tell you what."

"What?"

"I'll let you buy me a drink."

"A drink?" He sounded stupid even to himself, and tried to recover with, "Oh sure. Sure, yeah, we can do that. Where you want to go?"

"Phil," said his sister.

"I don't care. Anywhere."

"We could go the Brown Bear, or Sherlock's—"

"I like Sherlock's."

"Okay."

"Phil!" said his sister for the third time, in her *I am appalled* voice. He smiled at her and went out.

It felt strange, walking with an older woman. He wondered if any of the guys would see them. He wondered if she was a hooker. Then thought: Get serious. They don't apply for unemployment.

"So what did you do?" he asked her.

"What?"

"Before you got fired. What'd you use to do?"

"I was at the Style Shoppe. On Pine Street."

"Oh. Fixing hair?"

"Beauty culture. Yes."

Tuesday night, Sherlock's was almost empty. Phil looked around as he took her coat. Years of Catechism and his mother's warnings had given bars the same aura of seductive danger as women, or the Baptist Church. It seemed not too threatening now, just dim and scuzzy, smelling of old smoke and beer and chalk. He pulled out a chair for her, then stopped. He was standing there, unsure what to say, when she looked up.

"You aren't old enough, are you."

"Uh—no. Not in P.A."

"I'll get it. You sit down."

To his disappointment she brought him back a pop. They sat and looked at the silent old Wurlitzer. Finally he said, "My name's Phil. Phil Romanelli."

"Oh, sorry. I'm Jaysine Farmer."

"Uh huh . . . did you figure out what that stuff meant?"

"Stuff?"

"In your little book."

"Oh. No. What were you doing? Studying?"

"No. Something more important."

"What?"

He took a swallow of pop, thinking about it, and couldn't see any harm in boasting a little. "Well, me and another guy, an old guy, we're tracking down some criminals."

"Really?"

"Uh huh."

"What kind of criminals?"

"Midnight dumpers, they're called."

"What do they dump?"

"Toxic chemicals. Dangerous stuff nobody wants."

"They dump it in people's yards, or what?"

"No, no. On the roads. I caught one. We're reporting them to the state."

"Aren't you afraid they'll do something to you?"

"Like what?"

"Beat you up, or something—I don't know."

His tongue checked his loose front tooth. "I been beat up before. I'm not scared of that."

"You're pretty brave. You said you caught one? How?"

"Well, we took turns watching Route Six, down by Candler Hill. Finally saw one late at night, a tanker, just letting stuff run out the back out onto the road. I chased it on my bike and got a license number."

"You're pretty brave," she said again.

There was something strange in the way she said it and he looked quickly up at her. She'd taken her glasses off, coming in from the cold, and he realized again that she was kind of nice looking.

Now she got up and went to the bar and when she came back she was carrying another Coke. She pushed it over to him. It tasted funny. He realized it had rum in it. "Tell me some more."

He told her what he'd learned in the library. Halfway through it he pulled off his glove and showed her the rash. "Mr. Halvorsen got one like it, on his face. Must have breathed some, too, because he was in the hospital for a week. And there's a snowplow driver sick, and a family that bought some of the oil to burn in their furnace, and others, too, the doctor told me."

"What doctor?"

"Dr. Friedman, down at Maple Street. She's helping us on this."

"I know her." Jaysine sipped ginger brandy. She didn't feel angry at the doctor. She'd just done her job. It was Marybelle who'd decided that "taking precautions" meant humiliating and firing Jaysine. "Do you think they'll do anything about it?"

"Well, they've got to now we caught them doing it. Racks—
that's Mr. Halvorsen—he's reporting it, like I said, so all we're
doing now is waiting for them to get here and take charge."

"Well, I wish you luck," she said.

Phil asked her, "Have you decided what you're going to do?"

"My mom lives up in Four Holes. I might have to go back there.
I don't want to."

"Jaysine, why'd you quit your job?"

She had been wondering when he'd ask that. She thought about
telling him, but couldn't. "Oh, the owner tricked me into quitting.
That way she got to keep my equipment."

"What kind of equipment?"

She caught herself just in time; the kid didn't need to know that
about his sister. "Just hairdressing stuff. Anyway, thanks for the
drink. I needed one. Maybe I'll see you around town."

She got up, hesitated. "Or you could come up sometime. To
talk. I don't know many people in town. You know Gray's Drug?
I'm in the apartment upstairs, next door, over the Woolworth's."
She laughed softly. "I don't know for how long."

"Uh, thanks. Maybe sometime."

"Good night."

" 'Night."

He looked after her thoughtfully. What did that mean? He
wondered how well she knew his sister. He wondered if—

"Hey!"

It was the bartender, a big old guy, coming down on him like a
bear after garbage. Phil got up hastily. "I was just leavin'," he said.

"You better be. Don't come in here again till you're of age, kid.
I'm not losin' my license over you."

Outside, he stood in the street for a moment, looking at the
stars. Catching crooks, invited up by a blonde, and now he'd just
been thrown out of a bar.

He had to admit it, things were looking up.

Twenty-two

The old man stood at the top of the steps, looking at the sky. Behind his contemplative stillness a stand of blue spruce consulted in whispers. Below him Town Hill fell away, dotted with the tarnished silver of beech trunks. Above it all the clouds rushed past silent and swift and gray.

Jamming his numbing hands into his coat, shutting his eyes, Halvorsen squeezed the stale smells of the cellar from his lungs, then drew cold air like fine steel wire through his nostrils.

Snow.

He shivered—under the coat was only a sleeveless undershirt—and headed for the woodpile. Before he got there he stopped. Looked around again, frowning, though nothing moved and no sound came.

The spruces whispered, but gave no answer. He stayed alert as he selected five chunks of aged hardwood.

In the cellar, moving with the economy of old habit, he tapped his stove latch free and fed the embers. Then closed it, and looked around the dim interior of his home.

He'd found the basement rock-cold, coming back, and it had taken a couple of days to get back to living temperature. He'd cleaned up, not exactly energetically—he still felt washed-out—but now the cans were picked up and the floor swept and the trash burned. The fire was sputtering like oil in an iron skillet and he could hear the coffee starting to boil.

"Feel like breakfast, Jez?"

The puppy followed her nose out from under the couch. She sniffed and stopped by the door, looking at him and whining, and after a moment he bent. "You're goin' to be a big old dog, ain't you?" he said, rubbing her head.

By the time she was finished outside he'd found a handful of dry chow and replenished her water dish from the pump. He poured himself a mug of coffee and added sugar and slow-flowing Carnation. Then set to work, shuffling in and out of the cold room with his ingredients.

Cup of flour, pinch of soda, two tablespoons of shortening. No buttermilk, but a little vinegar in the condensed milk remedied that lack. He mixed it, dusting his hands with more flour. He cut the dough with absorbed deliberation, round as silver dollars, and slid the pan into the baking compartment.

After a time he let himself down into the chair and had hot biscuits and syrup. Gray morning edged slowly in to light the room, the reloading bench, old magazines, clothes hanging from ten-penny nails in the beams. Just as it had ever been, for years and years and years.

The puppy snarled in the corner, tussling with a deer skull Halvorsen had picked up on one of his treks. He cleaned the plate, carried it to the sideboard, and refreshed his mug. Then sat down again, chewing over the thought that had just occurred to him.

He was wondering if he ought not to go back into town.

Trouble with that was he didn't want to. He'd seen more people in the last few days than he cared to for a long time. He felt like laying up here for a couple weeks at least. Just thinking, maybe reading a western, or going for a walk before it snowed again.

On the other hand, balancing in his mind like a powder-scale, was his pension check. He didn't mind what he ate anymore, but a puppy should eat right when it was growing or it wouldn't have a nose. He'd got Jez the year before, after his old hound had got herself shot. Wasn't the same kind but he figured that didn't matter, not at this late date.

Yeah, his check, supplies . . . and there were other things he ought to be checking on too.

He sighed, resigning himself, and began hunting around for his boots.

Later, dressed, he stood in front of the gun rack. He took one of the bundles down and unwrapped a corner of the oilcloth.

His old single-shot .22 Hornet. His eyes crinkled as his mind gave him a sudden picture of a bird, wary, big, and beautiful.

He'd seen the flock as he worked on the lease; he'd come across their scratchings here and there, and at last realized where they were roosting, in a stand of white pine on the dark side of Lacey Knees Hill. That November he'd told Jennie not to buy a Thanksgiving bird and took the rifle out with him when he went to work that morning. A little after dawn he'd parked up the road, out of sight, and climbed up a ravine to a grove of chestnut oaks. He'd stopped a good distance off, but where he could see up into the grove, and settled behind a log, laying a broken-off brow over him and the rifle.

They'd come into sight half an hour later, hens and young toms, big this late in the year but still under the sway of the old male. Through the four-power Fecker he could see every feather. He heard their "prip, prip, prip" clearly, the scratching and fluttering, but he didn't move. Just rested the rifle-stock on dead wood and waited, so still that after a while he'd heard a stir above him and knew two squirrels were chasing each other.

When the old tom stepped out of the bushes it took his breath away. Its bronze-black was iridescent in the sunlight, and its beard dragged in the dry leaves. Facing him, still ninety yards distant, he knew it wasn't coming any closer. So he swayed the barrel, like a branch moved by the wind. To get decent meat off a turkey you had to place the bullet just right. The picket-post settled toward the wingbutt and he eased off the safety. The high-velocity crack scattered the feeding hens and bounced back from the hills.

They'd had all the folks over that year, and his mother had remarked on the nutlike sweetness of the flesh.

Smiling slightly, Halvorsen glanced toward the bench. He still had his molds for the old Loverin gas-check bullet. Now he thought about it there should be a box of loaded hulls someplace. Must be twenty years old, but powder didn't stale. He rooted them out and dropped a few into his pocket. He worked the action several times, then put some light oil on a rag.

He slung it over his shoulder and said to the dog, "I'll be back pretty soon. You be good now."

He went to the door, but couldn't get it closed. The bitch kept wedging her head into the crack and crying. At last he gave up. He stood at the top of the steps, watching his breath drift away on the wind, and adjusted the sling. "So," he said grimly, "you just got to come along."

The puppy frisked and barked ecstatically around his ankles.

Shaking his head, he set himself into motion, headed down along the side of the hill. The puppy hesitated for a moment, glancing at him and then into the woods, before she ran after him, flop ears flapping.

The old man marched steadily, grateful the snow wasn't too deep yet. He had a long way to go. He caught the last tang of woodsmoke, then lost it in the clear heavy wind that told him it was going to be cold, very cold, and soon.

Mortlock Run. He'd lived up here for more decades than he cared to remember, but there was always something new to see. After a while the road dipped sharply and the woods moved up to wall it in. The road turned left and followed the creek awhile, not as steep, but the descent good for a man who was getting on in years.

There was no hurry. He stopped three or four times, perching on the bank or on a stump, husbanding his strength. The puppy cast about ahead of him. Once she stopped to sniff at the remains of a raccoon, bare bone now, crow-picked, subliming. By next fall it would be earth again. Halvorsen called her sharply away, then went on.

He'd dressed warm but now he unbuttoned the coat and put his earflaps up. The woods were quiet, the only moving beings black-birds and a late hawk cruising far off.

He was thinking about the raccoon, and the other dead animals he'd seen along this road.

Who would do a thing like that? Dump poison where people lived, for money? He thought about it as he rested, worked at it as he walked. After a while it occurred to him to wonder why he'd taken the rifle along. The only answer he could come up with was that same nameless apprehension he'd felt at the woodpile.

He didn't get far along Route Six, a straight old man in red and black walking erect and a little stiff along the gravel berm, before a sedan pulled over. The rifle went in the back seat. The puppy was excited at being in a car and he held her on his lap the last few miles into Raymondsville.

They got out near Rosen's. Halvorsen thought of going in, saying hello, but remembered his missing check. Settle that first. He headed up Main Street toward the post office. A boy whistled at the puppy, but no one looked twice at the old man with the slung rifle.

There were three letters for him, all ad junk or *You May Have Won Millions*, which he dropped into the can by the ranks of brass boxes without opening. Then stood there, puzzled and a little annoyed. He generally got the check by the tenth, and here it was the sixteenth and nothing.

At the station the gas jockey said Fred was over in Olean getting parts, but he was welcome to use the phone. He propped himself at Pankow's desk, staring out through dirty glass at the pumps, and put a call in to the pension office. A girl answered and he said, "Lemme talk to Mickey."

"I'm sorry?"

"Mickey Zias, the manager."

"I'm sorry, sir, Mr. Zias is no longer with the company."

"What's that?"

"He's no longer with us. Would you like to speak to Mrs. Bridger?"

"I guess," he said grumpily.

After a while a woman came on the line. "May I help you?"

"This's William T. Halvorsen, Thunder Oil, retired. I ain't got my check this month yet."

"Let me call up that record. How do you spell your last name, sir?"

He told her. There was a pause, during which something tapped faintly at the other end. A deafening clang came from back in the repair bay, steel on concrete, followed by curses. One of the mechanics came out and looked at him, looked at the rifle, propped in the corner; then jumped back as the puppy attacked his oilstained boots. He laughed and went out to the pumps.

"Mr. Halvorsen?"

"Yeah."

"We have no record of your being a pensionable employee, sir. There was a W. T. Halvorsen who worked for Thunder Oil back in the thirties, but he was discharged."

"That's right, I was, but Dan hired me back."

"Well, we have no record of a rehire. I'm sorry."

"Wait a minute," said Halvorsen. "I got thirty years in with T.O. I been gettin' my checks regular since I retired. What's the trouble? Seems to me you better ask that machine again."

"I've checked our records, sir, and you're not on the pension list."

"Well, just call Mickey—"

"I've told you, Mr. Zias is no longer *with* the company, sir."

"Oh." Halvorsen thought for a while. "Well, call Dan then, he remembers me."

"Who's that?"

"What do you mean, 'Who's that?' Dan *Thunner*, don't you—"

"Mr. Halvorsen," the voice interrupted, brittle and young. "Mr. Thunner has taken no active interest in the company for years. If you think you deserve benefits, write us a letter setting forth your position and it will be considered. Have a good day."

Halvorsen stared at the receiver. Very slowly, his eyebrows crept up.

"I want to talk to the lady doctor."

"Just a moment, please."

When she came on the line he told her who it was. "Oh, Mr. Halvorsen," she said. Her voice dropped at the end.

"What's wrong?"

"Nothing seems to be going right this week. How are things with you?"

"Fair to okay. Look, you remember that paper I wrote up for the government? Did you send that in yet?"

"I sent it in that same day. Bad news, Racks. The inspector called back from Philadelphia."

"What inspector?"

"Apparently he stopped by the hospital, but I was out. He picked up the sample, though, from my secretary. He called me yesterday. Said he'd checked it out and there was nothing to report."

"What do you mean? He was here, you say?"

"That's right."

"I never seen him. And he said there wasn't nothing to it? Hell, I mean, heck, we got 'em dead to rights. And you did them tests. How can he say there ain't nothing to it?"

"I don't know. Something about the oil being residue, or something. I'm as puzzled as you are. But at the moment I don't know what else to do."

"Who's this inspector fella?"

"I have a number here . . . Hold on. Got a pen?"

Halvorsen found a ballpoint in the drawer. He tried it on the corner of a Champion flyer. "Yeah. Go ahead."

"His name's Nicholas Leiter, and the phone is (215)597–9370."

"That's a lot of numbers."

"How long has it been since you made a long distance call, Racks?"

"I don't know. 1958?"

"I see. Well, are you going to call him?"

"Maybe."

"Let me know what you find out."

"Okay."

Halvorsen hung up. He looked out at the street for a while, scratching the dog's head. At last he tore a piece off the flyer. FRED I USED YR PHONE TO CALL PHILLY. WILL PAY YOU WHEN I GET CHECK. HALVORSEN. Then he dialed in the numbers and listened to it ring.

"Office of the assistant director."

"This the operator?"

"The what? This is the district office, EPA, assistant director's office."

"Oh. Got a Nicholas Leiter there?"

"Yes, Mr. Leiter's the assistant director."

"This here's W. T. Halvorsen, Thunder Oil. Want to talk to him."

"What was that company again, sir?"

Halvorsen told her. A moment later he heard a young man's voice on the line. "Who's this? Brad?"

"This is W. T. Halvorsen."

"Who?"

"W. T. Halvorsen."

"Ah—well, how are you?"

"Fine, just fine."

"Is there something I can do for you?"

"It's about a report was sent up to you fellas last week," Halvorsen said. He leaned back, propping a boot up on the desk. "About some stuff bein' dumped on the roads up here. I wanted to see if you'd got time to look into it yet."

The voice went eager. "Yes, sir, I did. I remember your name now, sir. I traced that plate number. Then I flew up there and checked it out with the company that owns the truck. Turns out, thought, the sample's just residual oil. What's left in the bottom from a delivery. The driver left the valve open and a little of it dripped out on the road. Thanks for your alertness, but you don't have anything to worry about up there."

"What kind of oil?"

"Lubricating oil. SAE 30, I believe it was."

"I put in fifty years in the oil business up here, Mister. That wasn't no lube stock. You could tell that with your eyes closed, by the smell."

"Well, I'm afraid that's not what our analysis shows."

"Then your analysis's a lie," said Halvorsen.

Leiter sounded annoyed. "Mr. Halvorsen, I don't really know who you are—"

"Told you twice. Say, who'd you talk to up here?"

"Thunder Oil."

"Why didn't you talk to me? I'm the one filed the report."

"I'm satisfied with the investigation, Mr. Halvorsen. Unless you have something new to add I'm closing out the file on it."

"What was it they gave you? Money?"

"No money changed hands, Mr. Halvorsen, and I'd be careful about making remarks like that if I were you. There are slander statutes that can be invoked. I've got the sample bottle in front of me. There's nothing in it but Thunder Premium Lube Oil."

"Now, maybe," said the old man. He tried to calm himself. "Look, Mister, there's people sick up here cause of this. It's only going to get worse if it ain't stopped. You ought to think about what you're doing. You might be sorry you done it when you're older."

There was a peep on the line, almost too high for him to hear. "We're recording now, Mr. Halvorsen," came Leiter's voice, triumphant. "Please repeat the threat you just made."

The old man sat motionless in the overheated office, looking out at the gray sky. He didn't say anything, just listened to the electronic beep every few seconds.

Later he sat in the kitchen of the little house behind the station. His daughter was carefully pouring scalding milk into a mug of cocoa and saying, "Well, it's 'cause I worry about you."

"What's Fred got to say?"

"He'd be glad to have you. He's always complaining he can't get nobody to make change, clean up, things like that."

Halvorsen looked out the kitchen window, across the trodden-down brown grass of the back yard, to the garage. A rickety stair led up to a second-story door. Beyond it was the upper curve of the Texaco sign. In a sudden frenzy of barking the brown-and-black pup came tearing across the dead grass, followed by a Border collie. Halvorsen sighed and reached for the sugar bowl. Alma brought down some cookies. He selected one and dipped it in the cocoa.

"I don't think so," he said.

"I wish you would."

"Well, I ain't goin' to, and that's an end of it."

"What's wrong, Pa?"

"Nothin', Alma. Just gettin' tired of people trying to make me do what they want."

"Well," she said. Her rough red hands twisted together, her mouth unhappy. "Well . . ."

"Don't miss it till it runs dry."

She didn't smile; she'd heard the joke all through her childhood. He said, "Sorry. What was it you were goin' to say?"

"Well, there's other places you could go, than here." She looked past him into the living room, where the television set was telling them what to buy for Christmas. "I'd like you here in town with me, but just about anyplace would be better than out there in those woods."

"I'm happy where I am. Just need a loan, that's all."

"That's not the problem, Pa. You know I'll help with that. What worries me is, you aren't getting any younger. I worry since Ralph died. I dream about you falling down, getting sick, like you did last week—"

"That wasn't sick. That was poison."

"Whatever. I want you to get taken care of better."

He didn't say anything. She stared at him for a while, then got up and went into the front room. He heard the desk drawer. When she came back she put something white on the table in front of him.

"I didn't bring my glasses, Alma. You want to tell me what it is?"

"It's from a place here in the county. They got a special thing for Thunder retirees. A doctor brought this by. We had a talk. It's for me, but it's about you."

"What's it *say?*"

"Don't get mad, Pa. You have to promise you won't."

Halvorsen nodded, but his mouth was tight.

"It's about a place they just built, real nice. Look at the picture. It's up in Beaver Fork. You get to go in free."

"Free? Food and everything?"

"That's what it says." She smiled slowly, lips quivering.

"What do we got to do?"

"Nothing."

"Alma." His voice was quiet. "Ain't nothin' free in this world. Just tell me what they want you to do."

Not looking at him, she whispered, "I got to say you ain't in your right capacity. That's all. It don't have to be true. I just got to sign this paper. There's a doctor there, and people to make sure you get good care and good medicine."

Halvorsen looked at his hands, curled round the chocolate like sleeping men round a campfire; at the wrinkles and age spots and old scars. One of the nails was missing. He'd been holding a spike on a deadman in East Texas when the roustabout had missed with his sledge. Carried the mark of that hammer for forty years, he thought. Carry it to my grave.

"You goin' to sign it?"

"Not unless you say to, Pa."

"Better give it here."

He tucked it into his pocket. Then selected another cookie and munched it slowly.

"Why you carrying a rifle, Pa? Are you hunting again?"

"No."

"You ain't going to tell me what's going on?"

"Ain't nothing going on, Alma. I'm just trying to live my life, what's left of it, without bothering anybody or having them bother me."

"I wish you'd move into town."

"That's enough," he said sharply. She sat quiet a moment longer, pushing her lips out, then got up. When she came back she held out money. He nodded and took it.

"Want me to go down with you while you shop?"

"No need. Can I leave the dog? I'm too old to chase after a pup."

"Sure. Will you need a ride back? Fred's got the Dodge, but I can take you out in the tow truck."

A few minutes later he stood still and alone on the pavement in front of the garage. The wind came slow and cold and inevitable down the street.

Fight it, he wondered, or give in?

If he gave in they'd let him alone. Maybe give his pension back. But if he fought he'd lose not just his retirement but likely his freedom too. Even if they couldn't break Alma they could probably find somebody to put him away. He'd of trusted old Judge Wiesel with his life but there was a new man on the county bench now. A young one. And all too often to the young anyone who was old and set in their ways was senile, and anyone who didn't live like the rest should be made to. Especially if there was a way to come by a dollar doing it.

He figured he didn't have long to make his choice.

He wanted a chew. But when he put his hand in his pocket his fingers found first the commitment papers and then lead-tipped brass. Narrowing his eyes, jingling the cartridges, he began walking forward, into the wind.

Twenty-three

Later, in town, the streetlights buzzed and flickered on one by one. In their sudden brassy brilliance a woman sat in a window above Main Street. From the sidewalk a late shopper might have seen her: a solitary figure crouched on a window seat, hair tumbled forward, covering her face.

Jaysine was eating chocolate cake. She didn't look down, at the fizzling short circuit in one of the decorations, or the creche on Veterans Square. Nor did she look up, at the clouds that had wrapped the stars and put them away. She kept her eyes on the plate.

At a quarter of eight she disappeared from the window. A few minutes later the stairwell light came on.

She stood on the pavement, looking up at last. Her gaze focused between herself and the sky, on the moving air become suddenly visible.

The first flakes were falling. Airy, twinkling, they drifted earthward, as if coming home to rest.

She shivered, lifted her collar, and set out.

She'd passed the Reading Room a hundred times since she came to Raymondsville. Sometimes she'd stop and read the Weekly

Lesson through the window, the open Bible spread flat beside it, the matching passages highlighted. Once a gray-haired woman had smiled out at her. She'd smiled back, and walked quickly away.

Now an old man in a gray coat held the door for her as she approached. He said good evening and she said good evening, too.

The room itself was like all the others in all the other towns in America. Overstuffed chairs and reading lamps, shelves of *Sentinels* and *Journals* looking as if no one ever touched them except to dust. Through it was a larger room. She went in with her head down and sat in a left-hand pew. There were four others there, all old, seated near the stove. She felt better once she'd stolen enough glimpses to see she didn't know them.

The waiting silence was familiar. She sat in it for a long time with her eyes closed.

Her family had been Christian Scientists for four generations. The story as she'd heard it was that her great-grandfather had had some unspecified (and perhaps, she thought suddenly, in those days unmentionable) disease and had gone through the entire *materia medica* to no avail. Then one day he'd gone to Salamanca for a shay. He'd bought it, a Studebaker, and was looking for a saloon when he saw a practitioner's shingle.

He'd gone in, and been healed that very day and hour. And after that all her family had been Scientists. Right down to her.

Jaysine's mother was a practitioner, a devout dumpy woman who'd kept the house filled with the smells of canning and the lilt of hymns throughout her childhood. She remembered people coming to the porch, her mother taking them into the parlor and shutting the door. She'd peeped from outside, ankle-deep in the flowerbeds, hoping to catch her in the act of miracle. But all they'd ever seemed to do was talk.

She remembered her playmates at Sunday School singing around her, the circle of faces full of innocent confidence that her scrape would be healed or the glass would drop out of her finger. And it had seemed to her that often it had.

Till that spring night. Her father hadn't gone to service for years. And later there'd been long periods, weeks, when he wouldn't talk to her mother. He'd never said anything about the store, that he was sad or needed healing, or betrayed in any way what he was going to do. Till they heard the shot, and her mother, trembling, had sent her oldest son out to the barn alone.

Jaysine had stopped paying her Mother Church dues that fall. And gradually the whole idea of healing yourself through reliance on the Divine Mind seemed stranger and stranger, until now when people asked her what she was she just said Protestant, or some-times that she wasn't really anything at all.

At a scrape at the front of the room the old people stirred. She opened her eyes to the hand-lettered gilt GOD IS LOVE and the quotations from Matthew and Mary Baker Eddy.

The reader was Marguerite, from the Shoppe. Jaysine felt herself redden and her head go down, too late. She saw the older woman glance at her, but she only smiled briefly, and began the service.

Wednesday night meetings were simple. No sermons, no cere-mony. Just a few passages from Scripture and then the correlating ones from *Science and Health.* Someone played an organ, not very well, and they sang "Lead, Kindly Light." Then came the Lord's Prayer, said together slowly, and then a period of silence.

It seemed to go on forever; it could have been ten minutes. Jaysine began to tremble. At last one of the women stood, support-ing herself on the back of the bench.

"I want to tell everyone here about a wonderful healing I experienced some years ago.

"It happened when I had my grandchildren with me. My grand-son was ten, and one night he left his skates on the landing. I was coming down from the bedroom the next morning, and I stepped on one. My very next step took me onto the other, and I fell, not down the stairs, but over the banister.

"I remember while I was falling saying 'God is All.' It seemed to take so long that I think I said it twice. Then I came down across an end table near the bottom of the stairs.

"My husband and my daughter wanted to take me to the hospi-tal. It was hard to refuse, the pain was so great. Yet I kept reasoning to myself, and at last late that day I was able to get up and walk about. The practitioner came over that evening and she began my treatment.

"I progressed for some weeks in this way, and the pain lessened. But my husband said there would be a question of insurance, so I let them drive me to the hospital, just to put their minds at rest.

"The doctor looked at the X-rays and said, 'This woman has a broken hip, and I will need to put a pin in it. Admit her today and we'll do the operation tomorrow.' Well, I was dismayed at this. But I didn't protest or argue. I just told him quietly that I was a Christian Scientist and asked if there was any other way to proceed.

"And he said, 'How long has it been since you fell?' And I told him, six weeks. He said, 'Have you broken your hip before?' I said no. Then he said, still looking at the X-ray, 'It's interesting, but I see here, looking more closely, that the bones are beginning to knit. I've not seen that before, hips don't do that without pinning. Let's leave it alone and see what happens. I want you back in a month for another picture.'

"I went home rejoicing and continued my treatment. When I went back he said nothing, only asked me to continue whatever I was doing. When I went back again, he came toward me, smiling and holding out both hands, and said 'Here she is, the woman who heals herself.' He told me there was nothing left on the X-rays, that it had healed perfectly and he was very happy for me.

"I am very grateful for Christian Science."

She sat down. They rested in silence, and then a man got up and told how Divine Mind had rescued his daughter from smoking cigarettes. Then another woman, very thin, told about waking up without the use of her arm and how it had come back after an earnest session of prayerful thought. Jaysine listened, her tension growing.

Part of her regretted now that she'd gone to the doctors. It wasn't evil, but it showed lack of faith.

She'd been told from her earliest years that man wasn't a material but a spiritual being. Deny what was false, and it could no longer cause sin or sickness. There were no such things as diseases. They existed only in the carnal mind.

The trouble was that although she partly still believed, enough to make her feel guilty, she no longer had her childhood faith. Even if the people around her were right, she was too steeped in error and sin for it to work for her.

And if evil did not exist then *he* was not evil, and she couldn't blame him for what had happened. If there was anything Scientists believed, it was that one had to forgive in order to be forgiven.

But she couldn't. Not after the things he'd done. Given her this sickness, abandoned her, taken away her job, shamed her.

But still she stayed, standing from the polished pew, not needing the hymnal to sing:

> *I was not ever thus, nor prayed that Thou*
> *Shouldst lead me on; I loved to*
> *Choose, and see my path; but now . . .*
> *Lead Thou me on.*

For one moment, singing, she was able to try. *Tell me what to do,* she prayed. *If you would just tell me what to do, then I'd do it. Just tell me, please, I'm so lost and confused.*

She didn't really expect an answer.

Marguerite hurried toward her after the service. Her eyes reminded Jaysine of her mother's. She mumbled, "Good night," and fled.

In the hour she'd been inside the town had turned white. When she got back to her apartment, cursing the cold, the blue car was parked across the street.

For a while, standing beside it, she watched the flakes sweep down out of the dark, smashing themselves apart on the metal hood, then changing suddenly and mysteriously into shimmering ovals of water that reflected the streetlights in their hearts. Then she climbed the stairs, slowly, looking up toward her landing. She was starting to sweat, and she felt nauseated.

But when she got there it was deserted. She unlocked the door and let herself in, feeling a strange conflict of relief and regret.

A moment later her buzzer went off.

She knew instantly he was drunk. The smell came through the chained gap in waves. When she just stood there, unable to either close the door or open it, he grunted something.

"What?"

"I said, you going to let me in?"

"No. Go away."

"C'mon, damn it. We need to talk."

"What have we got to talk about? You told me to go to hell."

She was trembling. He'd come back. A week before she'd have been overjoyed. She'd spent hours fantasizing it. Then it seemed her love had turned, like wine left out overnight.

"Let me in. Right now. Or I'm leavin'."

"Brad, did you drive here? You shouldn't drive when you're like this."

"Hell I will . . . last chance."

She closed her eyes and imagined letting him go. I don't love him anymore, she thought. I tried so hard, but he doesn't love me.

But she didn't want him to go yet, either. There was intimacy here, a strange bond between one who inflicted pain and one who was hurt. Was being with him, bitter and wretched though it made her, any worse than being alone?

Rattling slightly, the chain pendulumed to and fro.

He lurched past her and half-fell into the couch. Big as ever, but tonight he seemed to have sagged. His tie was loose and something had spilled on his shirt. She stood by the door, paralyzed with contradictory emotions.

He rolled over, looked blearily at her, then toward the kitchen. "How's the wine situation?"

"I don't have any. You don't need any more to drink. Look at you. Do you want some coffee?"

"No. What else you got?"

"Chocolate layer cake. I just bought it. Do you want some of that?"

"No." His eyes ran down her. "You ought to lay off that stuff, Jay, it's starting to show."

She laughed. "What's it to you? Listen. I'm going to make some coffee."

He didn't say anything. She went into the kitchen. Starting to show, she thought bitterly. She hadn't dared weigh herself for two weeks. It was his fault, where did he get the nerve to reproach her? She was measuring drip-ground into the filter when his arms slid around her.

"You still care about old Brad, don't you, babe."

She closed her eyes, the spoon held out stiffly in front of her. Coffee jittered out and danced on the counter. She wanted to turn around and take him back. She also wanted to smash the Pyrex pot and grind the jagged pieces into his eyes.

There seemed to be no one inside her skull to choose between the two. At last she said, her voice thick and strange, "I don't think it's good for me to care about you, Brad."

"Oh, listen to this. You used to think I was. Pretty damn good, in fact." His breath stirred the hairs of her neck. The whiskey smell was overpowering. Out of nowhere, she remembered her father had smelled like that sometimes, and she remembered just for a moment the ceiling of the barn, so far away it seemed like heaven . . .

The image, the memory, vanished as she grasped it. She was struggling with this, trying to regain it, when he took the pot out of her hands and began unbuttoning her blouse. She hit him, once, on the neck, but it was as if she struck underwater; her hand was empty of all power. She put her head down, feeling dizzy, so dizzy

and empty that when his arms slid under her she could say nothing, neither in denial or desire, only turn her head away.

Lying beside him, exhausted, she eased her breath out with a
ragged flutter. She was still pulsing down there, still tightening and
loosening. No matter how she felt about him, the sex was still
incredible. Better than the magazines promised. Her lids sagged
closed. This was all she wanted right now, to lie here with her arms
around him, her head on his chest.

"You asleep?" she whispered, smiling to herself.

He grunted. Then swung his arm up. "Jesus!" he said, sitting up
suddenly.

"What's wrong?"

"Hell." She heard him groping in the dark, and the bedside
bulb came on. His belly sagged as he hoisted himself out. Water
rattled in the toilet.

He came out zipping his fly. He didn't look at her. The springs
creaked as he sat down. He smelled like sweat and whiskey and sex.
"What's wrong?" she said again.

"Got to get home."

"You said you'd stay here tonight. With me," she said, hearing
her voice gentle, sleepy.

"I can't do that. I didn't plan on this when I came over. Tell you
what, I'll call you tomorrow at work, okay?"

She remembered he didn't know. "Brad, I lost my job. I don't
work for Marybelle anymore."

"Is that right? That's too bad. Say, did you find my coat? Did I
leave it here?"

"Yes."

"Where is it?"

"I burned it."

"You what? Burned it?" He peered down at her and she wondered how much you had to drink to make your eyes liquid and
shiny like that. "You're different, babe, you know that? You even
look different. I bet you did at that. And my appointment book? I
hope you didn't burn that too?"

She came a little further awake. For a moment she thought
about giving it back. Then she thought: Maybe that's why he's here.
Through suddenly numb lips she said, "I didn't see anything else.
Just your coat. I took it out into the alley and poured lamp oil on it
and lit it."

He looked relieved and angry at the same time. But he didn't say anything, just started pulling on his shirt, getting the buttons wrong. She lay rigid, watching.

"You're pissed at me, aren't you."

"What a perceptive guy you are, Brad."

"Well, maybe you're right. Listen, I still got that money for you."

She almost told him what he could do with it, then remembered how much she needed it. Time to swallow your pride, Jaysine, she told herself. "All right," she said.

"Atta girl, now you're talking . . . Look, let's get something else cleared up. You calling Ainslee, that made me mad. Lemme tell you a little something, the way I operate. People treat me right, I treat them right. They try to screw me, I give them one warning. They don't take the hint, the next one goes between their eyes. I don't want you talking to her again, ever. Understand? . . . Hey, you sure there's nothing to drink?"

"No. Nothing," said the part of her that hated him. But then the part that kept telling her to do what men wanted added, "But I could go down to the store."

"Never mind, I got booze at home . . . Anyway, wanted to ask you, there's people around this town who're trying to hurt me. Make me look bad, the company too. You know anything about that?"

She thought instantly of the boy. The old man he'd told her about. "No, Brad, I haven't heard about anything like that."

"You sure you don't got that notebook? Leather cover, gold-stamped? I'd sure like to get it back."

She put her hands on her belly under the covers. It felt as if she was being twisted around a stick, tighter and tighter. "Was that all you wanted? To get your book, and a . . . free fuck? Or just your book, and then you felt *sorry*—"

"Hold on, Jay. Hold on." He waggled his head. "Damn! Look, I'd like to fix things up between us. But I can go the other way, too."

"What does that mean?"

"Well, look, I'm sorry I said those things to you. You know what things. I just got mad. I'm sorry you got canned, too."

"Is that supposed to make me feel better?"

He patted her shoulder. "No, but maybe this will. You lost your job? Here's what I'm gonna do. I got some positions coming open, nursing assistant positions. Doesn't pay shit to start, but you work out, you'll go to supervisor in a few months." He reached for his tie.

"And you have plans for us, too, I suppose?"

He smiled again, but he was looking toward the door. "I might get by once in a while."

"When? How often?"

"I don't know. Don't try to pin me down."

She sat up, aware suddenly he was leaving. She swung her legs out into the chill. "So basically you're saying, you'll hire me, then maybe come by and screw me when you're in the mood."

"Only if you want, baby, only if you want."

"You know what I wanted!" The pain in her belly was like a huge hot needle. So bad she couldn't stand; she huddled naked in the cold air. "I wanted to love you, and have you love me back! You didn't have to leave your wife. But you needed me, Brad. Believe it or not, you needed me."

She was crying and hiccoughing now, ashamed, terrified, but she had to say it all, get it all out. "I know I'm not pretty or smart. You think I'm . . . ordinary, and fat, and dumb. But I would've done anything for you. I could have hurt you and I didn't. Your wife wanted me to. I never told you that. Brad, they're going to stop you—"

"Who?" he said instantly. When she didn't answer he reached down and shook her. "I said, *who?*"

She said lamely, "Everybody. People around here. You can't keep treating them the way you do."

He gave a disgusted snort. "Okay. You've declared your scruples. Let's wrap it up, I got a headache. You taking my offer?"

"No."

"What?"

"I said no! I'm an electrologist, not a nurse, and not your whore!"

He looked so strangely at her that for a moment she forgot how to breathe. She was terrified at what she'd said. But she couldn't take it back. It was the truth.

He stood suddenly, huge, swaying. "Let's see. I apologized. I offered you bucks. A job. Chance to see me again sometimes. But no, you're like my fucking wife, you got to have everything your way.

"Well, you don't have a thing I can't get cheaper and better someplace else. And you don't scare me. These people are sheep.

"So fuck off, Jaysine Farmer, but listen to this: from now on, stay out of my way. And don't call my wife again, or I'll kill you."

"Brad, no!" she screamed. She lunged out for him as he turned, caught his legs, but he was already moving away. He dragged her from the bed, cursing and trying to free himself, but she gripped his suit with desperate strength. She was screaming incoherently. Till she heard the slap and then after a time, like thunder and lightning reversed, felt the pain.

She felt him kicking her off, like a dog. Then he was gone, leaving the door swinging above the windy blackness of the stair.

She crawled a few feet and then stopped, curling naked on the window-seat, holding her stomach and waiting, just waiting, filled with freezing despair. There was light below her, a bright copper glow. Somewhere in it red flared on, then dwindled away. But the snow was coming down too thick and hard for her to really see.

Twenty-four

P hil lay motionless in the room under the eaves, listening to the snow, staring up at the plywood sheet.

It'd be the fourth time today, but he was thinking of doing it again. The only thing that even transiently held his interest. For a few minutes he could forget this depression, this deadening nausea that had clamped down again, shorting out thought and emotion like a clamp over the poles of a battery. He no longer bothered to fantasize about girls he knew. Separating it from women, other than the ones in the photographs, made it somehow purer, less painful.

He sat up in bed, and reached for the thumbed damp pages.

When it was over he lay under the covers and stared at the darkened window for a long time. The last faint echo of desire ebbed back into the chill. His body was spent, his mind empty. He no longer wanted or cared for anything at all.

He thought, there's only one thing left to finish up. To make sure of or else to fail at finally and forever. Then he could go.

Take the gun, or the razor, and find the peace that would last forever.

Faintly, through the snow-hiss, the purr of a motor came to his ears. His father. Home early, he thought. He didn't wonder why. He stared at the ceiling, thinking already of doing it again.

• • •

Later someone called his name downstairs. He thought at first of
ignoring it, pretending sleep. Then he identified the voice, and
the tone. He threw back the covers and rolled out, ducking his
head without thinking, pulled on pants and padded down the
steep narrow stairs, sucking air through his teeth at the sudden
cold laid against his skin.

Joe Romanelli stood in the living room in uniform. Brown
striped trousers, uniform shirt, the lamb-lined bomber jacket with
the stitched-on flag. The badge, the gun, the cuffs. He didn't say
anything as Phil came down the stairs, just followed him with his
eyes. When he saw his father's mouth his step slowed.

"What you doin' home, Dad?"

"Where's your mother?"

"I'm here," she said, coming out of the pantry. "Joe, what are
you doing home?"

He said harshly, "Nolan put me back to night shift."

"Oh, Dad."

"Oh, no, Joe. Were you—you weren't drinking on duty
again—"

"It wasn't me this time," said his father, jerking his head up at
Phil where he stood on the stairs. Phil's feeling of nameless anxiety
deepened into dread.

"Joseph—"

"Maybe you better stay in the kitchen, Mary."

His father reached out as he neared him. Phil hadn't felt for a
long time how strong his father was. "Okay, living room."

The old dread was growing like a baby in his gut. Just like always.
It was just the same, nothing was ever new in the world, maybe that
was why there had to be new people all the time, so they'd think it
was . . . He followed his father's back into the living room and
stood waiting as he stripped off his jacket and threw it on the couch
and turned, his eyes cop's-eyes, folding his arms over the badge.

"Let's have it, boy, I don't want to have to make you tell me. You
and this crazy old guy, this Halvorsen, what do you think you're
doin'?"

"I don't know—"

"I told you, don't *give* me that kiddie-crap." His father hit him,
not real hard, but the way it landed made his eyes tear. He blinked,
cursing himself and thinking *I hate that. I don't care if he hits me but I
hate it when I cry.*

"Well?"

He didn't say anything. Couldn't think of anything, and didn't feel like saying it if he had.

Joe picked up the *TV Guide* and glanced at it, then dropped it back on the coffee table. He put his thumbs under his belt and said in his serious voice, "You're getting old enough to learn some sense. Learn about how things work. Now why don't we make this easy on both of us. What you up to with him?"

"We're on the track of some criminals."

The elder Romanelli laughed sudden and bitter, eyebrows climbing. "On the track! On the *track!* What the hey! Now he's a detective!"

"No, we—"

"You been reading too many books down in that library. I told your mother that, but she laughed." His father glanced hate toward the kitchen. "What kind of criminals? How come you ain't told me about it?"

"I didn't think you'd be interested. It's waste dumping, on the roads."

"Oh, Christ. You're right, I ain't."

Phil saw his mother's face, white and frightened, peering around the jamb at them. He tried to smile at her. Then switched his attention to his father, who was looking at the TV and slowly pulling his belt through the loops of his uniform.

"Nolan calls me in today, calls me into his office. Closes the door. Says: Romanelli, you keep an eye on your boy? I say, sure. He says, you know he's into something he got no business in? Stirring up trouble? Says, item one, teach me to keep tabs on what you're doing, I'm going back to night shift. Forget about the stripe. Can't supervise my kid, can't supervise a squad."

His father paused to light a cigarette, waved out the match, flicked it still hot to the floor. He looked at the ceiling, blinking in the smoke. "Item two, my pension. He hears about you again I won't have to worry about it. I'll be on the street. Reminds me I got three years to twenty. Seventeen years lickin' Hodges's shit, then Nolan's . . . See what we're talking?"

"Yeah."

"Yes sir."

"Yes sir."

His father coiled the belt, looking off to the side. "Get those pants down. You should be too big for this. But you don't got the sense of an adult, I can't treat you like one."

"I think I got enough sense."

"Shut up! Bend over!"

"No. You should be asking me who's doin' this—"

His voice went high then and broke and all at once he lost it. He knew it was stupid but he tried to slap his father back. Joe was inside his guard and had him doubled up in some kind of armlock before his hand reached where his father's face had been. Phil's eyes bulged and he cried out; it felt like his arm was being torn off.

But then, distantly, he heard his mother say "Joe—here, take this—"

He looked at her. Mary Romanelli stood in the kitchen doorway, one hand holding a rosary, the other arm rigid as a statue's. In her outstretched hand trembled a bottle of beer.

"Get back in there!"

"Don't hit him, Joe. Don't, he's not well—"

His father shouted and she came out of the kitchen. Then he slapped her too. There was the usual crying and carrying on, and somehow that toughened him and he got his mouth shut again. Bent over, biting his lips under the repetitive sting of the heavy belt, he was abruptly sick and disgusted. His whole being recoiled from the leather-wool-tobacco smell of policeman. He opened his eyes to find the worn butt of the service revolver inches from them, bent as he was over his father's hip.

He was still staring at it when Joe released him, slamming him against the wall with the same motion. He leaned there, drooping his eyelids as if bored, to hide the shame and anger.

"Okay, tell me what you learned." It was the phrase he used whenever he whipped one of them.

"Nothin'."

"Philip, tell him what he wants to hear, for God's sake!"

"I learned you're a coward."

His father looked shocked and sad, grim, as if this hurt him too, though Phil knew it didn't. He slapped his son hard on both sides of the face. Phil leaned his head back against the dark brown wallpaper. Behind his eyes he saw for a moment the inside of a house. He didn't recollect where it had been, somewhere his mother had taken him when he was small and they'd tried to leave; neat rows of brown pottery crocks, each filled with cookies, nuts, ground-up leaves and roots and blossoms that smelled so sweetly they lived like everlasting flowers all over the house . . . He shook his head and was back. His voice shook when he let it out.

"I seen you learn your lesson, Dad. About crawlin' around for the ones with money. I'm not gonna do it."

"You think it's any different anyplace else? I did too, once. We got our place here, Phil, and it ain't a bad one, all told. It's a hell of a lot better than some I seen."

"It ought to be better."

"You think I like it? You think I enjoy this? Christ, you're my son. Crippled or not, I got to show you how to get along. I want you to make it through in one piece."

"It ought to be better," he said again, knowing how he must sound, like a child crying to be given the moon; pretending he was being proud and scornful, but knowing he was really just bawling. "There ought to be more than just making it through."

"Maybe. But just doin' that's hard enough. You better face up to it. I sure as shit had to."

His father's voice was harsh, Police Lecture tone, but just for a moment Phil heard something else there too. He squinted up, startled, and Joe said, "Ah, both of you, just shut the hell up." He turned, and the door slammed behind him.

His mother was on him, crying. He pushed her away, then gave up and let her wipe his face and cry on him. *What the hell,* he thought then, feeling his twisted vicious and enraged victory, over them, over life itself. *Let her, she won't be able to much longer.*

He remembered, from deep in his childhood, going fishing with his father. Or maybe being taken fishing was more accurate. Or maybe being dragged off, forced to go fishing was it. This was one of those dim memories that you knew had happened, but you hadn't understood how little you were even though you might have been able to say a number when somebody asked you, three or four or five. Anyway it was summer, incandescently hot. He didn't recall where they'd gone. It couldn't have been far, but when you were that little you couldn't see over the bushes so you had no idea where you were. Now as he remembered it the pictures brightened, like a bulb coming on behind them. He could see it clearly even now, but different, as if the light of the sun had been different then. So different that he knew even if he saw the same place, the same creek they'd hiked along, he wouldn't recognize it.

Anyway he'd stumbled and run after his father for what seemed like hours (this was before his illness) till his legs hurt and things had bitten and scratched him and he was exhausted and crying.

And his father, towering up to the trees, would look back and yell angrily, "You coming? Or am I gonna hafta leave you here?"

And he'd run, frantically, tripping over roots and rocks and clumps of grass trying to catch up. When he did he'd reach up for a hand but it never held his for long.

When they got to the pond he was afraid of it. More water than he'd ever seen. The edge was slippery but his father sat him right at the brink and began showing him how to push the hook through the worm's belly. Somehow that afternoon he'd got the hook in his ear and cried and cried while his father cut it out with his knife. But he hadn't been afraid. It was the pain that made him cry, not fear. He knew his father would get it out. Just as he knew how to fish, and drive the car, how to do everything.

He remembered the fish too. It was huge and silver and dreadfully alive. It kicked itself around on the grass without legs. It snapped at the air and thrashed and then lay gasping for a little while before fighting itself in the dirt some more. His father picked it up by the tail and handed it to him, grinning, telling him he'd caught it all by himself, his first fish, telling him to feel how heavy it was. And he'd dug his fingers breathlessly into the slippery cold silver, feeling it buck and strain desperately to escape.

Then suddenly, he couldn't say why, he'd pushed it away, back toward the silver water. It hit the mud and bucked and was instantly gone beneath a thousand spreading circles. The men at the pond had laughed. He could hear them laughing now. Then his father had taken him into the bushes and whipped him for throwing away good food. And he'd pooped his pants and his father called him a name, and hit him some more, and at last took him down and washed his underpants there in front of them all right where the fish had gone back . . .

He lay under the plywood patching, the covers packed tight as gun-wadding around him, and let tears slide slowly down his face.

It wouldn't be hard to die.

It wouldn't be hard at all.

Twenty-five

D amn, it's cold, Halvorsen thought, leaning into the hill. Damn! Cold as he remembered it ever being. The wind seared the few exposed inches of his face like hot iron. He blinked snow from his eyelashes, peering uphill, into the falling dusk.

Why do I feel this way? he thought. Like there's something out here with me. Somethin' that, when I meet it, I won't like.

Around him for miles the deserted, leafless woods lay hissing-silent. This was the hill's northern face, and north of it was only emptiness. Old maps showed names there. But now there were no roads, no houses, except deep in a hollow the tumbled silvery boards of a long-abandoned farm. Only a slow heave and dropping away, like a white, empty, forest-covered sea. From here to the New York border, as this day dimmed toward evening not another human soul moved or lived.

Just now he was plodding homeward, following his drifting breath up between darkening sycamores. Swinging in his gloved hand was the light single-shot. Beneath his snowshoes crunched six inches of fresh fall. The shoulders of his coat, the crown of his hat, were frosted with what had come down in the last hour.

I don't know, he concluded at last. Must just be tired. Hiked a ways today for a man who still ain't feeling himself.

A few minutes later he came over the lip of a bench, a slackening in the hill's ascent. He paused there, glancing around, more from long habit of the woods than anything else. Beside him a lightning-shivered oak leaned into the reluctant embrace of a middle-aged beech, their upper branches tangled and partially intergrown.

He was resting against its massive cold bole, listening to the slither of snowflakes through the twigs, when a whine came from under his ear.

The old man sighed. He unbuttoned his coat. Lifted the pup out and set her down. Watched, as she sniffed around and finally squatted, blinking up at him.

When she was done he bent slowly to scratch her head. "You little devil. Getting heavier ever' mile. I think you better walk the rest of the way."

The puppy whined again, looking up at the furry broken thing that swayed by its ears from the man's belt. "You just wait," he said sternly. "You just wait."

A few hundred feet across the bench and then uphill, but not too far after that to home. Yeah, she's coming down hard, Halvorsen thought, planting one boot in front of the other.

He couldn't honestly say he minded. Maybe in a few more years, though. It seemed like the cold sank another eighth of an inch into his bones every year, and edged out, each spring, more reluctantly. Each year the slopes got steeper, till he could swear the hills were buckling upward.

But he wasn't ready yet to find a warm place to die. This was where he belonged. In these empty, chill woods, free of man and anything conceived of or invented by him, free of his pride and greed and relentless self-obsession.

He thought of Man with neither sneer nor pity but a deep regret. What other creature would afflict its God with its own image? Could admit with a snigger its irremediable sinfulness, craziness, murderousness, and in the next breath vaunt its similitude with the Almighty?

As for me, he thought, give me a god whose image is the tree. Silently uniting rock and sky, light and soil into food and shade for all manner of creatures. Or the deer: fleet and graceful, melting and moving like shadow; gentle, killing nothing, free as the wind. Or even the wolf: bringing death, but only to those no longer capable of life; destroying, but without treachery, without hate, without the masks of patriotism or honor.

He looked at the puppy, trotting along self-importantly in the marks of his snowshoes. But not in the image of a dog, he thought. They been keeping bad company.

He discovered he'd stopped again, half-crouching in the lee of a tree. Shoot, he thought, what are you doing? Acting like a spooked doe. But nonetheless he respected the instinct and stood still, a shadow in the driving snow, looking patiently between each stroke of gray in the dying light for motion or silhouette, up and down the hill. When he was sure there was nothing there, no one watching or stalking him, he resumed his climb.

A quarter-hour later the cover lightened, letting a little more twilight seep down. That meant the top lay just ahead. He was ready. He'd had to stop and rest every hundred feet of the last slope. This was the steepest part of Town Hill, damn near impossible in summer, when it was choked so tight with scrub and bramble a weasel would have hard going.

But he knew his way through it. He'd hunted and hiked here for sixty years, and at the steepest cuts had trees picked out to haul himself up on hand after hand. He did this now just below the crest. Then he was up and the puppy scrambled panting up after him. They stood for a moment, looking back down into the valley. It was almost dark there now.

"Couple minutes, Jez, we'll be home," he muttered.

He was turning, getting ready to hike on down the ridge, when he heard a motor. He cocked his head, but lost it. He couldn't even tell what kind of a machine it had been; airplane, snowmobile, car; only that it was far off.

He moved forward again, even more cautiously now. And behind him scampered the hound, hopping from one to the next of the shallow depressions his snowshoes silently embossed like ancient seals into the blank and yielding snow.

Some time later he stood motionless amid a copse of hemlocks, peering through their snow-loaded branches toward the clearing. Twice more, as he moved down the spine of the hill, the sound had come, swelled, then faded again behind the dancing veils. The last time he'd made it out: the growl of an approaching truck. Beside him the puppy keened once, low. "Quiet now, girl," he muttered.

It wasn't Alma's old Dodge. Wasn't DeSantis, he knew his Willys too. Beyond the stand of hemlock was a little space without trees. He bent stiffly, lowering his cap below the tops of the snow-covered bushes, and moved forward, cradling the old rifle.

He came to the edge of the woods. Past a vast old maple his land proper began. Twenty years before, a barbed-wire fence had marked this division. The open snow beyond it had covered sleeping flowers, when there'd been a woman to want flowers. On its far side, past the smooth white openness of the road, was his basement.

The sound came louder now, engine dropping into low gear for the last long climb up Mortlock from the base-valley of the river. Halvorsen fitted himself behind the maple, lowering the rifle so it wouldn't stick out. Behind him the pup dropped her belly to the snow.

When it came into view he did not so much as breathe. Only his faded blue eyes moved, following it. It dipped and swerved on the hidden road, throwing snow as a boat throws water. A four-wheel-drive, red, new, Japanese. It snarled up the last rise; then the back wheels spewed frozen mud and dead leaves as it left the road and swung out into the clearing at the top of the mountain. White vapor streamed from the tailpipe, hesitated, then was carried away in the chill steady wind.

Four men got out. One pulled a pump shotgun after him and leaned it against the bumper. They wore orange vests, heavy boots, flame-orange caps. Two lit cigarettes as soon as they were out of the cab. They were close enough he could make out the brands. Close enough, when one of them leaned back in and the engine snored down to silence, that he could hear.

"Christ, I got to piss."

"You sure this's it, Nickie? Looks like the ass end a' nowhere to me."

"That's what he said it was. Remote."

"Where's the house? Boulton said there was a house."

Silence for a few moments. One of the men, blunt-faced as the butt of a camp-axe, heavily bearded, floundered a little way off. After a moment steam rose from between his straddled legs.

Halvorsen watched it all intently, leaning against the cold black roughness of maple bark. The rifle hung motionless in his hand.

They looked like hunters. Or thought they did. But as they passed a flask, tossing back short hard nips while they waited for the bearded man, the faded blue eyes saw that their boots were new. All their clothes were new. And the license windows on the back of their coats were empty.

The blunt-faced man, apparently the leader, finished and came back to the truck. They stood around it, discussing something in voices too low to hear. Halvorsen's gray-stubbled mouth twitched. He'd been out long enough that the fire had burned down. Embered, there was no telltale of woodsmoke and very little smell. The basement lay so low beneath the snow it was indistinguishable.

The hatchet-faced man raised his voice. "Naw, goddamnit, it's gotta be up here. Tommy, you look over there. Mitch, down the hill. I'll go this way."

Cold blue eyes followed them as they trudged about the plateau. At last one shouted. The others turned and waded toward him. They gathered at the top of the steps, then went down, one after the other, into the ground.

When they disappeared Halvorsen looked down at the pup. "Well," he said slowly. "Guess you and me, Jez, we ought to get somethin' fixed for our visitors."

When they reappeared several minutes later, Halvorsen straightened. He edged himself slowly back into the woods. But they weren't looking in his direction. They were headed for the truck. He studied them with farsighted eyes as the blunt-faced man lifted out two red cans with spouts, let them drop to the snow—they sank into it, heavy—and shut the gate with a hollow slam.

He was opening the door of the Toyota when a whine floated out from the woods. The old man bent instantly, clamping his glove over the dog's snout, but it was too late.

The men turned, reaching into vests, pockets. Ah, thought Halvorsen, through the cold alertness that had taken him. He'd wondered why these "hunters" had no rifles. And only one long gun, when they should have had four, racked in the mounts bolted in the back window.

He straightened. Across thirty yards of snow his eyes met theirs. Holding their pistols out and ready, they slogged forward, toward where the puppy keened again, shivering, too hungry and too cold to stay quiet.

He stepped out, dropping the stock of the rifle into his left glove. His breath came warm and rapid, puffing steam into the bitter wind. It was too bad, he thought then, facing them, that the old falling-block was empty. He'd fired the last handload an hour before at the rabbit that dangled now head down, sightless eyes glazed open, from his belt.

"My name's Racks Halvorsen," he said quietly, into the mouths of the waiting guns. "And I want you boys off my land."

They stopped, facing him in a semicircle. The one with the shotgun moved sideways. The others moved too, edging apart, glancing to where the bearded man stood.

He said, loud, "What d'you want up here?"

"You Halvorsen?" said the bearded one.

"Just said so. Who're you?"

"That don't matter."

"What're we talking for?" said the youngest suddenly. "Let's get it done and get outa here."

"He got a rifle."

"So? Four of us, one a' him."

"You take him, then."

"Shut up," said the bearded one. To Halvorsen he said, "Put your gun down and come on out."

"I was you fellers, I'd get in that nice shiny truck and head back to town. You want me, come in and get me. You ain't going to like it, though, if you do."

"Can you count, old man?" said the one called Mitch. "You'd better come with us peaceful."

"Don't think so," said Halvorsen. He took a step back from the maple.

"Get him!" shouted the bearded man suddenly, raising the shotgun and letting go, pumping the forestock. The others took a moment to react, two aiming their handguns clumsily, as if unused to them. The shot whipped above him, rattling off branches. He didn't see or hear where the bullets went.

Halvorsen was already moving backward, crouched on the snow-shoes, when they lowered their guns and began running toward him over the field. He scooped up the puppy and stuffed it down inside his coat. Then he had trees between him and them, and he turned and set his face downhill, into the deepening darkness. He didn't know if they'd follow. He wouldn't, if he were them.

He still felt weak. But for the moment at least his heart pulsed strong, he felt warm, ready for a fight. He didn't know how long it would last, but it felt good. They were city men, that was plain. Unused to the woods, and not armed for it; the short-barreled guns they carried were concealable, but not very accurate. He'd have to watch the fellow with the pump, though.

He thought he could make things interesting for them.

Turning, now, he glanced back up the rise. To see the first, the fleetest or most eager, loom suddenly into view framed by the two trees Halvorsen had been standing between. The man was running hard. He was almost between the trees, the gun coming up in his hand as he ran.

Halvorsen, just to keep his eyes on him, stopped, turned, and waved.

The first man's name was Tommy, but he was usually called "Tommy Del." He had shot people before, but in parked cars, not in the winter woods, and they hadn't carried guns themselves; in fact two of them had been tied up at the time.

So that now, running heavy-footed ahead of the others toward where the old man had disappeared, he felt a little fear that made him slow for a moment, just before he entered the woods. Then he came to where the land started to drop, and looking down it he saw the old man, turning, lifting his arm.

Got you, you old bastard, he thought. He was raising his automatic when he felt the tug at his foot.

Tommy Del looked down, the upper part of his body still running though his legs had abruptly stopped, to see the loop of barbed wire rip up from under the snow. His arms windmilled, the gun went flying, and then he fell. He wondered, as he went down, whether it was some kind of trap. It didn't seem to be. Just wire. He was still thinking this as his eyes flicked to where his upper body would land. He caught the yellow gleam of whittled wood just before his hands struck the snow on either side of it.

Halvorsen halted at the bottom of the first slope, breathing hard, and listened. There'd been a hoarse shout as the first of them entered the woods, suddenly cut off; and then silence. Between them, now, the snow had drawn itself dense and sound-deadening. So even if they were still on his trail, he might not be able to hear them.

Or they him. The puppy was squirming and scratching at his chest. He unbuttoned a button to give it more air, but it kept on whimpering.

He plunged his hand into his pockets, hoping for an overlooked cartridge. The little single-shot wasn't much for firepower, but a .22 Hornet would do more than startle a fellow. His groping fingers found his old Case, the knife he'd used to whittle the stake-trap. Matches, he always carried them. Tobacco. But other than that his hand came empty out of the last pocket.

So that was that. He thought of dropping the rifle; it'd be that much less to carry; but then he thought, it'll make them keep their distance. Till they realized he had no ammunition. The end would come quickly after that.

He lifted his snowshoes and turned at right angles, heading east along the bench. The puppy whimpered again and without stopping he plunged his hand into his coat. Her fur was warm and her breath was hot against his chest. "Just hold on there, girl," he muttered. "Just hold on. This won't take long, one way or t'other."

The second man was the one they called Mitch. He had a part interest in a junkyard. Mitch Burck didn't like guns much, though he used them when he was told to. In his opinion it made smaller men dangerously equal. He preferred an iron bar, or better yet, his hands.

He'd been the second to reach the woods, and he'd bent over Tommy Del where he fell. He'd hardly grasped the meaning of the pointed wood that grew so oddly out of his back before Nickie was on him. The bearded man had shoved him, and he'd turned, snarling, and said, "Hold on a fucking second! Tommy's hurt!"

"We'll take care of him. You get that fucking old man or you're next."

Now he was ahead of the others. Couldn't see them, but they must be back there someplace. And ahead of him, somewhere in the falling snow, was the old guy. Mitch thought, What was that animal with him? Something small. Maybe a dog? He hoped it wasn't. He had six at home. But then he thought, Maybe I can get the old guy without hurting it. Then Nickie might let him keep it.

Okay, the old man . . . He stared around at the trees as he stumbled down the hill, using his left hand to steady himself when he started to slip. Keeping a sharp lookout for wires or stakes. He held the .38 snub out in front of him. Christ, he thought, it's spooky back in here. He shivered. And cold; the wind cut like busted glass. They'd bought wool pants and coats for the job but all he had on under them was cotton underwear, thin socks, an Italian silk shirt.

When he came off the slope onto the flat he felt relieved. It was hard for a heavy man to go downhill. He bent; the old man's prints were clear. The tracks moved on fifty feet or so and then made a sharp left. He grinned tightly and fingered the trigger. Yeah. He'd get him.

Burck trudged through the darkening woods, glancing around alertly. Getting darker . . . too dark to aim anymore, he'd just have to get close and give him the four he had left from the hip. Then charge. He'd crushed bigger men with his hands than this Halvorsen.

He was moving along, squinting toward something bulky and dark up on the bench, when he heard from ahead of him, low but unmistakable, the moan of a puppy.

He hunched down a little and moved forward, using the trees for cover. Just like a Indian, he thought. Ain't too much to this. It was in the woods instead of the unlit piers and abandoned warehouses of the waterfront. That was all that was different.

The dark ahead of him became boulders, huge rounded rocks half-sunk in soil. Their tops were white, their sides still bare and black. He moved cautiously in among them. They were higher than his head, but not so close he felt cramped. The falling snow melted invisibly on his outstretched hand, and he shivered again, hard. Somewhere ahead, or behind, around him somewhere, he heard a chuckle of water. And above it, again, the low wailing. It sounded close.

He stepped around the boulder and made out dimly ahead of him something dark and man-sized, with the straight line of a barrel jutting off to the side. At that moment the whimper came again, from directly ahead.

He jerked the revolver up, eyes wide—the old guy had a rifle—and pulled the trigger. The muzzle flash showed him plainly the stump, the rifle hung on it by the sling, and the puppy, crying at its foot with a head-sized rock on its tail. But his finger pulled twice more before his brain deduced from what it saw that the old man wasn't there. Wasn't in front of him. Might be, in fact, *behind*—

A terrifyingly loud crunch inside his head. His fingers opened and he fell. No, only started to, because he hadn't been knocked out. The blow hadn't been powerful enough. Or his skull was too thick. It just knocked him sideways. He kept going that way, rolling, and started to come up, hands spread, ready to grip, to crush.

Instead the ground slipped out from under him. The earth opened and before he could think rocks smashed into his side, his back.

He hit water with a cracking splash. Its icy shock revived him instantly. He went under for a moment and panicked. He couldn't swim! His feet groped. He flailed his arm wildly.

Then he stopped. He raised his head and looked around, feeling suddenly stupid.

He'd fallen down a short, rocky bank into a little pool. The chuckle he'd heard was a spring, bubbling idly out of the hillside and gathering here. There'd been a sheet of ice over it, through which he'd plunged, but it wasn't very deep. He had his feet on solid bottom now, and it only came to his chest. Something was wrong with his arm, though. It didn't hurt yet, but he suspected it was broken.

Burck realized suddenly that the water he was standing in was freezing. He waded clumsily to the edge and hauled himself out. Water poured off his clothes. But out of the pool, in the wind, it seemed suddenly a hundred degrees colder. He crouched on the rocks and beat his fist on his legs. It was like beating logs with a hammer, he couldn't feel either the fist or the legs, just a distant impact.

He looked up at the empty woods. He didn't see the old man. He couldn't hear the puppy anymore. He wondered where the others were. Nicky and Nate. He opened his mouth and tried to call, but all he could get out was a whimper. He couldn't feel his face or his tongue. He tried to climb up, but now his legs wouldn't move, either.

Well, he couldn't say he felt bad. No pain. His arm didn't hurt anymore. In fact, he was starting to feel warm.

Dimly, all alone in the dark, Mitch Burck realized he was going to freeze to death.

The two men stopped, halfway down the hill, and listened to the *pop pop pop* of a handgun echo from the trees and then, lower-pitched, come back seconds later from the night-shrouded hills.

"Burck," said the blunt-faced man, tasting the icy air.

"Yeah," said the other, the youngest one. "Think he got him?"

"Sounds like."

"I don't think Tommy's gonna make it with that stake in his chest."

"I don't think so either. Unless we get this over with damn quick."

The bearded, blunt-faced man with the shotgun was Nicodemo Asaro, "Little Nickie," a wiseguy from Saratoga Avenue who'd come up through charge cards, loan-sharking, brokering stolen cars, and heroin. He'd drawn a stretch for contempt and when he came out his family's distribution had been wrecked by a federal narcotics task force. He was working his way up again now in a different racket.

Till a few minutes ago this had been routine. Take three men. Drive out to the sticks, see a guy, do a job for him, drive home. He hadn't been told specifics till that afternoon, but they rarely varied; break somebody's back, torch his business, kidnap his daughter; whatever some guy said. This hadn't been any different. Go to this old guy's house, shut him up, go home. He was eager to get home. Tomorrow was his son's thirteenth birthday.

The younger man, who was twenty, was Nate Diamond. Diamond hadn't had much experience yet. He'd had a year of college on an athletic scholarship and realized he needed three more like a pig needs the Talmud. He had some friends in retail coke and when he showed them he could use his size for something more constructive than wrestling they'd passed him up the line. He was fast and ambitious and he kept himself in shape.

He also, unlike the others, knew how to shoot. He'd spent quite a few hours on the indoor range with the .44 magnum automatic he gripped now muzzle-down alongside his right leg.

Diamond didn't care about getting home for the weekend. He liked to see people die.

They came to the rockpile and threaded their way slowly into it, alert and primed. A strange whimper came sporadically at first, as they moved deeper into the maze, then ebbed away to silence. It hadn't sounded like a dog or any other animal they could name. So they took their time. Neither of them wanted to run into any traps. At last, perhaps a quarter-hour later, they came out on a clearing. It was too dark to see now, but then there was a click, and Asaro flicked the beam of a key-chain flashlight over a stump, a rock, a torn-up spot of leaves and snow, and a chunk of wood lying to one side. That was it.

"What the hell?" said Diamond in a low voice.

Asaro moved to the side. They looked over a short drop. It wasn't far down, maybe five feet, and then there was a sheet of ice. Beside it, sitting on a rock, was Mitch Burck. His arms were in his lap and he was smiling dreamily. Asaro kept the flash on him for almost a minute, but he didn't move. His open eyes glittered in the light.

Halvorsen was some hundreds of yards ahead of them by then.

When the splashing and cursing from below stopped he'd

dropped the length of wood and bent to free the dog. Then slung on the rifle again; and finally, bent to feel in the torn-up snow at the edge of the slope. At last his fingers touched the revolver. He broke the cylinder and took off a glove and rubbed his thumbnail over the primers. A five-shot, with one round left. He pressed the ejector, discarded the empties, and replaced the live round. He positioned it to the right of the forcing cone and snapped the gun closed.

Now he was trudging along the bench. He was tired now. The long hike down that afternoon, the long climb home again; the brief burst of fear-fed energy when he'd first seen the men; the swift pace since; they'd taken their toll. He felt his years on his shoulders now, each one like a pound of lead.

He consulted his mind. Though it was fuzzy on some things, like what he'd had for breakfast, or who the President was, he found his map of the land he walked on etched sharp and clear as a survey-or's plat. He was headed west along the slope of Town Hill, on the second bench. Half a mile farther was a saddle, then a creek, then the start of Lookout Tower Hill. No tower there anymore, hadn't been for years, but he remembered it. That was perhaps three miles from here, in the dark.

Could he outrun them? Go up the run, angle left down the valley, then over Gerroy into Dale Hollow and back down to Route Six? It'd be a hike. Eight miles at least. He figured if he had all night he could do it.

If he had all night. He paused and looked back. Under the overcast sky, not far back on his trail, swayed a faint glow. His mouth tightened in the darkness. They had a flashlight, then. They could track him. They were on foot, not used to the land, but their youth and strength would make up for that in a chase lasting several hours.

He thought then about foxing them. Red fox had a thousand tricks. One was to circle back and get on the hunter's trail. Sooner or later the man realized he was going in circles, and the fox, having more time on his hands, generally won that game. Hal-vorsen slogged on for a few minutes. He could circle back. Once behind, he could wait till the flashlight illuminated one of them, and then . . . No, that wouldn't work. He'd get one, but the other could take him at his leisure thereafter.

He was thinking this when something caught him painfully across the chest. His fingers explored iron, an inch thick, rough and cold. He recognized it as a rod line. So there was a powerhouse nearby . . . sure, he remembered it; how could he forget? It was number six on the Dreiser lease, a seven-spot pumping from second sand fifteen hundred feet down. He couldn't remember if it was uphill or down from this bench, but made sense it'd be uphill; power went down easier than it went up.

The next question was, was it still in operation? He felt his way hand over hand up the line. It cut through a tree, or the tree had grown around it; a few feet beyond that was a support post. His fingers found the slide fitting. The grease was fresh.

He wasn't sure yet what was evolving, back behind his mind, but it had something to do with the powerhouse. He felt his way up the line, stumbling through brush, barking his head on invisible limbs. He wished he had a light. Then thought: Better I don't. Then I won't depend on it.

At last, a few hundred yards up the hill, corrugated iron drummed faintly under his outstretched hand.

"Hold up," said the blunt-faced man, clicking off the light.

The younger one halted, blinking. Without the bright circle they'd been following he couldn't see a thing. "What is it?" he whispered, his fingers tightening on the .44.

"Listen."

Faintly, from somewhere ahead, came a thud. They stared up through the darkness. Asaro was thinking: Wasn't a gunshot. Too soft. Balanced there in the dark, fingering their weapons and straining their ears, they heard again, after a time, a second thud. A third.

Somewhere above them a great heart began beating; irregular and slow. And faintly too came to them through the falling snow a weird squeak and groan, like damp wood rubbed together, or ancient hinges turning.

"What the hell's that?"

"I don't know."

The older man scratched his beard. Thinking: Maybe we should go back. Somehow the mark had turned the job his way. Suckered them onto his turf and whacked Tommy and Mitch. He didn't like the feeling he was getting out here in the dark, in the cold, the weird metallic groaning getting steadily louder.

"Think we should give it a pass?" he muttered.

"D'I just hear Little Nickie Asaro pissing his pants?"

"Fuck you."

"Hey, fuck *you*, Nico-deemo. You ain't made yet. I'm going to get him. You coming?"

"Sure," said Asaro. He slowed, letting Diamond step out in front of him. He lifted the shotgun, pressed the safety off, and pointed it where the crunch, crunch of footsteps was. His finger came taut.

Then he thought: Let's get the old man first. Then I'll whack this mouth-off asshole. He pushed the safety back on and began to walk again, uphill, toward the thudding that he now recognized as some kind of engine.

The six-foot iron flywheel rumbled as it turned, filling the tin-walled, tin-roofed shed with slow thunder and the crying of cold bearings and the smells of oil and exhaust. In the darkness—there was a kerosene lamp, but Halvorsen didn't want to light it—the old gas engine made a blue flare out the through-roof exhaust every time the cylinder fired. He could see it flicker over the snow outside the two windows. It flickered too over the bandwheel, marching around with slow deliberation, one step left, one step right, pulling the pump-jacks at the ends of the rod lines through their nodding cycle.

Halvorsen had set them up by feel, hooking on whichever wells his hand came to first. He didn't know which the crew was pumping ten hours a day and which they pumped one. But he did know one thing, that he needed fresh crude in the stock tank.

Ain't got much time, he thought, sweating, though it was ice-cold in the shed. Not hard to figure this's where I went. It would take the men behind him a little while to find their way in the dark. A while, but maybe not enough. It depended on how long ago the day crew had left, and what lay in the sands below, deep in the earth.

Reaching inside his jacket, he fondled warm fur. "Just take it easy," he whispered, glancing out the window into the night. "It won't be long."

The younger man was sweating now. Not from fear. This was a good sweat, a workout sweat. Sure, he figured the old man was fixing something for them. Like he had for Tommy Del and Mitch. But he wasn't falling for it. They were coming round the back way. Uphill in a long loop, then casting around and coming downhill toward the noise.

It was spooky and dangerous on the slope. They weren't using the flash now. They'd take him by surprise. In the darkness they stumbled over stumps and rocks and ran into trees. The squeaking and groaning came from all around them, all up and down the hill, and they kept running into what seemed to be steel bars stretched across between the trees. He couldn't figure it. When he put his hand on one he jerked it back, as if it was hot. It was moving, going uphill two or three feet, then stopping with a jerk and then pulling itself back down again.

Weird, he thought. But not frightening. Not to a guy like Nate Diamond, two-twenty and in top condition, with a recoil-compensated .44 Auto Mag in his hand.

Behind him he head the Italian stumble and curse. He wanted to snigger but it could wait. The big mobster. They'd said he was tough nuts. Wait till he told them how some old geezer had wadded Nickie's panties for him.

Behind him Asaro could barely keep going. The Jew kid moved too fast. It'd be a pleasure blowing him away. He had other worries too. The thin kidskin gloves, his car gloves actually, couldn't stop the cold. The steel of the shotgun sucked warmth out of his flesh. He couldn't get Burck out of his mind. He'd seen men die, he'd put two inches in their mouths and grinned into their eyes as he pulled the trigger. But for some reason the image of the frozen man stayed with him.

Maybe because it could be him next.

They made out a black angularity ahead at the same time. Some kind of building. There was a blue flicker above it . . . exhaust? . . . all these rods led to it like an iron spiderweb. Asaro didn't know what it was and he didn't care. He was freezing. He wanted a drink. Time to finish this up.

He aimed the pocket flash and pressed the button briefly. The momentarily lit circle showed them a door before the world was black again. "Take the back," he snapped.

"I got this side."

"Take the back!" Asaro hissed, swinging the pump toward him.

"Okay. Okay, goddamnit!"

Diamond jogged away, thinking *That prick's not gonna make it back to the truck.* The old man could stand credit for three as well as for two. He reached the rear of the shed. Groping, he found a big iron tank and a batch of pipes going in through the wall. There was a window too. He crouched under it, the magnum held low, and over the irregular banging of the engine shouted, "Yo!"

"Take him!"

Up and over. The window burst inward. His feet hit hard and instantly scooted out from under him. He sprawled in something slippery, sucking in heavy, choking air, and scrabbled around in sudden panic until he found his gun again.

There was a heavy dull boom and the door at the far end blew inward. Asaro followed it, flashlight in one hand, the pump in the other. Their guns followed the beam as it swept the interior. It showed them machines, slowly revolving wheels, spokes, pipes, valves, and levers. But no old man. The light came back and down and steadied on him.

"What're you doing on the floor, Diamond?"

"I slipped."

"Christ," said Little Nickie. "Smells like a fucking gas station in here. Smells like—"

"Holy shit." Nate scrambled suddenly up, reaching for a pipe. It broke under his weight, and more of the slick darkness came pouring out of it.

"What?" said Asaro.

"We better get out of here."

They saw the face at the window at the same moment. It might have been there before, peering in at them from the night. But now it was suddenly and brilliantly illuminated, as if by a flare. Diamond jerked round instantly, bringing the pistol up. Asaro was turning too, lifting the shotgun. But neither of them had gotten close to aiming when the big wooden kitchen match, still sputtering in bright flashes of igniting phosphorus, came sailing lazily in to join them.

Halvorsen lay face down in the snow, waiting for burning things to stop falling out of the night. The initial eye-searing flash had been natural gas. The fireball that followed had been natural gasoline, the volatile fraction crude petroleum carried even before it was cracked. The major part of the thousand cubic feet of hell that now filled the roofless shed was the slower-igniting flammables: kerosene, naphtha, fuel oil, and paraffin. It was mixed, unrefined. But it was all there in the two or three hundred gallons of fresh-from-the-well, high-grade Pennsylvania crude he'd pumped out onto the concrete floor of the power house.

He lifted his head. Something was staggering out where the door had been; something that resembled a pitch-pine branch on fire. It didn't stagger far.

When the cartridges stopped cooking off Halvorsen got up. The fire was good on his face and he stood for a little while in front of it, warming himself.

This wouldn't end it. These four thugs had been strangers to the county. From outside. They'd been hired by somebody and told where he lived and what to do to him. So this was just the beginning. There'd be more.

Got to clear out, he thought. Fill a pack with food, ammo, his old down bag, and clear out into the woods.

And after that? Well, he'd have to think.

At last he judged it was time to go. He retrieved the pup, her belly wet from the sudden noise, from inside an abandoned drum and put her back in his coat. He got the rifle from where he'd hung it on a tree.

He reached for his tobacco, but his fingers stopped instead at a hard curve. He held the revolver for a moment—he hadn't needed it after all—and then tossed it into the fire, on the far side of the glowing outline of the engine. After a few minutes it went off with a pop and a little shower of sparks.

Biting off a chew, blinking thoughtfully, Halvorsen trudged slowly back up the hill.

Twenty-six

She sat at the window, by the telephone, in her pink quilted robe. Her face was swollen and red and she hadn't put on any makeup when she got up.

She was past caring about makeup.

I tried my best, Jaysine thought. In that last savage moment she'd finally managed to say it. That *if he'd loved her* she'd have done anything for him. Lie, sin, give up her profession. Anything.

Now she knew the truth. Her shame and her renunciation meant nothing to him.

She'd never meant anything to Brad Boulton.

She sat quietly in the growing light, looking down at the street with empty eyes. It didn't seem right, it didn't seem how things should be, that it was so hard to find someone to love.

Finally it was seven. She hadn't wanted to call too early. She positioned the phone book beside the telephone and dialed.

A woman answered. When Jaysine asked for Phil she sounded first surprised, then disapproving. At last she said, "Just a moment." While she waited Jaysine carried the phone into the kitchen and poured coffee. There was one doughnut left. Coconut sprinkles.

When he said, "Yeah?" it sounded like his mouth was full too.

"Phil?"

"Uh, yeah. Who's this?"

"Jaysine Farmer."

"Oh. Oh, hi. How are you?"

"Can I come over and see you?"

"What, now? I got to leave for school pretty soon. What, uh, what's it about?"

"It's about what we talked about."

"Oh."

From the pause she could tell he still wasn't sure what she meant. "About the chemicals," she said.

"Oh. Yeah."

"Listen." She took a deep breath, closed her eyes. Said, all at once, "I know who's doing it."

There. She'd done it. Up till that moment, she hadn't been sure she could.

"Doing what?"

"What you were talking about in the bar. Dumping stuff. Here in the county."

He didn't say anything. She stirred sugar into her coffee, hesitated, added more. At last he said, "How do you know that?"

"Remember the notebook I showed you? In the library? I'm not *absolutely* sure, but I think it's got something to do with it. Unless— unless you got it all taken care of already."

Again he didn't respond immediately. She heard a distant thud, scratching on the far end, as if the phone were being moved. Then his voice came back, lowered. "We ought to tell Racks."

"Who?"

"Mr. Halvorsen. The guy I told you was working on it with me. Look, can you meet me at the Todds footbridge?"

"Well—okay. When? After school?"

"No. Right away. And look. Dress warm. Wear boots."

"Why?"

"We're going to do some climbing."

She put on light powder and lipstick, just for the street, and went out. Before she'd gone ten feet she was glad he'd warned her to dress warm.

The boy was waiting for her when she got there, leaning against rusty iron, staring into the creek as if contemplating a jump. His jacket was cheap and worn, and he looked thin and sad. For a moment she stepped outside her own misery, thinking: He's unhappy too. It made her feel like hugging him. She said, coming up beside him, "Here I am."

"Hi." He straightened, looked her up and down, and blushed a little. She thought it was cute.

"D'jou bring it?" he asked her. "The book?"

"Yes."

"Okay, let's go."

She hadn't really understood what he meant by "climbing"; she'd thought, maybe walk up a road. Instead they went straight up past the houses into the woods. She followed him through deep snow for half an hour. As the town dropped away below them snow filled her boots and brambles clawed at her coat. She had to stop and rest twice.

She wasn't used to this. She was thinking about giving up when at last he stopped, looked around, and pointed. She looked, but saw only a pretty little patch of Christmas trees. Not till they were standing over a dead fire between two logs did she realize how artfully concealed the lean-to was.

The boy bent and looked inside it. Then straightened, looking frightened. "He isn't here."

"You lookin' for me?"

They both stiffened, looking toward the voice.

An old and evil-looking man stood back in the trees, holding a rifle. His face was grizzled white as ashes and there was an open sore on it. Dead animals hung from his belt. He looked cadaverous and sick and insane. As she stared he came forward a few feet, and she saw a little dog behind him.

"Ain't good business sneakin' up on a camp, boy. Better to call out, when you're comin' up. So, who's this?"

"Somebody I thought you should see. She's got something to tell us."

"Yeah? Well, looks like you about froze her." The old man came forward, short shuffling steps, and bent to pull off snowshoes. He propped the rifle against a log and squatted.

She couldn't see how he did it, but in less time than it would have taken her to brush her hair he had a little blaze going, shimmering the air but giving up no smoke at all. She sat on a log and stretched her hands to the heat. The puppy came up to her. She petted it and it gamboled awkwardly, one eye on the old man.

"Had breakfast yet, Miss?"

"No, just a doughnut, but please don't—you don't have to . . ."

But he'd already produced a knife. Before she had time to catch her breath he had the animals opened, gutted, and reduced to strips of meat. They went into an aluminum pot with snow and handfuls of nuts and sliced-up roots. That went on the fire, followed by a smaller pan with more snow. She watched, fascinated, as he stirred and seasoned with pinches of dried herbs.

They looked out over the valley as they waited for the stew to cook. She'd never been up this high before. She was surprised at how big the land was, and how empty; how small Raymondsville looked, huddled along the frozen river.

At last the stew was ready. She took a wary spoonful, followed with a sip of coffee. It was delicious. Meanwhile sourdough bread had been cooking on peeled sticks. Halvorsen broke it in his hands and they mopped the pans with it.

When the meal was over and everything scrubbed out with snow the old man adjusted himself against the lean-to, bending his gaze on her at last. "All right," he said, "Now who are you? And why'd Mr. Romanelli bring you up to see me? Go ahead, Miss. We're listenin'."

She remembered, then, why she was here. The brief sense of escape, of wonder at the view and breakfast on the mountain, disappeared. "My name's Jaysine Farmer," she started, nervous under the old man's intentness. "I work—worked on Pine Street, at the Style Shoppe. I've been dating a man. When we . . . split up, he left his appointment book at my place."

The old man nodded, pale eyes locked on hers.

"Anyway I ran into Phil down at the library a few days ago. He told me what he was working on. Then I got to reading the notebook."

"You were readin' it when I met you," said the boy.

"I mean, I figured out what it meant. Actually I— It took a while to decide to tell anybody this."

They both nodded. It was funny, they looked so solemn, like the Mormons who came to town in the summer on their bicycles. She almost laughed, then recalled herself. "Anyway, look," she said. "Right here, on this page. Where it says, 'Drop #12, Gould Run, 536.'"

"Let me see." The old man took the book. After a moment his hand moved to his coat for a pair of old-fashioned spectacles. He turned several pages. Then flipped it closed and looked at the front. "Whose is this?"

"His name's Brad Boulton."

• • •

Halvorsen had been thinking about the entries, but the name made him blink. What had the blunt-faced man said last night, the four of them looking like hunters and yet not, at least not of deer—"Boulton said there was a house."

It came to him now that yes, he'd met a man of that name, not long before.

"Who's he?"

"He's with Thunder Oil, in Petroleum City. He's important, the president, I think."

Halvorsen nodded, slowly, slowly. Sure. That was the guy.

He didn't like it, but it made sense.

You saw the big T.O. tankers on the roads so often you didn't think about them. They were part of the scenery, like the hills. The big black trucks with a jagged thunderbolt in a red circle, same as on the peak of his old green hat. No one looked twice at them around Hemlock County.

The ease of it suddenly came clear. They left the refinery full of gasoline for the stations. You saw them all the time, the big rigs pulled in close to the gas pumps, hoses snaking down to underground tanks, drivers standing talking to the owners or setting their valves. And the specialty products, fine grades of lube oil, feedstocks, headed east too in the same black rigs.

He'd never thought about it before, but they'd be coming back empty. He could see how a certain kind of a person might see that as an opportunity.

Holding that possibility suspended in his mind, he studied the pages again. He turned to a blank one and plucked a twig out of the fire.

Using the charred end and flipping back and forth, he noted each time the word "drop" appeared. Roughly twice a week, with the names of various roads or hollows, and the number—the truck, he thought suddenly. Sure, they had to have some kind of number so the dispatchers could route them.

He didn't like the idea of his company, he still thought of it that way, being mixed up in this. He smiled faintly. Oh, the old-line men were no plaster saints. They'd jump each other's leases, short-stick the pipeline companies, steal oil from each other with vacuum and crooked wells; they'd gamble and drink and fight like tomcats over a fancy girl; they might even, during Prohibition,

smuggle in boxcars full of—well, he'd go back and think about all
that later.

The smile faded. But they wouldn't have dumped poison in the
county they lived in. Or any other. They just weren't made that way.

But Thunder, like the whole country, was in the hands of a new
kind now.

"Lemme see," Phil said, leaning forward. It made sense; it made a
lot of sense. "New Jersey."

"What's that?"

"That's where it's coming from. There's a lot of dumping there.
Now they found a way to get rid of it out here."

Jaysine smiled at him. "Your face is getting red."

"Well, I'm excited!"

The old man handed him the book and leaned back, lips pursed,
eyes musing behind halfmoon lenses. Phil flipped the pages rapidly, thinking, What day was it Racks got sick? and remembered it
was a Saturday. He looked at the twenty-eighth. Nothing. Then he
looked at the page before it. The twenty-seventh. It said, halfway
down the page amid the other jottings, *Drop #14, Mortlock, 950.*

"Holy shit," he said. "You're right. This's a dumping schedule."

"Course 'tis," said Halvorsen, sounding irritated. "See that
soon's you open it."

Phil laid the notebook carefully on a dry spot on the log as
Halvorsen fitted another slab of split maple into the fire. There was
a brief silence, broken by the crackle as flames found the wood,
and then, far and faint, the nasal drone of a train. They no longer
stopped in Raymondsville, though the old man remembered when
they had. They watched it wind through town and over the trestle
over the river and creep off down the valley east, toward Couders-
port, East Towanda, Scranton . . .

"Okay," said Jaysine. "Now you talk. Tell me what's going on.
From the start."

Halvorsen and Romanelli looked at each other. Finally the old
man cleared his throat. He told her about the snowplow, his
hospitalization, and the diagnosis.

The boy broke in then with what the doctor had said about other
cases in the county. He told about their stakeout of Route Six, their
eventual success.

He stopped there and the old man took up the thread again.
This time he told of going out to Cherry Hill, his reception, and the

subsequent cutoff of his pension. He told about his call to the investigator, Leiter. Last he told them about the four men who'd come to burn him out the night before.

When they finished Jaysine sat silent. Part of her couldn't believe it. But she knew it was true.

"It's him," she said.

"You know him, you say?" said Halvorsen. "I've only seen him once. He's the type to do this?"

"Yes."

"He'd send out to kill somebody in this way?"

She thought about that one. She remembered his last words to her, when he was leaving, when he hit her. She took a deep breath. "Yes. I think he would."

Phil said, "What is this, a trial? He owns Thunder Oil. We know how he's been planning the runs. I'm convinced. The question is, what do we do about it?"

"Go to the police?" said Jaysine.

He told her about her father. "So that's worthless," he finished. "All that'll do is get this Boulton to send more thugs after you and me along with Mr. Halvorsen, if he hasn't already. No, there's only one thing to do."

"What's that?"

"Kill him."

Jaysine went cold inside. She thought suddenly, *They're crazy*. The old man looked it and the boy, with his hate-filled, bitter laugh, sounded like it. She felt sorry for them both, especially Phil. He didn't walk right and it was obvious just from looking that he'd never been loved. But talking about . . . what they were talking about, that was just crazy. "I don't think that would be a good idea," she said.

"Why not? It's the only way to stop it for good."

"It's wrong. That's why."

"What he's doing's worse. How many people are going to get sick, get cancer, die from that stuff? And there's no other way. We've tried."

"It's still wrong."

"No, *you're* wrong—"

"Hold your horses, boy. She's right."

Phil felt like shrieking at the treetops. "What? Mr. Halvorsen— he's the one sent those guys to kill you! Don't you want to—"

"Kill him? Not especially."

"But those crooks—you said you—"

The old man said coldly, "That was different. Right then it was them or me, boy. But if you're thinkin' to murder somebody, shoot him from ambush over at Cherry Hill or something, well, forget it. It could be done, sure. But W. T. Halvorsen won't do it."

"I'm sorry, I didn't mean that, exactly. I just thought—"

Meanwhile Halvorsen was sitting back, thinking. He reached for the book again. When the boy ran down he said, "Might be a way to make 'em listen to us, though."

"What's that?"

"We got to make it so this Boulton can't lay low any longer, or say he didn't do it and pay people to cover it up. We got to drag the whole stinking shebang right out in the open."

"How?"

"Stop one of the trucks. Hijack it, or force it off the road—something like that."

"Holy smoke," said Phil. He jerked slightly and started to smile. "Sure! That'd do it. That'd be great!"

"What do you think?" Halvorsen asked Farmer.

"I don't know. I guess if nobody got hurt."

"Can't guarantee it a hundred percent. Or wait, maybe we could . . . pretty close anyway." Halvorsen showed them the charcoaled page. "Look at this here. See what it says? On the nineteenth—that's tomorrow—truck number 223's going to be dumping out by Rich Falls. There's a dollar sign by it, too, I don't know what that means . . . Know where Rich Falls is?"

"Sure."

"I don't," said Jaysine.

Halvorsen swiveled to face her. "Nine, ten miles east of here, some rapids, used to be a dam. Iron bridge leaves the main road, crosses the river, and heads on up into the woods. There was a tavern-house and a planing mill and a tannery up there years ago, but all there is now's the oil leases and a gravel pit. That's Rich Falls. The next date after that, y'see, isn't till January."

The three sat around the fire, thinking.

Halvorsen hacked off another length of maple and added it to the fire. He was remembering another time he'd had to face up to Thunder, and to Forest, Kendall, Wolf's Head, and the rest of the Northwestern Producer's Association. That cold as shit, dangerous winter of '36. He remembered the florid face of the federal marshal, the line of brown-shirted National Guard. That time too they'd had no other recourse. No other way to turn.

Jaysine was thinking about her future. Once she'd dreamed of her own shop, a neat little place with a safe-tanning salon, a counter with her own line of beauty products. That was the time to sell them, when women were feeling lovely and wanted to stay that way forever. Then for a while she'd let herself dream about being his wife. If only she'd— No, she thought. It wasn't her fault. It wouldn't have happened, not ever. He's evil and he never loved me.

She didn't think about the future anymore, or if she did it was too dark to look at, like the sun in reverse. But she wanted the world to know what kind of rottenness was inside Brad Boulton.

Phil fingered his front teeth gingerly. Like the old man had said, they'd set again. He grinned bitterly inside. Funny how a guy who didn't care whether he lived or died could be glad he wasn't going to lose a tooth. He liked Halvorsen's idea. Hijacking a truck sounded exciting.

"More coffee?" said Halvorsen, reaching for the pot. They both nodded. "So. What do you think?"

"Isn't anything else *to* do," said Phil. "Except lie down and let him do what he wants. What he did to you . . . He'll kill us if he can't keep us quiet any other way. No, we got to stop him."

"It's me that's got to do that," said Halvorsen mildly. "I'm the one he's mainly after. I don't want you young people to get in any trouble. You got your lives ahead of you. All I might need's a little help. To get some things, since I can't go into town no more."

"Mr. Halvorsen?"

"Yes, Jay—Jaysine?"

"I'll help you any way you want."

"Me too," said Phil. "I got nothing to lose."

Halvorsen looked at them for a long time over the fire. They were so darn young. But maybe that was an advantage. Young people weren't afraid. They didn't believe in tragedy, loss, death. Whereas he'd seen it too many times to believe it couldn't, wouldn't, come to W. T. Halvorsen.

Well, if it came, he'd had a long, full life. And in some ways he was looking forward to Judgment.

"Okay, that's settled," he said. "Now the way I see it, we can't wait till January. We got to do her now, catch that truck tomorrow, or like as not he'll get us first. So we ain't got much time to put it all together. Going to have to work together, and work fast."

"How do you want to do it?" said Jaysine, scratching the puppy's head.

They waited; the old man stared down the hill. At last he blinked.

"If I done it right I could drop the bridge at Rich Falls, and the truck with it."

"Drop it? What do you mean, *drop* it?"

"Blow her up. Or at least fix it so's it goes down when the truck turns on to it."

"Yeah, but then what?" said Phil, unable to keep skepticism out of his voice.

"Once they got a truck sitting in the Allegheny River it'll be hard to pretend ain't nothing going on that oughtn't to be. Remember a couple years ago, when that tank collapsed at Ashland and a million gallons of diesel went down the Monongahela? They didn't have any drinking water in Pittsburgh for a week. I figure soon's it goes in, we call Bill Sealey, at the State Police barracks. I'm sure Bill's square, I've known him since he was a kid, but we got to give him a mouthful 'fore he can bite down.

"So here's the way I figure. Just tell me if you think of a problem, or of something better."

"Don't worry, we will," said Phil. He looked out over the hills, and pulled in a deep breath of icy wind. He felt as if the old man had offered him the world. He grinned boldly at Jaysine, and after a moment she smiled back.

"You listenin'?" said Halvorsen.

"I sure am."

And Jaysine said, taking her own deep breath, "We're ready. Just tell us what you want done."

Twenty-seven

Done, Boulton suddenly knew deep in his heart as the man across from him struggled to his feet, tugging at his tie, a lost, confused look in his eyes. It's a dodge. A fake. A bluff.

Because Luke Fleming was the biggest independent lease operator left in the state. A few years before he'd been next door to broke. Now, with tertiary recovery proving out, he held the key to millions of barrels of oil, locked like vaulted gold in the sandstone under the hills.

Their meeting had been good business. Thunder owned leases, but they no longer supplied all the crude Number One needed. This meant federal tax law put the company at a disadvantage. The depletion allowance let the majors, Exxon and Shell and Mobil, subtract revenue from domestic crude production from their pre-tax income. Since they lumped production and refining costs, they could charge themselves more for crude, and pay less tax on refinery profits than companies that had to buy on the open market.

That, with economies of scale, had gradually squeezed out their smaller competitors, and driven Thunder's margins down to where it couldn't afford to modernize.

Fleming, and five more men like him, were Boulton's answer. A few minutes before, Brad had offered him a directorship in The

Thunder Group in return for exclusive marketing of his crude. This would let T.O. exercise the same pricing and tax policies as the majors. If the producers accepted, the Group would be born as a mini-major, instantly dominant in the specialty lubrication market. The only threat then would be technological, the new synthetic lubricants. But no oil company had much interest in pushing them, for obvious reasons: they increased gas mileage.

Now, standing, he shook the broad soft hand and thought: Business is war. And as in war, victory gave herself not to the most deserving, the wisest, nor even the most ruthless, but to whoever lasted longest. Whatever it took—battle, borrow, lie, steal, scam—you had to just keep going. Till your vision proved itself or the receivers walked in.

When Fleming left, Brad ordered another drink. He looked idly around the dining room.

The Petroleum Club had been built during the oil rush, a hundred years before. The atmosphere was late Victorian, so old it was coming back into style: carved-oak balustrades, carpets, Austrian crystal chandeliers. Above the walnut wainscoting hung age-freckled engravings. Hundreds of timber derricks sprouted like forests, horsedrawn wagons plowed through mud streets, tiny figures posed in stovepipe hats and bonnets. In paling sepia gushers leaped skyward, a governor clipped the ribbon to an opera house, Adah Isaacs Mencken posed nude on a white stallion.

Now, at the bar, a white-jacketed waiter poured Heineken for a lawyer. Other members, all male, local executives and professionals, sat reading the *WSJ* or *Business Week*.

He finished his martini and signed the chit. Pulling on his new overcoat, he cycled through the revolving door, and stood tucking in his scarf, looking down the main street of Petroleum City.

The air was keen after the steam-heated club, sharp as an accountant's pencil. On the far side of town, above the dull brick of the college, Cherry Hill rose like a granite skyrocket. From habit he looked for the soaring towers, but caught only a flicker against the overcast.

He was thinking again of the fencing over lunch. Fleming hadn't agreed. Wanted to have his lawyers go over it. Something about a counter-offer from Kendall—

Brad held his breath. The wind moved past his face like icy water past a swimming salmon's, seizing his ears with steel pincers, touching his cheeks with tingling anesthesia. He lifted his suddenly brimming eyes to the hill again.

Fleming would sign. That's what his confused look meant. He was old, ready to quit. He was stalling, that was all, trying to carve out leverage for while they were roughing out the contract. Leverage that now, since he'd revealed his weakness, he wouldn't have.

Just that simply, he'd won.

Once the deal with Fleming was announced, the stock sale would be a pushover. The refinery would be rebuilt, and the new superclean fuel would reestablish Thunder as a leader in the gasoline market.

The Thunder Group was a reality.

The warmth of triumph, like the glow from a handball workout, faded after a block or two. His eyes fell gradually from sky to hill, to buildings, at last to the partially cleared sidewalk.

The reorganization would work, *if* nothing went off the rails in the next week.

But on another front, he had a major problem.

A car passed; he caught a waved hand; nodded back, recognizing Pretrick, from the Industrial Chemicals division . . . The phone call that morning had been upsetting. Of the four guys from Newark, only one was still alive, and he was badly hurt. Something about a stake in the chest. Boulton, remembering the shaking old geezer who'd come to Cherry Hill, found it hard to believe.

He'd told John to send his best team this time. They'd flown in this morning, in his view not a day too soon. This had to be closed off quick.

Had to be sealed off . . . He wondered if he didn't need someone full time for this kind of thing. It wasn't smart for a CEO to deal with it himself. Best to have a cutout between him and the muscle. For just a moment it occurred to him how dangerous this whole thing was.

Not just legally but . . . His neck prickled suddenly under the cashmere scarf. He glanced quickly around, searching faces on the lunchtime street. Halvorsen was loose, unaccounted for. They said he was a hunter, a damn good one. Old, sure. But he'd just killed three of the men who'd gone after him.

It occurred to him suddenly that he was totally exposed. It was a new and intensely unpleasant sensation. He twisted his neck, studying the rooftops. No one there. Yet a mounting fear hurried his steps. His eyes kept going to windows. He stumbled on a frozen dike of snow and fell to his knees in it. He jumped up quickly, dusted dirty snow and salt from his coat, and moved toward the Thunner Building, almost at a run.

When he had the portico between him and the sky he panted with relief. His kidneys ached. Drive from now on, he thought. No more parading around the streets like Joe Citizen. Joe Target.

Well, John's new boys would take care of Halvorsen. He scowled as he pressed the elevator button. Might be smart, too, to give the cops a call. Get Nolan in Raymondsville and Kaefer here in P.C. to alert their men. They could pick him up, when he showed in town for food. Then the boys could drop by and visit him at the jail.

He stood alone in the humming, slowly rising steel box. Was there anything else he should be doing? The old man and the kid were sealed off, or shortly would be. He'd bricked off the EPA and the media. But other agencies might be interested, especially if there was anything messy about Halvorsen's termination.

Was there a better way? What if he talked to the old man once they found him, offered him his pension back if he withdrew the report? Hell, if that worked he wouldn't need John's muscle, wouldn't need Leiter even. But even as he thought this he knew it wasn't really an option. Aside from the personal danger, every day Halvorsen lived, in or out of custody, gave him time to spread tales. Once the Thunder trucks stopped being invisible the dumping business would be over. Most deadly, any news break or even rumor would hammer down the price of T.O. stock.

That could wreck the reorganization. He couldn't afford to leave those stakes on the table. Putting it to bed now was the minimum-risk, minimum-cost strategy. He straightened his tie in the elevator mirror. For a moment he almost pitied the old man, fleeing through the winter woods, knowing no matter where he came out he'd be taken like a rat.

But Halvorsen and the boy, they'd had their warning. And ignored it.

When he stepped off on the executive floor his secretary was chatting with a refractories salesman. He nodded to him, but shook his head at her. Weyandt could see him. Twyla handed him a card but instead of looking at it right away he asked her to call Cherry Hill and have Mr. Jones come into town. Mr. Jones would be accompanying him full time for a while.

He drew coffee, deciding that his fright on the street had been due to the drinks at lunch. Here, five stories up, his fears seemed childish. He took a sip and headed for his office.

She sat in front of his desk. Blond, shoulder-length hair, tweed suit, heels. When he cleared his throat she twisted, looking back at him. After a moment he came the rest of the way in. He slid behind his desk, put his hands behind his head, and leaned back.

"Dr. Friedman," he said, his voice flat. "Nice to meet you."

"Hello, Mr. Boulton."

He examined her dispassionately. Intellectual. Thirty-five, thirty-six. A stripped-down model, serviceable, but basics only. "I don't recall having an appointment with you."

"You don't. I found myself in P.C. and thought I'd stop by. I think we're due for a talk."

"Is that so?"

"Yes."

"It wouldn't be about a job, would it? We have several openings for talented, conscientious medical people."

"No, Mr. Boulton. In fact, hell, no."

Brad made himself relax. Bitch break, he thought. She wouldn't like cigarettes either. He found the pack in the desk, lit one, and leaned back farther. "Talk to me, Doctor."

"I understand you've taken on a new physician. A Dr. Patel."

"That's right. He'll be overseeing our health care division."

"I suppose I know the answer to this one already. But I'll ask it just the same. Is he competent?"

"How would I know? I'm a layman. Vinny's a licensed physician. If he's good enough for you guys he's good enough for me." He waited, but the ball didn't come back. "Can I offer you a drink?"

"No."

"How about a quickie? I have a sitting room. The door can be locked."

"You're not amusing me, Mr. Boulton. You're not even disgusting me."

"Well, I must be doing something right. You're here."

"I'm here about your anti-social activities in this county."

"What activities are those?"

She held up fingers. "One. Poisoned heating oil. Two. Groundwater contamination. Three. Roadside dumping. Four. Your string of rip-off nursing homes." She rippled her other hand. "I'm sure there's more. But those are all I'm sure of at the moment."

"Do your directors know you're here?"

"Directors?"

He said patiently, "Of Raymondsville Hospital, Doctor. Barnett, Whitecar, Froster, Gerroy, et al. The men who hired you. They know you're up here tossing off casual insults at a major donor?"

"They will when I tell them."

"Or maybe sooner."

She laughed suddenly. "Wait a minute. Is that supposed to scare me? That I may have to take a better-paying job someplace I can see an opera or go to a museum? Find another button, Mr. Boulton. That one's not connected."

"Oh, I'm sure there's one." He thought about saying something witty about lesbianism, but instead found himself yawning. It seemed like an effective statement, so he did it again. "Look, did you have something substantive to say? If not, I'll ask you to peddle your bleeding heart on somebody else's carpet."

"Just that I know what's going on, and I intend to stop it. Hemlock County has a board of public health. So far it's dealt with rabies, mainly, but I think you're a bigger threat."

"You could have told me that on the phone."

"True. But I wanted to meet you. It seemed important, somehow, before I took you on."

"I guess that makes sense."

He wondered if he ought to make an effort here. Offer her a new cat scan or something. Then he decided, to hell with her. "Okay, you've seen me, we're enemies. Happy? Fine. Now get out."

When she was gone he waited a few minutes, till his pulse rate fell. It was time for a decision, and he didn't want to make it hastily or emotionally. He wanted to do it cold, cold as snow.

For a moment he felt fear again. This time not visceral, like his terror under the open sky, but a deeper disquiet. Word was spreading. How many had *she* told? Would his contacts, Ainslee's influence, the Thunner name be enough this time? He thought of his last trip to Vegas: the roulette table, up to a thousand from pocket change and putting it all on the red. The ball rolling, rolling, in its eye-riveting downward spiral. He had to decide. The shipment, and the payment, were coming in tomorrow.

But then he realized—suddenly, with relief—that he wasn't thinking straight. There was no "decision." This wasn't a choice, like the kind they made in high school plays, between good and evil.

This was business. He was acting for the company. For the stockholders, who'd employed him. For Dan and Ainslee. And indirectly, for Williamina. Thunder would be hers one day. And business sense, hard-headed logic, told him the only way to save it was to seal this whole problem off. Right now. Waffling or delay just meant more people would be hurt.

He thought about it for a few minutes longer, just to make sure. When he was satisfied with it, calm, he reached for the intercom. "Twyla."

"Yes, sir."

"Get me that number I gave you this morning. Over at the Holiday Inn."

"Yes, sir. Sir, how was that coffee this morning? Are you ready for a refill yet?"

"Yeah, that was great, meant to say something—is that the—"

"The Kona blend."

"Yeah, that's great stuff, babe. Get me that number now, will you?"

But before the outside call light came on the intercom beeped again. He pressed the lever, looking out over the town. His, by the grace of God. And his it would stay. "Yeah," he said. "Isn't he there?"

"It's an incoming call. Your wife, sir. She sounds, um, angry."

"What? What does she want now?"

"I'm not sure, sir . . . something about your daughter."

He had to close his eyes before he could force his voice into the empty cheeriness that was the only way, now, he could deal with Ainslee Thunner Boulton. When would it end? When would she be off his back?

Then he thought: You know when. As soon as the new board meets, and you run it. After that she's history, she and her taxidermy specimen of a father, and all her fucking forebears. And then, baby, it's a done deal and a new era.

"Okay, Twyla," he said, the cheerfulness real now. "Put her on."

Twenty-eight

The rear wheels whined, slickspinning on snow and frozen grass greasier than ice. Phil sweated, fighting the big Plymouth's slide toward the drop. The tires slid, grabbed, slid again.

Yet somehow the cruiser still trundled upward, skating wide around turns where the road canted bodily, as if the hill were trying to buck them off.

He glanced at the old man. Halvorsen sat motionless, one hand braced to the dash. Then pulled his eyes back to see treetops in front of him. He downshifted and jerked right, missing the drop by inches. "Jesus," he mumbled through dry lips. In back the puppy struggled to its feet, moaning.

Finally he couldn't stand it any longer. This was only the fourth time he'd driven a car. He hated to think what would happen if they got stuck, if his father woke to find the squad car missing. He wouldn't have dared take it again, but there was so little time before dark and so much to do. He cleared his throat. "Uh, I don't think we can get much farther, Mr. Halvorsen."

The old man grunted wordlessly and reached for his rifle.

When Halvorsen stepped out of the car his nostrils flared involuntarily. Raw, disquieting, the smell rippled like a danger flag on air that up to now, seeping through the window, had carried only snow and the astringent bite of evergreen. He lifted his head and closed his eyes, trying to decipher it.

The driver's door slammed. When he looked across the hood the boy's dark questioning gaze was locked on him.

"What is it?" said Phil. Something about the way the old man had hesitated, eyes closed, made him nervous.

Halvorsen grunted and shook his head. He reached his pack out, then narrowed his attention to the road. He studied it for several seconds, then lifted a slow regard to examine the woods, first to one side, then the other.

"What do you see?" Phil said, hearing nervousness in his voice.

Halvorsen silenced him with a downward wave. He shifted the rifle to his left hand and dropped the lever. He fitted a cartridge to the chamber. Then, a technique he'd learned hunting the big browns, he wedged three more rounds ready in his right, gripping them between his fingers, primers to the palm.

Holding the weapon ready, set to pivot instantly for a snap shot, he followed his searching gaze slowly up the last mile of Mortlock Run. Behind him, limping, came the boy.

The smell sharpened as they climbed. Halvorsen felt it seep into him, penetrate him, lodge like a sickness in his bowels. When he came out at last into the clearing he looked around once more, a long, searching examination of the bourn of forest and wind-smoothed snow.

Then sank to his knees, staring into the charred, stinking hole that had been his home.

Phil blinked at the old man's back. The flakes fell casually on it, one here, one there, glistening like diamond-chips on the faded wool. Then he raised his eyes to the woods, searching for whatever Halvorsen had been looking for. The thugs who'd torched his place, he imagined. Though it looked like they'd been gone a long time.

There was something else going on too. Something he didn't understand. And he didn't like the way the old man looked. Drugged, or worse, sort of scared.

That didn't fit his picture of W. T. Halvorsen. If he's scared, Phil thought, what chance have we got?

At last the old man got up, stiffly, using the rifle as a prop, and looked around with a brief blank glance. "What d'ya think?" Phil asked him.

"Ain't been long." Halvorsen's voice was unsteady. Phil heard him take a breath, let it out, to drift rapidly away from them toward the valley.

He looked at the basement carefully, trying to use his senses the way the old hunter did. He smelled burned wood and paper, a faint reek that might be gasoline. There was no smoke. The butts of the beams, where the fire had burned itself out, were frosted with gray ash. But then, concentrating, he felt heat on his face. It was still radiating from the rock walls. When at last he looked up Halvorsen's nearly colorless eyes had lifted to dwell on his.

He said, the words awkward in his mouth, "Somebody, uh, burned it."

"Right."

"And the other guys, the ones who came after you—"

"That was over there. On the north face. I imagine this second bunch picked up the bodies."

A moment later Halvorsen shook himself and said harshly, "Well. Let's get to work."

"You're going down there? Is it safe?"

"Let's see what we got, anyway."

Halvorsen let himself carefully down the steps, feeling weakness tremble his knees. He knew why. Forget that, he ordered himself. Sure it smells the same. But it's gone, over, years before and done with. So many years this kid beside him hadn't probably even been born.

He shook himself again and narrowed his gaze to the present.

The destruction was uneven. The flames (gasoline, he could smell it plainly) had destroyed the mud room and most of the front. He paused at the bottom of the stairwell, then stepped gingerly through a rectangular hole framed in black char. The smell was choking and to get room in his brain to think with he began breathing through his mouth.

Past that he was confronted by a fallen shatter of joists and floorboards and bridging, the floor-beams of the house. Burned out from below, they'd collapsed in the center and lay now pointed down into a pit from both sides. But their fall, the sudden descent of several tons of old ash, earth, and snow, had snuffed out the fire. Beneath the debris he could make out the blackened smashed frame of his armchair, and near the wall his sofa. The center of the room had suffered most; the stove was completely buried.

Yeah, he thought, right lucky Jez and me was out hunting when that first bunch come up here.

He put the rifle on safe and leaned it in the entrance. Clumsily, barking his knee, he got down in a crouch and crawled in.

The stink of burning, the peculiar sadness of familiar things reduced to ruin and uselessness . . . he tried to close his mind to emotion and memory alike. Moving like a ferret through a tunnel, he crawled over his sofa, circumnavigated the central collapse, and came out in the back. The roof had only sagged there, not fallen, swayed like a nag's spine. He stood again, cautious of his head. Enough of the winter light came through for him to make out his workbench. The descent of the overhead structure had dropped a beam through it. He eyed the timber, remembering how he'd hewed it out of the valley, dragged it up here . . .

No. No more memories.

He touched it, lightly as a cat, then gave it a shove. It didn't move much. Just enough to unsettle the debris above. Dirt came down, and dried grass and a layer of old ash. The ash drifted downward through the cold white light, the old falling onto the new, and both smells mingled and came up to him.

He sank to his knees, covering his face with his hands.

When he saw the old man go down again Phil hesitated, just for a moment, then ran down the stairs.

Stepping into the fire-stink was like entering an overchlorinated pool. It teared his eyes, and he sneezed violently. Then he was on hands and knees, crawling. A rusty spike bit and he hissed.

Halvorsen was squatting in a corner, staring at a pile of trash. Down his gray-whiskered, soot-smutted face ran white tracks of tears.

Phil crouched, puzzled. What was the old man crying about? What had he lost? Nothing in this hole to cry over. Then, all at once, he understood.

He moved forward, and reached out.

Halvorsen smelled of old wool and tobacco and his beard was rough. Phil felt his shoulders jerking under his gloves. "It's okay," he said. He wasn't sure of that, but it was all he could think to say. "It's okay, Mr. Halvorsen. That was a long time ago."

The old man said nothing, but after a moment Phil felt his hand. It clung to his shoulder, surprisingly strong; then pushed him away. He almost fell backward, but remembered the spike and scrambled up before he went down.

Halvorsen dragged a sleeve over his eyes. He blinked a few times, faded-denim eyes staring into the dimness under the collapsed roof. Then hawked his throat, and spat.

He pushed char and dirt off a tin wood-scuttle and began hunting around and throwing things into it. Phil watched him pick through bits of metal and cardboard. "What're we looking for?" he said at last.

"Nothin' . . . ah, here she is." Slow fingers brushed dirt off a little box marked Olin. It went into the scuttle. He unearthed a red can, a pair of pliers. "What are you doing?" Phil said again.

"What we're going to use don't touch off as easy as nitro." Halvorsen jerked his head at the box. "That there's shotgun primers. There's a pellet of azide in each of 'em. Put a bunch together and it ought to do for a cap. Take that up and come on back."

Phil looked at what the old man had gathered. There didn't seem to be much of anything there. Except the red can, and that looked to be barely a pint.

"Is this enough gunpowder to blow up a bridge?"

"No."

"Well, then, how—"

"That's what I sent the girl after," said Halvorsen sharply. "Don't worry about that. Just do what I tell you."

Phil resented the tone, but decided his resentment didn't matter. He crept out, cradling the scuttle. Carefully; the red can made him nervous. He left it on the snow.

When he got back Halvorsen had another rifle in his hands. Abruptly he turned, and Phil found himself holding it.

The old man watched him silently as he turned it over. The wood was scorched near the butt but the working parts looked okay. He stared at the muzzle. It was round and old and deadly-looking.

"Know how to use one of these?"

"No, sir."

"This here's a old Enfield. British, bolt action. See this magazine? Cartridges go in there. Make sure the rims go ahead, not behind. Then"—the old man took it from him and demonstrated, working the action rapidly—"Flip your bolt up and back, then down again like this. Set your sights, aim, squeeze her off."

"What are you going to use?"

"Oh, I'll stay with what I got." Halvorsen shoved aside a section of fallen rock, rubble, and dirt. "But some more ammo might come in useful. Give me a hand, let's see how hard this back door's jammed."

Jaysine shivered suddenly as she swung her legs down to the snow. Her eyes lifted to the cloud-veiled brightness in the west. She didn't know exactly what time it was, but it was getting late.

Well, her shopping was almost done, and her checking account with it. She tucked in her scarf, grabbing for the end as it flickered on the wind, and glanced into the hatchback. Big box of kitchen matches. Flour sifter. Two ten-pound boxes of confectioner's sugar. A length of tin stovepipe. And a twenty-five-pound sack of fertilizer from the Agway, the exact kind he'd told her. She stood now in front of the old Raymondsville Hotel, looking up and down the street. The wind howled down it, channeled by century-old brick walls, storefronts, false fronts.

The door jangled behind her, closed-in air scorched her cheeks. She stamped snow from her boots, glancing quickly around before her glasses fogged.

It was the kind of store her mother loved, packed solid with old junk. She listened to the chiming ticks of a dozen old clocks all going at different rates. There didn't seem to be anyone around, though at the counter a shadeless Art Nouveau lamp glowed candle-dim. She rubbed her glasses with the scarf, leaning to look at old medals, Zippo lighters, folding Kodaks, silver plate. She took a turn around the store. Comic books, old ones she'd never seen before. An antique glass washboard, porcelain, an interesting picture of two naked girls, or was it a girl and a boy, lying on a porch above a mountain lake.

She was peering at it when the door jangled and she started, remembering why she was there. The little man was whistling through his teeth, stripping off mittens. When he noticed her, he smiled shy and quick and dove behind the counter, just like a rabbit. "Hello. Just come in? I was over to Pickard's for some cough drops."

"Got a sore throat?"

"A little. It's the weather." He coughed to demonstrate. "Haven't seen you here before."

"Well, it's going to be Christmas soon."

"Sure is, sure is."

She paused, wondering how she could introduce this. "I wanted something for my brother. He's interested in old oil-field things."

It took a while to get to what she wanted. She had to consider and turn down a rusty oil lamp, a sounding stick, some strange tools. Then Rosen brightened. "I know just the thing! I took it out of the front room, but—just a minute. I'll be right back."

It was a wooden box, old but nicely made, with a wooden handle set into the top. She touched it gingerly. "What is it?" she said, though she knew, at least in general terms, from the old man's explanation that morning.

"It's a dynamite detonator. Old guy in here not long ago called it a 'spark box.' They used to set off charges down in the wells with 'em. You can get a nice shock if you hold those two knobs and push down the plunger."

"No, thank you," she said. "I don't like shocks." They both laughed and she said, "Gosh, I don't know. How much you asking for it?"

She could see him examining her clothing. At last he said, "I guess I could let it go for sixty."

"You have so many nice pieces here, I'm glad I came in. I see several things I like. Like that print of the girls and the mountain. And this dresser, my mother's been looking for one like that. I like this, this old thing too, my brother'd love it. But I can't pay that much."

"Make me an offer."

She hesitated. She'd drawn all her savings, and the other things had cost more than she'd expected. "As a matter of fact, I've only got twenty dollars."

"Twenty." The little man looked, she thought, dreadfully disappointed. She too felt balked.

"Wait a minute. Do you buy things here too?"

"Once in a while."

"Well, I see you have some jewelry in your case. This bracelet— well, a—an old boyfriend gave that to me. I don't want it anymore." Jaysine twisted it off. "It's silver and turquoise. Go on, take a look."

"Excuse me," said Rosen. He went into the back room with it. When he came out he said, cautiously, "I guess I could move it. It's not good stones, it's what they call 'male' turquoise, but I could give you . . . twenty dollars for it."

"How about if we trade? That, and—oh, I have a watch here too you can have—plus twenty dollars, for this?"

"Well. I don't know."

"I know my mother would just love that dresser," she mused, moving around it, touching the table lamp too, conscious of the little man's eyes following her.

When she came out, the box heavy under her arm and her wrists feeling light as air, the sun was impaled on the dead trees atop Town Hill. She examined the street again. Mr. Halvorsen had warned her to watch for police. None in sight. She put the box carefully in the back with her other purchases and got in.

She had the key in the ignition when the passenger door opened and a man she didn't know squeezed himself through it. At the same moment another materialized outside her window. It was done so casually that from the sidewalk, if anyone had been watching, nothing would have seemed out of the ordinary. She twisted, too startled to speak. The one next to her—not large, but with a heavy, cruel face she wished she wasn't looking at—said, "Go ahead, start it."

"Get out of my car!"

"You Farmer?"

"It's her," said the outside one. She heard him only faintly, through the window.

"What do you want?"

"Start your car."

She found suddenly she couldn't breathe. It wasn't the sight of the gun. There was something wrong with her chest. She felt dizzy, and put her head down. The man took the keys from her mitten. He looked out at the other one. "Too shit-scared to drive."

"You better take it."

The man outside opened the door. He shoved her over into the passenger seat. The one inside moved to the back. But his left hand lay extended forward, beside her, so that she could see the shine of the gun, chromed like a set of thinning scissors, where the seat belts buckled.

"Start her up," said the one in back. "Let's go south. There's a lot of woods down that way."

Phil felt doom heavy in him as he rolled backwards out of the hills. It was getting late. Odds were his father was awake already. He'd left the old man at the clearing. He had to get the cruiser back, and fast.

He turned it around, sweating bullets, on the first widening, and almost got stuck. But he didn't, and the rest of the way down was straightforward, though his fingers throbbed from clenching the wheel. He thought: wire, that's all we need now. He'd get home and crash for a few hours. They'd have to watch all day tomorrow, since there was no indication in the notebook of precisely when on the nineteenth of December a truck would rumble across the bridge at Rich Falls and into the empty woods beyond.

Dusk was falling. Across the valleyed road stretched the inchoate shadows of the hills. The cold snap had iced bridges and overpasses and there weren't many cars out. He pulled at knobs on the dash till headlights glowed on.

He was going up the flank of Gerroy Hill when he saw the rust-speckled little white car coming toward him. Its lights were off. He flicked his highs at it approached, recognizing it as he did so as Jaysine's.

It flashed past, and he saw in the transient illumination of his brights her face, not in front of the wheel but to the left. There were two men with her. Just their expressions told him instantly what they were.

Even as his foot slammed down he knew with instantaneous horror he'd done exactly what he shouldn't have. The tires lost all grip on the glare ice and at fifty miles an hour the world began to revolve.

He forgot the Toyota, forgot everything as he threw the wheel first one way and then the other. No response. The woods . . . the rear hatch of the white car, a blur of backturned face . . . the rusty guardrails over the drop to the river . . . woods again. He closed his eyes and bent, wrapping his arms over his head, waiting for death.

The Plymouth, spinning slowly around its center of mass, skated momentum-driven up the hill perhaps two hundred yards. Then, impelled by the crown, sagged off to the right. It crunched into the four-foot snowbank thrown up by the plows. The engine tried briefly to push the bumper deeper, and then stalled.

Phil sat with his eyes closed, shaking, and then opened them. He stared down into the river. He couldn't move for three or four seconds.

Then, all at once, his muscles unlocked. The engine ground

back into life. He threw the Plymouth into reverse, a two-point turn. Then aimed it downhill and slammed the pedal into the firewall.

Two hundred police-duty horsepower polished ice briefly with rubber before he wrenched the wheels up on the crown. The squad car leaped forward, accelerating with a howl. He hit the curve at the bottom at seventy, weaving and fishtailing on and off the berm.

The Toyota was a dot far ahead, visible for a moment around the arc of the river before forest screened it. His engine screamed like a panther and he came into the next turn, still gathering speed, to find himself head to head with a huge green Genesee Beer truck. Its headlights flicked in surprise, then it began spewing snow from under locked wheels. Finally it ran off the road, horn blaring. He hurtled past, pushed back in the seat by rigid arms, eyes blasted wide by speed.

Another turn . . . he eased his foot slightly for this one. He was beginning to get it. When the skid started you eased the wheel toward where the nose was going. The car would straighten with a snap and you were back in control. That is, if you were still on the road. So you took each curve on the inside, and trusted to luck there wasn't anyone coming your way.

Fortunately there wasn't for the next two. When he came out of the second, on a short stretch where the road ahead was visible along the river, the white car wasn't far ahead.

Maybe they hadn't seen him. It seemed odd that they wouldn't have looked back after a police car but then he remembered he'd flicked up his brights. In the dusk it was hard to see behind high beams. And then too, they'd have had no hope of outrunning him in the little Toyota. The grim-looking man driving might have kept his speed down to avoid official interest.

But now he had them. Now, he thought . . . now *what?* He had the rifle in the back seat, but he couldn't drive and shoot too. He had a fast car but only the luck of the stupid had kept him from wrecking it. If he tried to force them over he might kill everybody. He didn't have much time either. This was the last straight stretch between here and Petroleum City. Once in town they could lose him easily.

He was thinking he'd better do something soon when he saw again, turned backward toward him, the oval paleness of her face. He thought: What am I afraid of? The worst that can happen is, we all die.

He tramped the accelerator and mashed his hand against the dash. Sudden scarlet shafts stabbed out into the darkness, and the siren blasted out its two-tone discordance.

The squad car surged up on the Toyota, skidded just before it got to it, and ran up on two wheels onto the snowbank. The Toyota veered left, its rear wheels cutting up white roostertails. He'd expected that, though, and he jammed on his brakes with all his strength as his right wheels slammed down again.

The cruiser bounced, yowling. The small car cut right again as he dropped back toward it and he stabbed the brakes again, hard as he could, trying to do now on purpose what he'd done before by accident.

The squad car torqued instantly into the same sickening spin, plowing along at right angles to the road and to the oncoming sedan. Unfortunately it also slammed his head into the dash. He blinked broken light off his eyeballs and twisted, reaching back for the rifle.

When he poked up his head again both cars had stopped. The Toyota's doors were open, swinging idly. He gaped stupidly for a moment before he saw, on the bank above, two men in overcoats running for the woods.

He thought later that it might have been nice to think he had the presence of mind not to get out just yet. Or the courage to chase them. But actually he got the door open, on the far side from the now-vanished thugs, then found himself too busy being sick onto the glassy, tire-planed surface of Route Six.

Jaysine got to him first. She came hesitantly forward, blinking into the red and white flashes of the strobe.

She'd thought the police car was trying to ram them. Obviously her kidnapper thought so too. Fright had been plain in his curses as he yanked the wheel this way and that. Then, when the cruiser stopped dead across both lanes in front of them, they'd been out and running before her car stopped rolling.

She halted, puzzled, when she saw no one in the Plymouth at all. Then heard the retching, like a sick cat she thought, and ran around the hood.

"Phil! God, what was—what were you trying to do?"

"Hurt my head," he mumbled.

"Oh my God, you're bleeding. Here between the eyes—"

"Hit it on that radio thing."

"Hold still. Put your head back. I'll get some clean snow."

He straightened, still inside the car, then realized that blood was running down his face. He could imagine what would happen if his father found it on the upholstery. But he still couldn't walk. So he just sat down on the road.

By then she was back. He put his head back against the fender. The snow clamped down, cold and gritty, stinging for a moment and then numbing like Novocaine. He let her hold him and, after a moment, kiss him on the neck and the cheek and at last, at last, the lips.

Half an hour later they rolled back into town together. Phil, utterly drained, stayed at twenty-five. Like a short cortege the two cars crept beneath the streetlights, paused at the single stoplight, then turned up Sullivan Hill. He found his father's usual spot and cut the engine. He wasn't afraid anymore. He was too exhausted to feel much of anything.

When she rapped on his window he rolled it down. She was standing ankle-deep in snow, hugging herself.

"Why are we stopping here?"

"This's where I live."

"Oh." She glanced up State Street. "Well—I'm scared. Do you think you could, like, come and have a drink with me or something?"

"I don't know."

"Do you got to go home? Is that it? Maybe I could stay there too."

He had to grin at the idea of bringing Jaysine in, telling his mother she was going to sleep over. "I don't think that'd be too swift. Look, I got to get these keys back to my dad. He'll be pissed. It might take a while."

"I'll wait."

"Well, let's see how it works out." He checked his forehead in the mirror, then brushed his hair over the cut. They got the rifle and Halvorsen's scuttle out of the Plymouth and put them in her car.

Then the ascent to Paradise Lane, dragging his carcass up the stairs, heart heavy as his legs. He was late. Joe would have already been down to the car, to start it—he hated to start patrol cold. As

Phil came down the alley toward number 11 he limped more and more slowly.

On the drifted-up porch his father's tracks were plain. Phil sighed, straightened his shoulders, and limped inside.

Joe Romanelli sat on the couch in his uniform. A football program was on. A coach spoke gruffly about determination and pride. As Phil dragged the door closed his father glanced up at him through Camel smoke. Phil placed the keys silently beside him.

"At long goddamn last. Where the hell were you?"

"Noplace."

His father's hand cracked against his cheek, knocking him into the television. "You couldn't have done me the favor. Told your mother you were takin' it. Or left a note."

"I didn't think I'd be gone long—I figured you still got time to get to work—"

"No shit!" His father turned his face away. "The point is, stupid, since you didn't bother to tell me you had it, I called it in stolen."

Phil's mouth opened. "Oh," he said.

"Yeah. 'Oh.' So you tell me, smart-ass, whatta I tell Nolan now? That it wasn't stolen, you was just taking a joyride in it?"

He didn't have any answers for that. He kept his head down, wishing his father would hit him again, but at last he just shook his head. "You poor little bastard," Joe said softly. "What is it? You taking this Ryun girl out on the sly?"

It took him a moment even to recognize her name. His date with Alex seemed like years before. "No."

"You aren't still mixed up with this old guy? This Halvorsen?"

". . . No."

"That's good, 'cause we just got the word to pick him up. Armed and dangerous, they said." Romanelli shook his head again, staring at the TV. "I don't get it, I just don't. I could understand maybe a girl, you was trying to impress her. Stupid, but I could understand it. This other shit, I don't know. Is it worth licking you anymore? Does it do any good?"

He had the answer to that one, at least. "No."

"Then I guess I got to turn you in. You're a juvenile, they'll probably give you a suspended sentence, remand you to me."

"Dad—"

"Shut up!" The shout echoed in the cold little house. "Don't you get it, it's that or my job! And without a job, this is news to you I bet, we don't fuckin' eat! You got to clean up your act, boy. Your sister's making it out of here, college and all, but you're not going to, no matter how smart you think you are. Not with a record."

"Dad—don't you think . . . you can tell them somebody else took it, kids, you found it down the hill—"

"Shut *up*! Whether I do or not, you're grounded. Total. Permanent. Here or school, that's the only place you go. Understand me?"

He nodded.

When his father left he stood for a while, staring at the moving images of Bears and Redskins. Gradually his pain faded to a deadness within his ribs, as if he'd been cored, like an apple. He didn't really think his father would turn him in. It was just to scare him. But he didn't care. At last he pulled the volume knob off and pocketed it. The set went dead and he went into the kitchen.

His mother was sitting by the stove, eating canned pineapple. He wanted for a moment to touch her, share the misery; she'd heard it all, but he hadn't heard a sound from her, she'd probably been afraid to come out.

But he didn't. White hate was growing in him, not for her, not for his father, but for all the powerful, all those who oppressed and tormented others. It was too big a hatred to spare room for even the smallest love.

In the little room under the eaves he pulled boxes from beneath the bed, rummaged in them, dumped his scavengings into his Scout pack. He found the coil of wire he used for home-built radios and dumped it in too. He went back down carrying it. His mother looked up as he passed her. Then half rose, scattering can and fork to the linoleum.

"Where do you think you're going?"

"Out."

"But your father, he just told you not to. Where are you going with that? Philip, you'll get hurt. Something awful is going to happen, I feel it in my bones."

"I got to, Ma. I got things I have to do. I'll be back."

He was lying, of course. He didn't mean to be back. Ever.

"Oh, God, don't go!"

He was nauseated with her melodrama. He hated it even as he admitted its sadness. *If this is life*, he thought, pulling free from her clutching hands and wrenching open the door, seeing the world dissolve and melt in tears again even as the cold laid its hand across his face, *fuck it. I'm through.*

• • •

A hundred yards down the hill, he slid in beside Jaysine and slammed the door. He didn't look at her.

"Did you get what you needed?"

"Yeah. Let's get going," he said. His mother might come down after him. If she did he wanted t o be out of there. He wouldn't miss his dad, he thought, if by some weird and perverted whim God made you keep feeling things even after you were dead. But he'd miss her. That was the only thing he regretted. That after this last task was over, he wouldn't pull that trigger without hurting her more than himself.

But he didn't think that would stop him.

"Where to?"

"Well—we could go to your place."

"No!"

"Why? —Oh." He glanced over at her; her face was white. "You can't go back there anymore, can you? Because they'll be watching. Well—how's your heater?"

"What?"

"In the car, here. Does the heat work?"

"Oh. It works all right. It works good. Why?"

"Well, we could just head out toward the Falls, and wait till Racks shows up."

"Is there a place we could hide there?"

"There's some side roads."

"Will you drive?"

"No! I mean, you'd better." Phil shuddered, remembering the beer truck. "I'm never driving again."

He kept looking back as she drove slowly east, into the blowing snow; but they only saw two sets of headlights the whole time. One was a Thunder tanker and as it pulled out around them from behind he caught the bored glance of the driver. He wondered if this might be . . . no. It was headed east, not west. This one carried Thunder products, not poison.

"We getting close yet?"

"Better slow down. Look for a place."

In the end they went up a hollow south of the road, and found a cleared road leading back to a deer camp. He doubted anyone would go in or out before dawn. It would be cold, but they only had a few hours to wait. Four A.M., Halvorsen had said; that's when their vigil would begin.

When she turned the lights and then the motor off dark flooded in like black water. He blinked, unable to see her, the trees, anything. The only photons came from the luminescent hands of his Timex. The only sound was its faint ticking, their breathing, and the wind, sandpapering sheet metal with snowflakes.

"It's gonna get cold in here," she whispered. "I forgot, the heater runs off the engine."

"Uh huh."

She came over to his side and unbuttoned her coat. He took his off and they arranged them in a kind of tent, sitting close together. After a while, as it grew colder, they wriggled around to face each other. It was warmer that way.

Her breath was hot on his neck. Two pendant softnesses pressed against him. He thought about touching her, but only briefly. She'd just laugh. To a woman like this, he was just a child.

But as time passed the steadily deepening cold drove them closer, and with mingled guilt and horror he realized he was getting hard. Close as they were, she couldn't help but feel it. When she shifted again his now rapidly growing bone pressed against her thigh.

Jaysine had felt him stiffen, felt him begin to tremble. It made her smile. It was cute, a boy his age.

Then she remembered how the big Plymouth had roared ahead of her little car, the bloody mask of rage he'd raised when she came up to him being sick on the road. He'd risked his life for her, and saved her, too. She had no illusions about what would have happened once those men got her out into the woods.

She turned her head, searching in absolute darkness for the warmth of his breath. It smelled fresh. Unlike Brad's, sour with coffee and whiskey and something else she'd never been sure of.

"Usually, when two people get this close, they're kissing," she whispered into his ear.

A few minutes later she gasped. His hands were cold.

"What is it? I'm sorry, Jaysine. Did I hurt you?"

"No—wait. Wait, Phil. I didn't know you'd want to do that. I wasn't expectin' to, ever again. With anybody. Really."

"Why not? You're beautiful. I mean, I think you're beautiful."

"But we shouldn't—that's not what I mean. I think you're nice too. But I've got this—" She stopped, unable to finish that sentence. Not yet. "I'd like to make love to you. But we'd need . . . protection. You understand?"

He smiled in the dark. "Sure. No problem. I, uh, carry 'em all the time."

She had to help him when at last he wasn't sure how to do what he'd imagined for so long. When it was over they clung together, close, panting and murmuring, as if the only heat in the winter darkness was between them, folded like sleeping flowers in the night.

Twenty-nine

Halvorsen watched the dawn come that last day, as he had most of the twenty-five thousand mornings of his life. It began with a pearly foreglow not long, by his old Elgin, after five. But then it faded. For a long time none of the three who waited could have said there would be day at all.

Gradually the sky turned gray above Singer Hill. Light came slowly, as if it had to be pumped down through the overcast. Came gradually, creeping with the stealth of an old fox between the still-dark hills.

He remembered words he'd memorized long ago, declaimed aloud in a one-room schoolhouse. Something about the rosy-fingered dawn.

This dawn's fingers were a corpse's, pallid and cold.

When he could see the bridge he stood up. Beside him the boy did too, then the woman.

Halvorsen stretched his legs. When they were a little more limber he moved stiffly down the rise.

They came out of the trees a little above the falls. They were just rapids now, but the name remained. Halvorsen remembered saw-mills here, years before. Then when the forests were finished the dams had been blown up, or left for the Allegheny to destroy more slowly but just as completely.

He remembered the river as it was then. No bigger than a creek in July, but in spring brawny with glass-green snow-melt, a torrent neither horse nor man would dare. Up till the thirties it had flooded the towns along it regularly every few years. Then the WPA had tamed it.

Here, where the river narrowed, you could make out the bones of the old dam under the ice.

He looked northeast, into a rough Y, with himself between the arms. The river flowed toward him, propelled by the land's slope down from Potter County. On his left hand it went west, through Raymondsville, Petroleum City, Bagley Corners; then into McKean County, New York through Olean and Salamanca, then back into Pennsylvania. On his right hand Rich Creek was only a flatness under the snow. Must of froze early, he thought. Didn't matter, the springs that fed it would keep right on flowing. It would be seven, eight feet deep, under the bridge.

In a few days the water that was sliding past them now, deep beneath the ice, would join the Ohio at Pittsburgh to form the Monongahela.

The Rich Creek bridge crossed it about a mile from the newer span that joined the side road to Route Six. It was no great feat of engineering. Just a rusty iron truss, single-lane, with planks to take the weight of tires and feet. The north end sat firm on a New Deal concrete pier; the other, much older, was footed on hand-laid stone.

Halvorsen thought then, slogging across the ice, about tools. He patted his pockets. Pliers, Case knife, camp ax—that should do it.

This wouldn't be a complicated job.

Phil, a few feet behind him, edged out cautiously onto the ice. The old man had said the thing he cradled like a petrified baby was safe. He believed him, but he didn't want to test it.

He'd watched fascinated in the dark, holding the flashlight on a flat rock brushed free of snow, while the old man had assembled it.

It looked insultingly simple. Halvorsen wedged a cap onto one end of the stovepipe, then tore open the sacks. He measured the sugar and fertilizer into the other lid, then combined them with Jaysine's flour sifter. He worked deliberately, but still it wasn't long before the pipe was full, packed to the top with the gray mixture.

This was laid aside, and he held the flashlight closer as Halvorsen slid open the box of primers. Following his directions, Jaysine took each one apart with the needle-noses and threw everything away but the pill inside. These went one after another into an empty cartridge casing Halvorsen produced from a pocket.

That complete, Halvorsen asked for the wire and matches. He stripped a few inches and worked with his knife until one shining copper strand remained. This he carefully wrapped around the heads of two matches. This too went into the case, filling it, and he taped it shut.

He dug a shallow hole in the fertilizer/sugar mixture, poured powder from the red can, then stuffed the squib in till only the wire was visible. He put the lid on and rocked back on his heels.

"That's all?" Phil said after a moment. It didn't look like his idea of dangerous.

"That's it. You can buy the same stuff from DuPont in pretty cans, but this'll do the job. Got the rest of that wire?"

"Uh, yeah." He held it up: a coil of number sixteen. Halvorsen spliced the squib to it and taped the splices.

"And the box."

"The what?"

"Spark box."

"Oh."

The old man wet two fingers and placed them firmly on the brass posts. He nodded to Jaysine. She leaned her mittens on the plunger, and he jerked his hand back. He rubbed it, saying nothing, and Phil thought: obviously that works too.

And now dawn was here, and he gripped the tube as his boots wandered across the frozen surface. Snow and below that ice, glass-hard, grease-slick, and black as obsidian. He was happy when he was off it and climbing the bank.

Phil smiled, realizing suddenly what he'd just thought. That he was happy. Well, damn it, it was true.

Then they were at the bridge. He looked down it. The parallel lines of trusswork and roadway formed a square at the far end. It was still all but dark, still hard to see.

He realized then he'd lost the others. He turned completely around, pointing the three-foot cylinder like a bazooka. There was no one else in sight in the gray winter dawn.

"Hey," he said.

"Get down here."

It came from beneath him. He shuffled to the edge and peered over. At the crown of Halvorsen's floppy cap, at Jaysine's fur hat. The cap tilted back and the oilman's face appeared.

Halvorsen said, "What're you grinning about? Get off that road."

"Sorry."

When he bent beneath the planking he found they'd already quarried several rocks from the old pier. They were loose, jimmied by decades of frost and flood. He squatted, holding the tube.

"Okay," grunted the old man. "Guess that'll take her all right . . . hand it here."

Halvorsen worked it into the foundations. Then he and Jaysine packed rocks in on top of it.

"Anybody comin' yet?"

"Wait . . . no, all clear."

"Both ways?"

"Yeah, both ways."

Halvorsen came out, unreeling wire like a casual old spider. It disappeared into the snow, cutting a thin wavy slice. He headed for a patch of iced-over brambles thirty yards downstream. He threw the last of the coil over it and disappeared round the far side. After a moment he called, "You see me from there? Either of you?"

"No," Jaysine called back.

"No, but I might from the bridge," said Phil.

"Forget it, driver'll be worrying about those planks."

Gradually, in the slowly blossoming light, Phil made out the old man's standing figure. He was looking down the road. Finally he said, "Well, I guess that'll do her. You two can clear out now."

"Clear out? Hey, no way. I'm staying for the fireworks."

"Don't be stupid, boy. The girl's leaving and so are you."

"I don't have anyplace to go," said Jaysine.

"She doesn't have anyplace to go, Mr. Halvorsen. And neither do I. You might as well get used to having us here, 'cause we're going to stay."

They heard him grumbling. Phil grinned at Jaysine. Then suddenly they were kissing again, there under the bridge.

"What's goin' on under there?"

"Nothing," she called back, giggling a little.

"You two think of bringin' anything to eat?"

No," they said in unison. This time they both laughed.

"We'll probably be here a while," said Halvorsen. He came out from the bushes and squinted down at them sourly. Kids, he thought, a pair of kids, cuddling and sparking like it was their honeymoon. What am I doing out here with a pair of kids? "I wanted to get set early, but I doubt if anything'll happen till after dark. So if one of you wants to drive back to town, get something for us to eat, I'll set and watch."

"Uh . . . I'm broke," said Phil. Jaysine raised empty mittens and shook her head. Finally the old man, mouth grim, reached into his coat. He produced a pocket watch and pried the back off with the tip of his knife.

"Unfold it careful, that's a old bill."

"I'll go," said Jaysine. "But I don't want to go back to Raymondsville."

"There's a store in Roulette."

"You want anything special, Phil?"

Last meal, he thought. Well, why not? "Potato chips would be nice. New Era, or Wise. And maybe some chocolate, and peanuts."

She smiled, and cold as it was he felt warm again. "Junk City it is."

"Get something that'll keep us warm," said Halvorsen grumpily. "Stew or something."

"We've got enough here for both. And some Bisquick. I can make us some biscuits."

"That's some better," said Halvorsen.

Just then, out in the valley, they heard the whine of a distant car. Halvorsen crouched back into the bushes, and disappeared. "Romanelli, get over here with me," he called. "Jaysine, you go on. We'll be here, just honk."

She waved at them as she bumped across the bridge. The planks clattered under her wheels, but it felt sturdy enough. Only for a moment did she wonder: *What if it doesn't work?*

A few hours later, two hundred feet up the hill, Halvorsen spooned up scrambled eggs and bacon, bit into a hot pan biscuit dripping butter. Not as good as mine, he thought. But darn nice all the same after all morning out here in the cold.

He fed a little to the pup. She wasn't happy, tied to a tree, but she accepted it with only an occasional whine, a complaining bark.

A car droned by out in the valley, and he glanced down the slope. From up here, where he'd built the cook-fire, he could see the boy's stocking cap behind the bushes. Then the curve of the snowy shoreline, marked by the abrupt end of scrub and trees. Beyond that the bridge, a complication of triangles charcoaled above the ribbon flatness of frozen creek.

He kneaded his legs and sighed. He'd hiked near eight miles to get out here. Man my age don't need much sleep, he thought. But I got to be alert tonight. Well, he'd try to catch a few winks later.

He narrowed his eyes, but even farsighted he couldn't see the girl. That was good . . . He'd put her out toward the main road, overlooking the turnoff. That way, with the boy's little radio, she could let them know when the truck was coming.

If the truck was coming.

He groped around in his coat and located his plug. Only one chew left, a short one at that. He put it back.

No, couldn't let himself dwell on that . . . the possibility that Boulton, or those who worked for him, might have gotten skunked by him killing those men at his place, and canceled or postponed the run. He figured it was possible. But not likely. People like that didn't ever think they might fall. And that in the end was generally what brought them down. They'd told him a word for that years ago, in school. Greek word. Couldn't remember it now, too long ago.

He changed his mind and broke out the chew again. The wrapper snapped on the coals, shriveling to a wet-looking black wad before it suddenly popped into flame.

He tried to think of what might go wrong.

The driver should never see the girl. So any discovery or error would take place at this end. If it did go bad he and the boy had the rifles. He could cover them till the young people made it to the woods.

Timing. He'd never used this jury-rigged kind of jack-squib before, but it might take a while to heat up and go off. A truck making any speed would be across the bridge in seven or eight seconds. That didn't leave much room for mistakes.

He thought then, we ought to put something across the road. At this end of the bridge. So the driver would have to stop, get out, and move it out of the way. While he was out of the cab he'd touch it off. That got the driver out of danger too.

Halvorsen stretched, looking up. It looked like it might clear today; a little while before he'd seen a patch of blue in the east.

He decided he had time for another pan of coffee.

Jaysine played with the little radio with a mittened thumb. It looked like a toy. Silver and black plastic. Phil said he'd gotten them for fifty cents each at a pawnshop and fixed them. They looked like it.

Still, they seemed to work, for the few hundred yards between her, above the main road, and him, at the bridge. She looked at her watch. She was supposed to check in every hour. Coming up . . . she pulled out the antenna and pressed the button. She whispered, "I'm here. Are you there?"

"Check," came the voice, tiny and crackly, but recognizably Phil's. She smiled and said, "Can you hear me?"

"Yeah. Don't waste the batteries."

"I'm not. Are you cold?"

"Yeah."

"We stayed warm last night. Didn't we?"

"We sure did."

"I like you. You're a good lover, Phil."

"I . . . like you too. Don't waste the batteries! Over and out."

The radio hissed for a moment, and far off on it she could hear someone else talking: interference; but he didn't say anything. Then it went off.

She smiled. How differently this affair was starting out! She'd never had a younger boyfriend. It was funny to be the older woman, the experienced one. She closed her eyes, remembering how he'd tried to please her without knowing what she needed.

Then after a moment, opened them. Something else was nagging at her. What was it? It teased her, but wouldn't come out where she could see it.

Warm and comfortable in Halvorsen's old down bag, she stared down at the empty road, trying to figure out what it was.

They waited all afternoon and on into the night. Toward evening the weather changed. The clouds that had sealed off the valleys like paraffin on a jar of preserves slid west. For an hour, just before dark, the sky was a clear, dimming sapphire.

Phil sat on the hill, watching the day die. He'd made himself a clumsy flapjack from the last of the flour, and though it tasted burnt he made himself eat it all. It was all they had left, and there was no more money.

He hoped something happened soon. They couldn't stay out here much longer. He was slowly freezing, and he could see the wear on the old man. In a few more hours even Halvorsen would have to give up, go back. That would be too bad. He'd hoped to make a difference.

But even if he couldn't, the funny thing was, it didn't seem so all-important anymore.

He glanced at the rifle beside him. Short, ugly-muzzled, when the old man had handed it to him, he'd thought it would be the last thing he'd ever need. He'd planned to strike one blow as he went down, a blow against lies, and greed, and power abused. Then finish what Halvorsen had interrupted, up on the hill behind Paradise Lane.

But since then . . .

Could he have been wrong? Could it be possible for him to make contact with another human being? She'd said, what had she said—oh, yeah. That he was a good lover.

An unaccustomed thrill of joy made him tremble. Hugging himself with his good arm, he watched the inexorable approach of night.

Jaysine sat alone above the faintly glowing ribbon of road, snug and drowsy in the bag, her back against a log, looking up at the stars. It seemed so long since she'd seen them. So long she couldn't say when the last time had been.

It seemed like a long time since she'd been alone, too. Always there were people around. Too many people. And always she'd worried about pleasing them. Her parents, her teachers, Marybelle, her customers, Brad.

She was still lying there, looking up, when a funny thing happened.

She seemed, though she was still half-sitting in the snow, to be gradually rising.

Below in the starlight the trees fell away, and her sight seemed to expand. She could see now that the hills in all their folds were dark. Dark, but at the same time light, as if they were made of light. Dark light, folded and crumpled on itself into what looked like lifelessness, but to her eye now was filled with a dancing, burning radiance.

She blinked slowly and lifted her hand. Rising in front of her, white and frail in starlight reflected from snow, it too was made of the same stuff as the hills and the trees: the same changeless star-stuff, cold to the mortal touch, but filled with immortal, living fire.

She saw for an endless moment that what she'd been puzzling

over for so long was an illusion. There was nothing in the world but God.

She remembered now what she hadn't been able to remember before. It was summer and she was looking in through the curtains of the dining room. The cat, Thomas, had been beside her, polishing himself against her jeans. She'd been looking past her mother's shoulder at the widow, Mrs. Rogers, from down the road. All the kids knew her. She'd been harrowing her field, getting ready to plant potatoes, gotten down to open a gate, and the tractor had slipped into gear and ran over her. For years she'd walked twisted, as if her bones had been heated and bent, then cooled like that.

But she'd been watching that afternoon with the crickets going and the cat's little motor running against her ankle when her mother finished the reading and leaned forward, holding the widow woman's hand in hers. There'd been a long silence, so long she'd been about to turn away. Then without another word or remark the old woman got up, nodded to her mother, and walked out of the room.

And Jaysine, her legs suddenly belonging to some other child, had run to the front porch and watched as old Mrs. Rogers walked slow but straight up the walk and under the rose arbor and got into her car and drove off.

Now why didn't I remember that, she thought, the breath of stars hot on her eyelids. Why didn't I remember? Why did I deny?

She knew the answer, if she was honest. Because it was easier to deny than believe. Easier to be like others than bear witness to the Truth.

Guilt and terror shook her. Who could forgive such a betrayal? Yet in the next moment she knew, and was at peace again, with the stars glittering around her.

She'd been wrong about so much. About Brad. She'd thought him good, and he wasn't; then thought him evil. She'd cursed, hated, feared him. But she'd forgotten the single fact that made sense of life.

Evil didn't exist. Nothing existed save Him, and she was in Him, and He in her; and the same was true of every other being on this vast silent world, so dark in seeming, but in reality the white-hot heart of light. Her sin and sickness were only shadows cast by her error. She'd thought she needed the love of a man. But she'd always had something greater, more precious, eternal and inexhaustible.

Without knowing how or why, as if she'd just been handed a present, she believed again.

But if she believed, what was she doing here? This lurking, this scheming—it was hollow. Revenge only dealt more pain. *Be not overcome with evil, but overcome evil with good.* The only way to conquer was with perfect love.

She was thinking this, motionless against the log, when she saw something out on the road.

Not headlights; they were too dim. It took her a while watching them—not interested, just faintly curious, or perhaps it was only that the shadows were the only things in the world that moved—even to decide there was anything there. She blinked. Wasn't there something she ought to do? Something she ought to remember . . .

Without thought, her fingers closed on the radio. A moment later a faint voice asked her something. She didn't reply, only set it aside and began struggling out of the warmth. She got up clumsily, balancing on numb feet.

Whatever it was, it was coming toward her. She could make out the purr of engines, given back from the looming blackness of the hills.

Like walking in a dream. Her legs moved, but she couldn't feel them. Couldn't see the snow, as if all the world, hills, rock, snow, sky, gave back only the faint light infused in them at Creation. As if it all had been fashioned from the same pure silver, forged and tooled into the manifold shapes that tricked the eye. Surrounded by an immense comforting hum, she heard only distantly the squeak and crunch of snow beneath her felt-pack boots, the crackle of her breath as it drifted off.

She reached the bottom of her sentry-hill, hesitated, then began climbing toward the road. When she hit level she stopped, mittened hands tucked into her coat. She shivered, but didn't feel cold. She felt warm and happy.

There were no lights now. But she knew someone was coming. He meant to be invisible, but she saw. She was part of something now that knew everything, knew it and still loved it, no matter how misshapen or ugly, how sick or mired in error.

She waited. There was no one with her. But she knew she was not alone.

The first shadow came out of the black of trees. She heard the mutter of exhaust and the cry of the snow as the tires crushed it down. There was the faintest glimmer, someone lighting a cigarette. She stood motionless, hands in her pockets.

For a moment she wondered: Will they see me? Then she knew they would. There was the world as men perceived it: blind matter, moved by mindless chance. Beyond that lay another. She belonged to that world now.

The lead shadow slowed, and its engine dropped to idle. Then light blinded her. It lasted only a moment, then became two hot-red spots that faded through orange back into blackness.

She couldn't see now, dazzled, but she heard the grind of tires again. Someone called out. An electric window hummed, coming down.

Her outstretched mitten found the car. The voice was the one she'd been expecting.

"Who's that?"

"Hello, Brad," she said softly. "It's me."

Phil tried several times to get her to answer. At last he turned the walkie-talkie off. He sat silently for several minutes, turning his head from side to side, focusing all his being on the far end of the road.

He heard the motors then.

Oh, shit, he thought. To come all this way, risk everything, to have *them* win—

Jumping to his feet, he limped as fast as he could along the bank. The icy air whipped at his face, but he was past caring. His low hoarse shout, meant to carry but not far, preceded him. He saw the old man suddenly unfold.

"They're coming! I can hear 'em—Jaysine called, she didn't say anything but I think she must of tried to—"

"Shut up," came Halvorsen's voice, cold as the stars. "What're you doing, boy? Get where you belong!"

Phil realized he was right. He'd lost it, he'd deserted his post, and he was instantly shamed. He wheeled in his tracks, headed now back down the hill. Toward the river, toward the bridge.

He saw then that he would be too late.

She waited, knowing with mysterious certainty he'd recognized her voice. He didn't say anything right away. Then, sounding astonished: "Jay. *Jay?* What the hell are you doing out here?"

"Waiting."

"What for?"

"To warn you."

Someone else was in the car with him. She sensed a movement in back. But there wasn't enough light to see. She felt larger shadows behind his car. Then heard the crunch of boots, many of them, and voices. But she wasn't listening to that. She didn't care who they were.

"What are you doing out here?" he said again, and there was annoyance in his voice, and fear.

"I told you. Don't go on. There's people waiting for you down this road."

"What the hell are you talking about?"

"They know everything, Brad. It's your decision, to go on or not. But I have to tell you what God wants you to do."

"Oh, he told you, did he?"

He honed the question with contempt. She took a deep breath. Her fear of him tried to creep back, but she knew now how foolish it was.

Conquer evil with love.

"Give up, Brad. You've already lost. All you can do now is lose more."

He said swiftly, "To who? You say there's cops up there?"

"Not police. Just people."

The shadow that had come up behind her said, hoarse and lisping a little, "Who's this, Mr. Boulton?"

"This? This is the crazy bitch you let escape."

"What's she doin' out here?"

"I'm not sure. She says there's some locals waiting for us up ahead."

"That so? I'll tell everybody, get set for them."

"Good."

"We'll take care of her now too, if you want, Mr. Boulton."

"Do it," said his voice. She stood in the snow, hearing the mechanical whir again. She reached out, before they seized her. But her hands met only the smooth coldness of sealed glass.

They were pushing her into another car when she remembered Phil and Halvorsen. That she was supposed to warn them. But then she smiled, even as they twisted her arms behind her. There was no need for her to worry. God would take care of everything.

Down the road high beams came on suddenly, paling the stars. The road, the trees, the bridge leaped from nothingness to sudden bright relief. Phil tried to run faster and slipped. He screamed as his hip smashed into ice unyielding as concrete.

The lights reached the bridge. He heard the hollow clatter of planks, like machine-gun fire, then a sudden scarlet flare: brakes. He fought gasping through the bushes, their ice-cased arches cracking and tinkling around him. Thorns tore his face. He reached the detonator, crouched, and searched the darkness at the end of the road.

For just a moment, he saw something moving behind it.

There was a flash then at the near end of the bridge, where he and the old man had dragged the stump. Weeping with pain and rage, he fumbled for the wires. Halvorsen had warned him not to connect them till the last minute.

They slipped from his shaking fingers, and vanished into the snow.

He looked up through cold tears to see a car rolling off the bridge. Its brakes flashed again briefly before it accelerated up the hollow and disappeared into the woods.

He stood up, looking for the rifle. He didn't know what he was going to do with it. He was reaching for it when hands shoved him from behind and he pitched face-forward into the snow.

"Stay down." The old man's scratchy whisper. "That was just the advance man. There's something else comin'."

They lay in the snow, listening. Then Phil felt it in the ground, vibrating through frozen earth into his hands and arms and skull until he heard it not with his ears but with his bones.

Something heavy was coming up the road.

A rumble, a blackness against the stars. He trembled to the hollow roar of its exhaust, the clatter and mesh of gears, the yellow stack-flare above. Then saw faces, green-lit, hellish, high above, in the cab.

"Okay, I got them wires on. Get ready," Halvorsen hissed.

He scrambled to a crouch again, feeling wooden and detached. He couldn't take his eyes from the truck. His fingers grabbed for the plunger and drew it up.

"Not now! Wait'll I say. Remember, not just one push, that won't give her enough juice. Got to stroke it like a water-pump, fast, five or six times till she—"

The old man went quiet then. Phil looked up. His mouth came open, and his hands froze on the handle.

Two more cars came out of the trees, following the truck.

"Steady," said the old man then, and to the boy the voice sounded tired. Or maybe only resigned.

• • •

Halvorsen watched the truck edge out onto the trusswork. Moving slowly, as he'd hoped. But he hadn't planned on the cars. The first one he didn't worry too much about. It was on his side of the creek now, but as long as he could dump the tanker he didn't care that much about it.

But he knew what was in the others. More of Boulton's blacklegs, more of his hired thugs.

He wondered dully if he should go ahead. Or if it was too late. From what the boy said they'd gotten the girl. He was sorry about that. She'd seemed right spunky.

But since they had her, alive or dead, it meant there wasn't any choice about what he did. Whether he blew the bridge or not, they'd know about him and the boy. And be coming after them.

Halvorsen decided this was their only chance. From here on it was up to luck, or Fate, if you believed in Fate.

The truck loomed over the concrete piering. Old bolted iron groaned as it took the weight.

"You ready?" he asked the boy.

"Any time," Phil said. He'd turned his head, and though Halvorsen couldn't see, dark as it was, it sounded like he was smiling.

Kid's crazy, he thought. He switched his gaze back to the bridge. At last he judged it looked about right.

"Okay, let her rip," he muttered.

In front of him the boy straightened, then his shoulder dropped. Halvorsen heard the generator whir, then stop as the plunger hit bottom. He put out his hand but the boy was already hauling it back up. And pushing down again.

Halvorsen watched the bridge, head bent as if he was praying. The stars shone above it aloof and undisturbed as the black truck moved on, a little faster now, gears shifting upward as if its driver understood what they were trying to do.

Phil was racking the handle upward for the third time, his arms crying out, when he saw a faint red spark under the bridge. He thought for a moment it was a failed connection. Then the sound reached them and he knew it wasn't.

A heavy, muffled thud, not much louder than a shot, but deeper. Then blackness took the place of the stars. In it there was a rumble, and through choking smoke rocks started hailing down around them, whacking down into the ice like meteorites.

"Stay down," shouted the old man, behind him; but he didn't listen, didn't obey. Instead he stood up. A rock whacked down a few feet away, but he didn't care, he wanted to see.

The cloud swept past, and dimly he made out the trusswork down and a black whaleshape lying half on and half under the surface. Sharp cracks came to his ears, and the hiss of hot metal meeting icy water.

"Come on," Phil screamed.

"What?"

"We better get out of this smoke."

Halvorsen had to admit, the boy had a point. He reached for his rifle and followed him up the bank.

They were standing on it, looking across, when there was a flash and bang across the creek. A bullet sighed with expiring sadness over their heads. Then came a roar of motors. Headlights flicked on, wheeling into position, dazzling and revealing them as they stood surprised.

"Get down," said Halvorsen, shoving him. "Be with you in a second."

"What you want me to do?"

"Hold 'em off." Halvorsen bent and jogged stiffly into the darkness.

Another shot cracked from across the river. Phil bent double, slipped, and fell down the bank. The rifle jumped out of his hand and he grabbed frantically after it. The headlights lit everything around him, snow, rifle, sliding for the creek, the gracefully curved branches of the blackberry bushes. The ice a few feet out cracked suddenly and flew upward; bits of it stung his face.

Something moved in front of the lights, and he realized it was men, running toward the creek. Toward him.

He found a hollow at the shore, and threw himself gasping behind it. He lay there, hugging the rifle, and then remembered and turned and thrust it over the frozen earth, supporting the barrel against snow, rather than with his weak left arm. He tugged at the trigger blindly, then remembered the safety.

The muzzle-blast was deafening, and he yelped at the blow to his shoulder. His ears rang and a glow wavered over the darkness even when he blinked. Bullets smacked around him. But though he could see his own hands, lit by the headlights, he couldn't see anything to shoot at. He sobbed, working the bolt desperately, and got another shot off, aimed at darkness because that was all he could see.

Suddenly he realized that he no longer wanted to die. Not even heroically. He wanted to live. Not just with Jaysine, though he wanted her. He might love her. He wasn't sure yet. But through her, or in some mysterious way freed by her, he knew now that there were others out there to reach out to. Other hands, that would welcome his. Like a charm in a fairy tale, her kiss had toppled some prison wall he'd never realized existed in his heart. And if it was in his own heart, that meant he had built it. He wanted to destroy it, level it, and welcome in the crowd. How mysterious life was! How much he had to learn!

Christ, he thought, *Just let me live through this. That's all I want. I don't want to be a hero. Just get me home. That's all I want.*

From above and behind him came a sudden crack like a giant whip.

The corners of Halvorsen's lips twitched when he moved far enough out onto the stump of pier to look down.

No one would clear this without heavy equipment. The tanker lay with its back broken amid smashed and floating ice, half submerged. A nauseating stink welled up from it. The trusswork lay collapsed around it, the riveted box-beams crumpled, cables snapped and twisted like a net around a fallen elephant.

He nodded, and turned back toward the growing crackle of gunfire.

When he came out on the bank again things weren't looking any too good. The men on the far side had moved the cars to shine their lights in the boy's eyes. From time to time he was letting off a round, the old .303 making an impressive boom, but Halvorsen doubted he could see a thing.

He unslung the little single-shot and knelt down on a bare spot on the road, wrapping the sling around his forearm. A moment later he lay forward and steadied the sights. During the long forenoon he'd paced off the far bank at near about a hundred yards. Downhill, but not enough to matter.

His first bullet smashed through a headlight. He dropped the block, thrust in another cartridge, and fired again without taking his eye from the scope. The second light went out in a drifting fizz of sparks.

Working with the slow deliberation of long practice, Halvorsen shot out the lights on the other car. He shook the last four cartridges from the box in his pocket. Then paused, sweeping the now dark creek-bed with the old Fecker.

If they were smart they'd be hugging ice down there. If they weren't they'd be looking his way, trying to make him out. He'd see a pale blur, a face—

The little rifle cracked and jumped in his hands. Halvorsen sighed. After a while there was another crack, and then the sudden deep boom of the old British rifle, down on the creek bank, followed by a shout and the clatter of metal on ice.

Then for a long time silence grew along Rich Creek, silence and the glitter of stars. Then, gradually, a new sound crept into the valley. Halvorsen lifted his head. It came faintly against the wind, but it was there. The high sad keen of sirens.

"You boys hear me?"

A pistol-shot, far wide of him, he judged.

Halvorsen raised his voice. "Better put them guns up! I got one of them night scopes up here. I can see all you bastards plain as day. Crawl this way, you're dead. Crawl back, I'll leave you for the cops."

When he heard them discussing this he called down to the boy, "Hold your fire, men, let 'em think it over."

It didn't take them long. He hadn't figured it would. It would be cold as hell on their bellies on the ice. Plus they knew what kind of stuff they were breathing. Gradually a slow scraping rose from the pit of lightlessness that was the creek.

One of the cars started up. Its backup lights glowed suddenly, then cut off. The other started too. They pulled out, shifted, then howled, gathering speed down the hollow.

When they were gone the silence and darkness seemed twice as deep. Halvorsen began feeling his way down the bank. "Boy?" he called. Then, a little later, "Phil?"

He found him down by the shore. He knelt by him for a long time, till his knees turned to stone in the snow.

Halvorsen went over it all, kneeling there. What he'd tried to do, and what he'd ended up doing. What they'd tried to stop, and the price they'd paid.

How the boy had wanted to die, then found something to live for. But then had died anyway.

Only at least, Halvorsen thought, he'd died fighting for something he believed in. Something that would help the others. That had to count, didn't it? If anything counted at all.

He was wondering if there was anything he could have done

different when the hum of a powerful motor came down the hollow.

He left the boy as he lay and scrambled back up to the road.

It had to be Boulton. Waited till the shooting stopped, then come back to find out who won. Get over in them bushes—no, closer would be better. Next to that twisty chunk of bridge.

The hum grew louder, pushing amber foglights ahead of it.

The Jaguar came out of the treeline at high speed. Its brights snapped on, sweeping across the bridge, then steadying on its entrance. Then dipped, suddenly, as the brakes locked and the tires squalled, the car still tracking straight down the road, not skidding at all, aimed right for iron-framed emptiness.

It halted a dozen feet from where shattered asphalt hung like an extended tongue over black water and ice. It crouched there idling for a minute or so. Then the door opened.

It was the same man he'd met at Cherry Hill, big as he remembered him, in a tan car coat. Halvorsen saw him clearly by the courtesy light. He stood by the edge for a minute, looking down at the tanker. Then came back to the car and stood beside it, looking around. He seemed to be waiting for something.

At last Halvorsen got up. He went a couple of steps toward him before he said, "Hello, Mr. Boulton."

When the man turned he had something in his hand. "Who's that? Stay there. I'll shoot."

"It's W. T. Halvorsen."

"What've you done, Halvorsen?"

"Just an old man's foolishness," he said. "Blew up the bridge. Dumped your truck o' poison in the river. Won't be so easy to cover things up this time.

"Oh, yeah, and we chased your boys off. Once we evened the odds a little they lost their taste for a fight."

"Who's 'we'?"

"Me and some friends," said Halvorsen. "A couple of which got their guns on you right now. If you care to try me out one on one, though, you're more than welcome. After what you done to me, and my county, and my company, I don't mind seein' which of us is the better shot."

He could see now what the other man held. It was a little gun, aimed at him.

Boulton laughed. "You're a fool. You really think this'll do any good?"

"I figure it will."

"It won't. You might stop me, but you can't stop what's happening. It's business. Somebody else will take my place, that's all."

"Not in this county they won't," said Halvorsen.

It sounded okay as a comeback. But he wished the boy was behind him. His back felt naked. "Anyway," he said, "you better put the gun away. Cops'll be here soon."

"And if I'm not? If I deny everything—say the drivers were doing it on their own—"

"'Fraid not. We can prove you done it. Knowed about it, planned it, and took the money."

Boulton bent, glanced into the car, then turned back. His free hand went into his coat. It came out with an envelope.

"You mean this."

"Whatever," said Halvorsen.

Boulton looked across the blackness to where the lights and sirens were turning into the hollow. He tore open the envelope with his teeth. The old man saw what was inside.

"I guess this's where I ask you what your price is."

"Good a time as any."

"Well?"

"There ain't enough money in the world, Mr. Boulton."

Boulton fired. The shot missed Halvorsen, but before he could react the big man had slid back into the car. The door slammed and he caught the click of electric locks. But by then he had the rifle up. The sight framed the silhouette of a head.

Halvorsen pulled the trigger with the most complete and savage sense of justice he had ever felt.

The engine roared and the car leaped back, jerked around, and came at him, lights blazing. Halvorsen stood his ground, aiming at the windshield. An instant later he threw himself back, down the bank, just in time for the fender to graze him.

The Jag swerved, tires spitting snow over him, squealed the rest of the way around and accelerated up the hollow again.

Halvorsen got up slowly, feeling a numbness in his shoulder. He realized the other man hadn't missed, as he'd thought. He was glad he hadn't waited, taken that second shot. Some kind of armored glass on that car.

He thought quickly, sketching out the country to the south in his head. There was no other way out. Not in a car. A man could walk out, though, go to the end of the road and take to the woods. It'd be the devil of a trip at night, but a desperate man might make it.

The lights were drawing away rapidly, dwindling away uphill.

Let's see if we can't slow him down, anyway, he thought.

He thrust his last round into the action and fitted the butt to his wounded shoulder. In the scope he saw the taillights, the license plate light, the way the tires were kicking up snow. Must be doing eighty, he thought. He corrected upward, to where the snow was coming up lit red, and took a breath and let half of it out and squeezed off.

The lights staggered and slid off to the side. They jerked up and down, blinked, and stopped. Then they seemed, not to go out, but to be slowly eclipsed.

"Holy hell," the old man muttered.

As fast as he could, which was not very fast, he began running up the hollow.

When he got to the edge he stopped and looked down. The car was already sunken up to the doorhandles. He looked around. He felt like he ought to do something, but he didn't rightly know what. He'd go down too, if he got in that pit with it.

It was a slime pit, full of muck and old oil and the runoffs from the sandpumpings. No telling how deep it was. Halvorsen looked down at it. I was just trying to stop him, he thought. I didn't mean to send him into this.

The hood disappeared. The muck moved steadily up over the windshield, not fast, not slow, just steady, like a blacksnake swallowing its prey.

He could see something moving inside. The door had unlocked, come open an inch, then stopped, held closed by the pressure of the slime. Someone was hammering at the windshield with a gun. But only a faint tapping came through the thick armored glass.

Halvorsen felt suddenly weak. He's not going to make it out of there, he thought. Not unless somebody helps him.

A stand of tamarack stood not far away. He found himself under them, snapping off boughs as fast as he could reach. His shoulder hurt like a grease-scald now but he ignored it. Running back to the pit, he threw an armload between the dike and the door.

Something in his head, maybe the boy's voice, said *Forget it. Let him drown in it.*

"No," he panted aloud, back at the pines.

Leave him to die, said the boy. *It's what he deserves.*

"Ain't his God-damn judge," muttered the old man. "Shouldn't have shot anyway. Just got mad. Knew who he was. Just turn 'im in." He felt weak and dizzy.

"Let me help," said a deep voice from the darkness. Halvorsen spun, groping where he'd propped the empty rifle.

The man seemed made out of night itself; dark coat, dark hair, dark face. "Let me give it a try," said Lark Jones, holding out big empty hands.

After a moment Halvorsen said, "All right. But let's get us some more brows down first. I don't want that pit to eat nobody else."

The car slid deeper. The faintly glistening slime, viscid and greasy underneath a frosting of snow, was halfway up the door before they had enough branches down for the black man to move out cautiously onto them. The needled surface sank under his weight. Halvorsen tore more boughs from the evergreens. There were lights moving down by the bridge, but whoever was carrying them was too far away to help.

Jones got his fingers around the door and pulled. His shoulders bunched. Cloth tore beneath his coat. It yielded a little, with a sucking sound, but as soon as he slacked off it closed again; he was pulling against the direction of descent. "Throw me a piece of wood," he shouted.

Halvorsen couldn't find any that weren't rotten from lying on the ground. At last he passed him the rifle. Jones wedged it in and levered it. The stock snapped and his ankles disappeared.

But the door had yielded a little more, and he wedged the broken gun in it and folded his body over it and reached in.

The sinking car belched softly and started to turn over in his direction.

Something black and glistening slid out, looking like part of the slime. "Watch out, he had a gun," Halvorsen said.

"He's not moving."

"Clean out his mouth," said Halvorsen, putting a boot on the boughs and reaching for the feet. "Get him up here where we can work on him. Looks like he hurt himself when he went off the road . . . Yeah, lay him down there."

The lights came closer. "Hold up," said Halvorsen, glancing down the hill to where several men on foot were approaching, spread warily across the road. "Seems like I know them fellas . . . Hey! You there!"

"Who's that? Racks?"

"Up here, Bill. It's all right."

Bill Sealey was the sergeant from the Beaver Fork barracks. Halvorsen told him quickly what was going on. A couple of troopers set down their lights and bent to work on the body that lay, covered with the oily slime, on the dike.

"Where'd you fellas come from?" Halvorsen asked Sealey.

"Got a tip something was going on down here."

"Who was it?"

"Don't know. Anonymous call. Woman's voice. Real cold-sounding bitch."

"Did you get them others?"

"Five guys, three of 'em shot, and a girl."

"Kind of a short blonde? How is she?"

"In okay shape. Beat up a little, is all. She one of yours?"

"You might say that. Yeah."

Sealey asked him, "What the hell happened down there? At the bridge?"

"You better call the state water people," said Halvorsen evenly. "They're going to have a little cleanup problem on their hands."

Halfway through the explanation Sealey nodded, as if he guessed the rest. He looked down at the man, who was beginning to cough. "His trucks?"

"That's right."

Boulton moved an arm. It waved in the air over the pit. The car belched, shifted, lurched, pointing more markedly downward. All but the back window and trunk was out of sight now. The silver letters XJ glittered against the flashlights.

The hands grasped nothing, then came up to lie on his chest. Then, quite suddenly, he pushed off the man who was bent over him and sat up. He coughed savagely, as if trying to speak.

"What the hell's the matter with him?"

"Hold him! He's tryin' to go back in!"

Three of the troopers grabbed him, pulling him back from the edge. A low, animal moan came from the struggling man's blackened lips. His hands clawed the air. His eyes were startlingly clear, open and agonized, staring toward the car. His mouth gaped again. This time it made words, slurred, but clear enough to understand. "Get her out—she's still in there—"

Halvorsen turned. In the wavering glow of the focused flashlights they could all see clearly, in the rear window, flattened against the heavy glass by the pressure of the inflooding muck, the gay stitched smile of a child's rag doll.

The Afterimage

Could be the last snow this winter, that little bit last night, Barry Fox thought. He hoped so. This hadn't been a hard winter. Nothing like last year's. But he was ready for spring.

As the big plow snorted through a turn he lifted his fingers from the wheel, working each one separately, then returning to its job. Though the cab was warm he could still feel the sting of frost, a tingling afterbite that came whenever it got cold. The doctor had said he might always feel that, on and off.

He didn't mind a little stinging. At least he had his fingers. Hell, he was glad just to be here.

The blade clattered suddenly and the snowplow rocked. Damn, he thought, when're they going to get this stretch fixed? The damn state never spent a dollar till they had to spend a hundred.

He was meditating angrily on this when he saw the figure ahead. Old red-barred coat, tan pants, flop-eared cap, lace-up boots . . . he downshifted, and tons of salt and sand brought the plow rumbling to a reluctant halt. Cranking down the window, he leaned out. "Yo! Racks!"

The old man stopped, half-turned. He stared up, eyes blue and distant as winter sky, then nodded slowly.

Halvorsen hauled himself stiffly up into the cab, shoving a box in ahead of him onto the seat. He looked out the windshield. Then, a little reluctantly, said, "Hullo, Barry. Good to see you on the job."

Fox let the clutch back in. The plow reaccelerated slowly, rumbling like an empty oil drum rolling down the road. He dropped the blade and sparks danced under the skids. "Heard you got out. Figured I'd be seein' you along here, one of these days. How you been doin'?"

"I'm okay."

"You headed home? How long you been back?"

"Couple of weeks," Halvorsen said.

"Let's see," said Fox. "I don't really remember . . . We was reading about the trials and all, but I was sick, then when they let me out of the hospital we went down to visit my wife's sister that spring . . . it's kind of fuzzy . . . what exactly did they give you finally, there in the end?"

"It was pretty long drawn out," said Halvorsen. He stared out the window, remembering the months. The federal grand jury had indicted him even after he'd explained everything. Probably wanted to find out if he was telling the truth, though he'd told them right out that he was. Then after the federal trial there'd been the state one, just as long, and then after that they'd kept calling him as a witness to this and a witness to that; till towards the end he'd started to think he'd never go anywhere else; he'd spend what was left of his life in courtrooms, or huddled with Quintero going over what he was going to say.

"Well, it took 'em long enough," he said slowly. "But they finally got everything figured out, I guess."

"Pulled some jail time, didn't you?"

"Oh, they give me five years on the state charges. Judge said, blowin' up the truck while it was dumpin', he could of overlooked that. And the manslaughter charge they dismissed. But blowin' up state property, he meant the bridge, that wasn't something they could let you go scot free. Even if they did get a new bridge out of it . . . anyway my lawyer, she got me out early on what was left, account of how old I was." Halvorsen shrugged. "How're you?"

"About back to normal. But it took a while." The younger man scowled. "Doc Friedman says I got to get checkups the rest of my life, though. In case a' cancer. Christ!"

"Same here," said Halvorsen. "Well, you got your bills paid, anyway."

"Yeah, and *he* paid too. Though I wish—well, his kid wasn't to blame. She shouldn't have suffered because of what he done."

"Nobody should of. The ones he hurt, I mean. Trouble is, once you start doing things like that, can't tell where it's goin' to end."

"He won't be putting it to nobody else for a long time. Conspiracy, dumping, accessory to murder—what was it, twenty to twenty-five years? Must have been a clever guy, do all that without them knowing about it at Thunder."

"What's that?"

"That's what the paper said. Thunder had lawyers there, proved nobody knew about it but him. I don't think it's all settled yet, but looks like the company's going to come out of it okay. Hey, you tried that—no, you don't have a car. Anyway, I got me a tank of that new Thunder Green. Burns clean, got the zip of premium, like they say on the radio. Gonna sell a lot of that, I bet."

"That so? That's good. That'll bring some jobs back."

"Oh, they're already hiring again, down at the refinery. Told my brother that, he come back from Buffalo. He's goin' down, try to sign on."

Halvorsen nodded slowly, but didn't say anything. Fox looked at the seat between them. "Whatcha got in the box?"

"Chain saw."

"Firewood?"

"Roof beams."

"Oh, yeah, right. They burned you out, didn't they."

"About halfway," said Halvorsen, looking out the window at the passing hills.

"That reminds me." Fox reached across him to the glove compartment. "Got some things of yours here. Been holdin' on to them, figured you'd be back sooner or later."

"Thanks," said Halvorsen, looking down at the gloves and scarf. There was a black smear on the scarf. He folded it carefully, not touching the smear, and put it in his pocket.

"Say, what ever happened to them kids that was with you? When you blew up that truck? Wasn't there two other people?"

"Boy and a girl," said Halvorsen. He looked out the window, to where the moosewoods were starting to bud. "The boy got shot. Put up a good fight, though. They had his picture in the paper. All his buddies from the football team carryin' the casket. His dad wrote me he's some kind of a hero to a lot of the kids."

"And the girl?"

"Oh, she testified, but they let her off. She moved on. Said she didn't want to stay. Got religion, I think. Went on down south someplace, to live with her brother. Virginia or Florida or some such. Got a card from her. Says she's happy."

"Be warmer, either place," said Fox, peering out into the rear-view as he adjusted the spinner. "Not like this. Snow, snow, all the goddamn time. I'll tell you one good thing come out of it all, though."

"What's that?"

"Me and the wife. Remember, I told you we were havin' problems? Getting along a lot better. Ain't till you really need a woman, you find out how much she loves you."

"That's true," said Halvorsen after a while.

He didn't say anything more and for a long time the other man was silent too.

Rolling along high above the road, the old man thought how sometimes it all seemed to stem from the hunting. Men had come to be what they were fighting the other beasts for dominion. When the animals were conquered, gone, they'd channeled that drive into war.

And when war got too expensive and too dangerous, not just to the warriors but to everybody, that need to kill and win had become business. Just like the old human sacrifices had become animal sacrifices and then just to offering bread and grape juice, till people forgot even what it meant. They'd finally outgrown their terror of God.

But in a few that drive and need still went too far. When that happened the rest, the men and women who stayed sane, had to step in and stop them.

He leaned his head back, watching the sky as the truck rumbled along. Clearing snow. Seemed it didn't matter how often you plowed, it would come back, falling from the sky as it always had, inevitable and remorseless, without mercy or pity or regret.

But it could be cleared. And would be. Again and again. Till it was spring.

It's awful slow, Halvorsen thought. Terrible slow, and it ain't easy. But seems to me we might be making some headway.

Fox said, "Saw that old buck again. He must live out near you, you know?"

"Think I know the one you mean."

"Guess he's made it through the season again. Some of them deer, smarter'n you'd think. Hey, getting close to the Run. You want, I can maybe get you up pretty close to your place. Save you some walking, anyway."

And the old man said, his eyes narrowing in what might almost have been a smile, "That'd be just fine by me."

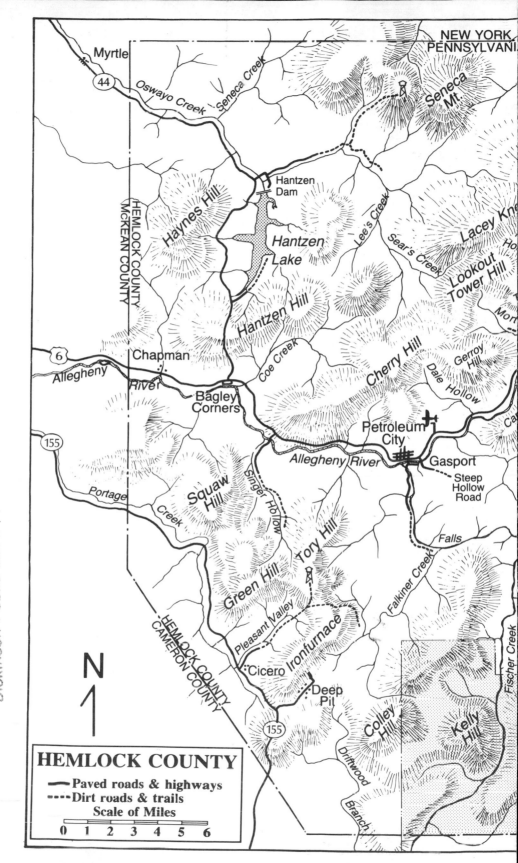

NEW YORK
PENNSYLVANIA

Myrtle

Oswayo Creek

Seneca Creek

Seneca Mt.

44

Hantzen
Dam

Haynes Hill

Hantzen
Lake

Lee's Creek

Sear's Creek

Lacey Knee

Lookout
Tower Hill

HEMLOCK COUNTY
McKEAN COUNTY

Hantzen Hill

Coe Creek

Cherry Hill

Gerroy
Hill

Dale Hollow

Mor

6

Chapman

Allegheny
River

Bagley
Corners

Petroleum
City

Allegheny River

Gasport

155

Portage

Creek

Squaw
Hill

Singer Hollow

Steep
Hollow
Road

Green Hill

Tory Hill

Falls

Falkiner Creek

HEMLOCK COUNTY
CAMERON COUNTY

Pleasant Valley

Cicero Ironfurnace

Deep
Pit

Fischer Creek

155

Colley
Hill

Kelly
Hill

Driftwood

Branch

N

HEMLOCK COUNTY

—— Paved roads & highways
---- Dirt roads & trails
Scale of Miles

0 1 2 3 4 5 6